ENDLESS

CRESCENT: BOOK ONE

MATT BONE

Published by Astro Impossible Books 2012
www.astroimpossible.com

Cover design by Al Greenall and Catherine Sulzmann. Cover
font design by Peter Klassen.

ISBN 978-0-9573025-0-1

For Cat,
and those who inspire me

'Life, I don't understand you.'

– Hjalmar Söderberg, *Doctor Glas.*

Prologue

John woke with a headache. He heard scratching at the door. A remnant of a dream – black lands and blue fire – flickered and vanished before he could grasp it.

He slid off the sofa and walked unsteadily to the kitchen to pour a glass of water, searching the cupboards in vain for aspirin. *Damn it.* His head pounded. The scratching continued.

It was Mr. Kirsch; Mrs. Kirsch's cat. She was the only person in the building who was allowed a pet, although John thought of it more as a piece of luggage that rarely left the considerable gravity of Mrs. Kirsch's body. That was probably the reason for the exception. Both creatures spent their lives in an equally immobile state within Mrs. Kirsch's antique shop on the ground floor.

The scratching went on. John was yet to hear the exaggerated whisper from Mrs. Kirsch that duly followed the tabby's rare moments of activity. After several minutes of the same noise, he moved to the door and opened it.

Mrs. Kirsch was there after all. She was at the bottom of the stairs that ended outside his front door on the second floor, and she was dead. Her neck was broken, her squat body lying on its side with her front facing away from him, her large face turned an impossible angle back towards him. Her eyes, open wide, looked up at him. Mr. Kirsch was sitting on his hind legs next to the body, also looking up at John.

John stared at the cat, then at Mrs. Kirsch. For a moment he felt a resentment at these twin gazes, accusing and expectant, as if this were all somehow *his* fault. But the feeling was soon replaced by the appropriate thoughts: *phone, ambulance, emergency.* Or was there another number he should call, given that she was dead already? *No, stick with the ambulance,* he decided. *They'll deal with it.*

He walked back into his apartment and dialled the emergency services. It seemed to be taking forever for someone to pick up. *Just stay calm.* Perhaps this was their regular response time. Perhaps they were busier than usual. The phone rang for minutes.

Eventually he returned to the corridor, and looked down again at Mrs. Kirsch. He was at a loss. Should he move the body? Maybe he should at least move the cat. His concern about the unanswered call to the emergency services was joined by a rising sense of unease – fuelled not only by the discovery of Mrs. Kirsch, but by an obscure feeling of something much larger, of something unaccountably *wrong*.

John attempted to ignore his anxiety and stirred his body into action. He picked up the cat – which felt as he had always imagined it would, an unresisting warm mass – and hurried across the hallway to knock on the door of his immediate neighbours, the Unsworths. The sound of his knuckles against the wood pierced a profound quiet enveloping the entire building. No answer.

He carried the cat downstairs and stopped outside a thinly whitewashed door. Clive's apartment. Clive had applied the coat of paint months previously, in a rare fit of domestic enthusiasm, but had never got around to finishing the job. The Unsworths were most likely at work – it was early afternoon on a weekday, after all – but Clive would be at home. He had been on sick leave with a mysterious back ailment for as long as John could remember.

But once again there was no response to his knocking. He tried the handle. The door opened, and John was greeted with more silence from within the flat. He stepped inside, the cat a dull weight in the crook of his arm. Something prevented him from calling out Clive's name.

He paused in the unlit hallway that led to the living room. A large chandelier hung in front of him, incongruous against the peeling wallpaper and low ceiling. Clive had never explained it. John envisioned some prideful last stand in a dead relationship – she got the wealth, the children, the friends, he got the chandelier and his life of exile. But that was John's own history darkening his imagination.

As he stood there he realised why he didn't call out Clive's name. A part of him already knew. He forced himself to walk on, into the living room. He glimpsed the back of Clive's head in his armchair. A few more steps revealed the television, the picture reduced to mute static.

He faced the front of the armchair and found the empty stare, the open mouth.

John didn't know how long he looked at Clive, or whether he checked for a pulse, or examined the man or the apartment further. He was suddenly downstairs, at the entrance of the building, and what he saw outside seared away all other thought.

The bodies were everywhere. Strewn along the road that stretched down from the building. Single bodies and small groups of bodies, scattered and unmoving like discarded playthings. Larger aggregations further down, where the busier high street began. He watched as a dog weaved through them, pausing and then moving to the next group, its yelps carried faintly up the hill. A distant alarm. There was little other movement or sound. A seagull pecked at a dark mass, thankfully too remote for John to discern any detail. Closer to him, shopping spilt out from the bags around a man and woman who were lying face down on the pavement.

Cars had smashed into the backs of one another, other vehicles had veered off the road and into buildings. Almost directly opposite him, a car had plunged through the front window of a restaurant. Some of the miniature fir trees used as decoration above the window had been detached by the impact, and lay about the rear of the car. Inside, the customers not struck by the vehicle were slumped over tables and chairs, indifferent to the intrusion.

The next thing John knew was that he was in his own apartment again, sitting upright on the sofa. Mr. Kirsch sat on the coffee table, staring at him. John stared back, unable to move.

PART I:
SEPARATION

1

John glanced at the rear-view mirror. *Nothing.*

His eyes back on the road, he swerved automatically to avoid some debris. He was simply imagining things. *Nothing there.*

Even if there had been, it was probably just an animal. Hunger made them lose their caution. Or was it the sense of a shift in the food ladder? Whatever the truth, it was enough reason not to take any chances. So today he would not take the turning.

He drove by heavy concrete buildings, some cracked, crooked, blackened, some already veined green with plant life, some seemingly unscathed. The turning was coming up. He could feel it pulling at him, dull yet insistent. But today he would head straight for home. *No point in taking the risk*, he repeated to himself. *A waste of time.* He accelerated past the turning, keeping his eyes fixed ahead.

He managed to travel a hundred yards along the road before slamming his foot against the brake pedal. *Damn it.*

Ten minutes later John was pulling onto a short gravel driveway. He stopped the car next to the broad steps of the hotel and surveyed the surroundings. Nearby, a faint wind rustled the browning leaves of a large ash. He remembered how it had once been, before the event, the tree standing alone in the centre of a meticulous lawn. But the garden had long since become wild; vegetation had sprung up unmolested, untidy and diverse. On the opposite side of the hotel, the car park was splintered by a similar green.

He looked at the building: a monumental grey slab, smothered with the inoffensive lack of character most large hotels seemed to adopt. The word *Entrance* was emblazoned above its doors, blue on white. The doors and ground floor windows were boarded up.

John reached onto the back seat of the car and removed a canvas bag from beneath a stack of petrol cans. He took a breath and climbed out of the vehicle, then hurried up the concrete steps to the entrance. After testing the handle – *still locked* – he pulled a key from his pocket and opened the door. He moved inside and locked it behind him.

The reception area was silent. Weak light bled through a small window above the door, giving shape to a reception desk and a few leather chairs. There was an odour of decay, damp, a faint dripping. Beyond the desk was the door to the stairway and, beside that, the wide arch leading to the lounge: a pitch-black cavern. John reached into the canvas bag and pulled out a torch, flicking a beam of light at the desk. Another key lay on it, untouched. He headed towards the stairs.

The hallway of the third floor was deserted and stale-smelling: better than most buildings. John had gone through efforts to ensure that. He walked slowly towards a door situated halfway along the corridor. The torch swung forgotten in his hand, the beam scanning uselessly across the floor. He didn't need it. He could walk the short distance with his eyes closed; he knew every groan of floorboard, every worn patch of carpet, every stain.

Next to the door was a neat stack of tins. He knelt to wipe away a thin layer of dust from the top, then pulled another tin from his bag to add to the pile. Apricot halves in syrup. She disapproved of tinned fruit, but would appreciate the gesture. She would understand.

He ignored the thoughts trying to force their way into the forefront of his mind. *Don't think, don't think.*

He stood and placed a hand on the door, fingers outstretched. It felt cold. He leant his forehead against the wood and squeezed his eyes shut. *Don't think.*

He turned and walked back towards the stairs.

John swore under his breath as he drove back towards his apartment. *Why do I put myself through this?* Again and again. Almost every day for the past two years he had gone to the hotel, and it was always the same.

Nothing changes anymore, he reminded himself, swerving around the wreckage of a bus. He ran a hand through his tangle of dark hair. *Why do you continue, John? Why don't you just –*

Something ahead caught his eye. *A light?* He slowed the car and leant forward to peer through the windscreen. He could have sworn that – *there.* At the junction at the end of the street, beyond the glut of cars. A brightness that was fluidic and somehow cohesive, alive in shape. And something huge beside it: lumbering, seething.

John stopped the car and leapt out. He stared down the length of the road, but the light had gone. For a second he thought he heard a faint crackling, an electrical hum.

He shielded his eyes and leant on the car to extend his tall frame. *Nothing there.* The sunlight reflected from an unlikely angle, that was all. He rubbed at his temples. Too many sleepless nights – and the headache again. It wasn't a surprise his imagination was beginning to rule his senses.

After a moment's hesitation he set off along the road, weaving through the cars, avoiding the broken glass and the skeletons. The debris increased towards the junction. He rarely travelled this far down the street, as it was impossible to drive through.

Upon reaching the junction, he scrutinised the adjoining

roads and the buildings about him. There was no movement, no light.

He sighed. The city was empty of all but animal life, he knew that. *It's a little late to start seeing ghosts.*

A short distance away was a motorbike that John recognised, propped up under a tattered shop awning. He remembered finding it a month or so after the event. Half of the yellow paintwork had been scraped away by the crash, by the long slide across the road. The rider had been another twenty yards away.

Something about the motorcycle had held his attention. A reconnection, perhaps: his past self had always wanted to try one out. He recalled hauling it up from the road, turning the key and listening to the engine's deep, satisfying purr – and then realising he didn't have the first clue about operating the machine. It was unreasonably complicated, a betrayal of a symbol of spontaneity.

Of course it wouldn't have mattered if he had tried and failed. There was no-one to judge. Yet some remnant of embarrassment had lingered, ridiculous and defunct.

And now? John told himself it was the impracticality, that's why he had never learned to ride it. A motorcycle wouldn't be of much use carrying supplies, and was more susceptible to the city's debris. It was more exposed, more at danger. *But danger from what?* The predatory animals were rare enough these days; the majority had left or died when the meat supply had run out.

The truth was rooted in apathy rather than fear. It was the same reason he had persisted with unexceptional hatchbacks for cars. He had always assumed that eventually he would pick up a more desirable vehicle. A supercar, flamboyant and reckless. Or a souped-up celebrity's jeep, as a minor concession to practicality. But he had never done so. In the early days after the event, it had been the shock. How could he have contemplated the choice of a car then? It would have been an admission that the rules of life had changed, or no longer existed. Later, the thought of obtaining such a machine didn't elicit any feeling in him, no matter how he tried to force it. The cosmetics of vehicles – status, power, personality – had eroded over time, and now they were simply tools, bare metal frames.

John walked over to the motorcycle. He moved his hand to its side, hoping to feel some emotion, anything. To his surprise, he did. It was as if a residue was disturbed by his touch: the sudden sensation of something reaching out into the air around him. Seeking.

His head pounded as he hurried back to the car.

John still felt uneasy by the time he arrived back at his apartment building. He parked the car on the pavement next to the entrance, then quickly unloaded the supplies into the hallway.

He peered out from the door when he was finished, but the street was as silent as ever. *Nothing changes.*

Inside, he avoided the noise of the portable generator and started lighting the gas lamps that were attached haphazardly along the walls. When the hall and stairway were adequately lit, he returned to survey the gathered supplies: two bags of tinned food, several water bottles, a dozen petrol cans, batteries of every size, an acoustic guitar, three violins, a box full of books, a pile of photo albums, a bag of cat litter, air-fresheners, paracetamol, amoxil, codeine, coffee, a few bottles of whiskey, toothpaste.

He had been fortunate with the petrol. Scouring the buildings on a residential street, he had discovered the garage of a scrupulous motor enthusiast. The house had belonged to a retired couple, John had concluded. They had been eating together on the sofa when it happened, folded newspapers under dinner plates.

John began transporting the supplies up the stairs. His left thumb, an adversary ever since a childhood accident, began to ache after only a few minutes, and quickly became stiff and unresponsive. The stack of photo albums became unbalanced and tipped over as he carried them, and he cursed as they tumbled down the stairs. He promised himself for the hundredth time that he would find a new building. One with an elevator that he would somehow get working. Or one with fewer stairs. Or a mansion, a villa. A palace, if he wanted. It didn't matter.

He began picking up the photo albums. Whenever he came across one in a house, he couldn't help but take it. Some day he would be brave enough to look at the photos.

2

Ceria crouched behind the tree in the darkness, gripping a vine attached to the trunk. The rain beat against the giant leathery leaves surrounding her. She could hear it all over the forest; a hundred drums, a thousand, as if proclaiming the hunt. The wind was an accompaniment, hurtling through the trees in periodic howls.

She caught her breath and peered out into the near-black beyond the tree. Not far from her hiding place was a dim expanse, a plain of grass, before the wall of closely packed trees began again on the opposite side. With the minor moons struggling to pierce the clouds, there was barely enough light to make out the vague shapes of trunks. But soon Ternerid would rise. Even with the thick cloud cover, the moon would add a great deal of light. Too much; the hunters would be able to see more clearly. The small chance she had would evaporate. She had to be quick.

She heard what might have been a shout carried on the wind, distorted and stunted. *Concentrate. Block out the noise.*

Listen.

A minute went by, and another, before she heard a further shout. Closer. Somewhere to her right, hidden in the congested foliage. She couldn't see the lights of their torches yet, but that didn't mean much. The forest was dense enough that they could be almost upon her before she saw them. *So listen.*

More shouts. A jumble of voices, a few men, at least one woman; a shrill shout, the low bark of an order. She dug her nails into the vine and fought the urge to run. *Wait, listen. Wait.*

Long moments passed, feeling like hours. Water dripped from her short black hair. A shiver of cold travelled through her body. Her thin layer of clothing, all she could gather in her haste, had been soaked through long ago. She waited. Finally she heard it: an animal's cry, an exclamation of pain and desperation that seemed to startle the forest into silence. An instant later the surroundings burst into life again with the clamour of shouts, the percussive thunder of the rain and wind. But she knew where it was now.

Ceria scrambled out from behind the tree and sprinted across the plain. Her bare feet gripped wet grass. She had to reach it before they did. The dark would hopefully be enough to mask her movement. She prayed that she had judged the direction correctly.

She plunged into the barrier of foliage, narrowly avoiding the looming forms of trunks. The large oval leaves lashed against her limbs, and she had to duck and weave to avoid the more substantial lower branches. The ground tore into her feet.

It was as she was beginning to question if she might be too late – the cry had not sounded again, and she should have been upon it by now – when she broke through to a small clearing, and found the jalren in front of her. An adult female, fully grown and nearly twice Ceria's length, its horned head adding another arm-span yet. The animal was lying on its side, an arrow protruding from its flank.

Ceria stepped forward. The jalren lifted its head and gave a deep grunt of warning. A wide ovoid eye followed her as she knelt carefully between the animal's legs. Flecks of foam dotted its muzzle. As she moved her hand to the arrow, the jalren summoned the energy to aim its curved horns at her. Ceria gave the antlers a wary glance as she leaned away: brittle blade-like growths spiralled their lengths, each as sharp as a dagger. As weak as the attempt was, even a minor contact could shred her arm.

She kept a safe distance as she gripped the arrow shaft with both hands, then wrenched it out of the animal's side. The jalren moaned loudly in response, but its movements were already beginning to lessen. The fight was leaving the animal. Ceria heard the shouts of the hunters once again, urgent and determined. So close now. *Concentrate.*

She laid her hands on the wound and felt the blood against her fingers, a slick warmth amongst the tangle of fur and the cold of the rain. She pressed down and began to feel for the flow, for the intensity she knew was there. If only she could manage to open herself to it, to allow it into her, and her into it. But she couldn't feel anything.

By now the shouts were a constant element in the noise surrounding her. The rain continued unabated. She wiped her eyes and glanced at the animal's head. It was still now, its gaze no longer on her. There was a reflection in its eye, and Ceria looked up to find Ternerid breaching the horizon, its pale silvery-green light already permeating the mass of trees. It wouldn't be long before the forest was bathed in the moon's glow – at another time a beautiful sight, but at this moment never more unwelcome.

Block it out. Come on. Ceria closed her eyes and concentrated on her hands, on the boundary of feeling between her and the animal. She could sense it, on the other side, something elemental and immense, a great swell barely out of reach. She urged herself toward it, attempting to overcome the resistance. She had to dissolve the barrier. Become exposed.

Suddenly it was there: an energy gushing into her, shocking in its violence and sweetness. It infused her, became her. A radiance glorifying every part of her.

The animal began to convulse. *No. Fight it.* She struggled to find herself. *Control it.* She battled to restrain the torrent, to ease the flow between her and the animal. Gradually the convulsions began to subside. It was an illusion of control, she knew; the energy could never truly be tamed. But for now she could exert her will to a degree.

She felt for the wound – a tear, a spreading void – and channelled the flow towards it. The damage was repairing, but so slowly, and taking so much. She could feel her body resisting, tightening. Almost there. Stretching, draining. Almost. Pain. Too much...

She collapsed backwards and the jalren immediately scrambled up. It looked around wildly, unsteady on its feet, before turning its huge bulk to face her. Ceria had difficulty focusing, but could see the animal's outline by the new light: its powerful legs and imposing carriage, the horns spiralling outward. A thick mane began under its muzzle, streaked by glimmering silver. The horns had more modest counterparts that trailed the jalren's back like a helical spine. The animal sniffed the air and snorted, then turned and galloped into the forest.

Ceria struggled to push herself to her feet, a deep exhaustion consuming her. She felt worn out and empty. But she had to move before they discovered her.

She stumbled into the undergrowth, pushing aside foliage and leaning against trees for support. The wind buffeted her, unsympathetic, eroding the small amount of energy she yet possessed. Her feet felt raw. She heard nearby shouts. *Hurry.*

Ternerid was entirely above the horizon, a vast orb coolly searing through the clouds and dominating the night sky, by the time she broke free of the forest. A false dawn perhaps, but enough to reveal her. *Move.* The ground became an incline and far ahead, at the crest of a long hill, were the stark silhouettes of buildings. An impossible distance away.

Ceria fought the urge to collapse and kept moving. The shivering was continuous now. The hunters' shouts had shifted to a tone of confusion and anger.

When she had progressed halfway up the hill, she looked back at the forest. Her vision was only becoming worse, but she could see how Ternerid's light had insinuated itself throughout the trees, producing a deep, complicated green. The rain had eased, as if in respect of the moon's exertions, and provided a softening haze for the azure glow that sat at the base of the trees, and for the silver that clung to the tops. Was that movement at the forest edge? *Just keep going.*

She turned and staggered toward the buildings.

Get to Telde.

3

John opened his eyes at a sudden weight on his chest, and found Mr. Kirsch looking back at him. A cuckoo clock sounded. The cat mewed.

"Yeah, I know." John's voice came out dry, foreign. He hadn't used it in days. "I'll get it if you get off me."

The cat jumped off as John sat up on the sofa, pressing a finger to his temple. His head ached more than usual, and he couldn't suppress a shiver. *A bad dream, that's all.* The window let in an early evening light. He had slept through most of the day.

At an impatient sound from the tabby, John forced himself to his feet and headed toward the most recent supplies. He searched out a tin of cat food, then hid it behind his back as Mr. Kirsch led him to the kitchen. Salmon in gravy – the animal would eat nothing else. Mrs. Kirsch's cupboards had been stocked with tin upon tin of it, but that supply had run out long ago. Now John had to go to considerable lengths each time to find more. *Too much effort for a damn cat.*

He opened the cupboard below the sink and made a pretend show of retrieving the tin. Mr. Kirsch wouldn't eat it otherwise. For the last domesticated creature on the planet, John reflected, the cat was infuriatingly fussy.

After he had filled Mr. Kirsch's bowl, John glanced back at the sofa. He was tempted to lie down again, but knew that he wouldn't sleep now. His headache showed no sign of receding, and his thumb was aching because of the cold. He needed a drink.

He moved back to the supplies, picked out a bottle of whiskey and took a mouthful large enough to make him wince. He looked at the wall behind the sofa, from which the sound of the cuckoo had originated. Vermillion and gold wallpaper striped between more than a dozen cuckoo clocks of all sizes. Mrs. Kirsch's clocks. It was her apartment. Over two years and he still thought of it that way, despite her being long dead. Despite ownership being a defunct concept.

It was partly because of the cat that he had moved here. *Moved here*; another extinction. It was simply where he slept and ate, and where he stored the supplies necessary to continue existing. Mr. Kirsch would not leave the apartment. Any attempt to carry him beyond the door resulted in a surprisingly animated struggle, from which John usually came off worse. It was as if the cat stubbornly awaited his owner's return. John resented that dumb expectancy, and envied it.

But the move was also due to his own apartment holding too many memories. He might have been living alone for the last few months before the event, but it was still his and Jessica's home. Their first together after university. They had agreed it was only until they found something better, and then stayed for the next five years. John liked to tell himself that leaving the apartment had been an acceptance of sorts. Of the way things were now. But that was a thin deception, a surface tension that allowed him to keep on moving. Their apartment was always below his feet. Sometimes he would lie on the floor in the night and imagine that he could hear voices below.

John looked at the clock that had sounded a few minutes earlier. A light-hearted domestic scene carved out of dark maple. Upon the striking of the hour, an aproned wife would in turn strike her tankard-drinking husband on the head with a rolling pin. The cuckoo, angular and white, black dots for eyes, had become stuck on its journey out of the miniature door, its spring exposed.

Not all of the clocks had been here originally. This was one of many that John had brought up from Mrs. Kirsch's shop at the bottom of the building. He knew that it was a cliché – a man with every right to insanity surrounding himself with cuckoo clocks – but there was a certain comfort in that: a cliché could only exist in the old world, where it had populations to thrive on. The clocks ticked a past presence. John pushed the wooden bird back in, and gently closed the door.

His thumb ached again, reminding him of the increasing cold. It was another comfort, despite the aggravation. The digit had been sliced off and reattached in his childhood; a traumatic memory, but soaked with so much emotion that nowadays it was precious.

He moved to the fireplace on the opposite side of the room, a Georgian remnant of which Mrs. Kirsch had spoken proudly and often. John took a newspaper from a pile, screwed the pages into balls and added them to the wood already inside. He searched out a match to light it, then took another swallow of whiskey as he watched it kindle. It needed more wood.

He walked back to the pile of supplies, picked up the guitar and without hesitation smashed it against the wall. A final indignant resonation issued from the hollow body. He did the same with the violins as Mr. Kirsch watched on disapprovingly from the kitchen. John ignored him. He gathered up the remnants and carried them back to the fire. The instruments didn't burn as well as other wood, but they were easy to gather, and he liked the smells they produced. Especially the violins, the varnished maple and spruce creating smoke that was rich and thick.

No, it wasn't just that. It was the pain that accompanied it. A sharp pang that came with the destruction of the hand-crafted instruments. Once he had burned one of the cuckoo clocks, and it had been the same. He liked to press himself against the point of the pain until he felt something. But it was becoming increasingly difficult to reach that feeling.

He remained by the fire until half of the wood from the instruments was gone. His thumb no longer ached and the bottle of whiskey was almost empty – the two facts not unrelated. Dusk was settling in, and he moved to the window to watch the light abandoning the city, street by street. He pushed up the window frame and leant his head outside, breathing in the cool air.

Something in the corner of his vision. Movement. Bright. He turned and hurriedly scanned the area. *There.* A building about a mile away. A flicker of light at a window. Gone – then reappearing at an adjacent window. Flooding it.

Get the binoculars. John reached behind him, fumbling blindly. *Damn it.* He moved back inside, finally discovering the binoculars a few metres across the room, then rushed back to the window. He pointed them towards the building and a trembling window appeared in his vision. Dark, no movement within. He struggled to hold the image steady as he shifted the view to the neighbouring windows. Nothing. He decreased the magnification so that he could see more of the building. Sandy-stoned, tall and narrow, unremarkable. It was fenced in on one side by a line of similar buildings, and on the other by a petrol station. No light, no sign of activity.

But surely he recognised the area. Wasn't it where the music shop was, from which he had collected the instruments? Wasn't it that very same building? He couldn't say for certain. From his vantage point the ground floor was obscured by the roof of a closer building.

John hooked the strap of the binoculars around his neck and leant his upper body out of the window, twisting so that he was perched on the sill. The binoculars' image shook as he gripped the frame for balance, but now he could make out the corner of a large window on the lowest level of the building, neatly bordered in red. It *was* the music shop. The same one he had visited countless times... including yesterday.

Yet there was nothing indicating activity. *What are you*

doing, John? So it was a shop he had been to – that was hardly significant. Simply a coincidence. He could point the binoculars in any direction and recognise a building he had visited, a shop he had plundered.

The window frame creaked in protest at his weight. John studied the dormant building for a short time further, before finally pulling himself back inside. Was this how it began? A trickle of illusion, accumulating until it was a full blown disease of the spirit? He closed his eyes and tightened his grip on the binoculars, feeling the reassuring weight in his hand. *Nothing changes, John.*

He opened his eyes and forced himself to look elsewhere: at the buildings opposite, stretching away down the hill. He followed them idly with the binoculars. The dim outline of a skeleton was visible through one window, collapsed over a desk.

He wondered when he had stopped seeing them. At what point the bodies had become scenery, debris. He would have never thought it possible in those first few months. They were inescapable then, he could hardly look at them. The smell had been unbearable. And the flies. He had moved some of the bodies. Those on the street outside his building, to keep the animals away. And those in the hotel, for her. He had cleared a pathway from the third floor to the entrance.

The dogs had been as bad as the flies. Worse. They were everywhere. They would leave him alone for the most part, as long as he was careful. John was sickened by what they did. But he came to appreciate it, in a way. If they hadn't cleared the bodies entirely, they had at least made them less recognisable. Less human. Just wreckage, inanimate blood and bone. Of course there were always places that the dogs couldn't reach.

He increased the magnification of the binoculars. The dark obscured most of the details, but he could make out the shape of a computer monitor on the desk, a phone in its holder. Nothing of use; he had thoroughly explored all of these buildings. They were some of the first. Some of the most difficult.

In those first few months he had expected a devastating reaction to follow the abrupt deprivation of human supervision in the world. A cascade of explosions engulfing the city, perhaps, or a distant reservoir breaking, a great obliterating wave. A power station overloading and casting out a wall of radiation, an invisible toxicity. A tidying up of loose ends. But nothing had happened.

He hadn't stayed in the same place for the two years. He had travelled, searched. England was the same everywhere, every city and town and village a similar scene of ruin. A dead land. Apart from the animals: the dogs, the rats, the birds. The Thames had burst its banks. The Channel Tunnel was gruelling, almost impassable, but he had made it through. He had driven the length of France and crossed the Spanish border. It was all the same. He had taken photographs of famous landmarks surrounded by bodies, a sadistic tourism to prove to himself that he had really been there, that this was the desolate truth.

Every body was the same as the next; there was no sign that anyone had seen it coming. Everywhere the same absence: no preparation, no expectation, no warning. The end had arrived without declaration. He could find no answers in the newspapers, no predictions or hints of an explanation. An African leader assassinated. A small earthquake in India. A flurry of suicides in Glasgow. An anti-war march in Washington. A rural town in Russia found abandoned. It was the lack of sensation surrounding the event that made it so unacceptable. The biggest story in human history passed without comment.

At least that silence had told him one thing: whatever happened had been instantaneous across the world. As if a switch had been flicked, and everyone had fallen down lifeless.

But not John. He remained. Without purpose, without

knowing why. He remained, with the cuckoo clocks, with Mr. Kirsch.

He put the binoculars down and closed the window. He turned back to the apartment. The cat was in front of the fireplace, licking the top of the whiskey bottle. John walked towards the sofa.

4

"You stupid idiot of a girl!"

Telde stood glaring at Ceria, hands on her hips, daring a response. When she didn't get one, she continued anyway. "We're meant to be keeping out of sight. And here you are chasing razorhorns and parading yourself in front of the whole fenning town guard." Her words were thick with a Ferolian accent; she struggled to hide it when she was angry.

Ceria sat on a stool beside the only window of the small, one-room shelter, her left foot pulled onto her lap as she surveyed the damage the forest bed had caused to her heel. The truth was that she could barely focus on it, let alone treat the wounds, but she was determined not to let the extent of her weariness show – Telde already had enough ammunition. At least the shivering had finally stopped.

Ceria wished, not for the first time, that Telde would get the scolding over with so that she could rest. She wanted to close her eyes and let a deep, heavy sleep consume her, to lie down for days and days. She stole a glance at the bed on the opposite side of the room. Telde pounced.

"Are you listening to me, Ceriande? This is serious. Don't you understand?" She glared accusingly for a moment, then began pacing the cramped room. She had succeeded in blocking the route to the bed, Ceria noted with regret.

"Of course you don't," Telde continued. "You never consider the consequences. You fly away doing whatever you choose and risking everything, with no thought for anyone or anything else. And for what this time? For some dumb animal."

Ceria felt the heat rising in her, despite the exhaustion. "It's not dumb. The dumb animals are those hunting it. They should have better things to do."

Telde was baiting her, she knew, but if she wanted an argument so badly then she could have one. She had done the right thing after all, even if it had meant sneaking out in the middle of the night.

"*Godsblood*, girl. What if they'd seen you? What if they saw what you did? It was a foolish risk."

"A risk to me, not to you," Ceria snapped back, and instantly regretted it. Before Telde could reply, she mumbled an apology into her foot. "I didn't mean that."

Ceria knew what Telde would have said, what she was probably still going to recite any moment now: that this was bigger than her, that people had sacrificed everything for their freedom. She located a large black thorn buried in her heel and pulled it out, only managing to stifle a gasp of pain by clamping her teeth together.

Telde remained silent. Ceria could feel her eyes on her. She knew the look: disapproving, disappointed. Much worse than her scowled anger. *She's only two years older than me,* Ceria thought, *yet she treats me like a child. What gives her the right to mother me? Why should I constantly apologise?* She stuck a thumb on her heel to plug a trickle of dark blood. *I should've told her where I was going. She couldn't have stopped me. Then I could have taken boots.*

She had overheard the guards during the day, whilst buying spiced bread from the town's baker – blacker and even staler than usual; Telde hadn't been pleased. The two men had walked a lazy patrol around the small town, and she had followed, soon learning of their night hunts. The commander from a neighbouring town would be along that evening, one of them had boasted. When Ceria had heard what their quarry would be, she had resolved to counter their efforts. She only had to prevent Telde from finding out.

That latter intention had been ruined when, attempting to climb unheard through the window after escaping the forest, she had caught her foot on the outside ledge and her fatigued body had crashed to the floor inside. Telde had sprung up and almost pierced Ceria with her blade – *did she sleep with that thing?* – before realising who it was sprawled on the ground. She had barely helped Ceria onto the stool and checked her condition before launching into the reprimands.

"But they're Queen's soldiers, anyway," Ceria said, looking up at Telde. "Even if they did see me with the jalren, they wouldn't have done anything beyond shouting insults or adding a few more bruises."

Telde made an exasperated noise. "Don't be so fenning naive, girl, you know better than that. We can't know where these guards' allegiances truly lie. Or how far the half-man's grasp extends."

The half-man. The name made Ceria's stomach turn. The monster who had subjugated her home, sealed it off from the world whilst he carried out his atrocities.

"It surely isn't this far," she said. "And he couldn't control every guard in such a large group."

Telde shrugged, a gesture she somehow made accusing. "Perhaps. But it would only take one – an eye can be as keen as a sword, remember. Even if none are tied to him, what do you think would happen if they found out we were from Ferol? Worse still if they discovered you were a Primitive. All of those being taken near the Ferol borders can't have escaped notice – the whereabouts of any Primitive is becoming valuable information. Perhaps it already goes beyond that."

"Stop using that word. Primitive. You know I don't like it," Ceria said. It made it sound as if those with powers were another species.

"Fine, yes. All I'm saying is that we've become commodities one way or the other. And soldiers' loyalties follow the coin. They might belong to the Queen, but we're a long way from the Central Seat." Telde moved to the window and closed the wooden shutters. She lowered her voice. "We can't take any chances. The half-man could find us, even here. We can't let our foolishness expose us, when so many sacrificed to get us here."

At least she said *our*, Ceria thought without much consolation.

"I was only trying to help the jalren," she muttered quietly. "Such a thing shouldn't be hunted for sport. It hasn't been done for generations."

"A lot is changing, Ceria. The Queen is less visible in her rule, especially out here in Ireldelor. There's unrest in the lands, and Ferol's closed borders only adds to it. Gods know how the Regency will try to take advantage. People sense that conflict is coming."

Telde let escape a small sigh as she moved to Ceria and knelt to take her foot. She had placed a cloth and a small bowl of water near the base of the stool, and began using both to wash the wounds. Ceria gave up the pretence of helping after Telde had slapped her hand away a few times.

She thought about how small her world had been before all of this, full with only Ferol. Naturally there was always talk of the Queen and her lands, when neighbouring Ireldelor was one of the countries under her rule. And you could barely have a conversation without someone cursing the Regency – the southern nation had been an enemy of Ferol for longer than books could recall. But that was as far as her experience had extended. She had grown up in the forests around Ferol city, and when they were razed she had moved into the city itself. She had always wanted to see the world, to explore all of Crescent, but not like this.

Both women were silent for a time as Telde continued to attend to Ceria's feet. Ceria ran a hand through her short black hair, still damp from the evening's exertions, and felt for the jewellery adorning her ears; one of the rings was missing. She gazed tiredly around the room. Pale wooden beams formed the crossed frame of the building, contrasting the dark clay of the walls. It may have been a well-constructed dwelling once, if a very modest one, but now even by the candles' sparse light Ceria could discern rotting sections, the woven sticks within the clay falling loose. They had stayed in better places in the months since escaping Ferol. But also much worse.

A splash of water brought her attention back to Telde, who was squeezing the cloth into the bowl. The liquid clouded a muddy brown. The lacerations on her feet were numerous but Ceria couldn't work up much interest, even with Telde's quiet curses. She was simply too tired. It was the dulling of her senses that always followed the use of her powers. It felt like several layers of sensation had been stripped away from her body, as if on each occasion she gave a significant piece of herself. That was an accurate enough explanation, as far as Ceria could tell. She didn't know how it worked exactly, it simply did. Most of the time.

She glanced at Telde who, her attention fixed on the treatment, briefly held a tender expression. When she didn't conceal herself behind guarded or fierce looks, Ceria was always surprised to find how young she appeared. And beautiful, no question there: her eyebrows sharp and angled towards her temples, and only severe when her expression matched it, a few shades darker than her auburn hair, which was set loose from its usual functional tail. Her pale green eyes, combined with her eyebrows, gave an inquisitive fever to her otherwise delicate features. Ceria wondered if others ever saw any of this. That scowl of hers was enough to keep most men at a day's distance.

But if Telde's sternness was a means of protection, then Ceria fell behind that shield too. Telde *did* look after her, she had to admit. She always had, ever since Climbe had introduced the barely twenty-year-old Ceria to Telde almost three years ago. The leader of the Ferolian resistance had told Telde in no uncertain terms that she would be responsible for the girl. Ceria smarted at the memory even now – she was no *girl*, and she certainly didn't need looking after. Telde was equally displeased. She was a soldier, she had snapped, not some nursemaid.

Yet both of them had lived with it. Telde never shirked her duty, and Ceria knew that she needed the shelter Climbe and his resistance offered. Even before the arrests had begun, Ferol's streets were a dangerous place for Primitives, and not a great deal safer for anyone else. The Hearts – who had always been fanatics, but were such a minority that no-one paid the religious order much mind – had suddenly grown in power, and wielded it with eager cruelty. Of course it had been the half-man behind their rise, though Ceria suspected that even the Hearts couldn't have imagined the scale of his plans. The horrors of his army.

The two women's companionship hadn't been easy, especially in the first months. They had often alternated between days of arguments and days of silence, both refusing to back down in either case. Climbe would eventually intervene, insisting that they stop acting like children with toothache, or in terms much less polite. The old man had a way of insisting in public, so that it was impossible to persist with their behaviour.

The arguments hadn't exactly disappeared over time, but their relationship had improved. They had grown close, and, though each was loathe to confess it, had come to rely on one another. Ceria had a way with people, Telde certainly did not; Ceria may have been streetwise to a degree, but she had no combat training unlike Telde, whose sword was an inseparable companion. When the resistance had arranged passage for Ceria out of Ferol, there was never any question that Telde would accompany her, despite how she must have wanted to stay and fight.

Ceria hadn't wanted to leave, either, but Climbe was adamant; he had been convinced that the half-man was on the verge of capturing her. So the two of them had fled their home, and headed deep into Ireldelor. They continued to run and hide, waiting for word from Climbe, and to meet up with the other resistance members who had escaped. Waiting to enact Climbe's plan to regain the city, whatever that might be – Telde was frustratingly reticent about it. Ceria had thought that once they were out of Ferol they would be safe, but Ireldelor held no shortage of threat, and not only from those under the half-man's influence. One of their most recent journeys had proved that.

Her weary mind began to drift and she couldn't stop it from placing her on a dusty road, hard-baked by the sun. She looked back and saw the large metal gates of Dereselon behind her. She was annoyed with Telde. Her friend had insisted they move on after only one night in the coastal city, where they had enjoyed the rare luxury of an inn. Dereselon had doubled its trade since Ferol's ports had been closed, and its diverse population was too talkative and keen-eyed for Telde's comfort.

As they were leaving the city, a group of Fivemoon priests joined them on the same westward road. They cheerfully discussed the receding gates, which were famed locally for the sculptures wrought out of the metal: tangled scenes of battle and celebration, proclaiming Dereselon's independence from both Ferol to the north-east and the Regent's lands far to the south. It was a city, the gates declared, answerable only to the Queen. One of the priests confided that the so-called glorious battles had no recognisable counterparts in history, with neither Ferol or the Regency ever laying claim to the city.

Ceria gained no little satisfaction from Telde's scowl as she encouraged the priests' chatter, but most of all she was curious: she had never come across Fivemoons before. Ferol had always been predominantly of the moderate Leafshade faith – before the Hearts, that is. The five men wore grey hooded robes, with the same closely cropped hair and beards. Only their facial markings separated them: each symbol depicted a different moon, they explained. They told of their pilgrimage to the Heartlands, the country that held the Queen's Central Seat and also the Fivemoons' holiest observatories.

But it was a false pilgrimage. After an hour's walk the priests' smiles turned sour. They circled the two women and demanded their possessions. Ceria saw her shock mirrored on Telde's face, but it took only a moment for the latter to recover. She drew her sword from the scabbard hidden underneath her cloak – the movement also revealing the gleam of crimson-plated armour – and stepped in front of Ceria, her challenging stance enough to make the men hesitate. The group obviously hadn't expected a fight, and their only weapons were the staffs previously wielded as walking sticks.

One of the men came at Telde nonetheless. She deflected his attempted blow, then countered by slashing at his arm; a warning strike, Ceria knew. The man's pained cry was enough to make up the others' minds. One of them barked a curse, and to Ceria's relief the group picked up their injured colleague and began to retreat.

Telde glared after them, sword gripped tightly, until they were out of sight. She would be furious with herself for being caught so unexpectedly, Ceria knew, but she could hardly be blamed – an impersonation of this kind was unheard of. Whilst many people didn't pay mind to religion or the gods, only a rare individual would risk angering them – or the men and women behind them. The Fivemoons were one of the factions that held sway in the Heartlands, and thus influence over the Queen's considerable armies.

They were desperate rather than practiced thieves, Telde said. Ceria somehow found that more concerning still.

She managed to shake herself out of her reverie, and looked down to see Telde wrapping her feet in bandages. Her friend was right, she thought: Crescent was becoming increasingly unsettled, as if it could sense a coming storm. People would do what was necessary to survive.

And she had seen this storm, this chaos. She knew its awful face. *The half-man won't stop at Ferol. He and his monsters are too hungry to stop.*

Ceria fought to suppress a shiver, but Telde didn't seem to notice. She was talking softly as she worked, almost to herself: "...more careful. You are important, more than you can appreciate. If we've any chance of regaining Ferol, then we need to use our wits. Await our chance. We can't be caught before the meetings. We have to be patient, and do things that go against our instincts..."

Even in her exhausted state, Ceria could see the direction of her friend's words. Her suspicions were confirmed when Telde looked up, a hint of apology in her eyes, if such a thing were possible.

"You want us to move again," Ceria said.

Telde nodded, her jaw set.

"We just arrived here," Ceria protested. "There's no reason to leave yet. We're not going to help by running away."

"I'm not running away," Telde said coldly, looking down.

"I know – I'm sorry. It's just that we get further from Ferol every time. It feels like we're abandoning it."

"I hate this as much as you, believe me. But we're following Climbe's instructions. There are other resistance members out here, and more will have escaped since we left. We simply have to wait until the meetings. Keep moving and remain undiscovered."

"Why hasn't Climbe contacted us? Do you think..."

"He's alive. I know it. The old man couldn't get himself killed if he tried. There'll be good reason why he hasn't." Telde waved the subject away, then stood and walked to the window. "I don't think we're safe here. We need to move."

Not safe. Had Telde ever felt safe on this godscursed journey? Ceria was close to repeating the thought out loud, but it was difficult to argue when her own actions had almost drawn such attention to them. And she had to admit that she felt a similar unease, especially since Dereselon. Perhaps they were better off being cautious, for now.

"Allow me one thing," Ceria said, finally. "Let me sleep first."

5

John stood on the edge of the roof, looking upon a city of shadow. The sounds of jazz drifted inconsistently from behind, struggling to permeate the thick quiet of the night. The building was tall, fourteen stories once serving as office space, and afforded a bird's-eye view of the city around it. Coated by the dark, that city appeared immortal. Black monoliths thrust up from buildings engraved at their feet.

Behind John, a torch on its side illuminated the asphalt surface of the roof. A canvas bag, portable stereo, and telescope were congregated around it, and a dim rectangle a few metres away marked the door back into the building. At the corner closest to him was a ragged patch of stone where a gargoyle once perched.

The buildings might appear immovable at night, John thought, but they were already crumbling. Fractured by vegetation, invaded by wildlife, worn down by water. Without humans the city was without its defences, its inoculators against the outside world.

The music had all but faded now. John stepped down from the ledge and walked back towards the stereo. He pulled out its batteries, tossing them across the roof to join countless others used up and scattered over the surface, then retrieved two new packets from the canvas bag. A faint hiss came from the torch by his feet. It possessed an inbuilt radio that he always left on, although it had been a long time since he had paid any attention to the emitted white noise.

After he had exchanged the batteries he searched the bag once more, pulling out a handful of compact discs and picking one at random. They were all instrumental – he couldn't endure any that featured singing, for the same reason that it was impossible to read. A voice was too close an echo, a thoughtless reminder of what was gone.

He began replacing the disc in the stereo, but was halted by a sudden, piercing pain in his head. It grew swiftly to a hammering so intense it made him nauseous, and he was forced to put out a hand for balance.

John swore breathlessly. The headaches alone were almost continuous these days, and now these additional spikes of pain were becoming more frequent. Medicine and alcohol didn't seem to make a difference. It was as if something was constantly attempting to bore its way into his mind.

And he could swear that there was another ache inside his skull, separate somehow, both in feel and intention. A nestled presence, probing but never revealing itself. He couldn't say which was the more disturbing. *Don't let them in, John.*

Let what in? He pressed a hand against his forehead as if to contain the pounding. *What's behind this?* Perhaps it was the onset of a serious illness. Cancer, or the prelude to a brain aneurism. Or the delayed effects of whatever had killed everyone else. Perhaps the universe had finally caught up with him and was dusting out the nooks of its prior extermination.

But *something* was happening, John was sure, whether its cause and consequence lay solely inside his mind or not. In the past week he had returned to the music shop, the building where he thought he had seen the light filling the upper windows. The entrance door had been broken off its hinges, and inside the instruments lay in disarray. Upstairs held a similar scene of destruction, with no indication that John could discover of why, or what was being sought.

Apart from the one obvious answer. He couldn't ignore the coincidence that this had happened in a building that he had visited so recently. *But what could be searching for me?*

Animals, maybe. They might be following his scent. But why now all of a sudden? It seemed far-fetched even for a starving predator. Yet there was something in the thought of being hunted that resonated faintly, deep within him. A subconscious itch that John couldn't quite reach.

His thoughts fragmented as the stabbing pain heightened. It was difficult to discern his own voice. He clenched his fists as the assault grew ever more insistent, ever louder. A will set on puncturing him, pushing him towards, towards…

He attempted to concentrate on the aching of his thumb. Compared to the pain in his head it was an encouraging familiarity, a call back to reality. He shouted over the din, finally managing to grasp hold of something coherent, some strand of himself. *Think John, remember. Names, places. Real things, physical things.* The apartment, the cat, the cuckoo clocks, the tinned food, the portable generators. John Bridgeman, Jessica Leary. The hotel, bright blue Entrance sign.

Gradually the pain began to retreat, until he could hear his own heavy breathing. He collapsed onto all fours, shivering and coughing. In the sudden quiet of his mind, he could feel it: the creeping presence, exposed momentarily. *One problem at a time.*

The assault wasn't over, John knew. These events lasted hours rather than minutes. But he had a little time to gather his strength. *Don't give in to it, don't let it in.* His fingers fumbled over the stereo as he searched for the play button. The music might help him through, bring him back.

There was another explanation for what had happened at the shop. A possibility that John feared to confront. Had he done it himself? Lately the world had felt increasingly unreal around him, and the headaches provided yet more numbing fuel. It was growing difficult to trust his memory and reasoning, his senses. What was there to detect or interpret in a dead world? Perhaps, deprived of input as it was, some bored sense was stretching out and crafting its own material.

He could be inventing all of this as a distraction, or a desperate grasp at purpose.

It was returning. A throbbing at his temples and behind his eyes. With a trembling hand he managed to find the correct button on the stereo, then rolled onto his side and curled up. He could hear the sporadic melody of a piano, but it was distant and insubstantial compared to the rising noise inside his skull. *Shut it out, don't give in. What's happening to me?*

John hugged his knees and looked into a sky that swam with light. Each star pulsed its own message: constancy, mortality, indifference, judgement, future, past. Pointlessness and purpose, heaven and hell. The universe had forgotten humanity and was moving on. Or it had suddenly remembered John and was moving in. He could feel the creeping presence, crawling closer. And now the roar of the assault was upon him, thundering to get inside, as the stars bled together, and the world became an engulfing whirl of light and noise and pain, closing in, seeping in…

*

John awoke, and for a few moments could not understand the world around him. The sky was a burnt orange, so bright it was painful to look at. Freezing air gnawed at his skin. There was a strange clicking, whirring noise.

It was the ache in his thumb that brought back his memory. The roof, the city. The asphalt dug into his cheek. *I'm still here.* For some reason the thought held an element of surprise. It wasn't that he was alive, but that the world surrounded him, that the same solid ground was beneath him.

The sound was coming from near his feet. He looked down to see the stereo tipped onto its back – the clicking was the disc skipping. He must have kicked it over during his… what, sleep? Unconsciousness? He could remember the beginning of the attack, but then only fragments: searing heat, heaving black, blue fire... There was no question that this latest episode was much worse than any previous. He doubted he could survive another.

He forced himself to sit up, then pulled the stereo upright and turned it off. The torch next to it was emitting the faintest hiss of white noise, its battery clearly dying. In the quiet John could hear the trills and chirrups of birds. That accounted for the light, too: it was dawn.

He got to his feet unsteadily, shivering in the cold. The pounding attack had left the usual dull headache in its wake, and he felt exhausted, but the surreality of the surroundings was at least fading. *You're still here, John. Still alive.* He stretched out his long limbs and started to exercise his thumb. It would be stiff all day.

He should go back to the apartment. Find something to eat, swallow some medicine. But he didn't feel like leaving yet – the apartment was somehow an emptier prospect than usual.

Instead he picked up the canvas bag and moved to the edge of the roof. The city had been substituted for another: in place of the monoliths were burnt out shells with glassless windows; below them rows of derelict houses, streets ragged with metal and plastic and bone. John was tempted to interpret the scene as an aftermath to the battle that had taken place in his head.

He wondered what it would be like when he was gone, and the final living remnant of humanity had disappeared. The world would continue unaware, growing over the concrete skeletons, digesting them. Some things would remain, though. The unpalatable parts, a few thin layers of strata reflecting the short-lived human flame: plastic, stainless steel, radiation.

He wasn't sure why it bothered him, why it was important that some trace of humanity remained. All that he possessed nowadays were memories of life, and he knew too well that they were only pale echoes. And yet there was something terrifying about being forgotten.

There was another layer of human construction that would be preserved, he thought, at least in a way. A century of radio and television transmissions, a blip of radiation fired out into the ancient universe. Then only static, the lifeless background noise. Like the torch.

He had visited a radio station a few months after the event. It was where Jessica had worked briefly as a news reporter, the first break in her journalistic career. John was still an out of work illustrator and often went to watch her through the glass screen, her voice disconcertingly emerging from a speaker behind him. He had returned, so many years later, with the vague hope of sending out some kind of distress call, a *Hello world*. It felt like something he should try to do. But there had been no power, and a great deal of the equipment was damaged by flooding. Even if he had managed to hook up a generator, he had no clue where to start with the overwhelming apparatus. At what frequency should he broadcast? What could he possibly say?

In those first weeks and months following the event he had been active, investigating, searching, *trying*, but it had been pointless. Nothing he could ever do would change anything. He was a ghost that didn't know its life was over.

John remembered a story he had once been hired to illustrate for a national newspaper. Jessica had put in a good word for him. A middle-aged man had surrounded himself with friends and family for all of his life, and found one day that whenever he was alone he couldn't help but fall asleep. It was as if he ceased to operate when there was nobody around to see him. Philosophers and scientists had clambered excitedly over the story, expounding theories of identities constructed by society, or rejecting the concept of the individual altogether. John and Jessica had laughed at it. She had claimed that it was when surrounded by her work colleagues that she found it difficult to stay awake.

He could empathise with the man now, however. He

understood the vacuum of meaning. *But you cling on, John.* A part of him refused to be consumed by an indifferent slumber. A faint bristling of purpose. It was surely a trick of the mind, some stubborn survival instinct, yet it made him continue.

John turned to the bag beside him and rooted out a compact camping stove, along with an aluminium cup and a tin of soup. If he was to keep on going, it wouldn't do to starve to death. He lit the stove and poured the soup into the cup. Carrot and coriander. He looked at the orange sludge with distaste. The survival instinct hadn't gone so far as to give him an appetite.

He left the soup to heat whilst he searched the bag again, emerging with a bright green coat and a sizeable fur hat. Both he had discovered recently in the one-bedroom flat of a traveller – photos and maps covering the walls, pins thrust into obscure countries. The dense russet fur of the hat seemed almost to have continued growing after it had been sheared off. John pulled both items of clothing on and huddled over the stove.

He looked at the building opposite. A number of small birds chattered along its periphery, yellow bodied with dark darting heads. A large black bird landed on the corner of his own building – a crow or rook, he couldn't remember how to tell the difference. It remained a wary distance. John must have been a curious sight: a lanky bearded creature hunched over some food or trophy, a fluorescent mass of a body with something resembling a dead animal perched on its head. He couldn't help but laugh, a sound that turned into a raw cough. The bird responded with a critical crook of its head and flew away.

John decided to look at the situation logically. If there *was* a reason why he was still here, what could it be? Perhaps names were important – what was that saying about God wanting mankind to label his creations? Was it in the Bible? He might have remained to preserve that kind of knowledge.

But if so, he was a poor choice. He was an illustrator,

unimportant, and he had never been a religious man. Jessica was the academic one, not him. He couldn't even identify the birds in front of him.

His sole talent was useless; he had been unable to draw since it had happened. How could it ever matter? Art had lost its meaning along with everything else. He had gone to a gallery after the event, taken all of the paintings he could carry and thrown them into the car. They had looked ridiculous and oversized in Mrs. Kirsch's apartment. The next day he had moved them to Clive's apartment and locked them inside. They went with the chandelier.

No, he wasn't the right man for the job. The accumulated knowledge of humanity, its inestimable bonds formed with the surrounding world, all had rotted away with the species. Now groups of birds were simply that, only that, and the stars were just light patterning the night sky. The reason he came up to this roof every week wasn't to observe the evening skies. It was because from this roof, using the telescope, he could gain a clear view of the hotel.

He turned off the stove and sipped the soup. It tasted about as pleasant as it looked.

Jessica always said that he had the right heart, but not the determination to follow it. She used his job as the prime example. He had the thirst for artistic freedom, yet he never made the leap. Instead he protested half-heartedly: he had worked at an advertising company, but quit to work as a freelancer. Jessica had seen through it. She had asked John how it was different when he took the same kind of jobs from the same kind of clients. She had fallen in love with an artist, she told him, not a mercenary.

It was one of the reasons for their frequent break-ups. Usually she would stay with her parents during the separations, until they had *thought things through*. She always returned, eventually, and would tell him that she believed in him, that was why she got so frustrated, didn't he understand?

But their last break-up had been different. This time she had moved to a hotel, and had started to look for another place.

After the event, John had gone to his parents' house, the homes of his friends, and those of Jessica's friends and family, and found what he had expected. He had buried all of the bodies. But the door in the hotel, her hotel, her room, he could not open. He had boarded up the windows of the building, so that no animals could get in. He had cleared the third floor hallway, and the route to the entrance. But he couldn't open that door. He had to keep her alive. The possibility. If he opened the door and found her, everything would surely stop.

John drank the soup, cursing inwardly. *Circles of thoughts, always returning to the same place. Never getting you anywhere, John.* He knew that he couldn't abandon the past, the leap was too much. Perhaps the part of him intent on survival was simple cowardice.

He flung the remains of the soup onto the roof, then reached into the bag. After a short search he found it: pitted brown grip, aged dark grey metal. The pistol felt cold and heavy in his hand.

He took aim at a distant bird, closed one eye, peered along the barrel. Squeezed the trigger, *click*. The bullets were in the bag, in a separate compartment.

It had belonged to Jessica's father, a relic of his service in the US Army. John was never sure if he had brought it legally to England. *My Colt, my workhorse, my lucky nineteen-eleven.* It was the only gun he could trust, he would explain. It had lived longer than him, and he expected it to live on after him. He would have had some pride in the truth of that prophecy, John thought.

When John had originally taken it, he told himself that it was for the animals. Just in case. He had never had cause to use it, and yet he held on to it. Perhaps he did so because it was one of the few objects in the world that retained a trace of its former symbolic power. Or because, when the day came, it would be easier than flinging himself off a building.

He tossed the gun back into the bag, and started packing away the rest. The torch he would take with him, but the stereo could remain here. As for the telescope... he hesitated as he looked at it.

Just do it. Get it over with.

John sighed, skipping the pretence of opposition for once. He brought the telescope to the ledge and began assembling its tripod. *Endless circles.*

Once the telescope was screwed into place upon the mount, he wiped the condensation from the lens and pointed it in the direction of the hotel. He looked through the finder scope, carefully manoeuvring it until a quivering, upside-down building appeared, its face a monotonous grey even in the enthusiastic morning light.

He moved to the telescope's eyepiece, and the building was transformed into a dark smear. He fine-tuned the focus until he could discern the features of a flag attached to it, the material hanging disconcertingly upwards. John adjusted the axis of the mount and at length the hotel's entrance slid into view. He started in surprise. His arm collided with the telescope and he barely managed to prevent it from falling over the ledge.

He desperately set it in its former position, fumbling to find the hotel again, a hundred frantic thoughts coursing his mind. *I'm not imagining it. Not this time.*

It seemed as if an eternity had passed before he could calm his shaking hands enough to regain the view of the entrance. When he finally did so, there was no doubting it.

The door was open.

6

The barn was a crush of people and sound. Groups shouted and cheered and argued around the gambling tables spread throughout the room, beneath an air choked by the blue-traced smoke of Spirit. There was a shriek, a glass smashing, raucous laughter.

Manvedian grinned. He felt at home.

He leant against a wall, picking out faces through the haze. There had to be over two hundred filling the vast space, and a disparate bunch at that. The majority were the rich – either the frivolously or shrewdly so – but there were many obviously poor too, those of only the desperate variety. In-between were those careful to mask their prosperity and identity. Like himself.

Manvedian watched men and women, young and old, their dress as diverse as their origins: here were the flowing gowns of the Queen's lands, meticulously white as was the current fashion; there the dark silks and sculptured headpieces of the L'pen Isles, a striking contrast to the desolation of their homeland. The colourful headscarves of the West competed with the dyed furs of Ranarin; the neat leathers and high collars of the Regency looked down upon the velvet tunics and fluted sleeves of Besgenin, more than half a continent away, as if they were a wayward cousin. There was no Ferolian fashion, naturally.

And, Manvedian noted with an inward curse, no sign of the Ferolian he was looking for. The man would come, he was certain, but the time spent waiting irritated him. Especially when surrounded with such opportunities. He whistled to calm himself, an old habit, but the tune was lost in the tumult.

Young servants shuttled between the tables, their platters brimming with pitchers of ale and clusters of exotic spirits. Manvedian snatched a thin glass of viscous purple liquid from a passing plate – Hedroth's Demise he guessed, by the tendril of smoke emanating from its surface – and swallowed it in one. He simply had to bear it, he told himself whilst the drink blazed a not-unpleasant path down his throat. There were more important things to attend to tonight.

At each end of the barn small stages had been erected for performers. Closest to Manvedian was a Tvennik throat singer accompanied by the traditional dancer. The contortions from both men were equally acrobatic, but went largely unnoticed by the crowds. On the opposite stage a man dressed in garish red was addressing a crowd whilst pointing to various markings on his face. Manvedian couldn't make out what his act might be.

The barn belonged to a wealthy merchant, Governor Banedete; the title was self-appointed. These *exclusive celebrations*, as Banedete referred to them, occurred once or twice a year and were an open secret. He and a large proportion of the guests had enough political swing to prevent objection to the nights' illicit attractions, but the secluded location helped: the barn was half a sun's ride from Dereselon, a city where such a gathering would have been under much closer scrutiny – and taxation.

The nearby village, hemmed in by Banedete-owned land, was an understandably amenable neighbour. Many of its inhabitants were in his employ, and the few guards, ostensibly Queen's men, had loyalties bought by Banedete long ago. Due to its position between Dereselon and Ferol, at the fringes of Ireldelor, trade in the village was sparser than ever. The nights' diversions were enough to draw the affluent from far and wide, and the village depended upon their liberal purses.

One such lure was the Spirit, smoked in such abundance here, but banned in most cities due to its unpredictable effects. *Especially on Primitives,* Manvedian thought. It could play havoc with their powers. And amplify them. The ancient belief went that the rare substance held the souls of the dead, which if set loose would possess an individual – hence, Spirit. More likely was that it brought out people's own demons and desires, Manvedian reflected.

Through the bluish haze, Manvedian could make out Banedete sitting on a high-backed chair on the other side of the room, looking magnanimous. He was known to be an eccentric if ruthless character, who would sometimes don an elaborate costume and roam the crowds. Manvedian had classified him almost immediately as an idiot. He was glad of that – it made things simpler. He knew the type and how to manipulate them, to stroke their egos and tempt their greed.

The invite had been easy to secure. He had given Banedete a crate of Ferolian Downberry. Since Ferol had closed its borders, one bottle alone had risen to ten times its former price. Manvedian had promised a cart-load more if Banedete was cooperative in other ways, and the man had already provided some useful information and contacts. He had ensured Banedete's continued allegiance with the carefully breathed possibility of entrance into Ferol – an irresistible opportunity for both the trader and egotist in the man.

He has no idea what he's walking into, Manvedian thought grimly. But he didn't pity him.

A roar sounded from the centre of the room, where the largest table was situated. Manvedian moved from the wall, pushing his way closer until he had a clear view. The table was at least twenty feet in length, with the competitors grouped together at one end and a row of full pitchers at the other. As Manvedian watched, one of the contestants flicked a white object from his palm toward the pitchers, resulting in a bout of jeers as his aim came up short.

Manvedian looked to the man next to him. "What's the game?"

"Tradition, ain't it?" he grunted in reply, not taking his eyes from the table. "Before the race tomorrow."

Of course. Manvedian had heard all about the race, and the juchen. It was one of the central attractions. "Tell me."

The man sighed, but seemed to reconsider his words as he glanced up at Manvedian. "Them's the riders on the left, them's their drinks over there. They each have their turn, where they take their teeth and –"

"Teeth?"

The man shrugged. "Tradition. Not *their* teeth you understand, it's the juchen's. The ones they'll be riding tomorrow. They get these big wooden pinchers and reach into their mouths and they yank 'em right out." He presented his own teeth in a crooked grin and demonstrated the procedure. "Then they take the teeth and try and land 'em in each other's ale. And when –"

The man's sentence was lost in another roar from the table, but Manvedian got the idea. One of the riders was being congratulated, whilst another was handed a pitcher with a large white tooth floating in it. He scowled and swore, then drank all of the ale down in one.

Manvedian's neighbour was still talking. "Last one left gets the best starting place tomorrow, but that don't matter much. It's more the bragging rights, ain't it?"

Manvedian looked at the celebrating rider. She was surprisingly young, with white hair that reached far down her back. She made short work of the glasses of liquor passed to her. "Who's the girl?"

The man's face soured as he followed Manvedian's gaze. "The latest hot shit, ain't she. *Godspit.*" He spat on the floor as if to emphasise the curse. "I got twenty royals on her, but the way she's sucking it up her blood's gonna be so thick tomorrow she won't be able to climb on the fenning animal."

The man continued to talk, but Manvedian stopped

listening. He watched the girl and felt an idea forming. He pushed it to the side for now, however – first he needed the information he had come here for. *Where is that fenning man?*

He left the table and aimed for the stage at the far side of the room, passing multifarious structures with only gambling and amusement in common: a huge Daktir table, its cobweb design scoring the surface; the squeals of rodents from Wilvarla's Maze; a man haltingly extending his hand toward a hole in the side of a tall, hissing vessel. The air glowed blue with Spirit above another table, but Manvedian couldn't see its origins through the thronged crowd.

Where a rare patch of floor or wall was empty, he saw evidence of dismantled stalls and troughs. Remnants of the barn's usual occupants: the juchen. Doused as it was in disguising perfumes, the place still smelt faintly of shit and piss.

How Banedete managed to acquire the uncommon creatures was a popular subject of speculation. Their home of the Black Sea was on the opposite, southern side of the continent, and the desert land remained unmapped and mostly consigned to myth. The animals were huge, fierce, and notorious for killing their riders. Banedete auctioned them individually. Most buyers would hire a rider to represent them in the race, but those less wealthy – or a great deal more eccentric – would risk themselves for the riches and celebrity awarded to the winner.

For tonight, the juchen were evicted from their stalls and kept in a pen outside. Manvedian could hear them now and then, a guttural rumbling beneath the din of the barn. The more antagonised they were, Banedete had confided, the better the spectacle of the race.

Manvedian reached a position from which he could keep an eye on the entrance, which was flanked by two guards. On the stage near him was the red-clothed performer previously too distant to make out. The man was blind, or at least claimed to be. The markings on his face were stars, one each on his forehead, cheeks and chin. His eyes remained closed as he challenged the sparse crowd: "Five royals to the lord or lady who can strike any of my stars!" But he warned that he would take five royals off those who failed to hit him within three attempts.

Cheap trickster or some weak Primitive, Manvedian couldn't tell, but if this was the sophistication of the performances then Banedete was lucky to have filled even half of the barn. A similar show could be seen in the backstreets of any city, and was what many Primitives were reduced to. Those with powers were rare, but such individuals had been around for as long as Crescent, and were generally accepted if not approved of. Although their abilities were of an almost infinite variety, most – like this man – were barely powerful enough to hold an attention. *At least he's safe from the half-man's interests,* Manvedian thought.

He watched as, following a few successful evasions, a volunteer landed a blow upon the performer's jaw. The latter complained about the smoke in the room and of disorientated senses, but received only jeers in response. The next challenger punched him in the stomach. Manvedian lost interest.

He waited until a servant passed, and grasped him by the arm. "I have a task for you."

The fear in the boy was palpable as he gazed up at Manvedian. He understood why: his shoulder-length black hair and similarly dark clothing, combined with his imposing height, meant that he appeared one of the more intimidating guests. *Good.* It would make sure the servant did as he was told.

"Where do you live, boy?"

The servant managed to splutter an answer about the village. "My father's the tanner."

"Do you and your family fear the gods?"

The boy's eyes widened.

"Good," Manvedian continued. "I'm going to give you the

opportunity to get on their favourable sides. And also –" he flicked a coin out onto his palm, long enough for the boy to register its silver glint "– the chance to help out your family at the same time."

The boy's expression twisted between fear and craving as he stared at where the coin had been. *He can't be more than fourteen*, Manvedian thought. *He's likely never seen a silver royal before.* They were worth fifty of the common bronze royals.

Manvedian allowed his words to sink in, and turned back to the stage. The previous performer had been hauled off, and he could see the next act waiting at the side of the platform. A cloaked figure, standing still.

"I will do it."

Manvedian turned to the boy at the abrupt response, and struggled to keep a straight face as he saw his earnest expression. The servant stood lankily, uncomfortably, but met Manvedian's gaze. *The kid has some mettle*, he thought, managing to hide a smile in a stern nod.

"I'll find you in the morning and tell you what's needed," Manvedian said. "It will be early. I'll need some letters taken, also. To Dereselon."

The crowd around the stage had quieted. Manvedian saw the cloaked figure standing at the front of the platform. That same stillness.

He looked back at the servant. "Are you able to do that?"

The boy nodded quickly.

"Good. Now go," Manvedian said, and had already returned his attention to the stage as the platter rattled away.

The figure had not moved. Head down, arms slightly outstretched. The crowd waited. A guard stood solemnly in front of the platform.

Then the figure looked up, and in a single motion untied and dispensed of her robes with a lack of ceremony. She was naked beneath.

Manvedian frowned. *What is this? A stripper – and not a very artful one at that?*

No, something was different about her. The smoky air seemed to shape itself around her, so that she could be seen clearly. She was starkly beautiful: entirely hairless, slim and black-skinned, her eyes a blue so pale as to almost appear white. But most remarkably, one side of her body was covered from foot to shoulder by intricate tattoos. Manvedian found it difficult to follow their sinuous patterns, as if they shifted as he watched.

They *did* move, he realised. The markings were slowly curving, twisting, converging, and eventually resolved into distinct forms with elaborate curls and tails. They started to snake around one another and the woman's body, coiling her leg and arm and breast. The patterns looped and danced, moving gradually toward the vacant skin on the other side of her body. They continued their graceful motions once the strange migration was complete, until at length they began to slow and settle, and the stilled lines glowed a scarlet resonance.

A momentary silence hung over the audience, before loud applause broke out. The woman remained motionless, staring only ahead. Manvedian was fascinated; he had never seen powers manifest in such a way before.

His attention was caught to such a degree that it took him a few seconds to register the disturbance over at the entrance of the barn. A man struggled with the guards, who drew their swords and pressed him up against the wall. *Shit.*

Manvedian hurried toward the entrance, shoving his way through the glut of people. The guards still had a hold of the man when he arrived, one of them lifting his slight frame with ease. Manvedian strode up and clapped a hand on the man's shoulder. "Causing trouble already?" He smiled at the guards. "This one's with me."

The guards looked questioningly towards Banedete who, after a lordly pause, gave a nod. They lowered their swords, and Manvedian swiftly walked the man away. *So much for an inconspicuous meeting.*

He tried to keep the annoyance out of his voice. "Quite the place, eh?"

The man had a fixed harried expression. Manvedian leant over and whispered in his ear. "*Gods*, Peledis, try not to look so fenning lost will you?"

Peledis managed a sheepish smile. Manvedian sighed inwardly.

A large gasp sounded from the crowd surrounding the stage as Manvedian dragged the man through, and he caught a glimpse of the performer's bare back. The half-man would no doubt wish to obtain the woman, like all the others, but he could learn of her from someone else. He had sent Manvedian after only one Primitive, and that was who he would deliver.

It was time to get to work.

*

"Have you seen any of the others?" Manvedian asked. He glanced across at Peledis, gauging his reaction.

Peledis gave a quick shake of his head. "You're the first. When I got your message... I wasn't certain whether I should come. You know what Climbe would say."

Peledis gazed into the large pen in front of him, his breath clouding out into the frigid night air. Massive shadows loomed in the darkness, which could have been taken for inanimate parts of the landscape if it wasn't for the deep grunts accompanying them. The noise of the juchen masked the two men's talk, although that was hardly necessary with the clamour continuing inside the barn behind them.

Manvedian studied Peledis' profile. The man was gaunt and nervous looking, and even thinner than the last time Manvedian had seen him. The few months since he had escaped Ferol must have been hard. He hadn't made it far, either.

Manvedian was surprised he had survived at all. His trail had been easy to follow.

Peledis looked back at him, dark rims beneath his eyes. "How long since you made it out?"

"Less than a month."

"Are things…?"

Manvedian shook his head. "Worse."

Peledis stared at his feet. "I would have left Dereselon by now. I never intended to stay so long. It's only… I've been waiting. For transport. *Safe* transport. It's taken longer than I thought, you can't trust anyone in that city. You know how it is." He looked up, seeking confirmation in Manvedian's eyes. "Some of the things we saw in Ferol, Manvedian… I can't sleep."

Manvedian waited, then said it carefully. "I need to find Telde."

"Why?" Peledis asked, warily.

"I have a message for her. It's important," he said, fixing his gaze on the other man. "I need to know where she's heading."

Peledis shifted uncomfortably. "I can't tell you, as I don't know. But I couldn't anyway. You know the rules. Especially where Ceria's concerned. You know how important Climbe considers her."

He's not the only one, thought Manvedian.

"Why didn't Climbe tell you?" Peledis asked.

Manvedian considered for a moment telling him that Climbe had disappeared. It was the truth, after all. But he didn't want Peledis to panic, or to turn to some impenetrable emergency plan that Climbe had surely instilled in the most trusted resistance members. Manvedian swore inwardly. *The old bastard is making it difficult, even now.* He continued to haunt him.

Manvedian shrugged. "You know Climbe. He never does things the easy way. Cautious to the point of paralysis."

"That caution saves our lives, Manvedian, you know that," Peledis replied, seeming to stand upright for the first time. "He knows what he's doing, and I trust him. With my life.

With all of our lives."

And he really does, Manvedian thought. Peledis was one of Climbe's most trusted members for good reason. But he was no soldier. He wouldn't have lasted much longer in Ferol amidst the half-man's slow strangulation of the resistance, and Climbe had known that. And now, away from the city, alone, he was a weakness.

Manvedian raised his hands in good-humoured resignation. "You're right, you're right. *Climbe's* right. He gave me instructions to follow, a contact to find. It's going to take me until fenning Godsfall to do so, mind. I was trying to cut a corner." He paused, leant on the wooden fence, adopted a sombre expression. "I suppose it's safer this way. We can't be too careful, especially now. We're being hunted like tick-ridden jallers. Did you hear they caught Neffede?"

Peledis gave an anxious shake of his head.

"A few days after he escaped," Manvedian continued. "They hauled him back to the city and took him to the courtyard in the Root District. Then they let the half-man's monsters have their way with him. Some say you could hear his screams all the way over in Sellsoul. They hung what was left of him from the Hearts Temple, as an example."

"Gods, Manvedian. *Gods*. Don't tell me these things." Peledis looked pale, even by his usual standards.

Manvedian shrugged an apology, and neither men spoke for a time. He whistled quietly to himself, his thoughts returning to Climbe. He seemed to be constantly battling against the resistance leader, even when he was absent. His words spoke through the members as if he gripped their jaws, and there seemed to be no end to his contingency plans. Manvedian wondered if the old man had seen his fate coming, if he had suspected a traitor amongst the resistance. He had managed to get Ceria out of the city with barely anyone's knowledge. But he hadn't been able to save himself.

One of Climbe's designs in particular had made Manvedian's life difficult: every member smuggled out of

Ferol had been given a location, and ordered never to say it aloud. It was an assembly point, in the event that there was no contact from Climbe. There were five such meeting spots that Manvedian knew of. But he didn't know which Telde and Ceria had been given.

He had gathered some useful information, at least. He knew the towns the two women had travelled through, the inns at which they had stayed. They had been close to capture in Dereselon, unbeknownst to them. Their trail went cold after they left the coastal city, but he could rule out two of the meeting locations by their south-west route through Ireldelor. Telemsis Waters, Candar'laon, or even Anat's Dark; it was impossible to conclude which of the remaining locations they were heading to. Telde would be too clever to make their destination obvious whilst she could prevent it.

Climbe refused to tell him the answer, no matter how hard he had asked. But Manvedian knew that a handful of resistance members had necessarily been given the details about the meetings. The most trusted members. He would get his answer another way.

He reached into a pocket of his leather jerkin and pulled out a thinly-wrapped tube of Spirit, then offered it to Peledis.

Peledis had been staring into the pen, but shook his head in reply. "Don't you know what those do to you?"

"Do I look like a Primitive? I reckon I'll survive," Manvedian said, and sought out a nearby torch to light the smoke.

"It's illegal," Peledis said.

"The best things are."

The juchen had moved closer. There were glints of hardened carapaces, and of the trio of horns where the rider's ropes would be attached. Peledis glanced nervously between the animals' profiles.

Manvedian knew there was no danger; the juchen were tied to stakes each the width of a man, and couldn't move beyond a few yards. He didn't tell Peledis. Instead, he took a few pulls of Spirit, exhaled slowly, waited. The blue-veined smoke fleeced the air in front of him, hanging unnaturally before it dissipated.

Finally Manvedian spoke, with a sideways glance at Peledis. "Can you get a message to Telde, at least? To let her know I'm coming." He asked it casually.

Peledis paused, momentarily caught off guard. "No. I can't."

It was only a split-second's hesitance, but it was enough. Manvedian smiled inwardly. *He knows where she's going.*

"Sorry. I had to ask," Manvedian said. He laughed and slapped Peledis on the back. "Listen, enough of all this. The night is a raw babe yet, and here we are wasting it out in the cold. Let's go have some fun inside, eh?"

Peledis looked as uncertain as ever, but allowed Manvedian to turn him back towards the barn. *He probably thinks this has been one of Climbe's tests. Poor fool.*

"You don't change, Manvedian," Peledis said.

Manvedian let him walk a few paces ahead whilst he picked up the torch. *No, Peledis, I don't.* He strode up behind the man, who was complaining about the activities in the barn, and swung the wood forcefully at the back of his head. It connected, dully. Peledis crumpled beneath him.

Manvedian tossed the torch aside and knelt down to check the man's pulse. He looked down at him for a few moments, exhaled some smoke. *Never fenning easy.*

With a sigh, he slipped his hands beneath the unconscious man to lift him up. He carried him over a shoulder to a small copse situated beyond the pen, a few hundred yards from the barn. Once a satisfactory distance within, he set the man down against a tree, then sat next to him. Peledis' head slumped onto Manvedian's shoulder.

He reached into a pocket and pulled out a small bottle of clear liquid, then forced some of it into Peledis' mouth. *At least he'll get that sleep now*, Manvedian thought. He sat back and took a sip himself; it would help him to fall asleep faster.

He took a few final inhalations from the tube, then flicked it away. The Spirit would strengthen his powers.

Manvedian closed his eyes. He would soon have his answer.

7

John sped the car through the city, swerving to avoid the scatterings of metal and stone. He knew the best route to the hotel by heart, but the way was far from clear. Often he was forced onto the pavement to bypass strings of stationary cars, and it was difficult to avoid the other debris – glass and plastic, bicycles and bones – especially at this speed.

Slow down, John, slow down. But even as he repeated the words, he knew there was no way he could obey them. The door was open. He must have stared through the telescope for over a minute to make certain, before grasping the canvas bag and torch and sprinting through the building to the car outside.

The hatchback shuddered in protest as it travelled over a broken section of the road. The morning sun reflected off the glass that remained in the shops and buildings, flashing in his eyes as he raced past. He tried to prevent his thoughts from progressing to questions that he didn't dare voice. To what, to who; to *if*, to *her*.

Just get there, John. Get there. He pressed his foot down on the accelerator.

The front of the car suddenly jolted as it struck a loose section of concrete, a piece of which flew up to collide with the windscreen; the glass was instantly transformed into a fractured latticework. John braked and veered away in reflex, realising his mistake too late as he was unable to stop the car from skidding sideways. He had a moment's glimpse of another vehicle before his own smashed into it and his head slammed against the driver-side window.

A blaze of pain. Splintered light. Shrill ringing.

His vision cleared stutteringly, a faculty struggling to remember its purpose.

He looked to his right, not quite able to focus on the crack in the glass that his head had created. He traced it slowly with a finger, then reached up to feel a dampness on his temple. Through the window he could see the crumpled bonnet of the other car. Two skeletons were inside, slumped against one another. The airbag had activated, and the driver's head and right arm were missing. The passenger leant towards John, its lower jaw absent.

Glass fell from somewhere behind and the sound snapped John out of his stupor. *Wake up.* He checked himself for further injury: other than the head wound and an ache in his neck, he appeared to be in one piece.

It came back to him: where he was going, the possibility of what might await him there. *Come on.* He wasn't going to let anything stop him, not when he was so close.

He climbed across the passenger seat and stumbled out onto concrete. He glanced about the street, attempting to regain his bearings. His mind worked sluggishly before it finally lurched into recognition: the hotel was less than a mile from here. He reached back into the car to retrieve the bag and torch, then turned and ran.

So close now. To her. *Surely her, surely. Please.*

By the time John arrived at the large gates that stood before the hotel's drive, his senses were returning. The wound on his temple had stopped bleeding, but there was a recognisable ache in his head: the hammering of the previous night's assault, if in a more subdued form. Was it weaker because of his head injury?

John pushed the question from his mind. *Keep going.* He

raced up the driveway, then the shallow steps of the entrance. He stopped in front of the door.

It was open. A small part of him was relieved by that fact, exonerated. But he frowned as he saw clear indications that the door had been forced. It hung at a tilt, and one of its hinges had been torn off. Inside he could see a bright smattering of glass on the floor, where one of the thick panes had shattered.

He felt a numbing panic creep over him. *Just keep going, keep going.* He stepped inside.

The gloom blanketed him. The shaft of sunlight issuing through the doorway seemed reluctant to venture more than a few paces in. It was silent, except for the fragments of glass crunching beneath his boots. He moved to the desk; the key was still there. The panic gnawed at him, a suffocating comprehension.

A noise. He was sure of it. From the lounge?

He rushed to the room's arched entrance, but couldn't discern anything within its pitch black interior. He switched on the torch in his hand, only for the light to sputter out almost immediately. *Batteries, damn.*

The noise sounded again, but more distinct: a heavy thud, followed by a strange rasping whine. It came from the dark at the opposite end of the large room.

He began searching the bag for batteries, but was stopped by a sudden light. It was as if a door had opened a fraction at the other side of the lounge; a strip of brightness bled from the aperture. *No, not a door.* The edges were too irregular, and seemed to be wavering. John struggled to make sense of it, until he realised with shock that the highlighted contours were vast limbs. A colossal figure stood in front of the light, almost as tall as the vaulted ceiling.

John stared in horror. The figure moved, and he glimpsed a giant made up of pallid flesh – but more staggering yet was what was revealed behind it. The source of light was unmistakably alive. Its liquid shape was ever shifting, yet somehow cohesive. These were the two creatures that he had seen previously in the city. They were real.

Then the light looked at him.

He could tell not strictly because of its movement – its form sharpening, twisting towards him – but because of the overwhelming pulse of emotion that he received: a cold purpose, a bitter malevolence. It was here to kill him.

For a moment John was frozen to the spot, before he forced himself to duck behind the wall. He hurriedly searched the bag, clutched the pistol, then delved deeper for the pocket that held the bullets. The crawling presence was in his mind, it revealed itself fully now: malicious, mocking. The same as the light. He was certain that it was different from the pressure that caused his pounding headaches. It was much worse.

Despite his fear John felt a surge of anger. These *things* were all there was. There was no hope, no humans, no *her*. The comprehension tore deep into him. He unzipped the pocket in the bag and pulled out the cartridge. *The bastards will pay.*

But as he loaded the gun, the light appeared before him, suddenly and blindingly. He stumbled backwards. It loomed over him: drifts and eddies, vortexes flowing and churning. Again John felt the pulse of feeling, as if the hateful broadcast were part of its physical make-up. He could feel the crawling presence communicating to him in an unknown language, but from which he could understand a plain message: *Found you.*

John watched in dread, unable to move, as a tendril of molten light coalesced within the creature. It snapped out from the body and entered his forehead without effort. *Deafening chaos. Teeming nothing. Ceaseless entities: inquisitive, hungry. Trivial being, are you the one? Energies swarming through him. Scouring, shredding. Tiny plaything, are you the one?*

Some distant part of him remembered the gun in his hand, and with agonising effort he pointed it upwards, pulled the trigger. The shot rang out loudly, the discharge knocking the pistol from his grip. A screech of fury; a whorl of turbulent light marked the bullet's trajectory through the creature. Then it vanished, leaving only whispers of vortices in the air.

John hesitantly touched his forehead, expecting an entry wound, a bloody fissure. But his skin was unbroken. *Christ, what the hell just happened? What did that thing do to me?*

He became aware of a crackling noise, a familiar electric hum. He picked up the gun and peered around the wall, into the lounge. The light was back beside the giant creature, which could be seen clearly now: a mass of raw flesh, humanoid in shape but hideously exaggerated, its muscular limbs twisted and irregular. Dark liquid eyes staring out from a contorted face. The giant harboured a light of its own, spitting erratically from blackened hands. There were two large metal bands fitted around its wrists, which it held together as if in supplication.

John felt a wave of revulsion, his anger rushing back. He lifted the pistol and fired at the two creatures in a wild spray of bullets, squeezing the trigger again and again until it clicked emptily. He was certain that at least some of the shots had struck the giant. A moment later an animalistic wail confirmed it, yet the creature stood unmoved.

With a noticeable change in pitch, the charged light in its hands grew until it was a ball of tumultuous lightning. The giant raised its arms toward him. *Oh shit.* John scrambled away from the entrance, but at the same instant there was a crack of thunder and the wall behind him exploded. Something heavy struck his shoulder and knocked him to the ground.

John picked himself up slowly, in a daze. His left arm dangled uselessly; his shoulder felt as though it was on fire. He ran towards the stairway. He had dropped the gun somewhere. The stairs were entirely black. *They must be following me.* He had nowhere to go, there was no escape. Yet he felt a strange calm, even as he ran from the monsters. It was relief. This was finally it, after waiting so long. The loose end tied up.

He kept on running, up into blackness. He could hear the giant behind him. The stairs were shaking. He felt his way towards the third floor.

It was pointless, he knew that. It had never been Jessica. These two creatures had been hunting him, and now they had found him. He collided wearily with the walls, increasingly disorientated. The dark was directionless and thick with vibration. It filled his lungs, weighing down his body, slowing him until his legs gave way and he collapsed to the steps.

Piercing noise: something hammered its way through his delirium. Like an old enemy, the pain inside his head shook him awake. He pushed himself up, breathed in air. *Keep going.* He stumbled up the last of the stairs to the third floor.

He staggered into the corridor and towards her door. It was closed, of course, and the tins remained where he had left them. He slumped down against the door, his exhausted body finally allowed to rest. The creatures would soon be here. He could hear the cruel voice in his head. But beside it was that other noise, the unknown force responsible for his migraines. Always pushing him, always trying to prise its way in.

There was static in the air, and John sensed a light at the end of the hallway. He closed his eyes, leaning his head back against the door. *Not long now, nearly over.*

But before the end he could manage one final act of defiance. He might not understand the hammering presence or its purpose – perhaps it was simply another method of killing him. Yet it was different from the light, from these monsters, and that was enough. *It can have me.*

John abandoned his resistance. He opened himself and could feel the noise coursing in, his mind twisting awkwardly and painfully to accommodate it, pathways altering to its design, and he used the very last of his energy to help it, to drive its disfigurement. At the same time he let go of the rest: the dead city, the echoes, the purpose, the hope. He finally let go of her.

Then something inside him snapped, and the world disappeared.

PART II:
GATHERING

Dark earth encloses him. Above, below, it presses against his sides. He reaches up a hand (his hand?) and feels cracked stone and roots and wet soil. Around him the earth is moist and alive, it resonates power. He is a spirit inside a beating heart.

He walks, he follows the tunnel. There is no light but he can see down here (is he the light?) and it is familiar somehow. Passages split and tangle and maze on and on, but he knows the way, he inexorably follows the right route. (Towards?)

There are runes along the walls, he sees them now. An ancient language engraved in stone. They tune the land, he knows, he is told, they are its eyes and mouths and hands and they are its disciples. They flicker blue, they whisper to him. Som'syere.

Earth reverberates, and part of him shudders with it.

He walks on (towards?). A network of tunnels suffuse the land, arteries and veins pulse animation. But too loudly: it hammers an outrage, there is pain and atrocity. (What is above? He knows it somehow.)

He steps into a wide chamber. There is a shadow on the opposite wall, an opening that is black and impenetrable and chaotic. He knows what is in there. He shivers terror and exaltation.

Out of the wild, deep dark, a slither of light.

Shiver turns to convulsion, refusal: no, he cannot. He knows what it is, preserver and destroyer, he knows what power it holds.

It cannot have him. He runs from it.

Now he is lost, the path is unknown. The earth shakes complaint. Sodden soil showers him, boulders block his way. But he is right. It is too much to risk. Its power: elemental and boundless, all-consuming and indifferent. (Turn back, grasp it?) With it he can be anything. (Preserver or destroyer?)

It is too much to risk. He runs.

He breaks free to the surface, he escapes the land to the sky. The day is choked by unnatural cloud. He is above, he swims in the storm, and beneath him the hills flow eternally on. But there are lacerations in the skin, it is scarred and gouged and pitted. A distant line scores the sea, bridging to a land he knows as well.

Somewhere below, a howl from deep within.

8

John woke to a blur of light. Bright streaks sliced through transient smudges; ghosts of shapes clotted his vision. His head felt fragile and worn, paper-thin.

He rubbed at his eyes, and as they adjusted to the light details eventually began to emerge. He was on a hard bed, in an unfamiliar room. The walls were a pale timber, almost white, and harboured several wide windows. Sections of cloth were attached to the frames, rolled up a short distance at the bottom. The warm light that entered bathed an eclectic array of plant life lining the room – none of which John recognised.

To his left was a doorway to another room, from which emanated the smell of a sharp spice.

A woman was humming.

John coughed, involuntary and raw. The humming ceased, and a few moments later a woman walked in from the adjoining room. She was short and stocky, a thicket of grey hair above a heavily lined face. She wore a simple brown dress and held a wooden spoon in her hand. She smiled at him.

"Well, it's past time," the woman said, shuffling up to his bed. "I thought you might sleep until Godsfall itself."

Was this really happening? After so long – a living, breathing human. *Where am I? How did I get here?* John's mind whirred but refused to settle on answers. He stared at the woman.

She seemed unperturbed by his reaction, and leaned over as if to examine him. John flinched, but she took his head firmly in her hands.

"Don't be difficult. Sit still."

He did as he was told – something in her manner was practised and reassuring. And yet there was another aspect that was wrong about this woman, John thought, apart from the fact that she was alive. He couldn't quite determine what it was.

Meanwhile, she busied herself with scrutinising him: his eyes followed the spoon as she moved it from side to side in front of his face; she clicked her fingers at each of his ears. She pinched his arm, then rapped the top of his head with the spoon. He hacked a protest.

"Well, your body seems alive, but your mind I'm still thinking about. Can you speak?"

He tried to say something, but it came out as a dry rasp. His throat burned.

"Stay where you lay," she said, and disappeared into the other room.

Through the doorway John could see shelves amassed with containers of all shapes and sizes. Odd-shaped roots – *vegetables?* – sat haphazardly in-between.

He glanced around the room. Was it a small cottage? The architecture was unfamiliar, and he couldn't identify the pale wood: its grain was flecked with silver. There were stone carvings placed between the plants, black and dark green and as varied as the vegetation. Close to his right was one of the largest: a female figure wreathed in leaves, her breath sculpted into delicate loops and whirls.

He remembered, as though it were a confused dream: the car, the crash, the hotel, the monstrous creatures, the corridor. *Did it happen?* It felt so distant.

"Drink this."

The woman had returned. She held out a bowl of brownish liquid for him to take. Whatever the other truths, John thought, here was another human. A real person, standing in front of him. An inexpressible joy flooded him. He sipped from the bowl with trembling hands. The taste was terrible and he couldn't have cared less.

"Improvement?" she asked.

He nodded in reply, but an instant later realised what was wrong.

"Why –" he spluttered, almost choking on the word. He swallowed, then spoke slowly, as if startled by every syllable. "Why can I understand what you say?"

The language she was speaking was not English. He did not know what it was – yet he could follow every word. And more remarkable still, he found himself responding in the same foreign tongue.

"I don't know how you expect me to answer such nonsense," the woman said, an eyebrow raised. "I'll tell you that your accent is peculiar to me. With that beard you could be a Ferol man, though it's been a long while since any of those travelled this way – you're not an escaped one, are you?" She peered at him, more curious than concerned.

"No. I don't know." The strange arrangements of vowels and consonants formed effortlessly in his mind, but tumbled uncomfortably from his mouth. He held his head in his hands. *What has happened to me?*

"Where am I?" he asked finally.

"You're in Milnadon village," the woman answered, watching his face for recognition. When he showed none, she continued. "We're about two suns from Candar'laon. No? A tensun from Edemon?" A short laugh at his blank expression. "Ireldelor? Crescent?" She said the last with a teasing smile, but it faded into a frown when she saw John's continued lack of comprehension.

She tapped the spoon against her forearm. "I'm thinking it could be loss of memory. I've seen such things before, but usually in the elderly, or those with head injuries – which I suppose could explain you. Don't worry, it sometimes comes back. I can help."

"I was injured?" John asked, whilst the woman foraged

around the room, evidently searching for a particular plant.

"What's that? Oh, yes – I'll tell you about it in a moment. But first – *there* – I have something that will help you."

Before John could say anything more, she had snatched up a slender plant and scurried into the other room.

He stared after her in a daze. *Could it really be a memory lapse? A concussion?* It was possible. He might have been in an accident that had wiped away his most recent recollections – what this place was, how he had arrived here, when he had learnt the language. It could have reset his memory to the last traumatic event in his life – the hotel. It *did* feel like a long time ago.

Despite its remoteness, a shiver passed through him at the recollection of the creature made of light. He touched his forehead. *Can such things really exist?* His mind and memory were a tangle. What was real and what nightmare? If there was a possibility that the events in the hotel had not happened, then what of the two years before?

But this is real, John told himself. *This place, this woman. Alive and real.*

She came back in – he realised he was relieved each time – carrying another bowl, which she delivered with an expectant look. The liquid was largely flavourless, apart from a vaguely bitter aftertaste that he could not identify. He sipped it politely, then cleared his throat.

"My name is John. What's yours?" It sounded ridiculous and stiff, but he had to start somewhere.

"John? Like the animal?" She let out a melodious chuckle.

John frowned.

"You must come from far away indeed." She chuckled again, then managed to compose herself. "My name is Wimda."

John set aside the question of his name for now. "It's nice to meet you, Wimda." He extended a hand, realising that he was naked beneath the thin sheet.

Wimda gazed at his outstretched hand for a few seconds,

75

before reaching out with her own. But instead of shaking his hand, she simply touched the tips of her fingers against his. She then pulled up a wooden stool and sat beside the bed.

"Ask your questions, John."

"How did I get here? What happened to me?"

"I can only answer so much. You were found nearby, in one of Mardhe's fields. You're lucky you weren't trampled by jallers – although that might explain you. When they brought you to me, you were as bruised and broken as battle. I'm the closest to a healer the village has after the gods took Tensid, Hethea bless him. I'm a herbalist, as you can see." She indicated the abundant vegetation in the room. "Healing draughts, skin ointments, pain-stopping tinctures – I provide the best sleep tonic this side of Ireldelor. A member of the Central Seat once asked for me by name. These are truths, not boasts. If you're sore of chest or temper, so it's spoken in the village, then go to Wimda – don't get impatient, I'm returning to your story."

She had mistaken John's frown. *Ireldelor? The Central Seat? Where were these places?*

"It's fortunate they brought you to me," Wimda continued before he could ask. "You were in a bad state. In your body, yes – your skull was damaged, and your shoulder – but I mean inside your head, also. There's some deep trouble there, I could see that."

John felt his shoulder, which responded stiffly. He realised the truth. "How long have I been here?"

"You've been unconscious for… well, it must be over a week now. Every day murmuring and twisting in your sleep. I said to myself, some bad thing has happened to this man."

"Yes, I think you're right."

The ache in his shoulder was from the segment of wall that had struck him. His head wound was from the car crash. It was real, all that had happened. The hotel, the light, Jessica. Everyone had died.

No, not everyone, he told himself. Here was a living person.

And something that Wimda had said suddenly registered: *They brought you to me. There were more.*

"How many more?"

Wimda shook her head, not understanding.

"Alive, I mean. How many more alive? That survived?"

"Survived what?" She tapped the spoon against her lap, contemplating him. "Yes, you're a peculiar one. I said as much to myself."

"Please, Wimda. Tell me. How many people live here?"

The urgency in his voice gave her pause. "In Milnadon? I wouldn't know precisely, you'd have to go to the village census keeper. But that was Tensid also, Hethea bless him, so I suppose there isn't one right now. Which is a problem we must fix – don't fidget, I'm answering your question." She took a few moments to complete some invisible calculation. "I suppose, yes, I would say, over a hundred."

"A hundred!" John bolted upright in the bed. "Alive here? Survived? That many?"

"I don't know what survival you're speaking about. The village is here as it always has been, thank Hethea," Wimda said. "But if you don't believe me, then listen."

She stood and walked to the nearest window. She rolled up the cloth covering and perched on her toes to hook it in place above the frame. Brilliant light immediately filled the rectangle, and John had to shield his eyes. The sky was a vivid, cloudless aquamarine. He sat up and strained to see more, but there was only a tantalising hint of land in the distance. He looked to Wimda. She tapped her ears.

For a long time there was nothing besides the sound of a gentle breeze and a few birdcalls. But finally, John heard a faint shout. Then, as he continued to listen and began to smile, there were further voices, a snatch of conversation, laughter.

He attempted to push himself up and out of the bed, but Wimda was across swiftly with a firm hand on his shoulder. "You must regain your strength."

"I have to see," John said.

Wimda sighed in response to his imploring look. "I will find something to give you a little strength, and then I'll show you – but only for a moment, then you're back to bed. Stay where you lay."

She left no room for argument as she headed to the door, plucking a sharp implement from the wall as she went. She shot him a warning look, then opened the door – John saw a snatch of land, tall grass, that dazzling sky – and closed it behind her.

He collapsed back on the bed, staring up at the low ceiling. Hanging from one of the pale beams was an ornate glass vessel that seemed to contain a fragment of blue rock.

It was all too much to take in. It was overwhelming. But it was wonderful. Finally, hope. Life. *I'm not alone.*

John wondered what country he was in. None of the places that Wimda had mentioned sounded familiar to him. Nor could he gather any clues from her appearance, or from the limited surroundings. Or from the language that he could inexplicably speak. Wimda didn't even seem to know of the human eradication, impossible as it seemed. Was this some remote, isolated village? An island? How did he get here?

There were still so many unanswered questions. But they could wait. *A hundred alive.* That was the important truth.

There was a knocking at the door, and before John had the chance to sit up again, a man had entered.

"At last you're awake! Can you understand me?" The man had light brown skin, short black hair, and wore a sleeveless robe. He spoke in a noticeably different accent from Wimda.

"Yes, I can. Who –"

"Incredible! How long have you been here?" the man asked eagerly.

John fought the disorientation caused by being so abruptly confronted with another living human. "I... don't know. Wimda said over a week."

"I know that. I meant how long *here.*"

John didn't understand the emphasis.

"Let me ask it differently," the man continued almost immediately. "Where are you from and how long since you left there?"

"I'm from England. And like I said, a week. I think. I'm not sure, this has all –"

"Incredible. So you only just arrived?" The question seemed to be rhetorical, as the man paced the room. His slightly portly shape always seemed to be in motion, his attention never settling on one spot for long. He was perhaps a few years older than John, although his abundant energy disguised the disparity. "And you can speak the language?"

"Yes, but I don't know how. I was hoping someone could explain it to me. I don't even know where I am."

"Incredible." The man fingered the fronds of a plant, then plucked off a leaf to study. John watched him from the bed, feeling more lost than ever.

The man turned to John, as if he had suddenly remembered he was in the room. "What's your name?"

"John."

"That's unfortunate."

"What? Why?"

The man picked up a figurine and then put it down again. "It's interesting about the language. It must be instilled somehow during the transport. What's the last thing you remember before being here?"

"I was in a hotel – look. Wait. How about you tell *me* some things? Like what this place is, and how it survived."

The man seemed to pause for the first time and look at him. "You are somewhere different entirely, John." A small smile crossed his lips. "Let me show you something."

The man moved to the door, positioning his back to it, then nodded toward the large statue next to John. John looked to the stone figure, not understanding his intention. He was about to ask, but then the statue moved.

John frowned, wondering if he had imagined the wobble. He glanced at the man, who for once was standing still, his concentration fixed on the sculpture. John pushed himself up in the bed and saw the dark stone shudder, a clear movement this time. Then, slowly, falteringly, it rose from the ground. The statue climbed a foot into the air, free of any objects around it, and remained there, floating impossibly in front of him.

John stared in astonishment. *What the hell is going on? Is he really doing that?*

The man smiled through his concentration. John followed the statue as it gradually descended to the floor. It dropped the final few inches, teetered unsteadily on the ground, then toppled into the adjacent plants.

"I'm improving each day," the man said. "A few months ago, I couldn't have held it in the air like that. Different materials present different difficulties." He sounded disconcertingly casual after such a display. "Do you have an ability? No? Perhaps you'll develop one. Perhaps not."

John felt dizzy. "Who *are* you?"

The man smiled his incessant smile. "I'm Jago, and I'm like you."

"What do you mean?"

The door opened behind the man and Wimda entered, almost colliding with him. She shot him an angry look. "What did I tell you about coming in here?"

She glanced at the toppled statue, which only served to intensify her glare. "And I've warned you about using your powers. This isn't the time to be open about such things. You will bring trouble on yourself – but even now you're not listening." She gave the grinning man a slap around the head and pushed him towards the door. "Out, now, out."

The man clutched at the doorframe and looked over Wimda's shoulder. "I'll show you, John." He beamed at Wimda, kissed her forehead, then allowed himself to be pushed out. "I'll show you!"

Wimda let out a long-suffering sigh as she slammed the door behind him. "That man is a thorn in my foot. Chew on this." She moved to John and handed him a thick stalk, shorn of its offshoots. He didn't risk argument and cautiously nibbled at the fibrous stem, which excreted a surprisingly sweet juice. He realised just how hungry he was.

"Jago has been bothering me day and night – chew it, don't eat it – ever since he saw those strange clothes of yours," Wimda said.

John attempted to get a grasp on the events and revelations so far, without much success. It seemed that instead of answers, all he encountered were more questions. He was god-knows-where, chewing on a plant, listening to a complaining, *alive* human, somehow understanding her foreign language, and he had just witnessed another person move a stone statue with... what, his mind?

He felt like the ground was slipping beneath him; he needed something solid to hold on to.

"Can you take me outside now?"

Wimda looked at John disapprovingly. "I'll take you to a window. You can see well enough from there." She offered him a hand.

He wrapped the sheet around himself and climbed out of the bed. His legs were weak, and he had to lean on Wimda's small but sturdy body as they moved to the open window. She moved a few plants aside so that John could lean on the frame. He stared out into the daylight, and was astounded.

The building was atop a slight incline, the view extensive. The sky was a shimmering blue-green ocean above a village alive with activity. Great white birds perched on wooden buildings that almost seemed to grow out of the land, their roofs made up of the same golden grass that lay in and around the village in vast swathes. A larger construction sat before a low hill in the distance, its upper tiers stacked implausibly. John could make out a herd of heavy animals at the village's edge.

And everywhere, everywhere there were people. Men and women and children, working and talking and laughing. John couldn't take his eyes from them.

"It's beautiful," he said, finally.

Wimda nodded approvingly beside him. "It's a healthy place. I can only hope it stays this way, with the world's problems rising as they are. You see the Spirit storm over there?" She pointed to a dark patch in the sky, which stood out like ink spilt on a pristine canvas. It seemed to shift and pulse as John watched. "I think it'll be here in a few days, a tensun at most. Previously we could go years without witnessing such a thing, but now we've had three in as many months. Crescent is in unrest, and I worry about what is to come. What are you staring at?"

John had barely heard her. He had seen something in the sky, to the left of the storm. It made the hairs on the back of his neck stand up.

A vast moon, silver and green. And beside it, a second, smaller moon.

John gripped the window frame, his heart pounding in his ears, the impossible thought seizing him: *Another planet. This is another planet.*

A movement caught his eye from below, and Wimda made an exasperated sound. He looked back to the village to see a man running up the incline towards them, waving something yellow. It was Jago. As he moved closer, it became clear that it was a piece of clothing.

John recognised it. It was a Brazilian football shirt.

9

Telde span and twisted with the sword, ducked and weaved and thrust and parried, one form blending into the next so that there was no visible separation, only fluent movement. Her footwork was precise yet light, her bare feet always poised for the unexpected attack, for the shift into the corresponding counter. The moonlight flashed off the double-edged blade as it sliced the air, picking out elegant inscriptions along its length. There was something dreamlike in her practice, a dance in the quiet of the night.

Ceria was bored with watching. Yes, she appreciated the beauty and discipline in the movements – though not as much as Telde, who could rhapsodise about it for hours on end – but she had witnessed a similar display every day for the past month. Telde was lost to the world each time, leaving Ceria to sit in silence.

She picked out pebbles from the flattened grass around her, tossing them towards the road a few yards away. Dark walls of trees crowded both sides of the dirt and stone path, which cut unerringly through the forest like an arrow cleaving a heart in two. At least that's how Ceria imagined it; the merchants were understandably grateful for the road that saved them a tensun-longer circumnavigation. The size of the forest could rival even those in Ferol and Ranarin.

She gazed past Telde's manoeuvres to the light of a campfire in the distance. They had been travelling with the merchant caravan for twenty or so suns – a ragtag band of all origins, most with no more in common than a talent for bartering and the appetite for a travelling life. The group included several like her and Telde, who had tagged onto the caravan for the security and company – the former important to Telde, the latter to Ceria. The disparate crowd meant that the evenings around the campfire were always interesting, not that Telde had allowed much socialising so far. And her fierce manner had scared away most other approaches. *Why does she always have to be so defensive?* Ceria thought. *Not everyone on Crescent is out to harm us.*

Part of it was continued punishment for the incident involving the jalren, even though it had been almost a month ago now. Telde had barely allowed Ceria out of her sight since.

But at least she had started to share more about their plans, finally trusting Ceria more than a child. Candar'laon – that was their meeting location, the end point of their months-long journey. Telde had explained how she had disguised their destination as best she could, taking convoluted routes to throw off any following them.

Candar'laon. Ceria had heard of it, in conversation and in books, but usually only in the same sentence as Edemon, the Ireldelor capital, of which it was considered a smaller – and much less grand – twin. But if it was anything like Edemon, she thought, then it would be a remarkable sight.

They weren't far away now. Since joining the caravan, they had made swift progress through the towns and villages on its route. Candar'laon was one of the merchants' principal destinations, and they hurried towards it after a lacklustre trade thus far. Once they emerged on the other side of the forest, another two or three villages, a few more nights, and they would be there.

And then? Ceria wasn't certain. She suspected that Telde wasn't either, and her friend would not be drawn on it – other than to state, vaguely, that they would better understand how they were to regain Ferol. *Climbe must have a plan,* Ceria told herself. *He must have a way of defeating the half-man and his army*. It would make all of this running, this inactivity while people in the city were suffering and dying, worth the sacrifice. *Regroup and retaliate*; Telde's words, a reassuring echo of Climbe.

Nonetheless, the evenings spent sitting idly were difficult to bear. Ceria was restless in the silence, a victim to her roaming thoughts. At least Telde had her forms to lose herself in. It didn't help either that Ceria constantly felt as though she were some prized and delicate baggage. She couldn't understand why Telde treated her like that – it wasn't as if she was unable take care of herself. And Telde was just as valuable to the resistance – surely more so. She was a skilled fighter, after all.

Ceria had her powers, but what use were they? She could only use them on animals, no matter what others might wish. Only once had she tried on a human, in her childhood, and it had ended in tragedy. She could never risk it again. She wasn't strong enough to resist the temptation.

Ceria fidgeted on the hard ground. She flicked pebbles at Telde's armour, left in a neat bundle on the floor while she exercised in a loose shirt. The metal shone a deep crimson in the moonlit night. The stones pinged off it.

Telde eventually sighed and paused her practice. "Do you have to do that?"

"Sorry," Ceria mumbled. She would have thought Telde able to withstand the distraction of a few pebbles, compared to the noise of battle for which the forms were intended. "Telde..."

"Yes, fine, go. If it means I get some peace," Telde said, waving her sword in the direction of the campfire. "Be careful."

She couldn't resist adding it, Ceria thought.

"And bring me back some food while you're there," Telde continued before she could reply, shooting her a grin and returning to her forms.

Ceria threw a pebble at her, then pushed herself up. She

walked towards the firelight, a pleasant breeze tousling her short hair. She passed the shadows of tents and carts, and the slumbering forms of jallers. Tied to the largest wagon was a huge shape, surpassing the size of the wooden trailer by half again. Ceria smiled at the outline of the joorun. The gentle beast was a prized asset of the caravan – not only for its ability to carry goods and pull carts, but also because the scarce animal would attract welcome attention whenever they visited the smaller settlements.

She moved closer and frowned at the heavy netting draped over the creature's back. Eyick had forgotten again – or was simply too lazy – to remove it for the night. Ceria had considered volunteering for the task herself, but Telde had talked her out of it. She was tempted to do it anyway.

But for now she left the joorun, and walked the final distance to the campfire. It was surrounded by the majority of the travelling group, a few of whom greeted her as she found a place to sit near the back. Most were absorbed in the conversation; the talk was of competing caravans, time schedules, goods that had dropped in value or were not wanted at all, towns that were not as welcoming as they once were. Ceria had the feeling that it was a well-worn topic. Someone passed her a stick on which an unrecognisable meat was skewered. Following a few leathery bites, she decided to save it for Telde.

She sat back, not listening to the conversation but allowing its sounds to flow around and over her, content to be in the company of people. It was tempting to close her eyes and lose herself in the warmth of childhood memories spent around similar fires, surrounded by similar forests.

After a few minutes, however, the mention of Ferol caught her attention. She leaned forward to listen.

"I've lost half my fenning supplies since they closed themselves off." Ceria recognised the speaker as Amese; she traded in rare stones and read hands. "I'll be as poor as Mercy's End before the year's up."

"Ferol is a symptom of a greater illness," said the grey-haired Holan, who dealt in livestock. "There's something wrong with Crescent – just look at the Spirit storms."

A few murmurs of agreement. The talk rebounded quickly around the fire.

"They'd had a Spirit storm up near Castout Rock, only a tensun before we ran through."

"I heard they had a giant one in L'pen'Mar. Razed all the Spiritstone bridges."

"It wasn't L'pen'Mar, it was L'pen'*Solan*. And it was only one bridge." That was Vers, the bootmaker.

"The point is they're getting worse, like Holan says. The last time we had so many was a hundred years back, in Wilvarla the Bright's time."

"It wasn't a hundred years, it was two hundred. I think you're getting her confused with Carisus the World Breaker."

"I know the difference between Wilvarla and Carisus."

"I don't. All those godscursing Primitives are the same to me."

"Watch your words. Ganrey's a Primitive."

"I meant proper Primitives, ones with real powers. Ganrey couldn't scare a jon."

"You don't get 'em like Wilvarla anymore. Powers are dying out."

"You do, you just don't hear of them. Ten royals says it's one who's causing all the Spirit storms."

"I got it from a sailor in Dereselon that the storms are making a whore's bed of the ocean up there – he reckoned they're coming from Ferol, from that island of theirs."

"Bet that ain't all you got from the sailor."

"I heard there was a revolt in Ferol, and everyone was killed. They're keeping the gates closed so no-one will know."

"Don't be ridiculous. How could they hide such a thing?"

"I heard it was water plague. Ravaged them all in a week."

"Messengers go in and out, explain that to me if they're all dead. Are they talking to spirits?"

"*Messages* go in and out, there's a difference."

"There's more than that goes in – what about all those Primitives over the Ireldelor border that've been grabbed?"

"That's just tales. They wouldn't dare take folk from Queen's soil. She'd have their balls."

"I heard monsters climbed out of Som'syere island. Beasts that feed on storms and breathe out fire."

"You have it wrong. Ferolians simply look like beasts – big hairy beasts." The speaker – Ceria recognised him as Raldeu, husband of Amese – made a clawing gesture with his hands.

A few laughs sounded around the group. Ceria shivered despite the fire.

"The only beast around here is you, Ral," said Amese, pushing her husband with a grin.

Ceria felt someone sit down next to her.

"Cold, precious?" It was Eyick. The large man – head shaved, beard braided in two – was uncomfortably close. He offered her the flask in his hand.

"I'm fine," Ceria said. She looked deliberately away, intent on the conversation.

"It wasn't Regent Liafur, it was Regent Amuur."

"Can I say one thing without you trying to correct me, Vers? The point is that the Queen's joining forces with Ferol to get rid of the Regency, final and forever. It's obvious they're preparing an army in Ferol for the task. Maybe even recruiting Primitives, too."

"If there's any truth to that, it'd be the other way around. The Regency is closer to the Central Seat these days than Ferol is."

"There's other ways a man could heat you up, girl." Eyick's sour breath in her ear.

Ceria pushed him away. "If I need warmth that badly, I'll jump in the fire."

Eyick crooked his head. "Got some spirit, do you? I like the ones that struggle."

"Leave the girl in peace, Eyick."

"What business is it of yours, Holan?" Eyick snapped back across the fire.

He took a large mouthful of the flask, then got to his feet and walked to the centre of the group. "You're all wrong, so that you know. It's plain what's happening." Eyick paused, taking in the faces around the fire. "The Endless are back."

A hush descended over the group. The flames crackled and hissed.

"Such things shouldn't be spoken aloud."

"I'm man enough to speak the truth, even if the rest of you aren't," Eyick said. "Look at you, helpless animals. You deserve what's coming to you." He spat on the ground, then stalked away from the group.

"What's wrong with him?"

"He's just drunk."

"When is he not drunk?"

"Do you think he's right?"

"Don't be foolish. The – those things he mentioned. They're myths. Night terrors. If they existed at all, which is a world's walk from likely, then they were wiped out by Fen and Hethea in the White Age."

The talk eventually returned to lighter topics, Eyick's outburst tacitly forgotten. Ceria didn't follow the conversation, but it was no longer a soothing inattention. All the warmth from the scene had evaporated. She couldn't help but think of Ferol. The attack.

There had been so many of them, and so suddenly. The half-man's deformities pouring in like some hideous herd, cruel and hungry. She remembered the initial bewilderment of the people, as if the city had stopped and looked up in disbelief. The lack of time for terror, for comprehension, before the massacre had started. That awful crackling. The screams, the stink of burning flesh. Then the lights descending, reining in the beasts and having their own fun. And the half-man, revelling in it all. Declaring his ownership of the city, closing the gates and sealing Ferol to its fate: the slavery, the executions, the hunt for Primitives.

How could we have known? How do you fight a night terror?

Ceria left the campfire shortly after, her head heavy with black thoughts. She didn't see the shadows, the tents, or even the animals as she walked. The wind was an accusing whisper, berating her for the past.

A sudden painful grip on her arm. She gasped and turned.

Eyick. It looked like he had continued drinking.

"Finally, alone." His broken smile held no humour.

"Get – off – me." Ceria struggled against his grip, but couldn't break free.

She felt a surge of anger. It would only take a hand on him. To open herself to the flow, to the fierce torrent that she knew was there. To take it from him.

He leant forward, his face close to hers. "I know what you are, little bitch. I know exactly what you are."

Ceria was startled by his words. But she recovered enough to kick out at the man's shins, and dug her fingernails into his arm. He released his grip, but a second later a hand came hard across her face, knocking her to the ground. She scrambled up, then turned and ran.

"Scurry back to your friend, precious," Eyick laughed from behind her. "She can't protect you forever."

Ceria felt both shock and outrage as she rushed towards Telde and their camping spot. And fear, too – although she couldn't say whether the greater cause was Eyick's physical threat or his words.

Or perhaps she was afraid of the urge that she had felt within her. Dark and thirsty.

She found Telde setting out their bedding for the night.

"You took your time," Telde said, giving her an appraising look. "Did something happen?"

Ceria hesitated. If she told her about Eyick, they would leave the caravan. Their journey would be delayed further – Telde might even choose to take a lengthier route to Candar'laon. She couldn't stand the thought of more waiting.

"No, nothing," she said. "They were talking about Ferol, that's all."

Ceria busied herself with arranging a blanket, then made a pillow from one of the bags. She faced away from Telde, glad for the dark. Her cheek burned.

He probably knows nothing, she told herself. *How could he? He's a drunken thug and no more.* But she would watch him. If she thought that he was a real danger, she would tell Telde. Right now there was no reason to worry her, or to alter their journey.

"Get some rest," Telde said. "Tomorrow is a better day."

Later, lying on the hard ground, the wind rifling through the trees behind her, Ceria thought of that moment with Eyick, the temptation of using her powers. To take it from him. That bright, saturating torrent. It could have been hers.

She felt the thirst, deep within her. To take it all from him.

10

"Do you believe in God, John?"

"What kind of question is that?"

"A simple one."

"Then no, Jago, I don't. How can you after what happened?"

"It's because of what happened that my belief is so strong. That's not to say it was easy. First of all I blamed God for all the death. Then I refused to believe he could exist. Finally, as I continued to live and breathe on Earth, I came to accept that he must, and that I had survived for a purpose. I think you felt the same in your heart, else you wouldn't be here now."

"That's a large assumption."

John sat opposite Jago, outside of Wimda's house, one of its walls shading them from the midday sun. Bundles of long golden grass lay on the ground around them. Except that it wasn't quite grass – at least not of any form that John knew. The stems were as thick as his arm, and of a material somewhere between wood and a malleable plastic. His and Jago's task was to cut away the tops – a crown of diaphanous leaves – and the massy, vein-like roots, then slice down the length of the stem and lay it out to dry.

It was laborious work. The basic tools that Wimda had provided were barely sharp enough for the task. John's hand was caked with sap, his thumb ached, and Jago was getting on his nerves.

The man was impossible. He rarely ceased talking, but directing that overspill of words was like pushing against a wave. It felt to John that for every question he managed to obtain an answer to, he had received five questions in return. Or lengthy expositions on subjects he had little interest in.

But part of the annoyance, he admitted, was because Jago had hit upon a truth. During his years of solitude on Earth, John had viewed his life as having a greater purpose. Jago had told him of his own experiences in Brazil, which were similar to John's: all human life had been suddenly and inexplicably extinguished. He had not found anyone alive in South America. It had seemingly strengthened Jago's religious faith, but John couldn't accept that it had done the same for him. The sense of purpose was simply a device used by his survival instinct.

Before the event John had been a mild atheist, his mind at least open to other possibilities – he hadn't been the cynic of religion that Jessica was. But he couldn't believe in any god that would allow such a meaningless fate for so many billions of humans. The truth was that the universe was indifferent: a sun giving energy to life or burning it to a crisp.

"Look around you, " Jago said, waving a golden stem at him. "This is a wondrous place. A planet that proves possibility is infinite. God is great, no?"

"You're a scientist. You must believe in rational explanations."

John had managed to glean some scarce details about Jago's former life. The man had been a geneticist, as far as he could make out. Jago had lost him with talk of proteomics and ubiquitination, seemingly unaware – or unconcerned – that John had no clue what he was talking about.

"I'm a scientist," Jago answered, "but that doesn't mean I can't be a man of God also. The two aren't contradictory. Science is understanding and exploration. A celebration of his creation."

Let it go, John; he had no urge to be drawn into a theological debate. Besides, he felt as though he began on unsteady footing, still overwhelmed with the new world around him – not to mention the return of human interaction. It was two days since he had first awoken in this strange place, and he remained in awe of it all. *Another planet.* The knowledge was surreal, it refused to settle into believable fact.

But at the same time, surrounded by humans again, it felt as if he were slowly coming back to life himself. Long dormant emotions were re-emerging, and even the irritation at Jago was a precious sensation. John imagined himself as a faded sketch, the colours being restored by other hands.

Jago was quiet as he examined one of the dense bundles at the bottom of a stem. He wore the same sleeveless robe that John had seen on the first day, light grey with large pockets stitched on around the waist. His sandals seemed to be made from plant fibres.

John was envious of the loose-fitting attire. Wimda had given him the borrowed clothes of a villager, who was evidently a smaller man than John. The leather boots crushed his toes, and there was a gaping hole in one of them. The leggings were of the same material – Jago had informed him that it was dyed jaller hide, whatever that was – and in a similar condition. At least the simple linen shirt was comfortable enough, its open neck admitting some much needed air.

On Wimda's advice he had trimmed his beard, despite not trusting the tool for close shaving that she had offered. He remembered looking at himself in the crude glass mirror: thin aquiline nose, thick tangle of dark hair, blue eyes that stared out from the face of a stranger. It had only added to his sense of displacement.

John used the dull blade in his hand to hack off the bottom of a plant, and placed it in a pile of others to his side. Jago had told him how every part was used by the villagers: the stems were for roofing; the fibrous roots could be made into rope, or ground up for medicine or soup. Wimda had asked them to save the feathery leaves for a pillow she wanted to stuff.

He looked to Jago. "What do you think caused it?"

"What happened on Earth, you mean?" Jago shrugged. John feared for a moment that he was going to call it an act of God. "I saw the same as you, and concluded the same. All human life ceased at an identical moment, with only us as the exceptions. It was an instant brain death, occurring globally. No disease has ever acted this way.

"I couldn't solve the mystery," he continued. "There were no unusual toxins in the air, or in people's blood. No injuries or symptoms suggesting the source. No abnormal solar activity or atmospheric change. The earthquake in India was not unusual. The sole event of interest was the town found deserted in rural Russia. It wasn't the only one – I discovered similar reports of isolated settlements missing their inhabitants, all over the world. But as these events seemed to have occurred not long before the global deaths, there was little time for the stories to be substantiated. There was truth to them I think, but I don't see it as a cause of what happened."

"Could they be here, like us?" John asked eagerly. He had read about the Russian town, but it had been such a trivial article that he had dismissed it.

Jago shrugged again. "I don't know. You should cut the stems along the ridge here, not as you are doing it."

"That's it? You don't know?"

"It's unlikely. Entire populations disappearing seems a different pattern to individuals like us being transported here – and it happened a long time before we arrived on Crescent. I've not come across any talk of the sudden appearance of hundreds of people."

"But that doesn't rule it out. They could be on the other side of this planet for all we know. Or separated. Or a hundred other things. They could be here."

"They could be."

John waited for Jago to continue, and was exasperated when he didn't. "Don't you care? They could be *here*! Or at least there could be more like us. Have you thought of that?"

John's mind leapt to possibilities that he was shocked he hadn't considered yet. "There could be a connection between us coming here and what happened on Earth."

"It's obvious there's a connection, John," Jago said simply, maddeningly. "Those creatures that you saw were clearly not of Earth. I'm sure we'll learn more about it eventually."

John sat staring, aghast at Jago's apathy. It wasn't for the first time. There was no question about the man's enthusiasm, which seemed boundless, but it was a selective, capricious thing. His interest didn't seem to operate by the normal logic of importance or relevance.

Jago showed him a stem, and demonstrated where he should be slicing it. John tried to ignore the gesture, as well as the urge to strike the man with his own plant.

"You've been here for three months, is that right?" John asked. "Have you found any connection in that time?"

"Not yet. And it's not three months as you know it. Time is different here. The days are longer, you must have noticed. The calendar is determined by the orbit of the moon, Ternerid. It suggests there aren't seasons like on Earth, or at least not as pronounced.

"A forty-day cycle of Ternerid equals one month," Jago went on, whilst John struggled to keep up, "in each month are four weeks, where a week is ten days, or a tensun. Ten months per year – although that seems to vary, and there's likely to be some cultural variation, or a compensatory measure if there *are* seasons, which could make the calendar partially solar-based also – but I'd need to observe an entire orbital period of Crescent to know with certainty. The sun here is incredible, isn't it?" he asked, not waiting for an answer. "It's slightly hotter than Earth's. Whiter. An F class I think. But it's further away, which would act to balance things."

John stopped listening as Jago continued about spectral classification and luminosity and spectroscopy. It struck him again how impossible a task it seemed to get a grip on the endless unknowns surrounding him, especially with the sources of information at hand: the unfiltered barrage from Jago, and from Wimda – like the other villagers he spoke to – conversation that assumed an implicit knowledge, abstractions and references that would be obvious to a child here, but not to John. The picture he was trying to comprehend was planet-sized, and it was being constructed with randomly placed pixels.

But he clung to those pixels protectively, though he didn't yet understand their wider implications. He gathered that he was somewhere to the north of a sizeable continent dominated by several powers: the Queen and her Central Seat – some sort of governing council, John assumed – who ruled this country of Ireldelor, amongst several others; Ferol, a city state to the north-east that had been closed off for some reason; the Regency, a land somewhere to the south that had often warred with Ferol. Then there was L'Pen, Besgenin, Gol Edge, The West, The Savage Lands – smaller powers or regions of which John knew even less – and Edemon, Candar'laon, Dereselon – which he thought might be nearby cities. There were religions and sects: Fivemoons, Transients, Hearts; Wimda had told him that she was a faithful Leafshade. Something was changing in terms of the weather, possibly related to a substance, figurative or physical, called Spirit. And there was a fear that even John could pick up on, an anxiety amongst the villagers of trouble on the horizon.

The things the people here took for granted formed a backdrop of more significant truths for John. They were humans, at least in all the ways that he could tell. The villagers might act and dress differently, but they were recognisable – another culture rather than another species. The level of technology seemed something from medieval Earth – though he should not confuse the two, Jago had warned. *There are deviations on Crescent that have produced different solutions,* he had said, *separate branches of progression.* As for the powers that some possessed, like Jago's... John had barely scratched the surface of that extraordinary truth. It was apparent at least that individuals with abilities had always been around, if in scarce numbers. They were called Primitives.

John collected as much of this information as he could, but didn't yet force himself to accept it as real. He wondered if he would ever be able to do that – if this reality would ever truly sink in. And he wondered what he and Jago, or the death of seven billion humans on Earth, had to do with an unknown alien planet.

He realised that Jago was still talking; he had somehow moved on to cell biology. John was relieved to see a villager approaching, until he saw that he carried more bundles of grass.

The man dropped the bundles on the ground, then nodded towards an area of the village below. "You seen them?"

John looked to see a group of soldiers congregated at one of the buildings, their armour glinting silver and white in the sun. "Who are they?"

"Queen's soldiers," Jago answered for him. "What are they doing here?"

"Don't know. But Fen take me if it's for anything good," the man grunted, then gestured to the right of the soldiers. "Look."

Emerging from behind another building was a soldier on a strange mount. John strained to see: the animal was a glossy black, as large as a horse but lower to the ground. Something in its movement was feline; it stalked, ready to pounce.

"A Queen's Claw. I've never seen one," Jago said, and shifted as if to get up.

The villager put a hand on his shoulder to stop him. "You'd be wise to avoid them, Jago. Curiosity around us village folk is one thing, but you go asking questions around the Queen's and you're like to get some unfavourable ones in return. Especially where you two are concerned."

Jago still had his eyes on the unusual creature as the

villager walked away. John feared that he wouldn't listen to the man's advice.

"What exactly is a Queen's Claw?" he asked.

"I've read of them," Jago answered. "They're reared in the Queen's Heartlands, tailored to a specific rider from birth – so the bond between them is unbreakable. Only the most renowned soldiers are awarded such an animal. Its name was even changed to Queen's Claw by royal edict..."

Something else had caught Jago's attention. John followed his gaze to see a procession of carts approaching the opposite side of the village.

"Come on, John."

"Jago, wait." But the man was already on his feet and jogging down the shallow incline leading to the rest of the village.

John watched him go. Something stopped him from following, but he couldn't put his finger on it. Perhaps it was simply the warning from the villager. He continued to work, hacking at the plants, deliberately not looking towards the village. *Just go, John.* Jago would land himself in trouble, and it might be an opportunity to find out more about this place. He felt a constricting sensation grow with his indecision, a taut claustrophobia. *Get up and go. Come on.*

Finally he threw down the tool and forced himself up. This was ridiculous – he would simply go and prevent Jago from drawing attention to himself. To both of them. He set off down the slope, towards the train of new arrivals.

By the time he had crossed the village – following its grass-enclosed pathways, as if navigating a waist-high labyrinth – a crowd had gathered around the newcomers. They were evidently traders – several were already setting out stalls or selling goods directly from wooden carts. The soldiers had moved to the travellers and seemed to be casually questioning a number of them. There was no sign of Jago, or of the Queen's Claw.

John walked along the caravan, which was rapidly gaining

the atmosphere of a marketplace. It seemed as though the whole village had suspended its activity to come and view the wares on offer. He saw colourful dresses and shirts and jewellery, hides and bows and boots – he was momentarily tempted by the latter, before remembering that he had no money; *What do they use here, anyway?* – as well as bowls and candles and foods and a hundred things he couldn't identify. There were entertainers amongst the sellers: a woman reading hands, a man performing something between poetry and song, a child dancing alongside a scaled animal; John couldn't help but stare. In the distance a man was dismantling his cart to construct a fence around more unrecognisable animals.

A crowd had gathered around what John initially took for an enormous wagon, until he realised with a start that it was alive. Lightly furred and seemingly placid, the animal reminded him of a picture of an extinct giant ground sloth he had once seen – although this creature was larger yet. Thick netting lay across its broad back, from which bundles of supplies hung. A heavy-set man with a braided beard was unloading them, whilst ignoring the buzz of questions from the children around him.

John carried dazedly on, still unable to spot Jago. He slipped between two carts – maintaining a wary distance from the bovine-like animals used to pull them – hoping to gain a view of the opposite side of the caravan. He almost walked into two women who were stood behind a cart, locked in tense conversation.

One turned fiercely to him. "Do you want something?"

"I was just… looking for a friend," John stammered. The two women were about his age, one with short dark hair and piercings covering her ears, the other with tied back hazel hair and striking green eyes – eyes that seemed intent on glaring a path directly through him. "Never mind. Sorry."

He hastily retreated to the busier side of the convoy.

It took several more minutes of searching before he finally spotted Jago. The man stood at the front of a small crowd around a woman demonstrating a ball and hoop game. A large bow hung over his shoulder and a collection of books balanced precariously under his arm. He had evidently volunteered for a turn at the game.

Instead of picking up the ball, however, Jago took a step backwards. A moment later the ball lifted as if of its own accord, and moved slowly towards and then through the hoop. There were a few laughs and claps, but also a hesitancy in those watching. The demonstrator was evidently irritated, and struggled to regain the attention of the crowd. John noticed two Queen's soldiers standing at the back, leaning on their swords. A look passed between them before they moved away.

John pushed his way through to Jago. He suddenly felt some of the anxiety he had previously sensed in the villagers.

11

Manvedian trudged along the dirt road, cursing under his breath. He could feel blisters forming on the backs of his feet, consistently rubbing as they were against his knee-high boots. He regretted the rest of his outfit, too: the day was turning to evening and yet the sun continued to beat down upon his dark brown leather jerkin and black leggings without mercy. The road was surrounded by long, low hills, a lone tree now and then not enough to disrupt the monotony. Mountains daggered the horizon far to the south. The only signs of life were the birds circling high above his head, in hope of an easy supper, no doubt.

He winced at a pain in his chest – a cracked rib, he suspected. His plan had not worked flawlessly, he had to admit. But it hadn't entirely failed.

The first part had been simple enough. After he was finished with Peledis, he had returned to Banedete's barn. It was much later by then, and the majority of the festivities were over. A small group lingered, however, including many of the riders as he had hoped. The white-haired girl was amongst them.

Manvedian had soon ingratiated himself with the group, sharing out his Spirit tubes and joining their drinking games. He plied the girl with more alcohol, asked her about the juchen and the race – he had acted one part fan, one part lecher. When the time was right, he had slipped another liquid into her drink.

A shame, as he was beginning to like the girl. With her brazen self-confidence and sharp tongue, he could see how she had held her own in racing circles. But the juchen race was one that she was destined to miss – the drug Manvedian had given her ensured that she was not rousable in time for the start the next day.

The owner of the animal she was set to ride – a Dereselon merchant – was suitably furious when her insensate condition was discovered. It was a lucky turn of events, then, when Governor Banedete happened to have an alternative rider in mind. Manvedian had accepted the merchant's subsequent offer of a hundred silver royals – half of which, being conditional on his arrival at the race finish in distant Ranarin, he knew that he would never see. The other half he had given to Banedete, for putting his name forward. The money wasn't important – he only needed the juchen.

Manvedian's mind took him back to the chaos of the starting line. The juchen surrounded him, jostling and snapping. Shaking the ground with their weight. The dense heat reeked of sweat and piss, and he was starting to question the wisdom of his plan. But if it worked, he would gain invaluable time on Telde and Ceria.

A deep grunt reverberated through him as his own animal barged into the enclosing wooden fence. The other riders shouted over the noise, fighting for position. Manvedian strained against the ropes attached to his juchen's trio of horns, keeping it near the back of the group. He was in no rush.

There was an abrupt quiet – and then the starting horn sounded. The front gates were opened and the juchen poured out like a ravenous tide. It felt as if he were atop a landslide. Two of the foremost riders were dismounted, their screams swallowed by the thunder of hooves. Manvedian desperately gripped the harness, engulfed by the furious noise around him. Collisions with the other juchen were like concentrated earthquakes.

Somehow he managed to cling on. Eventually the animals became more dispersed, the riders taking pre-planned routes or carried impotently by the juchen's will. Manvedian achieved some measure of control over his own animal – he was suddenly glad he had asked so many questions of the girl – wrestling the reins and using the spiked stirrups to force the creature in a south-west direction.

The speed was astonishing. In only two hours he managed the equivalent of two days' travel on a jaller. Every muscle burnt from clinging on, his mind was exhausted from the perpetual threat of being skewered by a horn, but he couldn't have been more pleased. At this rate he could catch up to Telde and Ceria within a day, now that he knew where they were going.

All of a sudden he was off-balance – in his distraction he hadn't noticed an irregular run of land – and he grasped for the harness or the reins or a horn, but the next bound of the animal flung him into the air. The ground rushed up and crashed into him. He tumbled and rolled, then managed to look up in a daze. A dark shape was hurtling towards him. *Oh shit.* He leapt aside barely in time to avoid the juchen's charge. Lying winded on his side, he was relieved to see the animal disappearing over the shallow hills. But the feeling was short lived as the realisation struck him: he had lost his transport. *Shit and godsfuck.*

And now he was left to walk this blasted, unending road. Half a day and counting. After the tempest of the juchen, it felt as if he were wading through quicksand. He whistled a tune through parched lips, and attempted once again to determine where he was. He remembered passing Hardlight Fort not long before he was dismounted, and the mountains in the distant south were the Coronal range that marked the Heartlands border. *Far west Ireldelor, then.* His best course of action would be to keep on the same bearing until he hit a settlement. With luck it would be the stippling of villages leading up to Edemon – from the capital he could gain easy transport to Candar'laon. Things might not have worked out perfectly, but he had still gained a great deal. He could be at Candar'laon within a few days, in time for the meeting.

He managed a wry smile at the thought. After so much careful play, two moves had jumped him almost within touching distance of his quarry. Once he found them, he would deal with Telde, and he would take Ceria.

There would be upwards of twenty members of the Ferol resistance at Candar'laon, he had learned from Peledis, provided all of them made it. Telde and Edodani were the highest ranking, and Benuitis, Ikdien, and Dem Cleaver were amongst the others. *Edodani. He could prove an additional problem,* Manvedian thought. The scarred man was more suspicious than even Climbe, and Manvedian cared for him even less.

But he had liked some of the members – it hadn't always been an act. A few were capable enough, and those like Dem and Benuitis knew how to have a good time to boot. He almost felt sorry for them now. With their little meetings, their painstaking plans, following Climbe's designs like a herd being led over a cliff. Their determination to fight the half-man and take back the city was ridiculous in the face of the forces that he could call upon. They would seek to involve the Queen's army, but they would still be playing into his hands.

He *almost* felt sorry for them. They had picked the losing side – it was a shame, that was all. A shame they weren't bright enough to see it, or how the half-man used the resistance as much as fought them. Their one, minor victory had been to keep Ceria from him. The half-man wanted her for her exceptional powers, to add her to his army – and the resistance sheltered her for equally selfish reasons, Manvedian reminded himself. But it was only a matter of time now before he delivered her. Peledis had provided him with everything that he needed.

He had entered the man's dreams on the night of Banedete's gathering, after he had dragged him to the copse.

There had been the usual flood of images and sensations to begin with. The danger of being overwhelmed. Manvedian had learnt to steel his will against it, to cling on to his awareness. Once he had sufficient control over himself, he had searched for the strings of consistency amongst the disorder; they represented the closest thing to a conscious experience for the dreamer. An experience that he could shape.

The dream world was one of chaos, illogicality. Manvedian relished it. There were fewer rules to restrain him: no cause and consequence, no permanence. What happened in the present would determine what had happened before: he had nudged Peledis towards the Hearts temple in Ferol, and his mind remembered being captured. Peledis was both outside – a regurgitated memory of gleaming white brick, a man hanging in front of a vast blood red window – and inside, tied down, priests surrounding him with rictus grins.

Manvedian had admired the man's creativity when it came to the torture; he had to do little more than wait whilst Peledis' fantasies took the most sadistic routes. He had blocked a tangent here and there, ensured that Peledis remained in the dream. Then he had delicately embedded his questions. It was always pleasing how abruptly exact the brain could be, how detailed the stored knowledge.

Once he had acquired the information – the meeting location for Telde, the names and dates, as well as other useful fragments of resistance plans – he had turned the temple into Banedete's barn and suggested to Peledis that he should run. Giving chase was a frenzy of Hearts, Banedete's guards, others from the barn, and any of the man's demons Manvedian could find at hand. He had left Peledis' mind to wander the wake. By then he was pushing the limit on how long he could safely remain in the man's dreams before his own would start to seep in. Too long, and they would succeed in wrenching him away – and those dreams he couldn't control. There his own demon lay in wait.

After he awoke, he had slung Peledis' body over his shoulder – the drug would keep him out for most of the day, if the blow from the branch didn't – and carried him toward the village. He had left him with the servant from the barn, telling the boy how they had been set upon by thieves. From the confusion he had introduced into Peledis' head, he wouldn't be able to tell otherwise.

It was too much bother to kill Peledis, Manvedian told himself. There was no need to get his hands bloody when he could avoid it. Besides, it was always possible that the man could be of use again in the future.

His thoughts were presently interrupted by a noise from the road behind him. He turned to see a carriage approaching, the jaller pair in front kicking up a cloud of dust around it. As it came closer, he could make out the driver perched before a closed carriage covered with a blue fabric, rows of tassels dangling over the passenger windows.

He hurriedly tidied himself, brushing the dust from his jerkin, fastening its buckles up towards his neck; he spat on his hands, wiped his face clean and flattened down his shoulder-length hair. He thought of the dagger tucked into his boot.

He stepped into the centre of the road, so that the carriage was forced to stop. Ignoring the barked demand of the driver, he strode directly to the passenger window. The curtain was partially drawn, enough so that he could see a woman inside; older than her close-fitting dress suggested, but going to obvious lengths to disguise the fact. She gave him a perfunctory glance – with a moment's surprise at his appearance – and then stared ahead, her head tilted slightly upwards. *Gods be fucking praised,* Manvedian thought.

Somewhat dishevelled as he was, he knew that he would still cut an impressive figure. He altered his accent: a slight piquancy, an indolent softening of the edges. "A fine evening, my lady. Do you have any water?"

"No, I do not," the woman answered frostily. "Driver."

The carriage resumed moving, at a trot. Manvedian jogged alongside.

"I'm just as parched intellectually. The road's as talkative as a L'Pen oathtaker. Perhaps you could spare a little conversation? It's clear that you're an educated woman, amongst other... qualities."

"If you're attempting to secure a seat on this coach, I can inform you that you won't succeed," the woman replied, not looking at him.

"I assure you that's not my intention," Manvedian said, glancing towards the driver. A burly man, watching him keenly. He could be handled, but it wasn't the preferable option.

Manvedian turned his attention back to the woman, allowing a faint smile to play across his lips. *Last chance.* "I wouldn't presume to sit alongside such a captivating creature. Lie beside, perhaps."

His comment earned him a sideways glance from the woman, her hand briefly touching her neck. Then, as if refusing to be cowed into embarrassment, she turned to look him up and down. "What are you? You don't seem the type to wander these roads."

"I'm a poet, an artist, and a lover," Manvedian immediately replied.

A raised eyebrow. "You have dirt on your face. If you're so talented, why do you walk this route like a vagabond?"

"I enjoy exercising my body as I enjoy exercising my mind. It ensures I'm able to fulfil all of my... intentions." He jogged backwards whilst he spoke, his gaze fixed on her.

"What are your intentions?"

"Seduction and satisfaction."

An amused laugh, followed by a silence. Then, as if she had decided to play along: "And what does that involve?"

"With a refined lady such as yourself..." He let the sentence hang as he gave her a long, appraising look. He moved closer to the carriage, placing a hand on the frame of the window and lowering his voice. "I could make you moan until you lost your voice. You would ache sweetly for a tensun after."

She reddened and looked away. "You mistake me for a different sort of lady."

But, Manvedian noted, she didn't call for the driver. She didn't ask him to move away.

"What's your name?" she asked, finally.

Manvedian grinned.

*

He stood on the balcony, a night breeze cooling his skin as he looked out at the city. Hundreds of torches dotted the vast bowled valley, giving shadow to the unending tide of buildings clustered and heaped together on its surface. From his position, halfway up one side of the valley and looking out from the Royal Quarter, he knew that the view before him was the Communal Quarter, a congested sprawl at least three times the size of its affluent counterpart. Above it was a thick strip of featureless black, where the city's enormous outer wall climbed up to blot out the stars.

Edemon. Manvedian closed his eyes momentarily, breathed in the air. It was good to be back.

It was only when he had stepped onto the balcony a few minutes previously that he had discovered, to his surprise, how much part of him had missed the place. Two years had passed since he had left, a time during which he had grown immeasurably. But Edemon seemed to have remained the same. Arriving in the city at the dregs of dusk, he had seen the giant gilded column of Edem piercing the sky, and, on the opposite side of the valley, the stain where fire had roared through the Communal Quarter, and superstition or protest prevented the nearby inhabitants, even as cramped as they were, from building on the most severe sites of ruin. For him the two sights neatly summed up the city's dual personality:

part glamorous capital, part slum.

But it was the intangible elements that were responsible for his nostalgia. The smell of the place, the restless atmosphere, the trembling of a city crowded with all the desperation and greed of Crescent. *Edemon, the Queen's Jewel.*

He had spent little over a month here originally, yet it had soaked into his bones. Remoulded him. He felt some regret that he wasn't free to take advantage of his time in the city, even if he had outgrown its petty power struggles. It would have been fun to visit some of his old haunts – the gambling stalls along Red Terrace, the black markets beneath Reverent Square, the Spirit dens and whore houses, both ripe with secrets. But he had more important matters to attend to, as usual. And they would start with Niscem.

He had known that the man would be aware of his arrival almost immediately – Niscem and his network of eyes knew of every person that came into the city. Not that Manvedian had made a secret of it; he allowed his face to be seen as the carriage had passed through the eastern gate. The message had come not long after. A note with a time written on it.

Manvedian turned his back on the lights of Edemon, and walked into the bedroom. Lady Wedlen was still asleep on the bed. He had learnt her name in the carriage, as well as the welcome news that they were travelling to her home in the Ireldelor capital. They hadn't made much time for conversation once they had arrived; he might have damaged another rib in the process, Manvedian thought with a grin. He snuck past her unconscious form, then downstairs to the building's entrance.

Niscem was waiting for him outside. Across the street, in the shadows; there was no mistaking that rangy, motionless shape. Manvedian moved towards him, and the shape gained a grey face and a frigid expression. *Same old cheerful bastard,* he concluded. He was surprised Niscem had come himself. It would mean that whatever he had to share was particularly important. Or unpleasant.

With barely a nod of acknowledgement, Niscem led him silently through a maze of side-streets and alleyways, until they finally stopped at the back of an unremarkable building. They were still in the Royal Quarter, but the heavily built man guarding the door gave Manvedian a good clue as to what was inside. They were ushered through and Niscem took him to a table in the midst of a room bustling with bodies and noise: naked dancers writhed to clamorous Gol music; masked groups engaged in various explicit acts in the corners. The air was thick with Spirit and the cries of pleasure and pain, the walls smothered in art accordingly erotic and violent.

It was a typical tactic of Niscem's, Manvedian thought wryly. He had never seen Niscem show a twitch of interest towards a woman or man, or even Spirit, and yet he often favoured the most sordid of locations for meetings. It was to gain an advantage over whomever he brought here; many would be distracted, overwhelmed, or at the least put off-balance. Niscem would know that such cheap tricks wouldn't work on Manvedian, so he took it as the man no doubt intended: an insult, a show of contempt.

Niscem himself was never off-balance. He never allowed emotion to show. The man barely moved – and when he did it was with a strict economy, precise and efficient. He had always reminded Manvedian of a predator, stock-still before the strike. Niscem's small pale eyes were fixed on him now, and a long silence stretched over the table. Manvedian was content to let it hang. There were only two men able to make him feel uncomfortable – one, his father, was long dead; the other could hardly be described as a man.

Hands knitted in front of him, spine rigid, finally Niscem broke the silence. "How does it feel to be back?"

Manvedian shrugged. He had never known Niscem to waste time with small talk. His news must be big. Manvedian was certain he wasn't going to like it.

He signalled a passing waitress and selected one of the

drinks that, by its faint blue effervescence, appeared to be laced with Spirit. He took a sip whilst looking across the table at the man who had recruited him to the half-man's service. After Manvedian had first arrived in Edemon, it hadn't taken long for him to gain a reputation in underground circles. His abilities helped – secrets were power, and he had a route to them that no others did. There was no hiding in dreams. He had soon attracted the attention of Niscem, the dominant force behind illegal trade in the capital. *He must wish he'd killed me back then,* Manvedian thought. Instead Niscem had sought to use him, and eventually sent him to Ferol, to the half-man. He had doubtless seen it as a shrewd solution, gifting his employer with an able body whilst at the same time expelling a potential threat, probably to perish in the growing turbulence of Ferol.

But it had backfired. Not only did Manvedian survive, but with the role he had played in infiltrating the Ferolian resistance, he had become as valued as Niscem. He doubted that Niscem had even met the half-man – not that it was something to be envied.

"The Queen's armies are moving in Ireldelor," Niscem said, after another lengthy interval. "By orders of the Central Seat. They will find and capture Primitives, and any with suspected ties to Ferol. The entire country will be scoured, down to the most insignificant village."

Blood and shit. So that was it. The Central Seat had been vacillating for months over taking action, as the half-man had pulled his strings – from a distance, always unseen – and those who he controlled worked their way through the bureaucracy and opposition, pushing to mobilise the army for the so-called anticipatory action. It was a decision of great consequence: no such widespread rounding up of Primitives had occurred since Wilvarla's era, no matter the contrasting motives that were claimed this time. Manvedian would have admired the weight of deception and persuasion it must have taken to achieve – and the neatness of the half-man making the Queen do his work for him – if it hadn't succeeded so soon. Now he understood why Niscem had wanted to tell him in person. The man knew how much this would disrupt Manvedian's plans.

"Good tidings, would you not agree?" Niscem said.

"Glorious," Manvedian replied, keeping his voice neutral. "When is it happening?"

Niscem paused, then gave the answer he had expected. "It already is. The last of the detainments will take place tonight and tomorrow. The timing has been impeccably orchestrated. Soon the majority of Primitives in Ireldelor will be in the Queen's hands – and, eventually, in the half-man's hands." The man was comparatively gushing now. "It's a pleasant bonus that they will weed out Ferolian resistance members for us. If not killed outright during the arrests, they will be brought here."

Brought to him, Manvedian understood his intimation. Edemon possessed the headquarters of the Queen's Ireldelor forces, and Niscem had wormed himself deep into it after all these years. He could easily arrange for certain Ferolian prisoners to find their way to him. Manvedian leant back, sipping at his drink. Niscem watched him, undoubtedly hoping for signs of anger at the news. *Fen take me if I give the bastard the satisfaction of seeing it.*

But he *was* angry. He was fucking irate. The Queen's soldiers weren't known for their subtlety, and their heavy-handed approach would likely kill as many as they detained. Telde and Ceria were hardly the types to surrender quietly, either. They could be dead already for all he knew. And even if they escaped capture, Manvedian thought, then gods knew where they would go. Not Candar'laon, that was for certain. His aim of catching them there had just been pissed all over.

Killed or captured or disappeared forever – it was all the same. It would be his failure if he didn't deliver Ceria to the half-man. Blaming the Queen's army or Niscem would be no excuse, as good as admitting weakness. He had no illusions as to what would happen to him. *Blood and Gods' shit.*

Niscem's lips curved almost imperceptibly into the ghost of a smile.

Later, Manvedian found himself back in Lady Wedlen's bed. He had needed the distraction, the time to clear his mind so that he could think.

As he lay there afterwards, sweat coating his body, Lady Wedlen mewling into his shoulder, he ran through the situation again: there was no possibility he could get to Candar'laon, or whatever outlying village at which Telde and Ceria were currently, in time to change anything. Whatever the result of the soldiers' incursion, it was out of his control. Ironically, he found himself relying on something he had been cursing all this time – Telde's ability to evade every trap in her path. The question was, assuming they managed to escape, where would they go? Where would Telde take her?

Manvedian swore inwardly. He had been so close, almost within touching distance, only for them to be wrenched away. But there was no gain in self-pity. *This is the reality now,* he told himself. *Adapt to it.* He had to find out everything he could about the arrests, when and where and who was involved. Fortunately he was in the right place for it – all of the information would filter through Edemon. If the two women were caught, then he would find a way to get to them before Niscem. If they escaped, then he would chase them down. He would be the one who brought Ceria back to Ferol. *She is mine.*

He turned his head to the side, and watched through the balcony door as one by one the torches of the city were extinguished, submitting to the light of a new day. *Where will you go, Telde?*

12

The fist came fast at John, and before he could react it had connected with his nose and knocked him to the ground. For one dazed second he reflected on how, for her height and build, the woman possessed a formidable punch, before pain racked his face and his eyes filled with water. Voices sounded above him.

"Telde!"

"I won't have violence in my home, young lady."

"She's sorry. Apologise, Telde."

A snort. "I'm sorry to you, Wimda. I don't apologise to *him*."

A face leaning over him, the tears in his eyes reducing it to a blur. "Are you okay?"

He recognised the voice of the other woman, the one with short dark hair. He began to splutter a reply but was interrupted by someone else stuffing a cloth under his nose, resulting in a renewed blaze of pain.

"Hold still. You're bleeding."

John was helped up and directed to the edge of the bed. After wiping his eyes, he could make out Wimda holding a bloodied cloth, whilst the dark-haired woman stood nearby with a sympathetic expression. The fierce woman who had struck him was at the window, peering out under the cloth cover. Jago stood by the door, watching them all with a look of fascination.

"*Godsblood!* They're searching every building. The Queen's Claw is out there," said the woman at the window – Telde, her name seemed to be. She turned to stare accusingly at John. He recalled those shockingly green eyes from the traders' caravan, when he had walked in on the two women's conversation. Again, they seemed intent on piercing him.

"Why did you hit me?" John asked. Instead of the angry demand he had intended, his voice came out nasal and self-pitying.

"Because it's your fenning fault, that's why!" Telde spat back. "You brought them here with your Primitive tricks. All because you had to show off."

"That was Jago!" John protested. "I don't have any powers – I don't even know what's going on!"

"I don't think it was either of these men, Telde," the other woman started. "I think that Eyick –"

"Eyick? The joorun owner?" Telde asked, her attention snapping towards her.

"I think he knew about us. Or at least suspected something. I don't know. But he probably talked to the soldiers, and that's why they're asking after us."

Telde glared at the woman. John was glad that for once he wasn't on the receiving end of those eyes. "Why didn't you tell me, Ceria?"

"I didn't think... it doesn't matter. We need to find a way out of here."

To John's surprise, Telde seemed to bite down her anger as she gave a curt nod. There was something else in her expression too, but he couldn't identify it. She paced the room.

John was still trying to disentangle the morning's events. It had been barely light when Wimda had shaken him awake, Jago alongside her, and hurriedly told that the Queen's soldiers were arresting people. They had started with the traders' caravan that had arrived the previous day, before turning on the village itself. They were searching for Primitives, she explained, and those with ties to Ferol – and also detaining anyone they deemed suspicious or argumentative. One of the villagers had been killed. Wimda had heard that the soldiers were seeking two strangers residing in the village, as well as two women who had been travelling with the merchants.

I won't let them get any of you, she had stated before leaving the house, her expression enough to prevent Jago from following. She could be the cantankerous type, but John hadn't seen that kind of fury on her face before. When she had returned, after many long minutes, she had brought the two women with her. She had barely started to introduce John and Jago before Telde had punched him.

The dark-haired woman – Ceria – took the cloth from Wimda, and knelt before John. She dabbed at and around his nose, the pain flaring despite her gentle touch. Her large eyes matched the shade of her hair, John saw. He found it difficult to meet them. The jewellery in her ears caught the light, which glimmered and streaked in his moist vision.

"I don't think any of you, or this Eyick, are to blame for what's happening," Wimda said, breaking the brief silence that had descended upon the room. "They didn't do all of this simply for the four of you. They're after *every* Primitive – do you think they'd confine their search to Milnadon, a small village in the vastness of Ireldelor? Yes, you've brought attention on yourselves – doubtless you're *all* to blame for that – and they seek you here because of it. But there is something much larger taking place that has nothing to do with you."

A concerned look passed between the two young women; evidently they saw the truth in Wimda's words.

"Could they really be arresting Primitives in all of Ireldelor? What could bring them to such an act?" Ceria asked, forgetting her tending of John, to his regret. "It hasn't been done for hundreds of years. There are laws against it, the Central Seat –"

"If it *is* country-wide, then the Central Seat and the Queen sanctioned it," Telde interrupted, then shook her head. "I always believed that local guards might do something like this, if their loyalties were tested by coin. But I never thought it could occur on this scale. Not the whole army."

"Do you think it's because of the half-man?" Ceria asked.

Telde scowled at Ceria as if she were being indiscreet. *Half-man?* John wondered.

"I don't know," she snapped. "At best it's to gather Primitives before he does. At worst it's a culling of a perceived threat – but the reasons don't matter," she added, cutting off Ceria's response. "If we're caught it'll be the end of us. We can't allow it to happen. We can't."

John realised what that something else in Telde's expression was – her words stretched tautly enough to reveal a desperation beneath. A second later it was gone, and her bearing turned to strength, determination.

She turned to Wimda. "You know the village and the land. Where can we go?"

Wimda frowned. "You wouldn't do well on foot – the closest village is more than a sun's walk to the west. They'd catch up to you, even if you managed to leave the village unseen. And what's to say the same offences are not already happening there?" She sighed, shaking her head. "As much as I would wish it otherwise, you're not safe here, either. The villagers are good people, but they have their lives and families to protect. Eventually the soldiers will be pointed to my home."

"Then I will fight them when they come," Telde said. "I can distract them long enough for you to get away, Ceria."

"That would be stupid," Jago said abruptly, to the surprise of everyone in the room. Telde turned to him fiercely at his remark, but he didn't seem to notice. "There's far too many, and fighting them would serve no purpose. The only option is to outrun them. There are stables in the village."

"The stables are guarded," Wimda said. "It was one of the first places they took hold of."

"How many guard it, Wimda?" Telde asked. "We can force our way through."

"No," Ceria asserted. She looked at Telde with the slightest suggestion of a grin. "No, I have a better idea. The joorun. I know the caravan will be guarded too, but not as heavily as the stables. They won't be expecting anyone to sneak in, let alone take the joorun. But if we succeeded... it's a lot faster than it looks. And what could possibly stop a joorun?"

There was a silence in the room as her proposal sank in.

"What's a joorun?" John asked.

"I've been eager to see the animal up close," Jago said.

"Can you even control such a thing?" Wimda asked.

"Ceria will be able to," Telde said.

"What's a joorun?" John repeated.

"We'll have to avoid the soldiers," Ceria added. "The caravan's on the other side of the village."

"We can do it – if it's only the two of us," Telde said.

"We can't leave them here," Ceria said.

"They aren't our responsibility," Telde insisted. But something in her manner suggested that she knew her friend wouldn't be swayed. "Fine, we don't have time to argue it. But they'd better be able to move fast. And quiet. If they give us away, gods curse me I'll kill them myself."

"Wait. Just hold on a moment. I'm not going anywhere," John said as he stood up, trying to ignore a momentary light-headedness. "I have no powers. I have nothing to do with any of this. Why should I go with you? I'm not on any side – I don't even know what the sides are!"

"Remain here then," Telde replied. She was already gathering the scant possessions with which they had arrived.

"They'll arrest you. Or worse," Ceria said, turning her large eyes on him.

"She's right, John," Wimda added. "You can't stay."

"Why would they arrest me? What could I have possibly done?"

Wimda gave him a look as if he was child asking why bad things happened in the world. John felt like screaming. He had somehow been thrown into the middle of this, into who knew what conflict. He had received a bloody nose for no reason, and now he had to run from an army for crimes he couldn't have possibly committed. It all seemed too absurd, like he should be able to shout *Stop* and the situation would become more reasonable, more comprehensible. Life would stand still, and he wouldn't lose his grasp on it.

But it didn't stop. Wimda was gathering food into a cloth bag, and the others were preparing to go. She pressed the bag into Jago's hands, then turned to the rest of them and cleared her throat. "I have lived in this village all of my life. I'm the longest here, now that Tensid has gone, Hethea bless him. It's *my* Milnadon – it'll be Godsfall before I let those soldiers or the Queen do with it as they wish. I will give a distraction, to help you escape."

"I don't mean to offend you, but what can one old woman do?" Telde asked.

"This *old woman* has had a lifetime to learn things you don't even know the letters for."

Telde accepted Wimda's rebuke with a nod, before looking to Ceria. "We have to go."

Ceria moved to embrace Wimda, and thanked her for her help. Jago did the same, and Wimda leant up to whisper something in his ear before giving him a gentle slap over the head. She then ushered them all, including John, towards the door. "Hurry, go."

John didn't say goodbye to the old woman. A part of him resented her for not allowing him to stay, for not protecting him.

But he didn't have time to dwell on the feeling. As soon as they were outside, Telde sprinted down the shallow hill away from Wimda's home. Ceria and Jago followed closely behind, heading towards the flat ground on which the majority of the village was spread. John stood frozen for a few seconds in the sharp morning air, before forcing himself to run after them.

He caught up to them at the bottom of the incline, where they were ducking behind the rear wall of a building. The village was eerily silent compared to its usual lively mornings. Only the occasional cry of a bird or grunt of livestock pierced the quiet, as if querying the change.

Telde led them in a low run towards the next building. They kept to the outskirts of the village, their movements partially masked by the tall stretches of golden grass. As John leant against the pale wood of another wall, he reflected on how unreal all of this was, as though they were play acting in some militant game of hide and seek. But there was a growing fear in him, also. Even if he didn't understand the danger, even if he was still numb to it, he could see it manifested in the tense expressions of Ceria and Telde. The latter was on her haunches, peering around the corner of the building.

Then, with a tersely whispered *Now*, she set off on a sprint through a dense swathe of grass. The rest of them followed, eventually emerging from the undergrowth to slip behind a short row of buildings. They hurried across the narrow alleys separating each to get to the furthest building, before the close sound of voices caused them to halt. *Inside the house,* John realised. Heavy footsteps, the scrape of a chair. They were probably only the usual inhabitants, but somehow the villagers had become as terrifying as the soldiers, as if all were complicit in exposing the fugitives. The four of them huddled beneath the rear window. Their collective breathing sounded deafening to John.

What am I doing? He needed a moment to think, to slow events down so that he could make sense of them. He glanced at the two women crouched next to him. There were strange markings on the back of Ceria's slender neck, a tattoo that began where her short hair ended and continued beneath her dark green jerkin. He could see the outline of a long sword on Telde's back, showing through her cloak. *Who are these people? Why am I following them?*

He looked up at the sky and saw that appalling emerald moon, a reminder that he was a foreigner here, an alien. To the right of the vast satellite, in two separate patches, the sky broiled and pulsed inky dark. *Spirit storms*, Wimda had called them.

He understood nothing of this world. *What am I doing here?*

With a hasty gesture, Telde sprang up and headed towards a dilapidated structure about twenty yards away. Ceria followed swiftly behind, but a hand on John's arm stopped him from doing the same.

"I have to get my things," Jago whispered. He had started down one of the alleys between the buildings before John could reply.

John rushed to the gap, uselessly mouthing Jago's name at his back. It was too late: Jago reached the front of the buildings, glanced briefly about him, then ran out of sight.

John felt a familiar immobilising uncertainty. He stared down the alley, waiting in vain for Jago to reappear. *Damn it.* He turned away, crawling beneath the window to the edge of the building. He dashed across to the two women, who were crouched behind what looked like a large, neglected hutch.

"Where's your friend?" Telde asked.

"He's not my friend," John replied, experiencing a stab of guilt as he said it. But he barely knew the man, after all. "He went to get his things. From one of the houses. I couldn't stop him."

Telde scowled. "I won't wait."

Ceria gave John a searching look whilst Telde moved to peer around the corner. A curse from the latter drew both of their attentions.

"Soldiers. One at the next building. Two more in front, towards the village. Getting closer."

John leant slightly away from the hutch, and was able to make out a cabin with an awning at its front. The soldier stood beneath it, his silver mail shaded from the sun. He leant against a pile of timber, facing away from them. John saw that there was barely any grass to obscure their passage. But they had little choice. The cabin was isolated on the periphery of the village, and if they moved further in they would surely be seen by the other soldiers.

He could hear the soldiers now: a murmuring of voices, a gruff laugh. *Have they stopped?* John became aware that his nose was bleeding again. He wiped it on his shirt.

"What do we do?" Ceria whispered.

Telde didn't answer for a time as she stared out from her crouched position, her sharp eyebrows knitted in concentration. "They're moving toward another building," she said at last. "When they reach it, we run."

"What about the soldier over there? What if he sees us?" John asked.

"Then the gods aren't fond of us. Get ready."

A minute passed – then Telde signalled. John scrambled to his feet behind the two women and sprinted across the open ground, not daring to look behind him. He expected the shouts from the soldiers at any moment. They approached the cabin in a wide arc, slowing their footsteps as they drew near its rear. The soldier still had his back to them. *He'll hear us,* John was convinced. He was only a few yards away. *He'll turn.* But Telde had made it behind the building, and now Ceria, too – *he must hear* – and finally John reached the cover, and the man hadn't turned, he hadn't seen them. *Christ.* John leant against the wall, catching his breath, almost collapsing in relief.

A sound from behind him. He turned – and saw with horror that it was the soldier. John stood dumbly before him, not knowing what to do. The man held his helm in one hand, a short sword in the other. Amusement in his eyes. He began to say something, but John only caught half a word before something shoved him into the wall – Telde, knocking him aside to get to the soldier. He couldn't tell whether it was her fist or elbow that collided with the man's head, it happened so swiftly. In almost the same motion she took hold of him and rammed his head into the wooden beam at the corner of the building. He slumped to the floor in a feeble clink of metal.

John watched stunned as Telde dragged the man out of

sight behind the building, helped by Ceria. She pulled John forcefully down, then took the soldier's short sword and held it out to him. He shook his head, but she pressed it into his hand. The grip was warm.

"I can see the caravan," Ceria said from the far end of the cabin. "But it's a long way. I don't think we can make it without being seen."

A questioning shout from somewhere behind them. John peered around the corner to see two soldiers looking towards the building. *Oh god.*

"*Blood and blackness,*" Telde muttered under her breath beside him; she must have seen the same. In her eyes was a ruthlessness that scared John more than anything yet. He glanced at the man's body near to him. A peppering of stubble was visible above the white gorget covering his neck, a scarlet insignia of a three-flowered plant inscribed at the throat. There was spittle at the corners of his mouth. *Is he alive? Did she kill him?*

The soldiers shouted again in the distance, insistent.

"Are you certain, Ceria?" Telde asked without turning.

"We'll be seen," she answered. "There's a large building in a clearing, with soldiers surrounding it. I think they're taking the prisoners there. We can't get to the caravan without crossing their view."

The building was Milnadon's equivalent of a village hall, John knew. Its stacked upper tiers would give the Queen's forces a considerable field of vision. *We're trapped here.*

"They're coming," Telde said, without emotion, then reached over her shoulder and drew the sword from under her cloak. John caught a glimpse of crimson armour beneath, a series of interlocking plates. She moved in front of him, the double-edged blade held before her. Inscriptions decorated its length. "Prepare yourself."

Suddenly, there was a soft whoosh and a burst of brightness in the distance. A house on top of a hill – *Wimda's,* John realised – was engulfed by blue flames. With another gust of sound the fire intensified, jade sparks fizzing around its fierce core. There were shouts from all over the village, barked orders, hurried footsteps.

"Come on!" Telde's urgent whisper broke John's stare. He followed her and Ceria as they left the cover of the cabin and sprinted towards the caravan. John risked a sideways glance – soldiers were pouring out from the village hall, joining others already rushing towards the opposite side of the village. To his relief none looked their way as they crossed the open stretch. He thought he glimpsed a dark, glossy shape loping ahead of the soldiers, but it was gone before he could be sure. There was another whoosh, followed by a loud crack, just as the three of them made it to the edge of the merchants' camp.

Telde barely slowed, twisting and turning between the carts and wagons of the procession. The caravan had widened considerably since the previous day, tents spilling out haphazardly from its side. They raced past a woman knelt over a man with bloodied bandages covering his chest, and John thought he recognised her as the palm reader. Numerous other people were scattered throughout the camp, the glint of silver mail amongst them, but most were gazing at Wimda's distraction. Strings of radiant blue were coiling out from the blaze, snatching at the sky.

Telde stopped abruptly before a huge shape, and John only narrowly avoided careering into Ceria's back. It was the gigantic sloth-like creature he had seen the day before. *This is the joorun,* he realised. *This is how we're meant to escape.* It was too incredible. Were they truly going to attempt to ride that thing? How would they even get it to move?

Telde and Ceria hurried to opposite sides of the animal, and began untying the thick ropes with which it was tethered. *This is crazy. Tell them, John. Tell them you can't* – a sudden blow from behind sent him tumbling face-first to the ground. A large hand scooped up his fallen sword. He looked up, expecting to find the silver and white of a Queen's soldier. But instead the man moving towards Ceria was in worn leathers, his head shaved, a braided beard hanging below a broken grin.

"If it isn't my favourite little bitch," the man said, pointing the sword at Ceria. He glanced at Telde as she stepped out from behind the joorun. "And here's your keeper. Stay there. Drop the sword." He moved his blade closer to Ceria, pressing the point against her chest.

Telde laid her weapon down in front of her and spoke slowly. "Let her go, Eyick. We can pay you."

"Pay me?" the man scoffed. "Do you really think you can match what the Queens'll give? They're sore for you two, especially after I told them you're from Ferol. Yeah I know your little secret, don't look so surprised. *I heard you.* Not that it ain't written on your fenning faces. You're spies, or traitors, or thieves. Gods know and fuck cares. What do you reckon Telde, will they be grateful enough when I hand you over to give me some private time with your girl?" He trailed the point of the sword over Ceria's chest to her stomach, his grin widening.

The sword then moved unexpectedly, angling downwards, its tip digging into the dirt. There was a moment's confusion on the man's face, and Ceria took advantage, kicking him hard between the legs. In almost the same instant John saw Telde react, advancing with that shocking swiftness to slam her forearm into the side of the man's head. He crashed to the floor in a heavy heap.

Ceria looked gratefully at John, to his confusion. No – she was looking behind him. He turned to see Jago, and then understood. Jago had used his powers to give them the distraction they had needed.

"Move, come on," Telde said whilst picking up her sword. She lifted the blade in a high arc above her head – for an instant John thought that she was aiming for the unconscious man – and brought it down upon a tethering rope, cleaving it in two. "Move!"

Ceria rushed past her to scramble up the netting draped

over the joorun, then crawled to its broad neck. Jago trotted to the other side of the animal, carrying a bow and a large bag. He scaled the netting with surprising athleticism.

"Come on," Telde repeated impatiently, looking at John. She had climbed halfway up the animal, and stretched out a hand to him. John's indecision abruptly and unexpectedly vanished. He pushed himself to his feet and hurried to Telde, who helped him onto the netting.

"Get a good hold – twist your hands and feet through the rope," she said, then turned toward Ceria. The other woman was close to the creature's vast head, whispering to it, her hands dug into its fur. There were shouts from within the camp; John saw the flash of chain mail. The joorun showed no signs of movement.

"Ceria."

"I know. I'm trying."

Come on. John willed the animal to move. Two soldiers were visible now. One shouted, pointing a sword in their direction.

The animal lurched beneath them, an extraordinary tremor. But it only moved a few yards. It buffeted an adjacent cart, emitted a resounding groan, then planted its feet again.

"Ceria!"

"I'm trying!"

Another soldier emerged from between the tents to the side of them. The man stopped and lifted a bow. Before John could shout a warning there was a *thunk*, and an arrow shaft trembled in-between him and Telde, where it had punctured the animal's hide. They exchanged a wide-eyed look, before a bellowing howl erupted from the joorun. The creature reared up onto its hind legs, and John clung on desperately as the horizon tipped on its side. He could see Telde losing her grip and slipping, and out of instinct he caught her wrist as she fell; she gasped in pain as her arm twisted beneath him. John strained with her weight but held on, he determinedly held on until she was able to swing her body around and regain a hold of the netting.

With a thunderous crash the animal's front legs reconnected with the ground, and they were barely able to prevent themselves from being thrown off in the opposite direction. John had a glimpse of the others – Ceria had her arms and legs wrapped around the joorun's neck, and the top of Jago's head was just visible over its immense back – before the animal charged, butting and trampling the carts and tents in its way. John seized handfuls of shaggy fur as he hung on, the ropes grating against his wrists.

The joorun broke free of the caravan in a shower of splintered wood, a terrified soldier leaping from its path. It let out another deafening howl, and pounded away from the village.

With some effort John turned his head, and saw the buildings dwindling behind them, a faint curl of blue rising into the sky above. *We made it.* The thought resonated slowly, incredulously. *Christ, it worked. It actually worked.*

He laughed and looked to the others. Jago beamed at him over the joorun's back; Ceria gazed back in exhausted relief, her head resting on the animal's neck. Telde was even beginning to smile – John was shocked how much it altered her appearance, how young she suddenly seemed.

"Telde. Look," Ceria said, flatly.

Telde followed her stare. Her smile evaporated.

At first John was unable to discern anything – but after a few moments he could make out a dark speck, between them and the village. "What is it?"

No-one answered. They didn't need to. The speck grew rapidly, until it became a feline shape, glossy and black. *The Queen's Claw.*

It consumed the ground between them, despite the enduring pace of the joorun. The animal bounded, half-leapt as it ran – it wasn't a feline movement, John realised, but something else entirely, an evolved motion that had no Earth equivalent. Sharp talons extended from its feet, and its powerful body wasn't furred but hard, gleaming. Its rider was incongruously still, as if detached from the violent strides beneath him. His plate armour was completely white apart from the scarlet insignia on his chest – the same design John had seen on the other soldier's neck: a thorny stem twisting into three lavish flowers. His helm mimicked the Queen's Claw, a squashed muzzle frozen in a snarl.

They were almost alongside now. The rider raised a crossbow. John sensed a movement beside him and turned to see Telde, further up the netting, crouch and push her feet into the joorun's hide, then leap towards the rider. She collided with the man in mid-air, and both of them and the Queen's Claw were sent crashing and rolling in a great plume of dust.

"Stop! Turn around!" John shouted at Ceria. *She jumped.* He couldn't believe it. The tangled bodies were already diminishing behind them. Were they getting to their feet? He thought he saw the flashing of swords.

Ceria was desperately tugging at the joorun's fur, pressing her feet into its neck. It was turning, but agonisingly slowly. John could only make out distant blots of colour: the white armour of the rider, the red of Telde, now apart, now knotted together. The black of the Queen's Claw, pushing itself up.

It felt like an age before the joorun finally approached the fighters. Ceria had bundles of fur in her hands as she attempted to slow the animal. John saw that the rider was now lying on the ground, unmoving, with Telde stood over him. But the Queen's Claw was on its feet and moving towards her. Telde gripped her sword in one hand, her other arm held limply against her body. She backed away as the animal thrust its head forward, snarling and snapping at the air in front of her.

The joorun had yet to come to a stop, but John glimpsed Ceria fling herself from its neck far above him. She landed nimbly, rolling on the ground and then scrambling up. In front of her the Queen's Claw lashed out at Telde, too fast for her to avoid. Its talon ripped across her stomach, the sword flying from her hand as she fell backwards. *Oh god.*

Ceria leapt onto the animal's back just as it was about to strike again. It jolted and jerked beneath her, then sprang repeatedly into the air. Ceria slipped down its flank but somehow clung on. *She can't keep it up,* John thought frantically. *She'll be thrown and killed.*

But something was happening. The animal was slowing – its throes were less violent and it had ceased jumping. It paced in a circle, tiredly snapping over its shoulder at Ceria, who was out of reach. The animal's limbs then seemed to give way, and there was a long, piercing wail as it collapsed onto its side.

John jumped off the joorun, whose momentum had taken it a short distance past the scene, and raced alongside Jago towards the women. He skidded to a halt a few yards away. The Queen's Claw was formidable up close: as tall as a horse, then wider, heavier. But it couldn't get up. The creature struggled weakly whilst Ceria lay across its chest, her hands pressed white against its stony black. Was she crying? The animal convulsed, lifting and shaking her body with it. Its talons scratched at the dirt. The huge chest was slowing, slowing, and, after a minute, it became still.

Suddenly Ceria was on her feet. Her eyes were unnaturally wide. She bared her teeth at John in a look of wild hunger. She took a step towards him, but in the same instant Telde appeared behind her; she brought the hilt of her sword down over the back of Ceria's head, then caught her as she fell.

John could do little more than gape. Telde dropped to her knees, clutching her stomach. The Queen's Claw framed the two women, its muscular legs lying either side of them. The rider lay in his brilliant white armour a few feet away, the ground dark where his blood had soaked the soil.

John glanced at Jago, who for once appeared as shocked as him. Above, the emerald moon stared bluntly down.

He understood nothing of this world.

13

Ceria clung onto the netting draped over the joorun's back. The animal let out another deep, protesting moan.

"Oh stop complaining," she said softly into its flank. She used a small blade to cut away the fur surrounding the wound from the arrow. Thick clumps of grey and russet fell to the ground ten feet below. The joorun turned its huge head back towards her; a fist-sized eye loomed, suspicious. It seemed to lose interest after few moments, however, and began to lick at the fur of its front legs. The action resulted in a gentle swaying as Ceria continued to work.

The arrowhead had gone deep, but it was only a minor wound for such a large animal, a thorn prick in its side. Treating it wasn't entirely necessary, she knew, yet it was their fault the joorun had been wounded in the first place, so it was owed any aid they could give.

She was simply glad the wound wasn't more serious. She couldn't risk using her powers. Not so soon after the Queen's Claw.

Ceria glanced over her shoulder. Telde and John stood close to the high banks of the river, sheltering from the afternoon heat under a line of trees. The amber leaves formed a dazzling canopy above their heads, as if set ablaze by the sun above, whilst the sound of rushing water provided a soothing contrast. Ceria was surprised to hear Telde's laughter mixed in with it. She was showing John how to use the bow in his hands, and let out a snort as he caught his ear with the string.

They were a mystery, John and Jago. Ceria wondered where they were from, what their stories were. Jago never stopped talking – asking ceaseless questions, giving answers no-one had requested, explaining things that made little sense to her. He had already thoroughly tested Telde's temper, but he never seemed to be daunted by her scoldings. Ceria couldn't help but like him. The man had wandered off now, ostensibly to scout out a crossing point for the joorun, but she suspected it was as much his curiosity and Telde's exasperation that had resulted in the mission.

She looked over at the other man, John. *Like the animal,* she thought with a chuckle. With those blue eyes, the long thin nose and his height, he might be handsome if he had a good shave and found some clothes that fit. *And if he stopped looking like a lost jaller calf.* He didn't talk as much as his friend, asking child-like questions and moving hesitantly, as if afraid that touching something would cause it to evaporate in his hand. He had regarded her warily ever since the Queen's Claw. *I can't blame him.*

She reached for a flask on the joorun's back, and began washing the wound with the river water contained within. It was a tributary of Telemsis, the great river that cleaved off the western edge of Ireldelor and signified an unofficial border with the neighbouring country of Ranarin. She knew from books and Elders' tales that the river ran from the Coronal Mountains bordering the Heartlands, to drain a hundred suns north into the Shimmer Sea. One of her favourite legends in her youth had been where Blue Branch, god and mother of Leafshade, weighted down by sorrow for her mortal husband's death, fell from the sky to be impaled on the Coronal Range. Her blood spilt south, fermenting the Heartlands' soil, blessing it with righteousness. Her tears ran north, seeking solace in the sea.

Ceria had always wanted to see the river, but the circumstances meant she had neither the time or mood to enjoy it. It had been a day since they escaped Milnadon, though it felt a lot less. No doubt that was because she had been asleep for much of the journey, knocked unconscious by Telde's blow. They had ridden due west away from the village, Telde explained when she awoke, until they came to the river. They had forded it and travelled south along the waters, hoping for their tracks to be erased before they turned back east. After a few hours they had stopped to rest, yet despite the tranquil setting none of them could sleep.

What will we do now? The resistance meeting in Candar'laon was surely ruined. Many members would have been caught if the arrests by the Queen's soldiers had been widespread. Ceria could only pray that some had escaped, or, like them, had not yet arrived. *Where will we go?* Ceria hadn't asked Telde yet, in fear that she wouldn't have an answer.

They hadn't spoken about what had happened outside Milnadon, either. Jago had been keen to, of course, questioning her almost as soon as she had regained consciousness: *What did you do to the Queen's Claw? What powers do you have? Can you show me?* Telde had railed at him for it. Ceria usually hated how she did that – how she always wanted to keep her abilities secret, as if they were something to be ashamed of.

But for once she was glad of Telde's shielding. She didn't want to answer Jago's questions. Because this time was different. She had used her powers not to heal, but in that other way, in the way she had sworn against. At the time there hadn't been a choice, she knew that. It was the only way to save Telde. Yet that didn't change what she did. It had happened.

If the bloody bandages and the throbbing of her head didn't prove it, the way the rest of her body felt did. Like an empty sky after a storm had roared through it. She remembered only fragments of the preceding events: leaping from the joorun, clinging onto the Queen's Claw, pressing herself against its huge chest. The pounding of its heart. Then using her abilities. Searching out that other boundary between them, pushing past it, opening herself to the elemental swell, letting it gush into her, and not stopping, widening the tide, taking more and more and more, taking everything. She had felt the radiance surge through every inch of her. *Gods, the power of it.* She ached for that feeling again.

Raised voices brought her attention back to the present. She turned to see John wave the bow at Telde, then throw it at her feet. Ceria hurriedly laid a makeshift bandage over the joorun's wound, using the heavy netting to secure the cloth, then shimmied down the rope to the ground.

When she reached Telde and John, they were standing tellingly apart. John was exercising his thumb in that way Ceria had seen him do a few times. She gave Telde a questioning look.

"I was simply demonstrating how to use the bow properly," Telde shrugged.

"You called me a jinua's arse," John complained.

Ceria couldn't help but feel for him; she knew from past experience how Telde was as a teacher. The woman had the patience of a starving jetten attempting to break a nut.

"We don't have any arrows, anyway. Jago didn't buy any with the bow, remember?" Ceria said, attempting to placate the two of them. "Have you injured your hand, John?"

"What? Oh, no. Yes. It's an old injury," John replied. "I lost it as a child."

"Lost it?"

"Yes, you know. In an accident. It was cut off."

Ceria frowned at the thumb. *Had it grown back?* He must have misspoke.

"It was reattached," John added. "It works okay, it's just a little stiff now and then."

Ceria thought that she might be missing some joke. He was an odd man. "Where are you from, John?"

Telde snorted. "He says he's from another world."

"I am," John replied, sparing a glare for Telde. "Jago's from there, too."

"That hardly strengthens your claim," Telde scoffed. "Besides, how would you know what a jinua is if you were from another world?"

"I *don't* know what a jinua is. But comparing me to its arse is hardly going to be a compliment, is it?"

"How can you speak the language then?" Telde asked.

John looked defeated by the question. "I don't know."

Ceria was worried that Telde would press her advantage, but was surprised when instead she gave a loud sniff and moved to her armour, which leant against a nearby tree. She sat with her back against the trunk, examining the wide tear in the crimson breastplate.

Ceria looked at John, who seemed to be immersed in anxious reflection. *He truly is lost*, she thought. His lack of knowledge seemed genuine. Of course they had been fooled in the past – Ceria remembered the Fivemoon priests near Dereselon – but what could he gain by acting so clueless? There had been ample opportunity to hand them over to the Queen's soldiers in Milnadon, if that was his agenda. And she would eat her boots if he was an agent of the half-man.

He deserves a chance, she decided. Telde's suspicious nature had been influencing her too much recently. Not everyone was out to get them. Perhaps he was from a distant place, the West or the Savage Lands – though he didn't seem hardy enough for that – or even from across the Shimmer Sea. Or he could have been involved in some battle and lost his wits; Telde had spoken of such things before.

Presently the man was staring with some unease at the canopy of leaves above him. Ceria followed his look but could only make out a small family of luminous jetten, which were hardly exceptional.

"I understand nothing of this place," he muttered under his breath.

"Perhaps I can help you, John," Ceria said gently. "What would you like to know?"

The offer seemed to catch him by surprise. He thought for

a few moments before speaking. "Why were those soldiers after you? And where or what is Ferol?"

"Ferol is our home. It's on the north-eastern coast, beyond Ireldelor – we're not part of the Queen's rule. It's principally a city of great size." She spoke uncertainly, embarrassed at stating such obvious facts. But there was only rapt attention on John's face. She could sense Telde's eyes on her as she continued. "Terrible things happened there. We escaped, me and Telde, with the help of others. We're part of a group that –"

"Ceria!" Telde interrupted.

"What's the point in remaining silent about these things anymore?" Ceria responded, surprised by her own vehemence. "Who's he going to tell? It's not like they're not after us already. And they were searching for him too, remember."

Telde glowered at her, but there was something of disquiet in the look, or even surrender. It pierced Ceria worse than any angry response, somehow.

"What terrible things?" John asked.

Ceria turned back to him, and gestured for them to sit. They faced the river, its waters a glimmering wealth below the parched banks. She could see the roots of the trees striking out from the dirt wall, bulbous stitches and tapering fingers. A large bloodfly whirred around John's head, which he waved away with unusual concern.

"It began six years ago," she said, "when Dalinde was elected – I suppose you haven't heard of him either? We saw it as a victory, most of the city did. It was an unexpected one, too. The government was shaped in such a way that despite his popularity, the council could have easily prevented him from gaining leadership. And Dalinde meant change to the regime, after all – he intended to break apart the governing council, and for Ferol to return to the old system of rule. Everyone presumed they would outvote his appointment. We expected change would have to be fought for.

"But he won, somehow he won. It seemed like a blessing. And he did everything he promised, at first. Do you remember the day the governors' mansions were torn down, Telde? We celebrated like Ferol had been reborn. It was back to what it once was – a true Ferol, not an imitation of the Regency." Ceria could see the question on John's lips. *Does he truly not know of the Regency, either?* Well, she couldn't explain all at once.

"Dalinde was a good man," she continued, "and noble in his intentions. I believe that. But he was also weak –"

"He was a fenning puppet," Telde muttered. She had removed the inner lining from her breastplate and was surveying the tear from the inside.

"It took some years before that weakness began to show," Ceria carried on. "But it became obvious there was much manipulation behind both his election and his rule. The Hearts began to grow in number in the city – before, they were only a small fanatical cult. Dalinde gave them more and more power, and this was a man who came from a gentle Leafshade family. He appeared less in public, and increasingly strict rulings were issued in his name. Soon the arrests started. The disappearances, the killings. High-ranking officials and prominent citizens, anyone who spoke out. Then the call for Primitives… at first it was only that, an invitation to the Hearts' temple. But by the end it was an undisguised hunt for every last one. Those caught were never seen again. The rumours said they were taken to Som'syere island, but we don't know for certain.

"The resistance reformed in the midst of this. They had disbanded when Dalinde was elected, thinking their work to be over. It was in a weakened state at first, with many members arrested or missing. But there was no lack of new volunteers, given the worsening conditions in the city. The movement soon gathered momentum. I was taken under their protection, like many others, and hidden as the Primitive searches escalated. In the following months, the resistance built towards the rebellion that would free our city. But..."

"We were used," Telde said, darkly. "We did the half-man's work for him. The whole fenning resistance. We helped him, gods curse us. The coup went perfectly. We overthrew the City Guard, left the city defenceless – we gave him the opportunity he needed. We were used. It's our fault."

Telde's words shocked Ceria. Her friend had talked about the resistance's mistakes before, but she never knew the guilt ran this deep. *How much does she blame herself?*

"We didn't know, Telde. No-one did," Ceria said. "Not even Climbe. How could we have predicted what would happen? How could anyone think such a thing? Even if the resistance hadn't gone ahead with the coup, even if the City Guard had been at their posts, they couldn't have stopped it."

"Perhaps. But the city wouldn't have been laid bare. We wouldn't have been animals for the slaughter. Some might have escaped."

"What happened?" John asked, following a brief silence.

Ceria paused, gathering her strength. "The Endless."

There was a blank expression on John's face. Ceria was bewildered; every adult and child on Crescent knew of the Endless. They were the whispered subject of the majority of night tales, their name often left unsaid out of superstition, even if most would never believe such creatures could exist.

"They came in the hours after the revolt. While we were still celebrating," Telde said quietly, not noticing John's expression as she stared down at her armour. She ran her fingers along the gash in the metal. "Suddenly there were so many. Monstrosities, beasts only nightmares can conjure. They tore through the city and the people like they were playthings. And then the Endless... spilling out of the sky, like the storm delivered them. They moved calmly, but were just as hungry for death. You couldn't fight them. You couldn't... they aren't physical, not blood and muscle. They're closer to gods – but they're not that. They're something else. No god could ever be so cruel." She looked up, her eyes fraught and angry. "You could *feel* them, revelling in the massacre. In the despair. They fed on it."

Telde lowered her gaze, and when she continued her voice was scoured of emotion. "They had won their victory instantly. There was already so much confusion in the city following the resistance coup – there was no organised force to fight them. The bloodshed was unnecessary. But it went on and on. It was a display of power. A demonstration. By *him*."

Ceria was absorbed in watching Telde, in reliving the awful events. She didn't hear John's question until he repeated it.

"Was it Dalinde?"

"No," Ceria answered. "No, it wasn't. It was Senthis." The name curdled in her mouth; she hadn't uttered it for a long time. "That's what his name was before, when he was on the governing council. He's called the half-man now, if anyone dares to say it. Because he's half one of them. Part Endless. Perhaps he always was, if you could hide such a thing. Or it might've happened at Som'syere, or the Endless did it to him, I don't know. But *he* controlled *them*. He was the one behind it all, behind Dalinde. On that terrible night he proclaimed a new era for Ferol, with him as its master.

"After that, Ferol was entirely shut off," Ceria continued, staring into the white whirls and eddies of water below her. "The ports were closed, and no-one was allowed in or out. The Hearts were given free rein. The monsters only showed themselves occasionally, during the executions, to have their fun. The city continued under this shadow, a shade of its former self. Countless numbers starved, many more were killed. Foundries ran day and night, and hundreds were forced to work without rest on a bridge connecting the mainland to Som'syere. The resistance, what was left of us, went into hiding. Climbe – our leader – knew we lacked the power to do anything meaningful. We concentrated on getting as many as we could out of the city, to regroup in meetings spread across Ireldelor. Then we would find a way to regain our home." As she said it, the notion sounded hopeless. She knew there were things kept from her, but what plan could possibly succeed against the half-man and his army? "We were helped to escape almost half a year ago. Gods know how the city has worsened since."

"Why would the half-man do this?" John asked.

"No-one knows for certain," Ceria said, shaking her head. "He's still after Primitives. And he's using Som'syere island somehow."

"He wants power and destruction," Telde said. "Ferol is only the start."

"Why has nobody done anything?" John pressed. "Aren't there other armies, other countries that could help?"

"Crescent doesn't know what's happened to Ferol," Ceria answered. "The Queen's lands probably saw it as a blessing when our borders were closed, sending all that trade to their cities instead. They have no reason to think it's any more than the rumours of some revolt or internal conflict. Why would they believe us if we told them the truth? The Endless are real. Gods of living light invading a city... no-one *could* believe that unless they had seen –"

"Wait, what did you call them?" John interrupted. "Are they made of light?"

"In a manner," Ceria said, taken aback by his urgency. "It's light, but like no other kind, always moving and changing... it's hard to describe." And she didn't like to, she realised. She didn't want to give those unnatural creatures a place in her mind.

"I've seen them!" John exclaimed, jumping to his feet. "The Endless – at least one of them. It was like liquid, chaotic and swirling, but held together. And they feel – I could feel it somehow. In my head. It had a tendril of light..." He paused to lightly touch his forehead. Ceria and Telde exchanged a frown.

"There was another with it," he eventually continued. "Something else, I mean. Massive and deformed. There were bands around its wrists, and it created something electrical. Like a ball of charged light. The sound – I remember the sound. A low hum. A crackling."

"How do you know this?" Telde demanded. "Have you been to Ferol?"

"Perhaps they're elsewhere," Ceria said. All of them were standing now.

"Yes, they are. They're on Earth, my planet," John said. "You have to listen to me. Something terrible happened there, even worse than what you describe. And these things were there, I saw them. They almost killed me."

"They attacked your people?" Telde asked.

"No, I... I don't think so. At least not how you described. And what happened to my people, it was over two years before I saw these creatures. They attacked me just before I was transported here. I think they were hunting me."

Telde looked at him for a long time, before waving an arm in irritation. "Tall tales."

Ceria wasn't so certain. *How does he know of the crackling?* Only few who heard that sound managed to survive.

"I said to Jago there must be a connection, a reason why we're here," John said. "This must be it, these Endless. They must have had something to do with what happened on my planet. What else can you tell me about them?"

"We've told you enough," Telde snapped. She moved to pick up her armour, before turning to Ceria. "We're leaving."

She stalked away towards the joorun without looking at John.

"You have to believe me. This might be why I'm here," John said, his eyes fixed on Ceria.

She found it difficult to escape his despairing expression, but after a few moments gave a faint shake of her head. "You should find your friend. Telde won't wait long."

As she moved away, John spoke quietly behind her.

"They all died, Ceria. Not just one city. Everyone, everywhere. They all died."

*

They were going to Edemon. Telde announced it once they were moving again on the joorun. They would find answers and other resistance members there, she explained brusquely. It would take three or four days of travel. She wasn't in the mood for further discussion.

Jago, who had caught up to them further upstream, an array of flowers in his hands, was delighted with the news. John was unmoved, not knowing what Edemon was. Ceria's first reaction was anxiety: a substantial number of Queen's soldiers would surely populate Ireldelor's capital city.

John was soon educated by Jago's voluminous descriptions of Edemon. Ceria watched him noticeably brighten upon hearing how large the city was, and how many thousands lived there. She thought it strange how much he seemed to enjoy company, or the prospect of it, when he acted so awkwardly around people. *It must be because of the events in his homelands.* She was surprised to find she so readily believed him in that. Or at least that something terrible had happened there. His eyes had contained the same grief she had grown to recognise in too many in Ferol.

John had said the events occurred over two years ago. *Perhaps not long before the attack on Ferol,* Ceria thought. *What if there is a connection?*

They forded the river after an hour of travelling south. The crossing was wide yet still waist-deep in places, and they had to climb off the joorun to guide the reluctant animal across. John was more talkative as they subsequently travelled east, the late afternoon sun working to dry their damp clothes. He truly was an unwritten book when it came to knowledge of these lands, Ceria reflected. But he seemed to have gained a new determination to fill those pages.

She left Jago to answer his questions, her attention drifting in the slow rumbling gait of the joorun, until she heard John ask what the events at Ferol had to do with the Queen's army and the arrests. It was a question she had asked herself many times in the past day. If it had been only a few soldiers involved, it could have been explained: it was clear the half man's influence – and his coin – reached far beyond Ferol. But this seemed to be the entire army. Across all of Ireldelor. *Telde's right,* she thought, *the Central Seat must be behind it. The Queen herself.*

Perhaps they had finally become aware of the events in Ferol, or some portion of it. They might have learnt how Primitives were being so zealously sought by the half-man, even if the reasons why were not apparent. Ceria had seen the groups of Primitives herded like jallers through Ferol's city gates, one of the very few exceptions to the closed borders. It would be impossible to entirely hide such actions, especially the further the abductions went into Ireldelor – into Queen's territory. Word could have made it to the Heartlands, Ceria reasoned, and the Central Seat had responded by gathering Primitives before Ferol did.

But the arrests seemed heavy-handed for that purpose. Too ruthless. *What could make them act so severely?*

"Perhaps the half-man controls the Central Seat already," Telde muttered blackly ahead of them, from the joorun's neck. "Perhaps all of this is by his hand."

"You don't believe that," Ceria said. "He can't control that much already." If he did, there was no hope.

"What happened to Dalinde?" John asked.

"What he deserved," Telde said.

She doesn't believe that either, Ceria told herself. She remembered the blood red window of the Hearts temple, the mutilated body strung up in front. *No-one deserves that.*

Silence fell over the group, and the two men were wise enough not to break it. Ceria gripped the netting as she watched the low hills roll sombrely past. The land seemed too bare here, the trees too lean. She tried to pick out mud burrows amongst the grasses, and followed the paths of the birds overhead. In the same sky she could see a pair of Spirit storms, hanging aberrantly, like pinched bruises in the skin of the world.

Eventually she moved to replace Telde at the neck of the joorun, and half-lay there, comforted by the warmth beneath her, the thick scent within the fur. She eased the animal eastwards, towards the Ireldelor capital.

The choice of Edemon made sense, in a way. Anyone still pursuing the group would not expect them to go there. It was the headquarters of the Queen's armies in Ireldelor, after all – not that that thought didn't have its far from comforting implications. But they *were* likely to find other resistance members there; she knew that many had been sent to the city. If they had evaded capture. Almost as importantly, they would find news. About what was happening in Ireldelor and with the Central Seat, perhaps even word of Ferol. News that might give them direction. Hope.

Ceria realised she had been steering her thoughts away from that dangerous territory: from the abandoned meeting in Candar'laon and what it meant for the resistance, for Ferol, for all of them. *How are we going to get our city back? How do we fight the Endless? What can we do?*

She prayed that they would soon find the answers.

14

John stood on the roof of the building, and looked upon a city teeming with life.

It was incredible. A living, breathing, beating city. He had thought he would never see one again. Never like this. It didn't matter that it wasn't on Earth. What mattered was that it existed, and it was full of people, it was bursting with humans.

Edemon.

The building was only a single storey, but the huge bowled valley in which the city sat – almost perfectly circular – meant he was afforded a panoramic view. The afternoon sun blazed down upon countless thousands of similar wooden buildings that lined the valley, a ramshackle mass huddled and heaped and stacked on top of one another, as though every whisper of space was a precious commodity. Jago described it as an alien favela, which seemed as accurate a description as any.

The only exception to the congestion John could see was an enclosed region to the south of the city. There the buildings seemed to be of stone, and neatly set apart – the subsequent avenues conspicuous due to their rarity elsewhere. To its left, about a third of the way up the valley, was an enormous column: dazzling white and gold, a blood red tip finishing hundreds of feet in the air. It was as if some colossal spear had impaled the world, and here was its point erupting through the other side. Its length cast an advancing strip of shadow, making a sundial of the city.

He hadn't needed Jago to explain that the valley was an impact crater, a product of some violent meteor collision eons in the past. John had seen one on such a scale before, a lifetime ago, in Arizona. One of his and Jessica's few holidays together – she'd had an aunt out in California. He remembered the story she told him as they looked upon that vast inverted blister: the businessman who had spent thirty years drilling its floor for meteoric iron, not knowing it was almost all vaporised on impact.

Edemon was infinitely richer than that barren crater. Not desolate but full of animation, a cradle of life. Not the end of the world but its nascence. Or its rebirth, in a site that sang of extinction.

People were everywhere. The valley shook with their noise. For so long construction hadn't been a signifier of life for John; he was used to congregations of vacant structures, to buildings that were nothing but mute frames. It was overwhelming to stand within a city that could barely contain its purpose. He looked down to see a woman hurrying along a tight passage below. She scolded her two children as they tangled in her feet.

So many people. John couldn't help repeating it to himself. So many thousands of lives continuing and independent and oblivious. The thought made him dizzy, and he had to turn his back on the view.

But the city wasn't so easy to escape: a swell of buildings now towered above him, reaching up to the foot of the monstrous outer walls. Edemon was engulfing.

The others were on the roof also, and it was a relief to direct his attention on them instead. Jago was sitting amongst a swarm of books and papers and other debris, undisturbed by the regular rearrangements the breeze made to his assemblage. Telde and Ceria stood in conversation at the back, a ragged tent near to them, as well as the top of a rope ladder. They glanced at the latter now and then; they had already been waiting over an hour for the resistance contact to meet them here.

John was glad for the pause. It felt like the first time they had stopped moving in days. The travel on the joorun had been monotonous – even with the scenery of a new world moving past him, and the novelty of travelling atop a gigantic alien animal, John had soon found himself languid in the heat along with the others. Wimda's food ran out after the third day, and all of them were famished by the time they had ridden through the miles of farmland that led up to Edemon.

Their first glimpse of the city had been the stone outer wall and spire, rising above the surrounding forests like some supreme ancient monument. Jago had gone ahead of them, with the joorun. He had managed to convince Telde he was up to the task – she had wanted to abandon the animal, but Ceria was opposed to it. They had settled on Jago posing as a lone merchant; it surely wasn't unusual for joorun traders to frequent the capital, argued Ceria, and when he was tested by a sceptical Telde, Jago had shown an exhaustive grasp of Edemon's imports and exports. John thought it likely the guards would let him through simply to save themselves from boredom.

As Jago had gone on to the west entrance, the three of them had hiked through the dense ring of forest around the city. John had been astounded by the twisting, silvery trees and the wildlife populating the woodland: innumerable examples of the luminous animals he had seen previously at the river bank; a pack of warbling creatures sitting amongst the upper boughs, fan-like tails hanging down; flashes of deer-like animals that disappeared into the undergrowth before he could get a clear look. Ceria named them all for him, a small smile on her lips. She had seemed immediately at home in the forest, pointing out dirt mounds on the forest bed and explaining how the jetten used them to store food – although many were false heaps to confuse other animals, she had quickly added, perhaps noticing the hungry looks on both Telde and John's faces.

When they had arrived at the eastern gate, Ceria had gone through first, with Telde and John following an hour later. Telde had wanted to take every precaution they could. Traffic into the city was reassuringly abundant, and the two of them had latched onto one of the larger groups as they approached the entrance. The gate was an immense thing, two hulking slabs of wood and stone, the slightest parting between them enough to fit a pair of jooruns; John had been briefly proud of his alien approximation. Queen's soldiers guarded the breach, plucking individuals from the influx on a seemingly arbitrary basis, for subsequent questioning or to search their possessions. John had tried his best not to stare at them – a subtle but painful elbow in his ribs from Telde came as a helpful reminder – and instead looked up as they walked, with no little vertigo, at the metres-thick stone arch a hundred feet above them.

Then they had been through, without incident, inside the city before John was prepared for the view that confronted him. It was as if the world had opened up, as if all human life had been collected and deposited within the walls. He had stood frozen at the sight until a fierce push in his back from Telde had made him move. There were plenty more soldiers inside – gleaming silver and white was around every corner. John couldn't help but think of the soldier in Milnadon, his body limp and unmoving.

Soon the ceaseless bustle of the city had surrounded them. It hadn't been difficult to learn about the arrests of Primitives; it was the topic of most conversations. The arrests had happened everywhere in Ireldelor, even here in the capital. However the reasons behind them elicited much more speculation than fact. The two of them had stopped at a cramped marketplace to satisfy their hunger, and encountered numerous explanations: the Primitives were needed for something important; they had been imprisoned for their own safety; they were after a single Primitive who was causing the Spirit storms; they were being exterminated for the good of

Crescent. Other rumours spoke of an army in Ferol, which had all of the other nations in agitation. Many more spoke of war, but the participants and motives varied.

The gossip or the soldiers or the packed city had put Telde more on edge than usual, and John had felt the result keenly and often. In the worst instance, he had asked a fruit-seller what a dimpled purple shape was, after which Telde had angrily thrown the fruit at him, resulting in a sweet-smelling explosion against his chest. *A fenning gamberry*, she had shouted at him, *stop asking idiotic questions!* John had decided against pointing out how her outburst could be considered much worse in terms of attracting attention.

Navigating the labyrinthine city hadn't done much to improve Telde's mood – John suspected she had been as disorientated as him, although she would never admit it – but they had eventually found Jago and Ceria at the predetermined location, a run-down inn. Jago had explained about stabling the joorun, and at length about the various other animals housed there, whilst Telde had entered the building. She had emerged with directions to a building not far away, explaining they would meet a resistance member called Tiyaden. To her frustration, however, the man wasn't on the roof when they arrived, and they had no choice but to wait.

A light breeze ran over the roof presently, and John saw a sheet of paper flutter up and away from Jago. Telde snatched it from the air as it flew near, handing it back with what looked to be a wry comment, which the wind regrettably took away. John glanced up at the sky, which had darkened, the sun partially hidden behind an increasing cloud cover. His eyes were drawn to the twin Spirit storms that hung either side of the city. They were a number of miles away, but close enough so that they were no longer just the pulsating stains on canvas they had previously appeared – now they held a third dimension, a dense volume. Viscous ink dropped in liquid.

As alien as this world might be, John thought, he had found a link between it and Earth. *The Endless*. The inconceivable apparition that had been on Earth, hunting him alongside the other monster. These things were on Crescent, too. In Ferol. He didn't know what it meant yet, and how it involved him, but it was something, a scrap of possible reason in the incomprehension surrounding him.

He remembered how powerful those creatures had been in the hotel, how intent on death. Hundreds of them had apparently invaded Telde and Ceria's city; John shuddered at the thought of so many let loose, at what they must have done to the inhabitants. And what if it was part of the same thing that had happened on Earth – would the same extinction happen on Crescent? If he had worked it out correctly, there had only been months between the event on Earth and the attack on Ferol. It seemed too close to be a coincidence. What if he should be doing something to stop it?

Telde didn't believe him about Earth or his encounter with the Endless, and Ceria was at the least doubtful. He had told them all that he knew anyway, which didn't amount to a great deal. But he was lost when it came to doing more. How could he help when he barely understood any of this? Was it even understandable? Perhaps he was scraping for reason in an unthinking universe, like he had been when alone on Earth. He was giving himself a purpose when no such thing existed. Perhaps he should forget it and concentrate on the chance he had been given here – to experience life again. *Why get more involved?* He was more of a hindrance to these people; Telde surely thought of him that way.

They can do without me. He would help how he could for now – answer any questions this resistance member might have, dig out details of the Endless or the events on Earth he might have forgotten previously – but then he would let them go their own way. He would stay here, in this city of life. There had to be a useful job he could do. He could draw, or utilise some common Earth knowledge they didn't yet possess. Or it might be better to find an innocuous occupation, a farmhand or the equivalent of a dishwasher, so he would better fit in, become a part of this new reality. He could let go of the past, Earth and Jessica and all the death, and he could live.

Across the roof, Ceria and Telde had stopped talking. Ceria moved to Jago, idly picking up one of the books and asking him about it. Telde looked undecided for a moment as she stood alone, evidently not wanting to go to Jago, before she finally walked towards John. *Not exactly a huge compliment,* John reflected.

She gave a short nod as she stood next to him, then looked out impassively on the city. John faced the same way, before risking a sideways glance. Her long cloak was wrapped closely around her, hiding the crimson armour beneath from any sharp-eyed guards. Whilst travelling the city she had slung two bags over her back, to cover the outline of her sword.

But if the soldier wasn't evident in her attire, it was clear in her stance and set expression. Another layer of defence. She was half a head shorter than John, her hazel hair tied back – he wondered briefly what it would look like loose – her dark eyebrows sharply prominent over those fierce green eyes. He remembered her outside Milnadon; his disbelief as she had leapt from the joorun onto the Queen's Claw rider. She had jumped in a heartbeat, without hesitation. There was something revelatory in the moment for him.

Telde raised an eyebrow at him, and John realised he had been staring. He quickly looked away at the city. He was reminded for what felt like the hundredth time that he still wasn't used to people.

"Are all the cities here this large?" He asked the first thing that came to mind, and inwardly cursed the artless result.

"Not all," Telde answered. "This is the capital of Ireldelor. But the Central City in the Heartlands is much larger, as is Ferol. And the Regency's capital, perhaps."

Silence followed. Both of them stared at the densely-packed valley. Telde was somehow more unnerving when she was quiet, John reflected.

"I hear some cities in the West are greater still, so much that the entire coastline is like a single, huge settlement," she added unexpectedly, with a slight awkwardness. "Besgenin would be too, I think, if you counted their tri-cities as one whole."

Is she trying to make conversation? As hard as John tried, he couldn't think of anything to say in reply. Instead he nodded idiotically, and allowed another silence to settle between them.

A gust of wind disrupted the quiet, as if in sympathy. The sky seemed to have darkened a few more shades, and there was the suggestion of rain in the heavier clouds. He looked to the Spirit storms, stark black and pulsing.

"What are they? What makes them?" John asked.

Telde followed his look and frowned. "It's like asking why there's wind and water, they simply are," she said, then continued quickly, perhaps regretting her bluntness. "Most believe they're related to Spirit, which is where the name comes from, but I doubt anyone truly knows how. They're as inexplicable as Spirit itself, and just as much a part of Crescent – though there's never been this many before. Ceria thinks Crescent is in distress, and these storms are the result."

"What do you think?"

"I'm not in tune with such matters," she said after a pause, as though she were going to say something else. "But I can tell you these two move strangely, even for Spirit storms. They've changed course many times, and now they're almost still, as you can see."

"Wimda said they were being drawn to one another," John said. "Do you think they'll pass over the city?"

Telde stared at the unnatural storms, as if willing them to disappear. "I don't know. A day ago I would have answered no, but they act so unpredictably. And now they simply sit there. I'm not an expert."

John could hear frustration in her voice, and imagined a number of uncertainties winding tightly around her. A tension comprising much more than the storms.

"Look who you're talking to, Telde. I don't know the first thing about Spirit storms," he said with a smile. "I don't even know what a gamberry is, except that it's all over my shirt."

To John's surprise this elicited a small smile in return, its appearance softening Telde's features far more than would seem possible. The change affected her eyebrows and eyes too, making her gaze not exactly more mild, but giving it the possibility of an intense warmth.

She started to reply, but was interrupted by a call from Ceria. Someone was climbing up the ladder.

Telde moved towards the other side of the building, then halted as the torso of the newcomer rose above the edge. The man pulled himself onto the roof and straightened to an impressive height. He was well-dressed, the dark leathers matching his shoulder-length hair. He grinned, wolfishly.

"Manvedian," Telde said, her expression hardened. "Why are you here?"

The man let out a short laugh. "That's all the welcome I get? You're still the same cold fish, Telde." He turned to Ceria, who had hurried to him upon his arrival, and gripped her shoulder. "It's good to see you safe."

Ceria responded with a warm smile and embraced the man. "How did you get here? How is Ferol? Have you seen the others?" she asked breathlessly.

"Where is Tiyaden?" Telde asked.

"He's not coming," the man answered. "Too many eyes on him, he reckons. Especially since the arrests. So he sent me instead – lucky escape for you really, Tiya'd bore your balls off with all his talk of city politics. You'd think moving to the capital would've broadened his interests." He held up his hands as Telde stalked up to him. "Alright, alright. I've got your answers, and more besides. But how about we get out of the wind first? The sky looks like it's about to unbuckle and piss all over us."

Telde gave a brusque acquiescence as he nodded towards the tent. All five of them subsequently clambered through the tent opening – though John suspected Jago came mostly because he didn't want his collection to be soaked. Inside was expectedly cramped. A few scant possessions lay strewn about: an empty bottle, some leftover food, bundles of clothing pushed up against the yellowing fabric.

John found a place between Jago and Telde, folding his legs uncomfortably beneath him. The resistance man, Manvedian, sat opposite. His dark brown jerkin – the silver clasps reaching to his neck, the leather scored with diamond patterns – and the sleek boots that extended to his knees made John feel like a peasant in his too-tight leggings and shirt stained with blood and fruit. He realised it had been a long time since he had felt self-conscious about his appearance.

Manvedian had found a small flask amongst the untidy effects, and sniffed and sipped it, before offering it around. John thought the man flicked his eyes momentarily toward him and Jago, and had the distinct impression he was sizing them up.

"What news of Ferol?" Telde asked impatiently. "Why are you here?"

Manvedian looked at Telde, with a slight incline of his head toward John and Jago, the meaning clear: *Can I speak in front of these?*

"They're with us," Ceria answered. John felt a mixture of emotions at the comment, which he could not quite untangle.

"I can't say I understand your tastes, Telde," Manvedian said, "but better strange men than none at all, eh?"

"Get on with it," Telde snapped.

Manvedian shrugged with an amused smile. "I got out of Ferol about a month back. Tiyaden had gone silent on us. You know him – the man couldn't find a courier worth shit if you threw one at him. But Climbe wanted to be sure, and knew he could trust me to get here in one piece."

"Climbe's alive?" Ceria asked keenly.

"We haven't had word from him in months," Telde added.

"He's his usual jaller-headed self, believe me. Chances are the messages were intercepted – or he thought it safer not to risk it." He shrugged again, but had assumed a more serious aspect. "Ferol is a lot worse than when you left. The resistance is squeezed tighter every day. Iomel is dead. They found out his ties to us. Killed his whole family, as one of their examples. We lost Temm'l and Neffede, too, amongst others. Kese switched allegiance to the Hearts. They had her husband, can't blame her. But the rest of the city has it worse – we're out of sight, the rest of the population isn't. The bridge is finished, so there's even less reason to keep the people alive. Be it by starvation, slavery, the Hearts, the City Guard, the Endless, the flesh beasts, life is being choked out of everything.

"The good news is we're getting some attention, as you must've noticed. Outsiders are starting to listen, and Climbe's doing everything he can to fill them in. That's partly why I'm here. Edemon's the ideal vantage point to keep an eye on how the Central Seat's reacting – though I doubt even Climbe expected the response we got."

"Candar'laon, and the other meetings?" Telde asked. *Not hopefully,* John thought.

"You didn't make it, then? Ruined, as you'd expect. Candar'laon's close, so I've learnt plenty about it. Three of ours were killed – it sounds like Dem Cleaver gave a bloody battle. The rest were captured, though a couple might've escaped. Edodani's description wasn't mentioned, and you'd surely remember that face. We can assume a similar story from the rest of the meetings. Fenning typical of the Central Seat. When they finally get off their royal arses and do something, it's as clumsy and excessive as ever. But it's given us the chance we need."

"Clumsy? Excessive? *Gods curse you* Manvedian, they're

killing and capturing our people!" Telde almost spat the words at the man.

"You're not seeing the greater purpose, Telde. There's consequences much more important than the disruption of our meetings," Manvedian responded coolly. There was something in the way that he spoke and moved that unsettled John, something beyond his cocky assurance.

"I don't need lectures from you about the greater purpose, Manvedian," Telde said.

"Does the half-man control the Central Seat?" Ceria asked abruptly, as if she had been working up the courage to say it.

"Gods, no. Like I said, word is getting out about the situation in Ferol. They know about the half-man and his gathering of Primitives. Most of the rest is jaller-shit and rumour, but at least they've finally realised there's a threat. At least they're doing something. And there's more," Manvedian said, pausing for effect. "All the arrested Primitives, they're being taken to the Regency."

"The Regency?" Ceria asked, disbelieving. "Why?"

"The Central Seat has allied with them," Manvedian answered. "They'll mount an attack on Ferol together, if they're convinced it's needed. Which they will be. Two armies, and the Primitives. It's our chance."

"Blood and gods," Telde said angrily. "You see this as a good thing, Manvedian? They'll tear Ferol apart."

"What did you think, Telde? How the fuck else are we going to get back the city? Our meagre band of resistance?" Manvedian replied. "You know we can't fight the half-man's monsters. We need the other countries. We need armies, real numbers. It won't be pretty, but Fen take me if there's a better choice."

John struggled to keep up with the conversation, but he could at least understand Telde's concern: he recalled the Regency was an old enemy of Ferol. The possibility of a war, and its loss of life, made his stomach turn.

"Even if they manage to defeat the half-man and his army,

they'll divide the city between themselves as the spoils," Ceria said. "And what do they think the captured Primitives can do anyway? Even if the Central Seat ignore their own laws and force them to fight, the majority are likely just village Spirit mediums, or Primitive-remnants at best."

"They're better off fighting the half-man than in his hands, don't you think?" Manvedian responded. "And I'm not disputing the Queen's and Regency will have their own agendas. Especially the Regency. But we can deal with that situation afterwards. *Them* we can fight, if it comes to it. We can't fight the fucking Endless. For now we need to get to the Regent's lands, and join up with the forces before they go north."

Telde shook her head. "You think we'd have a say in the Regency? They won't listen to us. *Gods.* Have you not seen how Primitives and Ferolians have been treated so far? They'll never view the resistance as an ally. And the feeling is fenning mutual."

"I'm not saying we should climb between their legs, Telde. We just have to make sure they win. The resistance can give information from within the city itself – they'll listen to that. And if they don't, there's other ways of influencing things." Manvedian leant back with a slight shrug. "It's not like we have much choice. Either we go, or we miss the show."

"*Show...* gods fuck you, Manvedian," Telde said, giving the man a look that could make a sun shiver.

Rain had started to drum on the tent, streaking and blotching the fabric. Next to John, Jago was rifling through a book; he eventually leant over to him, tapping his finger against a picture. John saw what looked like a woodcut of a vast city, intricate palaces rising above tiered walls. *The Regency,* Jago mouthed.

"We'll go," Telde announced as he looked back up.

"Telde!" Ceria protested.

"We have to."

"But we don't know if they'll even march on Ferol."

"They will," Manvedian said.

"*If* they decide to attack, we need to be there to influence them," Telde said.

"But it'll take months to get to the Regency," Ceria said.

"We can do it in two," Manvedian said. "We go through the Heartlands pass, stick to the bottom of the Coronals. Then south-east from there – detouring around Central City, obviously. That'll slow us down, but we could still make it to the Regency in time."

"No. Not the Heartlands," Telde said resolutely.

"What other way is there?" Manvedian asked, then evidently saw the answer in her face. "You can't be serious. Through the Sea? The baby-eaters? Gods, Telde. They don't call it the fenning Savage Lands for fun."

"Are you talking of the Black Sea?" Jago asked.

Ceria said something that John missed, as Jago was whispering excitedly in his ear. "Big desert, very hot. Warring tribes. Spirit source. Mostly unmapped – travellers rarely survive."

John didn't care. It didn't matter, as he wasn't leaving this city. The others started discussing travel routes and methods, but he determinedly didn't listen. He had come to the right conclusion before – he would be no help to these people. It was better for everyone if he stayed in Edemon.

Yet he felt a clinging guilt at his resolve. A familiar, constricting claustrophobia. He had to get outside.

He crawled towards the tent opening, ignoring glances from the others. The rain was coming down heavily now, but he was willing to endure it to escape the suffocating air. Once outside, he saw how much more the city had darkened. The clouds must – *oh Christ.*

The Spirit storms had moved impossibly. They were at the very edges of the city, seething black nebulas that took up the majority of the sky. He could see their shadows creeping over the outer walls on opposite sides of the valley, enveloping row upon row of buildings. Advancing towards one another.

The two storms were going to meet directly over the city.

He shouted desperately to the others inside the tent. Eventually Ceria stuck her head out. "What is it, John?"

But the words died in her mouth as she saw the sky beyond him. She turned and said something urgently into the tent, before scrambling out to stand beside him.

"Gods protect us," she breathed.

In short order all five of them were out of the tent and standing in a gaping line at the edge of the roof. They watched as the Spirit storms slowly progressed over the city, their turbulent bulks closing up the remainder of the sky.

"They're going to merge," someone said.

"They can't."

But it was obviously true. Long tendrils of twitching blue light could be seen at the fronts of each cloud, stretching towards their opposites, touching in spasms of snarled brilliance. The main bodies of the storms seemed to hasten in their movement, as if made impatient by the precursory contacts.

"It can't be chance," Jago said. "It's impossible."

"What will happen?" John asked.

The question went unanswered, but the city held its own response. The atmosphere had changed drastically, from bustling noise to a tense hush. Hundreds of people were perched on roofs or leaning out of windows, watching in astonishment. The narrow streets and alleyways were deserted apart from a few who scurried about in search of cover. The rain ceased abruptly.

John continued to stare alongside the others as an increasing number of tendrils connected the storms, vivid stitches drawing them together, sewing the sky shut. The section of open air gradually diminished, then finally disappeared as the two storm clouds met. The city was plunged into blackness. John held his breath.

For long moments nothing happened. The clouds thickened, perhaps; a rippling of effervescent blue through the heavy black. The silence was as thorough as the dark. John hoped, unconvincingly, that this was all there was to it.

Then the sky began to hum. A low-pitched thrumming that came in pulses, each more resonant than the last, and accompanied by vivid blue synapsing through the clouds. The reverberations throbbed louder and louder, a vibration from the deepest bowels of the sky, its force enough to shake the building beneath John.

Suddenly a beam of light struck down from the cloud, its intensity illuminating the entire valley.

"Jesus Christ!" John cried out, stepping back out of reflex.

The twisting blue pillar was at least three times the width of the average building in the city, and as wild as lightning – but a constant, it showed no sign of dissipating. John could see fire at its base, structures torn apart in a fury. It was moving, he realised, churning a trail of destruction. Another beam shot down, lancing ruthlessly into the urban sprawl, a strike to the heart no matter where it landed. And now a third and a fourth, and John thought he heard screams amidst the thunderous drone of the sky.

This can't be happening, he thought desperately. He looked to the others, who appeared to be as shocked as him, even Manvedian. *What can we do?*

A pillar flashed down nearer to them, leaving a glaring imprint on John's vision as he shielded his eyes.

"We've got to get out," someone half-whispered.

Something else was happening, however, and it held them in dreadful fascination. Where the two storm fronts had met, a great rent was opening. But it wasn't the previous sky that was revealed, it was different entirely, a black maw of nothingness – but somehow active, chaotic. The space seemed to unfold as they watched, or fold back onto itself – a movement too contradictory for the eye to interpret, as if it involved too many dimensions. On went the creases of blackness, of swarming emptiness, and it became clear they were increasing in frequency, disgorging ever more black, unfolding and reaching in further and further until finally a skin was peeled back, and something was exposed.

Then, out of the laceration in the sky, an awful light began to spill out. It floated to the ground in a stream of bright forms that John recognised. *Oh god.*

"We've got to get out. We've got to go." It was Ceria. She repeated it, and Telde reacted, as though broken from a trance.

"Come on!" she shouted, pulling and pushing at each of them.

The five of them ran toward the rope ladder on the other side of the roof. As John hurried down the rungs after the others, he was able to see through a window into the building. A family huddled beneath a table stared back at him. *This can't be happening,* he thought, dread and resentment filling him.

He reached the ground and sprinted with the rest – through lean alleys and steep passages, aisles with slanting walls and uneven ground that was the roofs of buildings. Structures jutted out and forced abrupt corners. John could only ever see a few feet ahead in the midst of the wooden maze.

The streets remained mostly deserted. The majority of inhabitants they encountered were leaning out of windows, straining their necks to look up. A sickly blue flushed their faces, like it bathed everything in the city. The throbbing in the sky continued, the bass sound distorting in John's ears, too low or too loud. Buildings trembled out of focus. He tried to keep his eyes on Telde and the others, but it was impossible not to glance upwards. The stream of light continued from the centre of the storm, a dream-like vortex. He knew what those hateful shapes were. The Endless, descending to the ground. The Endless spilling out of the wounded sky. The storm cloud pulsed its blue veins as if in ecstasy.

There were countless more beams, sundering through the city. Some seemed to have touched down beyond the outer walls; thick rolls of smoke were rising into the air.

It can't be as bad as it seems, John told himself. *Something will stop all of this. It will be reparable.*

Ceria gave his arm a fierce tug, pulling him towards the sharp turn the rest of the group had already taken. In front, Telde was yelling for them to hurry as they continued their winding route. Their progress uphill was often hindered by passages that forced them along level stretches or veered unexpectedly downwards. Twice they met a dead end and had to turn back. They passed through an enclosed tunnel, buildings spanning above their heads, and emerged into a rain of splintered wood. From nearby, a dull roar and an inferno of blue, too bright to look at, confirmed the cause.

They raced away from the light, and suddenly the tight pathways were filled with people, as if everyone at once had come to the decision to flee their homes. Terrified faces surrounded them, ran with them, pushed and helped and cried out. The blue glow coated everything, and with it, barbing the air, a malevolence.

John looked at the people in despair – he wanted them back inside, not admitting these events, not giving truth to the full scale of the horror. But through his frantic thoughts he knew the reality: it was happening, the worst was coming. *No, no. Not the city, not the people. Please, no.*

They came onto a rare wide avenue, but the crowds had stopped in a glut ahead. The five of them struggled their way through, but a crackling noise made them freeze. Moments later there was a crack like thunder, and the foremost rows of the crowd erupted. Brilliant white fire. A blast of torrid air. Then screams: from those not immediately incinerated, from those covered in flames and still alive. There was a crush as the people near the front turned and surged into the multitudes behind. As they shifted, John glimpsed the source of their terror. Through the flames and over the wounded and the dead, there it was, as he knew it would be: a giant of distorted, tumorous flesh. And behind it, felt as much as seen, a shape of liquid light. Watching. Revelling.

"Move, John!" Telde shouted at him.

He rushed after her as she led the group into a short side alley. They clambered through a window at its end, through the subsequent tiny room and out its door into another wood-lined passageway, and another, and another, until John simply followed numbly. It was everywhere now, inescapable. The charged crackling, the screams. The stench of searing flesh. *No, no.*

There were tears in John's eyes, hot tears rolling unstoppably down his cheeks. Life was being torn away from him again. But he wouldn't be left alone. Not this time. If everyone died, he would go with them.

They kept running, merging with crowds small and large and crushing, before Telde or Manvedian pulled them in a new direction, a better route upwards. Or away from churning blue light, or from screams, or from crackling. There were always more people around the next corner, and John often saw the silver of a Queen's soldier running with them. But there were pockets of fighting, too: at the end of a street a group of soldiers surrounded one of the flesh beasts, which batted their bodies away as if they were gleaming insects.

They turned into a passage little more than a foot wide, shuffling sideways, pushing themselves along walls of pale wood. Jago was struggling behind John, and he reached back for the man's hand to help him through. Emerging onto a wider path, they joined a group of twenty or so and headed upwards with them, ever upwards towards the distant, towering city walls. The group coursed through an alley and into an enclosed square, piles of wood on the ground marking it as a construction site. They crossed the space to the only other exit, a gap between two buildings – but those in front suddenly halted with a gasp. John saw fringes of light bleeding around them. They retreated, pushing the rest of the group back into the square, and John saw it clearly, gliding unhurriedly towards them. A form made of swirling liquid light. The Endless.

The group turned to run, but as it did so there was a crashing from behind, and a giant shape tore out of a building next to the alley through which they had arrived. A mass of seething flesh, grotesque exaggerations for limbs. John stared in horror. Viscid hair grew from one side of its deformed head; on the other an eye was lost behind a swelling of tissue, and a mouth hung like a wound. It blocked the only other way out of the square.

Someone was making an attempt at escape, John slowly realised. A woman, darting towards the side of the flesh beast. *No, don't*, he thought imploringly but couldn't force out the words. At first the creature showed no sign of movement, and for a fleeting second it seemed she might slip by it, she might make it. But then it pulled back a massive arm, and with shocking speed swung at the woman, delivering a blow to her head of such force that John, ten yards away, felt a warm spray of blood on his face. The giant moved to her body – *oh god she's still alive* – and used a leaden lump of a foot to pin her, like a squirming newborn, and now it had her arm in its blackened hand, and it was pulling, and the woman's damp scream ended abruptly as her limb was wrenched from her body with sickening ease.

The screams were taken up by the crowd. Someone next to John was vomiting. The giant was still ripping, tearing apart lifeless meat.

John turned and saw that the Endless had moved closer. A terrified man backed into him. The light hovered at the border of the crowd, within touching distance, causing them to cluster ever more tightly. *What are you waiting for?* He remembered Earth, the hotel, the tendril of light. The man in front of him stumbled backwards, and John stared directly into it: the brilliant vortices and drifting eddies that somehow comprised a sentient whole. He felt it. The malevolence. Disdain and hunger. It floated closer to John, blinding him, and he detected something else: surprise? Recognition? A curiosity, followed by gratification. *What the hell are you waiting for?*

There was a crackling hum from behind, and John felt the Endless ripple with pleasure. *It's herding us,* he realised. Packing them into a neat group for the flesh beast to incinerate. A fresh wave of wailing arose around him. Prayers and desperate pleading. A voice that might have been Manvedian's saying *No, wait, wait.* Telde was struggling to draw her sword in the cramped group. But John knew there was nothing she could do.

He began to feel that familiar suffocation. The constriction. He stood, unable to move.

Then, as he looked into the maelstrom of light and felt the rage he had experienced in the hotel, recognising that this monster was the end of hope, that Edemon and Earth and Jessica meant nothing to it, the constriction holding him was pierced and he was suddenly free. He stepped forward and reached a hand inside the Endless. The creature emanated amusement, contempt, as he grasped at only emptiness.

But somehow he was able to push beyond his fingers to touch a substance beyond, and the whirls of light near his hand began to quiver and thicken. He could feel the light, the fibres of being, and he willed it towards his hand. Shock filled the Endless, a lurch of disbelief. It was trying to pull away. But he had it in his grip, it was connected to him, and he pulled and twisted and tore at the fibres, and as they tightened and broke apart he felt an energy gushing into him. *Go to hell, you bastard.* He broke more and more, he drained the creature without mercy. The energy gathered, built inside him, until it was overflowing and agonising, and he raised his free arm towards the flesh giant and released it. A brilliant torrent of light shot out of his hand and across the square, setting the air ablaze and striking the monster squarely in its chest. A few moments later the torrent dissipated as abruptly as it had appeared, and a gaping hole was left where it had cut unerringly through the giant. The ground shook as its

165

lifeless body collapsed. In front of John the Endless gave a piercing howl as it evaporated into fragmented wisps of light.

John stood staring at where it had been. His arms were still outstretched, and there was blood covering the hand through which he had directed the torrent. It was wrong somehow, and he realised in a daze that his thumb was missing. A heavy wave of exhaustion hit him, as if his body had been scoured of all its energy, and someone caught him as he fell.

Telde's face was above him, looking down with a stunned expression, her green eyes like otherworldly fires.

He must have passed out briefly, because when he opened his eyes again he was somewhere else. Not in the square but on a street, and the city's outer walls had doubled in size. He felt empty and faint, and struggled to make sense of the world around him. There was a flood of people. Jago and Telde were carrying him towards the walls. *No, no,* he tried to shout to them, *leave me here, leave me in the city.*

He closed his eyes and there was another shift in time: the outer walls loomed enormously above him. He gazed along the barricade of stone, which in the distance turned into a pillar of bright blue, and John couldn't understand what he was seeing. He looked back in front of him and there were animals, houses full of animals, and Ceria was opening doors and chasing them away. Blood was dripping from his hand and Telde was wrapping something around it. She was shouting at him, but the sound swam wordlessly in his mind.

Then he was being hoisted into the air, onto a wall of fur chequered by rope. The joorun, he realised, it was the joorun, and it was Jago with his arm around him and speaking into his ear *I got you I got you.* John reached out his hand to someone below, but his gesture was mistaken – the person was helped up onto the joorun when John had wanted to be pulled down, to be taken back into the city. More were clambering around him, arms and legs and faces, and he found that his arm was tied into the netting and he couldn't get it loose.

They were moving now: a juddering gallop over flattened houses, and John floated above and saw them as a rat covered in ants. The floor of broken wood turned into a mountain of stone that the joorun struggled up, and as the angle steepened John felt someone fall over him, fall with the square boulders and rubble around them, and he remembered photo albums tumbling down a staircase in another life. They crested the mountain and he saw the pulsing black cloud above and the great walls either side and he understood they were climbing over a collapsed section, and away from the city. *No, no.*

Down the mountain of stone they went, plunging into an inferno. Walls of fire surrounded them, flames the shapes of trees. A million fireflies billowing about. The heat, the heat. The joorun broke through to a road that hummed electrically and there were monsters made of white fire – no, they were people, and their blackened bodies covered the road and cracked under the animal's feet.

Away from the city. He looked back. The land hung from the sky via tethers of lurid blue. It tipped abruptly at an angle. No, it was the column, he realised, it was slanting and falling. It disappeared beneath the veil of the walls, and there was an instant of world-shattering noise before what remained of his hearing faltered and gave up.

He was losing consciousness again. He couldn't keep his eyes open. The heat, the endless heat. All life was burning away.

Leave me in the city.

PART III:

GOD IN THE MOUNTAIN

Warm earth embraces him. It smothers his body, encloses all parts of him. But he is not afraid, he is not threatened.

He is welcomed, he is taken below, swallowed deeper, and he is placed within its veins. He is in the passages where ancient runes resonate blue. They glow encouragement. They whisper him towards it, through these living tunnels that he knows (how are they so close?).

Urgent yet fainter now (than when?) they speak to him: their breath is being taken, too much, it is used to shape and foul the above. They tell him. Here, in the heart of the land. Here, where he is always brought and they tell him he is needed. Where it awaits him.

He continues along the passages that pulse the land. They open for him, urge him further in. The moist walls swell and thrill and beat. It feels good, this alignment: the tunnels move and he moves with them. It must be right, what he is doing, what he is moving towards (what is it?). A flicker of knowledge, fear, doubt, there then gone. The land draws him further in.

He reaches the edge of the chamber and he knows. This is where it is kept (imprisoned?), he knows what it is. He remembers the shadow inside. Black and wild and chaotic. The opening through which it comes.

But it has emerged already, he realises as he steps forward. He feels it. Boundless elemental presence (preserver or destroyer). He does not face it, he cannot, his eyes cannot contain it. He keeps his back to it, he side-glances and glimpses: it is darkness and light, no separation, no distinction. Black inverts and light bulges out; light unfolds and black shines within. It is shifting unstill, bloom and ruin.

It touches him. He senses the limitless power. Unrestrained and undirected. Turn, embrace it, the land wills him. Take it and all is possible (how will he use it?).

But he remembers himself and resists: he fears. No, he convulses rejection, he shouts and screams, No (why don't they understand?). It cannot have him, he cannot have it. It is too much risk.

He tears his self away. He runs from the land and from it. He cannot be trusted with such power (how will he use it?). Thick mud is cloying at him, heaving and pulling, but it cannot hold him, and *he bursts upwards, and he breaks out of the land. There is pain below. A howl, longing.*

He is in the black air above and he looks down upon rolling hills that he knows, that are so close to him. Som'syere: gouged and broken-skinned and violated.

The land shudders and becomes something else, and he sees further and future. Desolation envelops the lands. Sterile all: the land is silent below and the above is unvoiced. No seed, no song.

Possibility or reality, he does not know. He is being shown this by the land or by the runes or by himself (his destruction?). If he takes it, how will he use it?

The land shivers bare beneath him. He cannot take the risk.

15

"Did you ever think about killing yourself?"

"What?"

"When you were on Earth. Did you ever think of killing yourself?"

"Christ, Jago. That's some question."

"Well?"

John opened his eyes and glanced to his side. He could only make out the top of Jago's head beyond the joorun's broad back. The man walked alongside whilst John lay on top of the animal, which was wide enough to allow two outstretched bodies at once; Manvedian currently lay asleep next to him. But it was a far from comfortable bed, the rope netting scratching against his spine, the joorun's pounding gait quaking through the rest of him. Above, the morning sky was a tremulous aquamarine, threaded with pinkish wisps of clouds. John closed his eyes to avoid looking at it.

"Yes," he said, at length. "Yes, I did."

"What prevented you from doing it?"

John took a breath; he knew Jago would continue badgering him until he received his answers. "I don't know. Hope, I suppose. Or… or a disbelief of sorts. I didn't believe that this could be all there was, if you know what I mean. That everyone could die and that was the end of it. The times when I lost that belief, and saw there was no reason behind any of it, that's when I considered killing myself. It seemed pointless carrying on."

"And now what do you believe? Does your life have purpose?"

"I'm trying to sleep, Jago."

"Does the universe have meaning again?"

"Christ, I don't *know*. Maybe. There's life here. And we must've been brought to Crescent by something or someone – so yes, it's possible we have a purpose connected to that. Maybe we're meant to prevent what happened on Earth from happening here. Or at least what happened at Edemon. I don't know. It's hard to believe in meaning after what we've seen. We just have to do what we can."

John surprised himself with his last remark; he knew it reflected a change that had taken place within him. His thoughts drifted back to the events in Edemon, to the Endless. To what he had done. The power he had wielded was a part, either symptomatic or causal, of this change – even if he didn't understand where it came from, or how it worked, or what it was for. If it was for anything. It didn't feel like some divine gift, bestowed upon him so that he could fulfil his purpose, his destiny – such notions were laughable in the chaos of reality. All he knew for certain was that whatever he did in Edemon had left him exhausted to the point of death afterwards. And with one less thumb.

He turned onto his side, pushing himself up on an elbow. Beyond Jago stretched an expanse of predominantly flat land, peppered by slender trees with close coats of tawny leaves. Further out, the trees eventually congregated into scraps of forest, then, as they climbed towards the mountains on the eastern horizon, turned into swathes of brown spilling over the land, interrupted only by the snowy slashes of an unknown bloom.

The range was the Coronal Mountains, Jago had told him. The other side of which was the Heartlands, the territory inhabited by the Queen and her Central Seat – the governing body of most of these lands, as John understood it. They were going to bypass that domain, however, and instead cut south through the Savage Lands, a region not controlled by the Queen or her forces. To reach the Regency, another of the dominant powers in this world. John repeated it all in his head, attempting to force significance upon the details: he was determined not to lose his grip on the events surrounding him.

The wind had all but disappeared, its voice lost in such vast tracts of land. John could hear the faint murmur of conversation between Telde and Ceria as they walked out in front. He glanced at Jago, whose face was shaded by stubble and looked thinner than it once had.

"Did you?" John asked. "Consider suicide, I mean."

"No. Not me."

"No?"

Jago looked up at him. "The morning it happened, I went into the biomedical institute where I worked, as if it was a day like any other. I was close to finishing some research, and was determined to continue with it. The mind can be a powerful delusional tool. The bodies surrounded me but I pushed the knowledge away. It was only as I waited for a bus hours later – of course it didn't come – that I finally confronted reality. It was a crushing thing. The weight of the dead falling upon me. The silence in São Paulo. In Butantã, Morumbi, Pinheiros, Jardim Paulista. The silence stretching along Paulista Avenue, where previously you'd find the noise of the world. It all came down upon me in a moment, the entirety of the loss. It's too much for any mind to realise."

Yes, it is, John thought.

"That was the hardest time," Jago continued. "I lost control of myself, I can't recall those days. I may have been close to suicide, I can't say. But that wasn't me. When I came back to myself I was in Rio de Janeiro, where I grew up. Eventually, although sooner than you might think, I came to accept the change that had come over the world. Death was everywhere and yet I was alive – it felt like I was blessed. You don't understand that, do you? The world may have died for you,

John, but it still lived for me. There was an entire reality to be experienced, an infinite amount of knowledge within my country alone. Constants of the universe that exist with or without humans. I was chosen to see this. It's true I had my low points, as I always have. Times when I'm not me. But in my lowest I knew my life still held value."

Several questions came to John's mind: What low points? What constants? What knowledge could be worth living on like that, with no-one to share it with? But he decided not to break the silence Jago had subsequently settled into. He knew what kind of answers Jago would give. He didn't have time for God right now, or any of His purposes.

John rolled onto his back again and closed his eyes. The thick bristles of the joorun tickled his neck, the ropes dug into his skin. His bandaged hand ached. He tried to sleep, but knew it was a futile effort. Something buzzed close to his head: another of those god-awful flies. Bloodflies, Ceria had called them, laughing as she had watched his attempts at waving the fat-bodied insects away. The joorun seemed to attract droves of them.

But it wasn't the extraterrestrial flies, or his discomfort atop the joorun, or even Jago that prevented him from sleeping. His head was loud with too many thoughts, a restless energy that had spread to his body. It was understandable, after resting for most of the last two weeks of travel. Edemon had left him weak enough that Ceria had feared he would not recover. She told him he had barely stirred during the first week – *ten days, a tensun*, John reminded himself; he had to get used to the rules of time here. All he could recall of those days were dreams: swirling light, a hanging mouth, broken stone and shattering wood, screams and fire. Energy searing through him.

In the last few days he had begun to recover his strength, however, and Telde had soon insisted he take turns walking like everyone else. She had been keen for him to explain what he had done to the Endless, what he *could* do. She wanted to know if he could do it again. John had frustrated her with his lack of answers. He couldn't tell her how he had done it, or if, like Jago's ability, it was something he could call upon when needed. He didn't understand it himself. The source had been instinctive, indecipherable, and was now buried deeply enough to be out of reach – if it truly resided within him at all.

He could tell her the power was bound inexorably to the Endless, but how to explain the abstract connection, the threads of being pulled out of nothingness into reality, contorted until they bled pure energy – things that were beyond words and sense? How to explain the force so raw and overwhelming it had ripped his thumb away? Outside of that state it was like describing a fire that had burnt out on the other side of the planet.

Ceria had better understood what he couldn't express. She had spoken to him about her own ability, about boundaries and tides and temptation, and the thinness she always felt afterwards. There was a great deal that John didn't recognise in his own experience, but at the least both involved similarly inexplicable energies. She seemed to be as relieved as John to have someone to share it with.

The shock of Edemon had still been apparent in her, like it was with the others. But while comprehension of the events was fresh for John, the two weeks that had passed for the rest of the group had shifted the subject into an unspoken tension, a concealed wound that each dealt with in their own way. Ceria was subdued and on edge. Telde was determined, pragmatic. Jago didn't talk about Edemon, which John found telling. Manvedian shrugged the events off, but a few sharp remarks suggested they had their reverberations within him, too. Perhaps partly in compensation for the slips in composure, he said the attack did have its positive sides – now the Central Seat and the Regency had no choice but to march on Ferol. Ceria had snapped at him for it. Surprisingly, it had been Telde calming her, and declaring Manvedian was in the right.

For his own part, John felt a weight fill his stomach whenever he thought of Edemon. He struggled to suppress the events, the inconceivable loss of life, the devastation of such a teeming city – he wanted to question it out loud, to say he couldn't believe it and be reassured that he was right, it couldn't have happened. But he remembered the column falling, slow and dream-like. The mast of the city broken. He remained quiet, like the others.

There was a guilt in him too, John realised. Because despite all of the terrible things, the destruction of Edemon, the existence of the Endless, the prospect of future atrocities and wars, the immediate peril of their journey – Manvedian seemed to revel in telling tales of the brutal tribes populating the Black Sea – despite all of it, at some point during these last few days, to his surprise, he had started to feel good. Not physically – although partly that, too – but inwardly. He felt good; and he had changed.

He wasn't upset about losing his thumb. Not as much as he should be – it was almost a relief. For so long he had dreaded its capability deteriorating, the prospect of a lifeless appendage, and now the worst had happened and he found he was okay, he continued. It could be shock but he didn't think so – it was similar to the constriction that had previously held him, the rigid indecision that had shattered when he had seen so much life lost around him and realised it wouldn't be safe even if he stood still. A freedom. That was the change in him. *We have to do what we can.* Yes, and he was willing to do that now. He was free to touch the world.

So now he cared they were going to the Black Sea. He memorised travel plans, the details of the lands around him, the politics and rulers and histories. He allowed himself to care for those around him. He touched the world and it responded; it became significant, alive, and he became a component part. Not in some *greater scheme* sense – he was simply an active element instead of a passive one. He had acted in Edemon and changed things, saved people. He took that step forward, and it mattered.

"Do you think this is real?"

It took a few moments before John registered Jago's question. "What?"

"This world, all that's happened. Do you think it's real?"

"Of course it is, what do you mean?"

"It could all be taking place inside your imagination. Or mine."

John didn't know how to respond, or if Jago expected him to. Or if he wanted to. He kept his eyes closed and pretended to sleep.

"It makes no difference if it is, obviously," Jago continued after a minute.

John let out a sigh. Jago would carry on anyway, he knew. It was best to get it over with quickly. "Why is that, Jago?"

"If you believe something to be real, and you commit entirely to that belief, then it's really experienced."

"Is that so."

"Yes. It's obvious. Say I never left Brazil. Say I'm still there – I've gone insane. From loneliness or despair. I've had some kind of breakdown that's led me to invent this new world, and all the people and creatures and forces in it. It doesn't make a difference to me if it's true or not outside of me – because I'm inside of me. It's no less than real to me."

There was a whirring close by. Something touched John's face. He waved away the fly with a curse, and without opening his eyes. On his left hand he could feel an unsettling phantom; a thumb made of air, refusing to vanish entirely.

"Say I pushed you off the joorun, so you fell to the ground."

"Why would you push me off?"

"Say I pushed you off, and you broke your arm from the fall. I would feel guilt and shame for causing you that harm. The feelings would be real to me. It doesn't matter where they come from, or if the cause is imaginary or real. Do you understand? The emotions are really felt. Say someone else pushed you off the joorun –"

"I don't seem to be very popular."

"If they pushed you off and you fell, and I caught you before you were hurt. The pleasure I would feel, from your gratitude –"

"The gratitude of an imaginary me for being saved from a hypothetical fall in a world only existing in your mind?"

"The feeling of pleasure I would experience – as long as I fully committed to all of this being true – would be the same whether it's really true or not. Do you understand?"

"Yes."

"To give another example –"

"I understand, Jago."

"Perception is our reality, that's what I'm telling you."

"What about food?"

"What?"

"If the real Jago is imagining all of this in Brazil, then what about food? Won't he starve to death?"

"Perhaps I will. Perhaps I'll become weaker and then die. Perhaps time is different in this imagined world, and while months have passed here only a day has on Earth."

"So you've got about a year left, give or take. That's not so bad."

"It's also possible that I *do* nourish myself, and part of me is aware that I'm imagining this world. That part keeps me alive in the real world, whilst hiding these mundane truths from the rest of me."

"That's pretty far-fetched."

"So is an alien planet populated with humans and supernatural forces."

Touché, John thought. "Does that mean you invented Telde?" he asked.

"It would mean that, yes."

"I left a cat back on Earth. Do you think real Jago can pop over to England and feed it for me?"

"I don't think you understand what I'm saying, John."

"His favourite is salmon in gravy."

"What's sammenin grey-vee?" It was another voice: Telde's.

John sat up abruptly, his eyes open and the brilliant sky pouring mercilessly in. He grasped half-blinded at the netting and clumps of fur in order to restore his balance and not fall to the ground. The joorun grunted unhappily beneath him.

He recovered his composure enough to speak, if not in as steady a voice as he had hoped. "Jago was explaining how we're all figments of his imagination."

Telde raised an eyebrow, which somehow managed to convey a voluminous condemnation of such frivolous talk. "It's your turn to walk. Wake up Manvedian."

Ceria and Jago duly replaced him and Manvedian on the joorun. John felt sorry for Ceria; if Jago continued in his philosophical mood she wouldn't be getting much rest. Talk was conversely scarce as John walked alongside Manvedian and Telde, who only broke the quiet for the rare muttered necessity – direction, distance, time – and didn't take to John's attempts at striking up conversation. The sky clouded over as they walked, the joorun pounding steadily behind them, the low land stretching out prodigiously in front. And so extended the silence between Manvedian and Telde. There was a tension between them, an invisible field of knowledge and history that excluded John. He was obscurely jealous of that connection for a moment, before dismissing the feeling.

There remained a faint tickling of familiarity at the back of John's mind when he regarded Manvedian. Who or what did the man remind him of? It was difficult to place it, especially with Manvedian apparently determined to avoid him – or simply having deemed him unworthy of his time. Perhaps John merely disliked the tall, self-assured man. He was still becoming reaccustomed to emotional attachments, after two years where they had been as good as absent, and to untangling their often deceptive shapes into explicit meaning. He had overheard Manvedian a day ago, complaining to

Telde: *Why are we shouldering those two lunatics?* Jago had previously, blithely, told him that they came from another planet.

But he had to admit part of him was glad to have Manvedian travelling with them. There was steel beneath that arrogance, John was sure, a shrewd resourcefulness. He was a good man to have on their side. Perhaps that was how Telde saw it, too.

He walked on in silence alongside the two resistance members from Ferol, a city that had been attacked like Edemon, although not destroyed, and where this *half-man* was. John recited the details to himself as he gazed at the distant mountains to his left, which in their sheer-faced stillness seemed to regard the group's progress with contempt. It struck him that believing all of this was imaginary as Jago had suggested would make the incomprehensible – and the terrible – bearable. It would make the loss of Edemon bearable. But he quickly rejected the thought. *It's a coward's way out.* A method of avoiding the risk, of not living.

No, he told himself, he had to keep this as real. He had to stay involved. The resultant vulnerability was terrifying – and exhilarating. He was coming back to life.

He continued walking, into the world.

16

Over the last two days of travel, the land had changed. Ceria watched it, from on top of the joorun, or walking ahead, feeling the terrain harden beneath her feet. The grassy plains became dryer, rockier, and only the most stubborn of plants grew out of the parched soil. The trees, previously slender and adorned with their thick coats of foliage, turned bony, anxious, their leaves thinning into needles. The Coronal Mountains were finally diminishing as the range hauled its great ring north-east, away from them, as if wishing no part in their subsequent journey.

Telde spotted the figure first. She put a hand on Ceria's arm and gestured towards a high rocky bluff in the distance, where the man stood motionless, watching them. He was clad entirely in black, his head wrapped in the same cloth that covered his body. *A sentry,* Ceria concluded. As the group moved close enough to see the long bow on his back, the man pulled an object from under his clothing – Ceria sensed Telde flinch next to her – then raised it to his mouth. The sound emitted was somewhere between a horn and a whistle, a penetrating series that seemed to share several notes with the wind. The figure wordlessly raised his arm to point ahead of them.

The group had no choice but to follow the instruction and hope they were being directed towards a settlement. They required supplies if they stood any chance of crossing the Black Sea. The food and water they had obtained from the farms and villages close to Edemon had been barely enough to sustain them for two weeks – with the villages thronged by hundreds of refugees from the city, Ceria reflected, they were lucky to have gathered even that much.

She couldn't prevent the memories from resurfacing: the escape from Edemon, the monsters, the fire and death; then, away from the city, the innumerable faces, dirtied and bloodied, crying or searching or wide-eyed, staring; *saved*, they had seemed to say, *but for what?* The group had been fortunate, Manvedian had commented, that most of the refugees were too lost to think of necessities – meaning there was enough left to buy for themselves. *He can't be so cold-hearted,* Ceria thought.

It reminded her to be grateful. Even if for the last week they had suffered the same daily meal of dried talonroot, supplemented only by the meagre pickings gained from short forages ahead of the joorun – Telde had been more single-minded than ever since Edemon, and barely allowed any breaks in their travelling. Ceria's stomach was twisted in knots from the diet, but it wasn't *real* suffering.

Be grateful, she told herself, because the same could have happened in Ferol as in Edemon. She felt a keen guilt for thinking that, for being glad Ferol hadn't been destroyed like the Ireldelor capital. But perhaps her home was worse off for it. News had soon reached the nearby settlements that the Endless and the flesh beasts had abandoned Edemon as abruptly as they had arrived – the city left broken, buried, a mass grave. But those soulless things still inhabited Ferol. Rotting its core. Perhaps that was worse.

Three hours after passing the first sentry there was another, similarly wrapped in black. Then two more as afternoon turned to evening, and the sun began its slow descent. Each encounter was the same: the sentry would watch them, unperturbed or unsurprised, before sounding the piercing horn and pointing them onwards. The solitary figures made the group uneasy; it was a reminder they were trespassers in this unknown territory, they were no longer in control. Ceria knew Telde would hate that. Manvedian too, probably.

On the few occasions in the villages after Edemon when they had asked about the Savage Lands, the responses had been invariably laced with surprise and suspicion. They had been informed many times over how foolish the notion was of treading those barbaric lands. They were told how no decent Queen's folk – with the implicit accusation that they consequently couldn't be such – would want to be within a tensun's ride of the border. It didn't seem to be an exaggeration; before today, the group had seen no hint of a settlement for over a week.

The only useful information had come from a wounded trader to whom they had given a place on the joorun for the length of a few villages, alongside the then unconscious John. The Savage people sometimes came to Ireldelor markets, he had told them, bringing with them hides and jewels and other, less lawful items. They were from tribal towns on the border, but he knew of no-one except travelling merchants who had set foot there – and none of those for many years.

As she hung one-handed from the netting covering the joorun's flank, watching the darkening sky, Ceria thought of how they would soon be stepping into one of those tribal towns. They had crossed the border into the Savage Lands days ago, she supposed. Their position in regards to the Coronal Mountains told as much, if she remembered her maps correctly. Not that there was any defining line in reality, apart from the gradual alteration in the land. But that was hardly a surprise, despite what Ireldelor folk might think. *Life is life, border or no.* Campfire talk in Queen's lands would give the impression that all Ferolians or Besgeners or Westerners or Regents were some wild, unknowable breed, but they were simply men and women the same, yawning in the evening, hungry in the morning. Even John and Jago – who came from this unheard of land – were recognisable and intelligible beside a few eccentricities. The so-called Savage people would be the same in all the essential ways too, Ceria was sure.

No, it wasn't the tribes she feared, no matter the tales Manvedian told. It was the Black Sea. That was truly different; a change worthy of a line on a map. Even with the hardening landscape around her, it was difficult to believe the great desert was so close. Part of her didn't want to believe it, she knew.

In her childhood, living in the forests outside of Ferol's city walls, she had heard many of the legends surrounding the Black Sea. She remembered the most common tale, best enjoyed when Elder Nefehed told it in her slow and authoritative voice as the camp hushed around her: the land now known as the Black Sea was once exceptionally fertile, so the story went, but was forever changed after the third war of the gods. The scores of deities on the defeated side were punished by Hedroth, leader of the victors, to death in the mortal realm; their spirits, bodiless but immortal, were bound for eternity to a land where consequently no seed would bloom again. *Fouled by the mournful spirits, only death could ever take root in those black lands*, Nefehed would always finish. Other Elders spoke of a civilisation that had once flourished there, growing powerful on the gods' remains, before eventually, inevitably, paying with their lives.

Ceria worried that Telde and Manvedian underestimated the Sea. Telde didn't believe in spirits, good or bad, and Manvedian wouldn't consider any land a match for his wits. They needed more than supplies, they needed advice – an understanding of the unnatural place they would be treading. Ceria couldn't escape her dread of that unnaturalness: the desolate lands, the lack of wildlife and vegetation, the absence. *You can't be where Crescent don't want you to be*: Nefehed's words resounded in her skull.

She shook her head, trying to dislodge the past. Why was she thinking of Elder Nefehed and those times now? It must have been John's latest questions, which she had avoided answering. He had wanted to know when her ability had first emerged, and how she had learnt to control it. She hoped her reticence hadn't put him off; it had been good to talk about her ability with someone who truly listened instead of a disapproving Telde, or Jago who tended to study her like one of his books.

But there were some things too precious or painful to share. The answers would have stirred up memories of a forest that had been torn down, and of the Elder who had been mother and guide to her, directing her supposed *wild will* when others had long since lost patience. Nefehed had called her ability *a gift from Crescent*, and with a firm hand had helped her to both constrain and enhance it – and to be proud of what she could do. Mindful too, she warned, but never ashamed. Ceria wondered as she always had since, bitterly and pointlessly, if Nefehed had known that her student would cause her death.

Her thoughts were brought to a sudden halt, along with the movement of the joorun, as the group crested a long rise. A walled settlement was visible not far from the foot of its opposite slope. The sight came as such a welcome distraction to Ceria's reflections that it took a moment for her to grasp the significance. *The border town*, she realised. *We're here*. The town gleamed white even in the dimming light, its outer wall forming a square around equally symmetrical buildings within.

"Come on," Telde said, breaking the instinctive silence that had settled across the group.

Ceria jumped off the joorun and descended the slope along with the others. She led the animal by a rope hung loosely around its wide neck – although she was sure it would have naturally followed them by now.

As they progressed down the incline, the white of the town's walls rose like a covering sheet, gradually obscuring the buildings within. Ceria couldn't escape the impression that the town was raising its defences. The feeling was only strengthened by the numerous black-clad figures dotted around the perimeter of the walls.

"I don't like this," Manvedian said.

"They have no reason to attack us," Telde replied.

"They have no reason not to, either," Jago added.

They headed towards an entrance in the outer wall, flanked by two guards. The robed figures didn't react until the group was within twenty paces, at which point they pulled the bows from their backs, nocked arrows and aimed at them.

The group froze. Ceria heard Manvedian swear under his breath. One of the guards barked an unintelligible sound. Then silence, each side facing the other. She glanced across at Telde, who stood rigidly, but with a calm expression. Ceria tried her best to mimic her.

It felt like hours until the excruciating stand-off passed and a tall figure appeared in the entrance, immediately striding up to the group. He wore the same clothing as the others: a black robe wrapped around his rangy frame, a strip of leather tied around his waist – a pair of daggers were hooked by their hilts – and a head covering that spared an opening only for his eyes. Those eyes, clear and blue, stared out from a strip of skin as black as the cloth, and seemed to coldly appraise the newcomers.

"We are here to trade," Telde began, stiffly. "We need –"

"Come," the man interrupted, uttering the word bluntly. An order. He turned and marched back towards the entrance. He gestured to the guards, who lowered their bows in response, if not removing the arrows.

Telde glowered after him, before giving a brusque nod to the rest of them. They followed the man as he entered the border town, a noisy scratching of rope against stone behind them as the wide bulk of the joorun squeezed through the opening.

Inside, the pristine white of the rectangular buildings was a striking contrast to the dark, busy shapes of the town's inhabitants. The majority of the figures were clad in the same black, women as well as men judging by the varying frames. But some of the smaller forms wore a lighter shade of grey – children, a braver selection of whom ran closer to inspect the strange newcomers and their giant animal, followed by remonstrations from adults. The rest watched the group warily, a spreading lull in the activity of the town the further in they ventured.

Their escort led them at a brisk pace across the well-trodden, dusty ground. Between buildings, Ceria glimpsed a curious ceremony in the distance: a woman and a man standing together on a small platform, both naked and pale-skinned. The woman was taller, but seemed to be leaning on the man as if for support; he in turn leant on a long upright bow. *Some kind of binding ritual?* Ceria wasn't certain – there was only one other person in attendance, a man in noticeably different clothing, a medley of browns and greys.

Before she could make out further details the group was led on and her view was blocked. Black figures stood conspicuously in front of white stone, whispering to one another, watching. Ceria couldn't help but feel exposed – they had been outsiders ever since leaving Ferol, but here they couldn't hope to hide it. In Ireldelor she had grown to hate that hiding, the lies and the *blending in* – she had longed for the day when she could shout where she was from, proudly and regardlessly. Yet the eyes on her now reminded her of the safety anonymity had held.

The group passed a clearing where numerous townsfolk were at work in the fading light: breaking apart huge chunks of black rock, sorting fragments into piles, chipping away at stone with smaller instruments. Ceria didn't need to see the brilliant blue shards amongst the fragments, or the vague indigo of the dust cloud surrounding the work, to know the rocks contained Spirit. She could sense it, feel its obscure resonations within her. *Where is it all from? What are they doing with it?*

Their escort hurried them on, away from the clearing and

past a line of animals that looked like jallers, albeit larger and shaggier. A Tvennik breed, she suspected. Several grey-clad shapes were brushing and watering the animals, one of whom ran up to Ceria, obviously intending to take the joorun's leash from her hand. She refused, gripping it closely.

"Ceria," Telde said, firmly.

Ceria shot a glare at her. She knew her friend was in the right, and there was little choice in the situation – but it didn't give her the excuse to act like the empress of Crescent. At least the tribe appeared to treat their animals well, she told herself. *The joorun will be fine.* She took her time in handing over the rope nonetheless, and added a meaningful look at the small grey figure as she did so.

Telde turned to their escort. "We want to trade for supplies. We have –"

"This way. Come," the man interrupted again, dismissively. He spoke with a thick accent, the words harder yet to resolve due to the cloth covering his mouth.

Ceria saw a scowl on Telde's face – she couldn't help but feel a small satisfaction in response – along with the pursed lips that usually signified an imminent argument. But the man was already moving away, unconcerned by her indignation. Without sparing a glance at the rest of them, Telde stalked after him. Ceria thought she heard a quiet snigger from Manvedian.

The four of them followed in Telde's wake. John and Jago looked around themselves as they walked; John apprehensively, Jago with a smile. Manvedian stayed at the back, indolent, relaxed – but alert, Ceria knew.

The tall escort led them between more buildings, until they came upon the ceremony she had glimpsed earlier. None of the three individuals involved had moved. Ceria looked at the woman and realised with shock that she was dead. There was a sizeable wound above her left breast, sewn up, purple and red, and her filmy eyes stared out at nothing. Her feet were noticeably pink in comparison to her pallid body. The man beside her – who was alive; Ceria could see him breathing, sweating – had his arm around her. Somehow the woman stayed upright. The other man watched the two impassively, his clothes a rugged mix of cloth and leather with no head covering; his lengthy blond hair was tied back. Neither of the men seemed to take note of the group's presence. Telde gave John's arm a sharp tug as he stopped to stare, then glanced at Ceria. *It's okay*, she mouthed.

They were finally ushered towards a building twice the size of the others. Its stone walls were complimented by sections of decorative wood, woven intricately into vertical zigzags. Several etched poles of varying widths and heights stood outside.

"No weapons," their escort commanded as he stood in front of the cloth-covered entrance.

The group obeyed grudgingly. Telde drew the long sword from under her cloak and leant it against the wall. Jago took off the bow for which he had no arrows. Ceria dug out the small knife that she used for almost everything but violence, and threw it onto the ground. John said he was unarmed. Manvedian shrugged and claimed the same, which Ceria struggled to believe – though part of her was glad for the deception. The man patted each of them down, then, once satisfied, lifted the fabric covering the doorway and led them through.

Inside was a single spacious room: guards stood at each corner, whilst in the centre a great stone seat dominated, its sides decorated with symbols and carved faces. In the throne sat a naked man, his skin exceptionally white except for a black band painted across his eyes. He was fat-bellied, and his bald pate gleamed; the face below wore its years in countless lines, the skin stretched tightly across his prominent cheekbones and flat nose.

"I've been expecting you," he declared in sonorous tones.

There was a sound from John that Ceria could have sworn was stifled laughter, if she had seen any reason for it. He mouthed an apology at the staring Telde. *It must've been a cough*, Ceria decided. The air was especially thick in the room, after all.

Thick with Spirit, she realised. It suffused the air, lined the walls. Bright blue was all around them: the eyes of the larger statues, the bodies of the smaller ones, the frame of a looking glass, a line of arrowheads, the fluctuating glow of Spirit lamps suspended from the ceiling. She could feel the Spirit, as she had in the clearing, but it was much more concentrated here. It clung to her, permeated her; her senses were sharpened, overwrought. She felt a little light-headed.

"It told me you would come," the seated man continued at length, leaning forward to look at them. "I am Onuor, Spirit Seer of Rele'ba, province king of Nightsteppers tribe." He spoke with a heavy but musical accent. His teeth were stained blue.

Telde introduced each of them by name. "We need supplies. Food and water. We can pay or trade."

"Unimportant. There are things we need to talk of. Do you know what a Spirit Seer is?"

"Seers are guides for their people," Ceria answered. "They use visions to make judgements and forecasts."

The man, the Spirit Seer, gave Ceria a blue-toothed grin. "Your answer has truth in it, although no Seer is the same as his brother or sister. We singly have our godgifts. One will use simple wisdom to lead his people. One will open his mouth and the voices of the gods will emerge. My gift lies in dreams." The Seer paused, leaning back in his chair. His movements held the slow weight of a man accustomed to being listened to. "There is a god in the mountain, in the east of what you call the Black Sea. He speaks to me in my dreams. He has told of your coming for many suns, and he has a message for you."

Ceria saw Telde clench her jaw. She knew her friend wouldn't want to waste time with this kind of talk. She jumped in before Telde could speak. "What message?"

"The message is for your ears, not mine. It is my duty to make you listen. You will go there."

Ceria wasn't sure how to respond, but felt as if she had taken up the responsibility for the group. "How do you know it's for us?"

The Spirit Seer gave her a look that suggested how self-evident the answer was. "You are unmistakable. Each separate from the next."

Ceria glanced at her companions. He was right: each of them was distinctly different, in appearance, in character. They were a surprising band. *What bonds hold us together?* The thought made Ceria aware of the effect the Spirit in the room was having on her – causing her mind to drift and wonder in an air suddenly swarming with interconnection.

"I will fulfil the god's wish, as I must," the Seer continued. "But while you are in my province you belong to me, and I have other duties to realise. I need to know who it is that will step my sacred land. I will see you closer."

The man moved his hand to a bowled indentation cut into the arm of his throne, which was filled with a fine blue powder. He took a large pinch, brought his fingers to his nose and snorted the Spirit.

The Seer closed his eyes briefly, before stepping out of his chair. Ceria sensed Telde shift uncomfortably next to her as the man, with his small but heavy frame, his bare whiteness – there was a faint powder residue on his skin, suggesting the paleness might be exaggerated – walked to within a pace of the group. Blue stained his upper lip and nostrils, and he smelt of herbs and sweat. He moved in front of Ceria. On his wrist were markings, she noticed, tattoos that – *it can't be.* Without thinking she took hold of the man's wrist to look closer. The guards and the tall escort reacted around her, daggers instantly in their hands – but the Spirit Seer halted their approach with a quick signal. They retreated as he gave an irritated wave.

"Do you know this rune, child?" he asked.

Ceria lifted his thick wrist and studied the tattoo. A roughly square arrangement of three intricate symbols made up of fluid lines and loops, the lower symbol twice the width of the two above. It was the same. Of course she knew it – she had known it her whole life. "Where is it from?"

The Seer gave her a questioning look, then turned her wrists in his hands – but they bore no markings. Ceria glanced at Telde, who gave a slight but firm shake of her head. *But he has to see*, Ceria argued silently. *I have to know.*

She turned, so her back was to the man. He saw it immediately; she felt his breath on her neck, then his hand tugging down her collar to see how the tattoo, its tip visible on her nape, continued beneath her clothing. He lifted her jerkin from the bottom, and she helped by lifting her arms. He would find the same design, Ceria knew – large enough to cover her back, and rotated so the square became a diamond, but unmistakably the same markings. His fingers traced the curve of a line, and Ceria wasn't certain if she imagined the tingling in her skin that followed his touch. She felt her face redden; the others must be watching her, seeing what she had allowed so few to witness in the past. But it didn't matter – she needed the answers the Seer held.

"Now I am certain," the Seer said, finally. "You will bring no harm to Nightsteppers or to my land."

"Tell me," Ceria said, pulling down her jerkin and turning back to the man. "Tell me about the markings. Please."

"It is an ancient rune of Crescent," the Seer replied. "Very powerful. It is sacred to my tribe – even the heathen Pors recognise its divinity. It calls upon the land, the gods, the spirit world, the mortal world. It signifies unity and preservation. The ancestors held this knowledge. Much of their wisdom has been lost, but this symbol has endured the centuries. Nightsteppers have discovered it many times, marking my Sea from deep within."

"Do you mean it's from here? I thought... doesn't it come from Ferolian lands? From Som'syere?" Ceria was confused;

the Elders in the forest had known very little of her markings – and as an orphan delivered to them in her infancy, there had been no family to ask – but were consistent in the opinion that it originated from Som'syere's ancient past. *How is the symbol here, too, a world's walk to the south?*

"It belongs to many lands," the Seer said. "The ancestors stepped far across Crescent, although most of their marks are now buried. Your Som'syere is a place as significant as my Sea. There the mortal and spirit worlds are also in conjunction, and the ancestors' presence remains strong. Our two lands are linked more closely than mortal feet would realise."

"Who were these ancestors?" Ceria asked.

"They were a people with great understanding of Crescent. This is what made them so powerful – we are ignorant babes in comparison. Let me show you." He turned over his wrist, and began indicating the markings. "This heavy line beneath the others is Crescent, the land and mother of all mortal life, on which we are all dependant. The curve here, like that of a bow, is our mortal concerns. It is also our responsibility, the need to protect what has been gifted to us. See how it points here –" the Seer indicated a symbol with the appearance of a half-open eye "– the gaze is upwards, towards the gods. Faith. The bow defends our faith but also defers to it. We in turn submit our fates to the gods, who are impossible to convey in mortal lines. It is a rune of balance, used to draw upon the essence of Crescent."

Ceria felt overwhelmed. She tried to take all of the information in, and pick out a coherent response from the disarray in her mind. Jago spoke first.

"I haven't come across ruins of these ancestors," he said, curious rather than sceptical.

"There's nothing but hills at Som'syere," Telde added. She was right; Ceria had snuck onto the island when she was young, years before the half-man's attack. Despite its powerful atmosphere, she had been disappointed by the otherwise featureless downs.

"You haven't looked deeply enough," the Seer replied. "Land covers the tracks of the past for mortal eyes, but the mark is always beneath the surface. Crescent does not forget. But mortals do, and this blindness has led to abuse." His expression darkened, and his words held a sudden hostility. "I have dreamt of Som'syere. I know of the violation there. Your treatment of it damages my sacred land."

What treatment? Ceria wondered. She remembered the storms above the island, the rumours in the city. No-one had been allowed near Som'syere to find out for certain. But the bridge was finished now, Manvedian had said. Linking it to the mainland. *And all those Primitives being taken to the island... what evil was the half-man doing there?*

"You're mining Spirit yourselves. To sell in Queen's markets," Manvedian said, unexpectedly.

"We sell small amounts of the Spirit we gather, to sustain us. It is nothing like what you do in the north. You are savages, taking what is not yours, exploiting the powers of Crescent without comprehension. Your ignorance and greed will bring great suffering." He almost bellowed his last words, before staring accusingly at the uneasy group. Manvedian stayed wisely quiet. The Seer walked back to his chair, leaning on its stone arms with his back to them.

Eventually, turning with an unsettling smile, a change of mood too abrupt, he spoke again. "But now I am certain. You will do something about this offence. It is why the god brought you here."

"We just want to cross the desert," Telde said.

The Seer ignored her and moved back to Ceria. "Give me your hand, I will see you."

"Wait," Telde said.

"It's okay, Telde," Ceria replied.

She did as the Seer asked, and felt his cool palms enclose her hand. His eyes were wide and starkly white against the black band on his face, and it came as a relief when he closed them. After a few seconds she felt a prickling sensation, starting at her fingers but soon spreading to the rest of her, spreading *inside* her. The Seer crooked his head, as if listening, and Ceria felt herself respond: a surge of energy flowing outward from her, into him, then swelling rapidly back; she gasped as she felt the thirst, the urge to saturate herself with that energy, to take all she could. But the Seer withdrew his hand a moment later, and the feeling instantly subsided.

He nodded slowly, his eyes open again. "You have power over life and death. It is no surprise you bear such a rune."

Ceria's head was swirling. *How did he do that?* He had triggered her ability somehow, experienced it with her. *Life and death.* He knew what she hated to admit, what she dreaded and refused but could not change: her ability took life as willingly as it gave it, perhaps more so. *Why does it have to be that way?* Ceria glanced at Telde, who was gazing at her with an expression she couldn't recognise – satisfaction, or desire, or... But the look vanished abruptly, and Ceria was left uncertain what she had actually seen. She felt disconcerted, dizzy, and found it difficult to focus on the events in the room.

The Seer had moved on to the others, taking their hands one by one. He smiled at Jago and told him the world would stir at his command. John was met with a frown; the Seer said he was unclear – damaged or altered somehow. Manvedian shook his head and stepped back as the man moved toward him.

"Don't trouble yourself. I'm no Primitive."

"Come on Manvedian. There's no danger," Jago said.

"Yeah, come on Manvedian," John added, a hint of challenge to his voice.

Fenning men, Ceria thought, attempting to involve herself in a scene from which she felt increasingly distant. She looked to Telde for agreement – or was it for a hint of that previous expression? – but her friend's attention was fixed on the Seer.

"We are crossing the desert," she said, resolutely. "All that we wish from you is supplies."

The Seer paused. He gave Telde a long stare, his jaw faintly working, as if chewing on her words. "*My* desert," he said.

He returned to his stone seat, taking a generous amount of time to position himself. His movements seemed a little tired now, Ceria thought.

"You will go to the mountain," he said. "You will be accompanied by a guide."

"We appreciate your kindness, Seer, but we don't need a guide," Telde replied. "And we truly haven't the time to visit a mountain."

"I am losing patience with you, child. These are not requests. You will do as I say, or you will not leave this place." His words carried an authority, even with the edge of fatigue. He made a signal with his hand, and their previous escort moved to him to receive a whispered instruction. The tall man nodded in response, and strode across the room to exit the building.

When the Seer spoke again, it was with a softer voice. "You will come to see that both of these things are necessary. You would not survive my Sea for more than a sun if you did not have a guide. The sacred land is especially dangerous at this time. We war with the Por tribe once more. Many provinces have been lost, as well as two of our kings." He gave a slight shake of his head. "The god in the mountain is a blessing, yet its presence causes disruption and battle. My Sea is wounded from the abuse at Som'syere. It coughs out storms and agitates into madness the mortals treading its surface. I fear the outcome of these unruly days." A weary sorrow seemed to have supplanted the Seer's anger now, and it was almost as though he were talking to himself.

"We will supply you with what is needed," he continued after a long pause. "But the journey is harder than you have known. I cannot say if you will survive, that depends on the gods and your own strength. We will give you food, water, cloth for shelter, two jallers and a guide. You will give us your animal."

In her disorientation, Ceria was slow to decipher the meaning of his words. *The joorun.* She hadn't thought of losing it. The Seer noticed her frown.

"I offer you this trade only because of your journey's importance to Crescent. Do not offend me with your concern – we understand the relationship between human and animal better than any northern savage." He gave a dismissive wave of his hand. "It would not survive where you are going."

Ceria gave a reluctant nod. She felt too unsteady to argue – and he was right, anyway. The joorun was not made for crossing a desert. Neither were they, the Seer's eyes seemed to say. *But at least we have a choice*, she thought.

The robed figure returned, entering the room alongside a blond-haired man. The observer from the funeral, Ceria realised. He wore that same emotionless look, and she couldn't say whether it was borne out of deep anger or true unfeeling. Not that there was much difference in the end.

An image suddenly in her mind: the stitched wound, the dead woman. She couldn't escape it – it was as if she stood before the woman, close enough to touch her fetid skin, to meet her gauzy eyes. She was filled with her death, her emptiness, her repulsive absence of energy. Ceria was left nauseous and trembling as the vision finally dissipated.

"I will talk to your guide. Leave me," the Seer said, with another wave of his hand. The tall man directed the group to the doorway. Ceria was relieved to be able to escape the thick, affecting air of the room.

"I will not see you again," the Seer spoke after them. "May my Sea leave your souls intact."

17

The sight was breathtaking: a sheer drop of more than a hundred feet, then a black plain that had no end. *The Black Sea.* Even the blazing sun had little brightening effect on the colourless rock, as if the land soaked up the heat and was sinking with the weight of it. To his left and right the cliffs continued at a consistent, imposing height above the desert, until they disappeared into the horizon. Manvedian couldn't help but be both impressed and appalled by the vista – and wonder just what they had got themselves into.

We have to cross this damned thing. He should have pushed harder for taking the route through the Heartlands. But he had simply been too elated when Ceria and Telde had turned up in Edemon – he had scarcely believed his luck when word had come from his informers that they had entered the city and asked after a resistance contact. The game had turned suddenly and unexpectedly in his favour, following the set-back of the Ireldelor-wide arrests. He had learned previously that the two of them had not been arrested at Candar'laon, but was frustrated by the lack of any further news of their whereabouts.

That after so much chasing, and almost losing the women altogether, they would simply walk back into his grasp seemed like a blessing. He had had to act fast: first to get Tiyaden out of the way, then to reach them before Niscem, who would have no doubt received the same information as Manvedian. But Niscem wouldn't have known the contact or the meeting location immediately, unlike Manvedian – he had

Peledis to thank for that – and the small advantage was all he needed. There wasn't time to plan how he would hide them, how he would take Ceria away from Telde. But that would have fallen into place easily enough. Perhaps even without violence; it would have been simple to split them in the city.

But then the attack had happened. The game had changed again. *Fucking half-man.* Of course there was no warning. Manvedian doubted anyone working for Senthis had been told. Anyone human, at least. Certainly Niscem hadn't known. He almost felt sorry for the bastard – he had lost all of his power, and probably his life, in one swift move. The half-man wouldn't care about that. He utilised people when they were useful – and they felt the benefits – but didn't hesitate to discard them when they lost that use, or when something or someone of more value came along. He would only have eyes for what the attack achieved: the Queen no longer had a choice but to join up with the Regency and move on Ferol. The trap was set.

Manvedian had to admire the half-man's unwavering focus. And yet... and yet the attack seemed an act too far. He had expected an escalation in events, some measure from the half-man to push towards his desired end – but not what had happened at Edemon. Destroying an entire city was... unnecessary. Melodramatic. The slaughter went beyond achieving his aims, it was a statement, or an amusement. Because he could.

It wasn't the loss of life, Manvedian told himself. It was the waste. He remembered the Endless, the fluidic tendrils emptying minds; the flesh monsters rending apart bodies. *A waste of a fine city.* The loss of countless opportunities.

Forget Edemon. It's gone. It wasn't his concern – the city had been in the way and now it was gone. The inhabitants were too weak to do anything about it. If you lived without the power to protect your own interests, Manvedian reminded himself, if you relied on others to do so or on some universal goodwill, then you only had yourself to blame when someone with power came along and consumed you. *Forget it.*

He looked out at the Black Sea. There was no going back. The desert appeared utterly featureless apart from a distant patch that was a different shade of dark, slightly raised – a forest, perhaps. But it seemed too sparse for that, too black. There was a suggestion of movement; probably a shimmering due to the heat.

"Do you think they're trees?"

It was Ceria; she had come up from behind unnoticed. He silently chastised himself. *Focus, Manvedian.*

He shrugged as she moved to stand next to him, and they both gazed upon the bleak panorama. "Couldn't say. Maybe."

"I didn't think there would be life. But Yeoba says there is – plants, animals. He says they're few and far between, and not like on this land. But there's life."

Yeoba. Manvedian was still getting a measure of their stoic guide. In the few hours it had taken the group to reach the edge of the Black Sea, after setting off from the border town earlier that morning, he had barely spoken a word. The man was another complication, alongside John and Jago. But nothing Manvedian couldn't handle.

"I don't like the unnaturalness of it," Ceria continued. "It looks so… desolate. But if there's life, it might not be so terrible."

Manvedian glanced across at her. She had wrapped a small section of black cloth around her head for protection from the sun. Only a hint of her dark hair could be seen at the edges, a glint of the jewellery in her ears. He couldn't help but think back to the Spirit Seer's room, to Ceria's bare back: slender, flawless. Even the markings that covered her skin flowed with her, were a consonant part.

But they also stood her apart. *Remember that, Manvedian. Remember her importance to the half-man.* At one time he had assumed that she simply represented a danger to Senthis – Manvedian knew of Telde and Climbe's plans – yet now he was certain there was more to it. Who knew the true scope of her abilities, or what she could become? But it didn't change anything, except to make her even more valuable. He had to remember why he was here, the months of work to get to this point. *Don't be distracted.*

Manvedian put an arm around Ceria's shoulder. "It won't be too bad, kid. Hot as a guilty god's armpit, no doubt, but a little sweat won't kill us." The *kid* remark earned him a dig in his ribs.

He shielded his eyes and stared out across the desert, but couldn't detect any further disruption to the black as it extended dully into the skyline. Ceria's body felt warm against his.

"Do you think we'll get our home back, Manvedian?" she asked.

"The Queen has a formidable army," he answered, after a moment's thought. "And they'll be pissing daggers after what happened to Edemon. The Regency's numbers could be almost as large, I reckon. The force heading north will be enough to make the gods flinch."

"I just hope they remember Ferol isn't the enemy. We didn't do this. It's never the normal people, they don't have a choice. I hope the city doesn't end up paying even more for one man's evil. The Regency won't need any excuse to damage Ferol."

"That's where the resistance comes in. Us on the outside, Climbe and the rest on the inside. We'll remind them who the enemy are. Direct them. We'll make sure."

Ceria nodded, but didn't seem convinced. Manvedian wasn't surprised.

Climbe's face entered his mind: gaunt, bloody. He forced it away mercilessly.

The sound of laughter from behind made them look back at the camp. John and Telde were standing a little way from the campfire, Telde with arms folded, scowling at a grinning John who held her sword in his hands. Jago knelt next to the guide, Yeoba, pointing out something on the spits they were using to cook on the flames.

"Do you trust Yeoba?" Ceria asked.

Manvedian inclined his head towards her, indicating the obvious response. "Do you know he's from the Por tribe? The ones at war with the Nightsteppers. I asked around in Rele'ba before we left. He's bound by honour, apparently. Can't say it fills me with faith." He nodded towards Jago, then John. "But he's not our only dubious companion."

"John saved us in Edemon. Jago's done the same for us before," Ceria replied.

"Yes, John did. You have to wonder how, eh?" John's ability had certainly come as a surprise, though admittedly it had been welcome at the time. It was an impressive feat – Manvedian had never seen anyone but Senthis able to affect the Endless – yet it could bring John more trouble than it saved; there was little chance of Telde getting rid of him now. Manvedian wondered how valuable he might be to the half-man. "Jago likes to ask a lot of questions."

"Don't, Manvedian," Ceria said, untangling herself from his arm.

He gave a slight shrug. "All I'm saying is we should be careful. There's too much on the line to be throwing our trust around like Besgin whores."

"Let's get some food," Ceria said flatly. She walked towards the others.

Manvedian followed, trying to ignore the irritation gnawing at him. He sat close to the fire, cross-legged on the hard ground. Ceria sat away from him, next to Jago, who immediately began explaining the origins of the vegetable he was roasting. The two jallers were tied to a rock a small distance away, whining at the smell of the food. After a few minutes Telde and John joined the rest of them around the fire, and Jago handed out a number of unappealing blackened husks. Telde was shaking her head, and Ceria asked her what was the matter.

"John says that where he is from, there are cities made of

buildings taller than the Edem pillar," Telde answered, "where thousands of people live high enough to touch the clouds."

Manvedian noticed that although her words carried a familiar tone of cynicism, it was more gentle than usual.

"They don't live there," John said, awkwardly. "Not mostly. They're offices – people work there. Used to work there."

"The Mirante do Vale is five hundred and sixty feet high and has twelve elevators," Jago said.

"What could so many people work at inside a building?" Telde questioned.

"Do they live with birds?" Ceria asked.

"*Godsblood*," Manvedian interjected, perhaps more sharply than he had intended. "We haven't got time for this nonsense. Why are we sitting around here anyway, when we could be travelling?"

"We travel at night," Yeoba replied. He took a bite of the vegetable in his hand; juice ran out and sizzled on the rocks surrounding the fire. His long blond hair was tied back, and a white slither of a scar severed the stubble on his jaw. Manvedian arrowed a questioning look at the man, until finally he continued. "Nightsteppers do not tread the Sea during the day. They believe this is when the godspirits are punished by the sun, and you would be ill-fated to walk alongside such tortured creatures."

"But you don't believe this?" Jago asked.

"The Por'uhiin tribe do not," Yeoba answered.

"Then why are we travelling at night?" Manvedian asked.

"The Seer Onuor insisted. Also, because you would not survive the day." The guide said it matter-of-factly, before taking another mouthful of his food. Manvedian was glad to see that Telde was as riled at the comment as he was. "Night will better hide us. It's wise with such a conspicuous group. You are trespassers, and a prize to be taken. It would not be good for you if you were captured."

"How long will the journey take us? What is our route?" Telde asked.

"The time depends on how much you slow me. If you are capable, we may reach the mountain of the god within two tensuns."

The reference to the god in the mountain was met with a scowl from Telde. She remained determined not to waste time on that foolishness. Manvedian was still wondering if he could turn it to his advantage.

"Also, it depends on the Sea," Yeoba continued, "and how it receives us. We will not progress far if our journey is not blessed. Storms are more common recently, and to reach the mountain we can only cross Hoa Lake when it is calm."

"There's a lake?" Ceria asked.

"Many, far into the Sea. But not as you know them. They are dangerous places, not meant for mortals."

Nor is any of this godscursed place. Manvedian thought of the endless monotony of the desert that lay ahead. He loosened a few buttons on his jerkin to combat the stifling air, stroked a lock of wet hair from his face, then risked a bite of the vegetable. Beyond the tough shell the pulpy inside was surprisingly juicy, if unsurprisingly bland. Ceria threw a few pieces of hers over to the jallers.

"Are there juchen in the Sea?" Manvedian asked.

"Not where we are travelling," Yeoba answered. "They are found to the south, near Tvennik borders. Why?"

"No reason," Manvedian said.

"It would be incredible to see a juchen," Jago added. Manvedian entertained himself with the thought of introducing the man to one.

"Was that a funeral you were at in Rele'ba?" Ceria asked the guide, who looked briefly down in response. "Sorry. You don't have to answer."

Yeoba met Ceria's eyes at that, as if insulted. "No, I am proud to speak of it. It was a ceremony for a great warrior. My wife."

"Your wife?" John asked.

"She was felled in battle with Nightsteppers, by the man who stood beside her in the ceremony. Before her body is returned to the Sea, this rite decides the fate of her spirit, and of the one who killed her. At the beginning, I ask her to speak if wrong has been done. I ask her to speak if her fall was not the work of the gods. My wife stood silent for a day and a night. It was a good ceremony."

"Don't you feel anything for her killer? Don't you wish revenge?" Telde asked.

The guide seemed puzzled by the question. "What sense is in that? My fight is with Nightsteppers tribe, not the one who felled her. It was an honourable battle – he is a godsblessed warrior who defeats my wife. He observed the traditions and honoured her in the ceremony. I am indebted to him and his tribe for that."

No-one spoke for a time. The fire crackled weakly, its flames slowly sputtering out, as if unwilling to compete with the scorching sun above. Manvedian ate some more of the tasteless vegetable.

"Why do they call you baby eaters?" Jago asked Yeoba abruptly.

"Jago!" Ceria exclaimed, slapping the man's arm.

Manvedian almost laughed, despite himself. The man was either daring or entirely tactless.

"It's cruel gossip, is all," Ceria said quickly. "To make those in the Savage – ...the southern lands – seem more foreign to us. To encourage hate."

"There is truth to it," Yeoba stated unexpectedly. "You northerners would never understand, but we are not offended by your names. You think you dishonour us, but you remind us of our strength – and expose your own weak hearts."

There was silence around the dwindling fire. Ceria looked abashed.

Yeoba carried on. "Almost a hundred years have passed since the famine that threatened to end all tribes. The Sea was angry with mortals, and in its spite spread poison to the surrounding lands, killing our crops and animals. Province kings took many measures to help their people survive. Some held obvious wisdom – the elderly or weak were asked to end their lives. Some were foolish. It's told that a number of tribes hunted Unnhoa for food, even when all know their flesh is godtouched and unable to be swallowed by mortals. Many tribes, including the Por'uhiin, decided to consume newborns. They were fated to die anyway."

"What about the parents? Did they allow it?" John asked.

"Of course. We are a tribe, we suffer and prosper as one. To refuse would bring shame upon your family. Only one child could be taken per mother, and the kings' offspring were not excluded. It was a sacrifice that proved our strength. It was necessary."

"He's right," Telde concluded, following a period of silence.

The group was quiet, inevitably subdued by the conversation. Even Jago found an end to his questions. Most stopped eating. Ceria eventually stood, and walked away from the fire towards the jallers.

Manvedian glanced across at Telde, who was staring at nothing, lost in contemplation. *Of course she would agree with the sacrifice*, he thought, contemptuous. *That shit's in her blood, righteous and stinking.* He wasn't the only predator disguised with the smile of a friend. Ceria might even be better off in his and the half-man's hands.

He took a final bite of the vegetable, then tossed its remains into the fading fire.

*

The desert wasn't flat. Instead the surface was made up of innumerable peaks and troughs, spilling out endlessly to the horizon. Manvedian could understand why it was called a sea. The jagged undulations were only a foot high or deep, but it was enough to make it impossible for a brain to rest; failure to consistently pick out a careful route inevitably led to a painful trip on the black rock.

Night time made navigating the craggy terrain even more difficult. Ternerid was a thankful presence in the sky, its ethereal green preventing a pitch-black landscape, its induced shadows reminding that the sea was static when the imagination insisted otherwise. The rest of the sky was teeming with stars, striving to win back dominion from the moon through sheer weight of number. The temperature had barely cooled from the sweltering day, as if the million pinprick suns conspired to produce the exhaustive heat.

They had been walking for hours, and it was gruelling. More than Manvedian had anticipated. He had removed his jerkin long ago, revealing a sweat-soaked white shirt beneath. His knee-high boots reminded him with every abrading step they were not made for such an excursion. He wondered if he would ever be able to peel his leggings from his sodden limbs. *Fenning Sea.*

Naturally he didn't let his suffering show – and at any rate he was coping better than the others in the group: their heads down as they searched for the next fleeting foothold, hands poised for when they stumbled. They looked weary and weak, and made Manvedian feel better. But Yeoba didn't. The guide strode ahead, holding the ropes of the jallers, always sure of his direction, untroubled by the uneven ground. A parent leading its awkward hatchlings. No doubt he was revelling in the outsiders' struggle, Manvedian thought, feeling even less inclined to exhibit his frustrations. He was at a disadvantage. He needed to gain control of this place, push the game back in his favour. *Godscursing Sea.*

At one point the ground started to shudder beneath them. A faint vibration through the rock. Yeoba told them it was normal and didn't stop moving.

They had set off from their temporary camp at dusk, skirting the cliffs that bordered the desert until Yeoba had turned onto an almost imperceptible track descending the precipice. The path had zigzagged down, its precariously thin ledges forcing the group to shuffle sideways, hands pressed flat against the stone. The dimming light had made it no easier, except to partially conceal the plummet beneath them. Once on the ground, Manvedian had looked back to see enormous, glowing blue symbols covering the cliff faces. *Songs for the Sea*, Yeoba had called them.

On they walked in the dense, arid air. Three or four hours now. The sweating was continuous, as if the air was intent on wringing every drop of moisture out of them. There was no change in the uniform black landscape. The miniature waves played with the mind: it was adrift in this scorched ocean, thirsty for land.

Jago wouldn't stop talking. He took gasps of breath between sentences and provoked a flurry of sharp remarks from Manvedian and Telde – and Yeoba, who said all of them were too loud – none of which seemed to deter him. Telde eventually sought refuge with John a distance out in front. She would sometimes fall back for a few paces, whispering a new astonishing detail about Earth. *Fenning Earth,* Manvedian cursed to himself. He had had enough of that place, too.

Although… if he could get John or Jago alone for a time, he was sure to pry some interesting answers out of them. *A pointless risk,* he quickly cautioned himself. It wasn't what he was here for. *Focus.*

Ceria was sullen, depressed by the landscape. Yet Manvedian saw how she was buoyed by the traces of life they encountered, infrequent and sorrowful as they were: a sinewy plant here and there, wedged into a crack; the meagre droppings from some unknown animal. She complained when Yeoba took the group on a route far around the patch of forest they had spotted from the camp. He told them it held nothing but death.

Manvedian's thoughts strayed to the Endless, and to Ferol. Would that city end up like Edemon? He wasn't sure where the half-man would stop – *if* he would stop, when he won his victory. Would he rein in his Endless or set them loose on the weakened world? There was a chaos to his appetite that was unsettling.

Manvedian's reflections were interrupted as his boot caught on an edge of rock, and he was only narrowly able to prevent a fall. He cursed inwardly – but at least the constant exertion of traversing the desert deterred such idle speculation. *Focus on the present. On getting the job done.* The rest didn't matter. He couldn't control it, and he didn't have to. He simply had to ensure he wasn't in the way.

Ternerid had moved overhead, ploughing a path through the stars, by the time the group came upon a tall, statue-like structure in the empty land – its presence communicated by a curious whistling minutes before it was visible. The vaguely bulbous shape was sculpted out of the dark rock, its base a substantial cube. If it was meant to resemble something, Manvedian couldn't tell what. Several holes of different sizes and angles were cut through it, producing the fluting sounds even in an almost non-existent wind. The flatter slab of stone beneath was covered by inscribed symbols to which Yeoba, pulling out a knife, presently added. The way-post told him the location of other posts, the guide explained, as well as nearby Sea wells.

"It records who passed here and when," he added, "so their bodies can be recovered."

As the group trudged away from the stone, Jago came alongside Manvedian, and began explaining what a Sea well was likely to be. Manvedian told him to go away.

The brief distraction of the way-post was soon forgotten, submerged by the boundless black of the desert. Manvedian felt fatigue seeping into him. He whistled quietly to himself and looked ahead at the slurred horizon, where the land and sky were inseparable, welded together. The world was a complete container, its insides lined with darkness. The moon and stars smeared themselves over one half, whilst the six figures were left to crawl a vacant crust on the other. And filling the space between: the heat, the swaddling, suffocating heat.

Over the next two hours, the few features that disrupted the repetitiveness of the serrated plain did little to rouse Manvedian from his drowsiness. Once in a while, a rock flecked with brilliant blue. An arrowhead, a section of wood, a bone. For a brief moment there had been a sound suggesting movement above their heads; Yeoba made them stand silently for several minutes, his hands held over the muzzles of the jallers. But nothing happened. Manvedian half-suspected a deception to further unsettle the group.

Occasionally an unnatural fragment lay embedded in the desert surface, as if thrown up by the rocky drift: a smooth stone bearing unknown markings, a crumbling segment of a carved relief, a tellingly neat angle of black. Jago was tiresomely exultant over every glimpse. Yeoba explained they were remnants of the ancients, his tone disapproving. He didn't share the same reverence of the ancestors as the Spirit Seer.

"They were fools, wrong doers. As bad as you northerners at Som'syere."

He was missing the point, Manvedian knew. Like all of them. The Ferol resistance, Climbe, Telde, Ceria, the Queen and her armies, those in Edemon… *they* were the fools, unaware they were on the losing side, that right and wrong didn't matter a damn. Morality offered no protection, held no power against what was coming – there would be winners and losers, nothing else. Manvedian would not be caught on the losing side.

Finally the dark was lifting; the light of an impending dawn began to bleed into the Black Sea. The desert responded by rolling out its rugged tide towards the brightness, the monotonous black lengthening to ever further, unfathomable distances. Yeoba would soon make them stop and set up camp, so they could sleep through the searing day. Despite his exhaustion, Manvedian didn't want that – he wanted to keep going, to get the job done. He wanted to make the next move.

He looked towards the light leaking in at the horizon: an opening in the sealed container. A way out. Soon he would take his quarry and escape with her. *Focus.*

18

"Do you notice the difference in the air?"

John gave Jago a blank expression by way of reply, the momentary distraction enough to cause him to stub his toe painfully on a jag of black rock.

"The air quality," Jago continued, not seeming to notice John's suffering, "the thickness of it. It's different somehow, don't you think? It's slightly off. You can taste it."

John couldn't taste it. Up until now, he hadn't given any thought to the air quality – except to note its exceptional heat and density, even when they travelled at night as they did presently. It was like trekking through a stifling sea; they were at its bed, suffocating in the incredible pressure, whilst above them the shimmering stars and great torch of Ternerid represented a distant, unattainable surface.

"It's fascinating, really," Jago went on. "It could be the gas makeup. A tiny percentage of a difference in the constituent elements. The minutest change would have effects. Perhaps the whole of Crescent has this difference. We wouldn't be aware. Who knows what it could do to a body brought up on Earth atmosphere?"

John gave Jago a look he hoped would convey all of the unconstructiveness of his commentary. But Jago continued talking as they walked in the dark, scrambling over the ragged crests of stone that had become larger, more chaotic, if lower in frequency. The rest of the surface had been shattered into an immense jigsaw, the irregular black shapes puzzled together by some meticulous overseer. John could feel the warmth of the rock through the worn soles of his boots.

Jago went on: he described trace elements and solar radiation, atmospheric pressures and absent pollutants. John tried to ignore him, and looked instead at Telde's outline. She was striding ahead, head held high, confident enough on the terrain now to scan the surroundings. A hunter. Or someone being hunted, wary of a predator. *Always on alert*, John thought. *What does she expect to happen?*

It had been days since they had first stepped foot on the desert, and nothing of real note had occurred. The same black landscape repeating ad infinitum, the same tedious and demanding terrain. The same routine: largely ineffectual attempts at sleep during the scorching day, tossing and turning in sodden clothes; this wearisome travel during the night, any progress indiscernible in the reiterative dark. Once: a far-off Spirit storm, a patch of sky where the stars were missing, a fleeting filament of blue giving it away. The land continued to shudder periodically.

Jago grabbed John's arm. "It could kill us, you know. A shift in the percentages either way and *poof*, dead. We would never be aware." He said it quite cheerfully.

"Isn't there a fascinating rock somewhere you can study?" John replied hoarsely, through dry lips. He realised he hadn't uttered a word for some time – although it didn't take long for the heat to crack lips as efficiently as it did the desert surface.

"It's Spirit," Ceria said, coming up from behind to walk alongside them. She gestured upwards, towards the star-crammed sky, and it took John a moment to understand what she meant. *In the air.*

"It's here," she continued. "Like it was in the Spirit Seer's building, but... everywhere, like the air's infused. It's a part of this land. Its breath." She appeared both animated and anxious, her dark eyes wide. "It's getting stronger, the further we travel into the Sea."

Jago breathed in the air, then smiled. "You could be right. Incredible."

"Can you feel it, John?" Ceria asked.

John shook his head. If there was Spirit in the air, then he couldn't detect it. But he hadn't felt it in the Seer's room, either.

Jago took the bow from his back and held it out in front of him. He stretched out his fingers and the bow remained upright, balancing on his palm, before rising a small distance to float in the air. It subsequently completed a full revolution before he grasped it again.

"It's easier here," Jago said. As though to add further proof, he pointed a hand towards Ceria, and a moment later her head covering lifted an inch into the air. She laughed and pulled it back down.

Damaged or altered. That was how the Seer had described John. *What did he mean by it?* He remembered the disconcerting sensation of the Seer looking into him; the prickling inside his skin that had triggered a faint resonance from within him – but only that: a flicker, an insubstantial echo. Ceria and Jago had both described how they had felt their powers respond, as if they were using them. But in John nothing had happened, like some vital catalyst had been missing. He knew what that catalyst was. He resented it – the thought that part of him was connected to the Endless, that his power might be reliant upon them. He didn't want to share anything with those monsters.

Altered... did the Endless in the hotel do this to me? Had it given him the power he had used in Edemon, or had it twisted something he already possessed, an ability previously more pure, like Jago's? Could he do it again, Telde remained eager to know. John translated her meaning: *Are you of any use?*

Jago had extracted his latest batch of roasted vegetables from a satchel, and was presently moving several of the misshapen tubers through the air in a loose circle. Telde looked back, making an irritated gesture for the three of them to hurry up.

"Where do you think the powers come from?" John asked Ceria. "Not yours," he added quickly, remembering her reluctance to speak of her ability's origins, "in general, I mean. All of them. The Primitives." He cringed, remembering her dislike of that term.

Ceria absolved him with a smile. "They're from Crescent," she said, after a moment's thought. "Yours too."

"But we don't come from here," John said.

"You're here now," Ceria replied simply, with another smile. She snatched a vegetable from the air and walked away from them, towards the jallers lumbering alongside Yeoba.

John watched as she helped the guide lead the reluctant animals over a large rocky wave – Ceria using the vegetable as an effective lure – which resulted in a sharp curse from Manvedian as one of the jallers lurched down the incline and barged into his back. John was glad to see the man sweating as much as the rest of them, his apparent cool not entirely invincible.

"Do you think the people on this planet were transported here at some point, like us?" John asked Jago.

Jago floated a vegetable over to John before replying. "Do you know why they call this planet Crescent?"

John didn't need to shake his head, Jago was already continuing.

"I've encountered numerous versions, but most share a comparable origin. An ancient myth concerning Ternerid." Jago pointed out the spectacular orb in the sky, as if John didn't already know it. "It was believed the moon was a reflection of the land that people lived on, and that the land swelled as the moon did. It was a fat Crescent, it was a thin Crescent. The name has remained, even as beliefs have changed or been abandoned.

"Wimda considers Ternerid to be a sort of spiritual extension of Crescent," Jago carried on. "It signifies the will and temper of Crescent, and expresses this in ways the material body cannot. It will block the sun when Crescent is in great agitation. It will gather the lesser moons around it when Crescent is covetous or lonely. This anthropomorphism is common amongst the Leafshade religion. Ternerid is assigned a strong personality itself, playful and impulsive and narcissistic. Its cycle of waxing and waning reflects the cycle of life – it grows fat and prosperous, grows old and fades, disappears entirely until it's reborn in a slither of light. It's obvious why Ternerid dominates many calendars here. Wimda also used it in an astrological respect, predicting Crescent's future moods depending on the sections of sky the moon visited.

"The priests of Fivemoon have a much more rigorous astrology. It governs their religion. I've read their book – one of them, at least. It's written in a confusing prose, half formless poetry and half detailed scientific measurements, but there's a section entitled "On the diagnosis of mortal malady through study of the trajectories of the immortal moons" which has some very –"

"What's your point, Jago?" John interrupted, starting to will for the poisonous air.

Jago glanced at him. "I've learnt a great amount since I've been here. I've talked to people about their lives, about different lands, cultures, ideologies, theologies. I've read of wars ancient and recent, famed figures and legends – I should tell you about Wilvarla the Bright sometime – as well as civilisations long extinct. I've seen books written in an archaic form of what we speak now, and in languages that are no longer recognised." He paused reluctantly for breath. "This is their home, John, and has been for a very long time. If they were transported here like us, then it was at the least many thousands of years ago, likely before written history began."

Jago took a large bite of a vegetable, marking the satisfactory delivery of his argument.

But what he said *was* right, John had to admit. Crescent felt ancient. It was thick with the accumulated layers of human history, as dizzyingly cultured as Earth. Or how Earth once was, before it was scoured bare. The microscopic yet overwhelming sample of Crescent he had experienced so far proved it to him. The inescapable sense that even as he grasped a tiny fraction of meaning it was merely a surface comprehension, shallow and adolescent, as if that fraction held a thousand interdependent fractions rooted beneath, and those a thousand more, embedded in the collective memory of the planet. How would he ever begin to understand this place?

"It could be the other way around, obviously," Jago said. "That we were the ones transported, to Earth from Crescent. It's possible that life started here. But the two planets are not interchangeable," he added, waving his vegetable admonishingly at John, as though he had suggested otherwise. "There's a fundamental difference here on Crescent. Something connected to its structure or composition. Or perhaps something more elaborate, interactions with exotic dimensions that have created new rules of reality, or warped the ones we're familiar with."

John chewed on his own vegetable, which tasted about as good cold as it did hot. The bland flavour echoed the surroundings, as if the Sea had a sterilising effect on all that touched its surface. He held the vegetable unsteadily in his thumbless left hand.

He looked at the night sky, which held the promise of pristine, cold air – it made walking through the oppressive atmosphere of the desert surface feel like an everlasting form of drowning. Ternerid was an insistent light to the upper right of his vision, its face three quarters full and covered by a complex pattern of silvers and greens. *A reflection, a mirror.* John could appreciate that intuition. But in truth it was wholly separate, another alien planet. *Is life there, too?* The thought shot exultantly through him, leaving in its wake the impression of a universe swollen with sentience.

And yet an unease lingered. The ghosts of Earth, of Edemon. They warned that life was defenceless, that a gust of inclination from the universe could wipe a teeming planet clean. *Is that the direction of things?*

John put a hand to his temple, his head heavy with conflicting thoughts. It felt as if the dense air of the Sea had leached into it. The increased load spread to the rest of his body, weighing down his limbs, making each step more arduous than the last. He tried to distract himself with lighter concerns.

"What's wrong with my name here?" he asked Jago. "When we first met you said it was unfortunate. Others have reacted in the same way."

Jago tore a chunk from his vegetable, taking his time to chew and swallow it, savouring the knowledge.

"There's an animal here called a jonun," he said finally. "Often simply jon. It's a kind of rodent."

Great, John thought.

"It's probably used as an insult," Jago added helpfully.

John considered the possibility of using his surname, Bridgeman, as a designation. Or his middle name. Unless Miles happened to be the name of some unfortunate bodily function here.

He decided to abandon the subject, and luckily Jago didn't seem intent on pursuing it. Though that was more likely due to a lack of interest on the man's part rather than any abundance of empathy, John reflected.

He settled for silence and his tired, heavy limbs.

An hour later they came to a disturbance in the monotony of the desert: a wide and roughly circular construction of black stone. Nearby, an upright rock emitted fluting noises similar to the way-posts they had encountered previously.

"A Sea well," Yeoba announced.

The hand-drawn mechanism of the well was frustratingly slow, as if drawing water from a considerable distance below. It required two of them at a time to haul up the giant wooden bucket at the end of the rope. But the water was mercifully cool and plentiful when it arrived, and the group hastily drank, refilled waterskins, and doused themselves with the liquid.

"Do not drink too much at once," Yeoba said. "The water is not pure. It can cause you to dream while awake."

John had thoroughly soaked his head and clothes before he considered the well's incongruity in the parched land. Jago was already asking Yeoba about it, who explained that it was from the ancestors' age. On one side of the well was a deep trench filled with untidy hunks of rock, as if a past attempt at an excavation had been abandoned. John could make out exposed layers of sediment inside the pit: the metre-thick black crust of the surface, then bands of greys and ruddy browns. The well had its own boundary a distance down, where the coarse rocks forming the structure above ground became an immaculate curve of unbroken stone. *How advanced were these ancestors?* John wondered.

"Hundreds of Sea wells are known to us. There are doubtless hundreds more hidden by the Sea," Yeoba said. "Por'uhiin wise-men tell of the great ocean far beneath, in the land that is an opposite to this one. The ancestors were given this secret by the trees that have no end, who once tasted the sun of this world with leaves larger than men, and who drank from the magic waters of the ocean with their roots in the other world. But the ancestors betrayed this knowledge for their own greed, and were punished by the Sea. The Sea told the sun to burn the water away from their lands, and told the trees to poison the great ocean for mortals and their crops. The trees were allowed to survive, but as penance their leaves were withered into ugly boughs."

Manvedian sat on the edge of the well, one long, booted leg pulled up onto the rock, whistling to himself in-between swallows from his waterskin. John had that niggling sense again: there was something familiar about the man, something not quite right. Manvedian looked at him, head

221

tilted. John looked away.

When they set out again, John moved alongside Telde, adjusting his stride to keep up with her fast step. She had removed her cloak, yet despite the heat still wore her armour – the crimson breastplate with its interlocking plates, its contours enfolding her upper body as if the metal were shaped for her figure alone. The black chain mail under her arms matched that of her leggings; further sections of deep red plate protected her thighs and shins. John could make out the ghost of a design on the front of the breastplate. *A tree?* It was difficult to be sure in the gloom – and the motif was interrupted by the laceration caused by the Queen's Claw.

"How long have you known Manvedian?" John asked, quietly.

Telde's pale green eyes were questioning. "Near two years. Climbe himself recruited him to the resistance, after Manvedian's wife was executed by the Hearts. He has as much reason as any to fight for us. Many of our successes wouldn't have been possible without him. He may possess the head of an arrogant, obstinate jinua, but his actions speak his heart."

Telde aimed a challenging look at him, daring him to disagree, or to offer evidence to the contrary. John remained silent as they walked on. Her expression had also seemed to enquire: *What have you done to prove yourself?*

John already regretted his question, and hoped he hadn't pressed Telde into the defensive humour that almost seemed her default attitude. Or worse, pushed her toward thoughts of John's usefulness. If she began asking about his powers again, it would end the same way as previously: his lack of answers exasperating her until she snapped at him or stormed off.

But after a few minutes of walking in silence, he was surprised when Telde asked what he thought of the desert. Neutrally, yet a touch awkwardly, as if she weren't accustomed to unnecessary conversation. The question made him study the black plain as though there might be something new to influence his opinion. The nothingness, the starvation of the senses reminded John of Earth after the event. The empty city, the repetitive and inconsequential substance of days. Before he could stop himself he was telling Telde this, the words tumbling out of him.

But she listened. Patiently, with interest, nodding once in a while as they picked their way over the dead landscape.

"It was the quiet that was unbearable. Before it happened, the city I lived in had a constant sound. A background noise. People, cars – imagine a trailer, powered without jallers. I never really noticed before, but afterwards the absence was overwhelming. Deafening, if that makes sense. I couldn't escape it. It reminded me with every step that I was alone, it forced me to listen to that truth."

"In this event that killed your people, did you lose family? A partner?" Telde asked.

"Family, yes. My parents, grandparents. As for a partner... no. Yes. We weren't together at the time it happened. I'm not sure if we would've stayed that way or not." John glanced at Telde, who stared back with those piercing eyes, under the scrutiny of which it was impossible to hide. "I lost her, yes."

"What was her name?"

"Jessica."

Telde nodded, a gesture somehow enough to convey both her sympathy and the weight of loss involved – something futile to try and put to words.

They continued walking. John lost his balance as they mounted a miniature ridge – his grip hindered by the sweat on his palms and his missing thumb – but Telde's hand was there to steady him.

"Tell me about cars," she said.

John did so. And about buses, trains, cruise ships, and flying machines that could lap the world in a day. He hoped that he didn't sound like Jago.

He couldn't say why, but Telde seemed taken with his stories of Earth. And John found pleasure in the telling – in seeing her mask of stoicism drop for an instant, her sharp eyebrows furrowed in wonder rather than determination or argument. He wasn't certain if she believed him entirely, or at all, but that didn't seem to matter. For a moment, in the trace of a smile, John envisioned the worries of Crescent falling away from her.

"Did you lose family or those close to you in the attack on Ferol?" John asked, after exhausting his limited knowledge of hot air balloons. He was surprised to find himself asking such a direct question.

"Many friends. Most belonging to the resistance," Telde replied. "My mother and father were already dead. Ferol has a history of turmoil, long before this."

"Tell me," John said. He felt an obscure thrill, like a barrier had been lowered and he was daring to step beyond.

"Ferol has long warred with the Regency," Telde said. "It's unclear where the enmity began, it seems to have always been this way. Some say the massacre at Tursen Fens a hundred years ago is the cause, and our ancient stories were coloured to fit. A string of outlying Ferolian towns were slaughtered by Regency forces, igniting many of the conflicts that followed. But most believe the legends hold the truth, and that they explain the irreparable differences between the two lands. They date back to the White Age, to Fen and Hethea. Do you know of them?"

John shook his head – Hethea sounded familiar, but he couldn't place the name.

"Both were born of gods but led mortal lives, so the stories go. Hethea was from Ferol, and Fen was of the Regency. Both were powerful and venerated warriors of their people. There was a great love between them, enough to unite the lands. But after Hethea's death... her final, perfect breath, you haven't heard of this?" Telde asked, then carried on after inferring from John's expression that he hadn't. "After her death Fen grew bitter and resentful. He blamed the Ferolians for her passing, and there were many ensuing wars. The celebrated hero turned into the terror of our lands. He showed no mercy – he wanted only to cause pain to the world that had pained him so. Those in the Regent's lands would tell you a different tale, naturally. Whilst Hethea is revered in Ferol and a large portion of Ireldelor, especially by Leafshades, the Regency's religions worship Fen, and believe that he was wronged. The Hearts in Ferol hold similar beliefs."

Telde gave a dissatisfied wave of her hand. "Ceria is better to talk to about such things."

"You mentioned there were recent conflicts?" John said, encouraging her to go on.

Telde nodded. "Too many to describe. Twenty-five years ago there was perhaps the largest battle between Ferol and the Regency, fought at a pass near Gol Edge." She paused, a note of uncertainty in her expression, but continued after a moment. "My father and mother met on the eve of that battle. Both were young soldiers in the Ferolian army. They fought alongside each other for three days. My father was badly wounded, but both lived to witness the terrible result. For each side the losses were unimaginable. Ferolian history books will say victory was won that day – as the Regency's scribes doubtless claim the same – but those present knew there could be no such distinction.

"They were bound together soon after, and I was born a year later. My mother remained in the army, but my father took an official position due to his injury. The battle had changed things in Ferol. The severe consequences of the war began to weaken peoples' resolve. There were new tensions within the city, different political factions emerging. With every ensuing clash with the Regency, even if smaller in magnitude, the clamours for peace became louder. One faction in particular, led by some of the richest Ferolian houses, took advantage of the discontent. They made promises of peace and prosperity, and steadily gained in influence. Yet there remained many in positions of authority who recognised the group's true motives, and these voices barred their route to real power.

"The faction made their move sixteen years ago. We call it the Night of Knives. I was still a child. They went after key figures in the city, the ones that stood in their way. They came for my father in the night. He knew they would, so he had already hidden himself and me behind a false wall in our home. But not my mother. She had refused my father's protests and attended her guard duty for that night.

"They dragged her in, two of them. They wore animal masks and furs, I remember that – outfits worn on the days of our Bounty festival. We could see through a crack in the wall. They beat her, and they raped her, but she would not tell them what they wanted. She would not give up my father. He knew that she wouldn't. As they both knew that his role in the future of Ferol was too important to risk his life to save her, that the sacrifice had to be made. They cut open her throat and left her on the floor. My father waited until morning before he let us out. He covered her body and took her away. He didn't cry, and told me to stop."

John tried to say something, he didn't know what, some inadequate consolation, but it was stuck in his throat. Telde went on after only a few seconds' pause.

"It didn't take long for the faction to take power after that. My father declared allegiance with them. He feigned hatred for the pro-war group who were found guilty of the killings – the Bounty outfits had been discovered in their buildings, and of course they were executed before they could speak out. He knew it was in the best interests of Ferol that he secure a place within this new ruling power. So he gained their trust, he spoke for them in public – my father was a man of popular standing in the city, which made him a valuable asset. He was given a prominent place within the regime, not far below the governing council itself. This council at first fulfilled their pledge and made peace with the Regency – the first such in at least a hundred years. But as the years passed, the true colour of their rule began to emerge. Their corruption and avarice, their disregard of the people and our traditions. They even began to refashion parts of Ferol to emulate the Regency. The forests surrounding the city, where Ceria once lived, were torn down to provide wood for the governors' mansions. The resistance was born, with my father's assistance. He used his position close to the council to great effect – the evidence he provided of their corruption allowed the resistance to inform the people, and to fuel the growing unrest. Eventually this culminated in the city-wide riots that effectively deposed the governors.

"Ceria already told you the rest – how Dalinde was elected, how the mansions were razed, how we hoped for a return to a true and fair Ferol." Telde shook her head, embittered. "Dalinde was a fenning puppet, his laws not his own. The Hearts were granted increasing power, and soon the city was as oppressive as it had ever been under the governors. Years after it disbanded, the resistance was reborn… and we consequently managed to let in something worse still. We have to bear responsibility for what happened."

John glanced at Telde, who held the same dark expression as when Ceria had first described the resistance's coup, and how their actions had left the city defenceless to the half-man's attack. He remembered Telde's account of the invading Endless and flesh beasts. He had soon witnessed such horrors first hand in Edemon.

"What happened to your father?" John asked.

"He was killed in the riots, before Dalinde was elected," Telde answered. "The crowds weren't aware of his involvement in the resistance. Much of the resistance didn't even know. But he had accepted the risks. He knew he would be seen as an enemy of Ferol, a traitor. It was necessary. My father knew the price that had to be paid to free his city. He knew the worth of sacrifice. And so do I."

Telde stopped speaking, and it was clear that she would say no more.

She walked on in silence, her eyes forward, and it felt to John like a door had closed on a light.

*

Jago had changed. Suddenly, without warning, he had become silent and sullen. For the past four nights of travel he had remained in the same mood, and wouldn't be drawn as to the reason why. John couldn't understand it – the desert was as gruelling and monotonous as ever, but that very consistency meant there was no ready explanation for such an abrupt shift in character.

It had taken its toll on the group. As irritating as Jago could be, his incessant enthusiasm had served to distract them from the bleakness of the desert; his chatter was reassuringly casual. But now the severe reality of their journey was exposed.

John spent most hours of the night-time treks in silence. Telde seemed reluctant to talk, a grim determination set on her face. There was something unsettling in that resolute focus. Manvedian and Yeoba were openly hostile – not that John had much inclination to strike up conversation with either man. The lifeless gloom of the land was slowly wearing Ceria down.

One of the jallers had been killed. The animal broke its leg slipping from a crest of rock and Yeoba had finished it quickly, without fuss. They had eaten well that day, for the first time in an age, although John couldn't help but feel a pang of guilt at his substantial enjoyment of the freshly cooked meat. That guilt had soon been assuaged by the subsequent necessity of having to carry more of the supplies as they travelled. Ceria had eaten as much of the jaller as any of them. *It would be a waste not to,* she had explained, puzzled by John's surprise. Still, after that day she had been noticeably more downcast, and attended to the remaining animal almost relentlessly, to the annoyance of Yeoba. All of them were becoming increasingly short-tempered in the clinging heat.

John frequently tried to recall how long they had been travelling the Sea. *Nine days? A tensun?* It was a difficult determination when the characterless nights merged as they did. He had the reoccurring impression that it wasn't the six of them moving but rather the desert; they were static, stuck fast in the soupy air as the rock flowed beneath them, the craggy waves clawing spitefully at their legs. The lack of any perceptible progress over the days only encouraged the notion.

They encountered more way-posts, another Sea well. The land trembled intermittently. There was a closer Spirit storm: a blackness laced with electric blue, as if someone had placed a finger on a star and dragged out a chaotic course.

John was thankful for every interruption, even the worrisome ones. He treasured that anxiety, the sharpness of it. On Earth he had become numb and unfeeling – he never wanted to return to that passive existence. On this planet there was life, significance. And he was beginning to care. For Telde and the others, for what they were trying to prevent.

It was a risk, he knew that. Now he had become involved he was vulnerable, it could all be taken from him again. But there was no other choice; without the risk it was impossible to live.

They were halfway through the night – their tenth here, John was sure – a night almost complete in its blackness, as Ternerid had failed to rise and the other moons, roaming the sky like unattended children, provided little in the way of light, when Yeoba quietly announced that they were being followed.

The guide immediately changed direction, and led the group at an increased pace. John struggled to adapt to the urgency after so much monotony. His aching muscles wouldn't respond quickly enough, the lethargy worn in deeply by the repetition of their journey. He waded sluggishly after the others.

Yeoba wouldn't say who or what was following; he signalled for silence and marched on. Telde and Manvedian glanced warily about themselves. Telde had her sword drawn, and Manvedian had produced a long, silvery-white dagger from somewhere. John's heart pounded heavily. He noticed Jago lagging behind, and hurried back to grasp his arm and urge him forward. *Of all the damn times, now he's got no bloody energy.* He dragged Jago along whilst staring into the surrounding murk, unable to detect anything in the unyielding dark. *What's out there?*

A noise in front of them. A whistle? John froze with the rest of the group. Yeoba sounded a brief trio of whistles – a reply? – and hastened them on with a wave.

Figures abruptly materialised out of the darkness, only a few yards ahead. John was alarmed to discern the shapes of bows in their hands. But Yeoba stepped forward to greet them, and in turn the figures began to lower their weapons. John could see that they were clothed in similar leathers to the guide. *They're the same tribe, the Pors*, he concluded with some relief.

There were a number of tents behind them, and a tiny campfire, almost entirely hidden by an enclosing square of rocks. Yeoba took one of the individuals a distance aside, leaving the two groups to an uneasy silence. The men and women of the camp, at least six in number by John's count, eyed them with suspicion. Each seemed to possess the same contradiction of fierce unfeeling that was evident in Yeoba. As they waited, a faint vibration passed through the land. Yeoba finally returned.

"Who was following us? Are we safe here?" Telde immediately asked him.

"Sheathe your sword," Yeoba said brusquely. "Come."

He directed them away from the camp, dropping his bags on the ground after twenty or so paces. John followed suit, glad to be relieved of the baggage, which left a ghost of its weight on his shoulder. Yeoba began unpacking his tent. Telde stood in front him, hands on her hips.

"Well?" she demanded.

Yeoba glanced up with annoyance, but was met with an equal stare. "It was probably Nightsteppers or Disciples Of The Stone," he answered eventually. "Both tribes have been spotted in this area recently. We will stay here tonight, and travel tomorrow."

"Why don't we camp with the others?" Ceria asked.

"It's better the less they know about you," Yeoba said. "For now they believe you to be the belongings of this province's king."

"Belongings," Telde repeated with distaste. "Don't you trust your own people?"

"You can't trust any of these fenning tribes," Manvedian added almost immediately. "We should keep moving."

Yeoba ignored both of them, unrolling the cloth for his tent.

"Do you hear me?" Manvedian asked, taking a step towards the man, who was instantly on his feet in response. Ceria was quick to move between them.

"We have to listen to him," Ceria said, looking at Manvedian, then pointedly at Telde. "He knows this land, we don't. It's *his* land."

Manvedian muttered something under his breath, but after a few moments moved away. John had to admire Ceria's diplomacy – and her nerve.

"How far have we to go, Yeoba?" Ceria asked, turning to the guide.

Yeoba stared after Manvedian, then looked at Ceria. "Another three nights and we will arrive at Por'syere. Then, if the Spirit storms relent, we will travel Hoa Lake to reach the mountain where the god lives. My duty is then complete, and I will no longer be honour bound to Nightsteppers."

"Do you mean you'll leave us after that?" Ceria asked with concern.

"My duty is to guide you to the mountain, no more," Yeoba answered.

John shared Ceria's apprehension. How did honour dictate the man's treatment of the group after the mountain? He wondered if Yeoba might truly consider them belongings, items to be traded – or to be put down like the jaller. He saw Telde frown, and imagined similar thoughts occurring to her. She was already frustrated by what she considered a foolish errand, when they should be heading with all haste for the Regent's lands. But they needed Yeoba in order to navigate the desert, that much was obvious by now.

"What does he look like, this god? Have you seen him?" John asked, hoping to eke out a clue as to the man's intentions.

"No. But others in my tribe have. He is a god of light."

A visible shock of comprehension passed through the group. John felt his stomach turn.

"It's an Endless?" Telde asked disbelievingly.

"We don't call them that," Yeoba answered. "It is a god."

"Blood and blackness!" Telde exclaimed. "You think you're going to take us to a fenning Endless?"

Manvedian and Ceria and Yeoba all spoke at once. John was deafened by his own thoughts. *It's an Endless in the mountain. An Endless we're supposed to meet. One that knows about us and our journey across the Sea.* The others were pressing Yeoba for more answers, but he refused, and told them angrily to be quiet or risk arousing suspicion in the adjacent camp.

John sat on the ground, feeling nauseous. The group continued to argue in low voices. Except for Jago, who stood apart, staring into the blackness. If Telde had been reluctant to visit this so-called god before, John thought, she would be vehemently opposed now. He was comforted by the thought of her contesting the journey – that he wouldn't have to confront this Endless. Yet there was a part of him, quiet yet adamant, that wanted answers. It wanted revenge.

Finally the rest of the group began to unpack the tattered stretches of cloth that passed for their tents. But John could see in Telde's scowl that the argument was far from over. He began setting out his own tent, which he shared with Jago; the latter's lack of help and John's preoccupied mind turned it into a lengthy chore. After considerable effort coercing the short wooden poles into narrow fissures in the rock, and weighing down the edges of the fabric with what scant stones he could find, he achieved some semblance of stability and moved to sit hunched beneath the low shelter. He dreaded the coming day, when they would be stuck here, unable to travel under the blazing sun, unable to sleep through the fever of heat and troubled thoughts.

He glanced over at Telde and Ceria, who had long ago finished erecting their own tent. Ceria was lying within, whilst outside Telde washed her face with a handful of liquid from her waterskin. The frustration of the following day would surely be worse for her, powerless as she was to take action, knowing that they were reliant on Yeoba. He guessed at the questions going through her mind; they would be the same as his own: *What is an Endless doing here? Why has it asked to see us? Is it alone? Is this a trap?*

John rested his head on a bag and stared up at the dim canvas of cloth above him, which held little chromatic difference to the sky beyond, or to the darkness waiting behind closed eyelids. He felt the warm rock against his body, and tried to ignore the growing sickness in his stomach. *What does it want?*

The land shuddered beneath him, as if an insect had brushed its skin.

19

The stone jutted monolithically out of the land. Its hot black surface – like the fine dark sand covering the ground – was flecked by brilliant blue. Ceria crouched behind it, the blazing sun roasting her back. A bead of sweat trickled down the nape of her neck. She was certain she hadn't been seen.

She leant to her right and peered around the edge of the stone. What she had glimpsed in snatches during the sprint here, between the formidable rocks that burst through the land like the fingers of a buried giant, now took her breath away with its explicit presence. A cavernous fissure, a hundred feet deep and five times that in width, teeming with human activity. The thick black crust of the desert surface protruded over the rear of the cavity, and elsewhere expanses of fabric were stretched across the space for some degree of shelter from the sun. Inside were the unmistakable ruins of structures: walls, columns, arches, all formed from the same dusty yet remarkably smooth blue-veined stone. Some were barely recognisable fragments, whilst others were almost complete in their imposing dimensions; a number even bore angular reliefs carved out of the stone.

But most striking of all, everywhere about the ruins, disrupting and disfiguring, were billowing outgrowths of shocking blue; misshapen bulges climbing walls or clinging to columns or tumorous globes suspended in the sedimentary rock. The protuberances were static yet held an aspect of motion, as if during the act of escape an opaque smoke had been frozen into solid form. The abundant dust of the site seemed unwilling to settle on their surfaces, and so the substance – *some form of Spirit,* Ceria thought; she *felt* – was left unobscured in its vibrancy, and appeared even more alien in the muted surroundings. Innumerable figures chipped away at the stilled eruptions with picks or smaller tools, dangling from walls and ramshackle wooden platforms. Others hacked at the packed rock between the ruins, and Ceria could see tunnels where the excavations had burrowed further in.

In the distance beyond the vast fissure she could make out another site of busy animation, another rent in the land. *How far does this buried city extend?*

Por'syere. That's what Yeoba called this place. *But it doesn't belong to his people,* Ceria thought. *They didn't build it.* Near to the main excavation were the Por tribe's camps: countless tents interspersed with simple wooden structures, and surrounded by the thin blue haze that filled the air here. Jallers carted loads about, and there were numerous guards, patrolling in pairs, or standing with bows ready, their gaze often, inexplicably, searching the skies above. Almost everywhere else people were at work on the quarried rock, hammering and paring and sorting beneath long horizontal tents and makeshift shelters, creating a continuous, chiming din. The majority of workers were dressed in Por leathers, but Ceria could see a group in black robes, similar to those worn by the Nightsteppers, and others in robes and garments unfamiliar to her. *Are they slaves? Or bound by honour somehow?*

A noise brought her attention back to the excavation site: a small collapse of stone within, followed by shouts, an engulfing plume of dust. Dark shapes scrabbled out of the cloud, retreating to a broken pillar a short distance away. After a minute had passed, they crept back to their original positions.

The city was built by the ancestors, Ceria was certain. The same people who had built the system of wells throughout the Sea, who had wielded exceptional powers over the lands, and over Spirit, and doubtless much more beyond her imagining.

Yeoba said the ancestors were punished for their greed. Had the Elders from her childhood been wrong? The legends they had told described a war of gods destroying the lands, and of a civilisation thriving off their fallen remains – but it was surely the ancestors themselves, mortal people, who had brought about this ruin. They had created the Black Sea. *But how? What could have done this?* Ceria couldn't help but imagine the lush, rolling greens of Ferol, its wild rivers and forests, transformed into a similar wasteland. *Will the same happen to my home?*

An empty cart drawn by a pair of jallers and led by a woman had emerged from the Por camp, and was evidently en route to the excavation site. Ceria saw that their course would bring them close to her position, so she moved out of sight behind the stone and waited for them to pass.

It was the Spirit that had attracted her here. It was so strong in this place; its noise made it difficult for her to think clearly. She had felt it as soon as they had arrived during the previous night, setting up their modest camp nearby but – by Yeoba's insistence – out of sight of the city. The guide had been adamant that none of them approach Por'syere. But the draw of the Spirit and her curiosity of its origins had proved too much. She had to see it.

She had slipped away from the camp as the others slept; Yeoba had pushed them hard to reach here before dawn, and for once exhaustion had won a swift victory over the difficulties of sleeping through the heat of the day. Except for Ceria, who had kept her eyes resolutely open, aided by the insistent voice of Spirit resonating inside her. But there was good reason for the subterfuge besides her own compulsion, she told herself; the Seer had said that this land was linked with Som'syere, and so any information she could gather could be valuable to their cause. Telde would be glad, in the end, if Ceria discovered something of practical use. And if she didn't, well… she would be back at the camp before they knew she was gone.

Ceria thought she could sense that bond between the two lands. Or at the least feel a similar sensation to that which she had experienced when visiting the island of Som'syere all those years ago, long before the half-man's attack. The pulse of the land there, the beating power held within it – even if on the surface only boundless hills could be seen. She hadn't understood the significance then. But if it held as much Spirit as here... that might explain the half-man's interest. Was he also mining the precious substance? For all their talk, then, the tribes of the Seer and Yeoba were just as bad.

No, it isn't the same, Ceria told herself. The tribes *did* care for the land, and they understood the importance of Crescent, its fundamental role in all – even if they had to carry out ugly necessities such as this in order to survive. And besides, they took from land that was already damaged. The half-man wouldn't stop at mining Spirit. He wanted power, domination, not riches alone. She had seen the horrors shaped by that heartless desire. *He must be using the Spirit somehow.* All of those Primitives taken to the island. The Spirit storms. The Endless and the flesh monsters. It was all connected. *What is he doing there?* Ceria wished she had returned to Som'syere to see for herself, but not even the resistance could find a way onto the tightly-guarded island afterwards – or if they did, those involved never returned.

The Seer had said that what was happening at Som'syere – what the half-man was doing – was wounding the Sea. Damaging Crescent. *He has to be stopped.* Even if it meant siding with the Queen's armies and, worse, with the Regency. Even if it meant helping a Regent's army into Ferol city. Ceria understood why Telde had resigned herself to that bitter choice now.

She inched towards the edge of the stone, then looked beyond to see that the jallers and their escort had gone. She pushed the distracting influence of Spirit from her mind and studied the excavation, endeavouring to seek out something of importance. Were those runes etched into a column? She

237

leant forward, squinting.

A hand suddenly on her shoulder. She whirled, stumbling, her back colliding with the rock.

For a moment she was blinded by the fierce sunlight framing the figure, but then the tall outline resolved into familiarity. *Manvedian.* A surge of relief ran through her.

"*Gods,* Manvedian. You scared me," Ceria said, pushing herself to her feet and shielding her eyes. She thought that she detected a serious aspect to his expression, but it was difficult to tell in the dazzling light. "Are the others…?"

"Still asleep," Manvedian replied. "I'm surprised you got away unnoticed from Telde."

"I'm well practised," Ceria said, rubbing the small of her back, then dusting black sand from her leggings.

"It'll get you into trouble, one day," Manvedian said. There was an odd, detached tone to his voice. *Is he angry with me for coming here?* The last thing she needed was another Telde, watching over her like an overprotective parent.

"Why are you awake?" Ceria asked, determined not to be cowed into admitting wrongdoing.

"Bad dreams," Manvedian responded with a small shrug, then moved to the edge of the stone to peer past.

Despite herself, Ceria felt a faint relief to be out of the man's gaze. But if there was something slightly off in his behaviour, she reasoned, then it was simply the result of fatigue. He wasn't the only one affected, after all. Jago was much worse. All of them had had their personalities stifled by the heat, and by apprehension, especially after the decision about the Endless in the mountain.

"It's unbelievable," Ceria said, as Manvedian stared out at the rift. "There's a whole city under there. One of the ancestors', I think. The Pors are mining Spirit – do you see those collections of blue? Have you ever seen anything like it?"

Manvedian remained quiet as he looked out. His shoulder-length hair was wet from perspiration, his white shirt patched with analogous damp, and a growth of stubble darkened his jaw. It was the closest to untidy that Ceria had ever seen the man. The hilt of a dagger was visible where the long blade had been tucked into his leggings, and he carried a bag on his shoulder.

"Do you think the Endless is here because of this city?" Ceria asked, attempting to break him out of the silence, and, she had to admit, to escape her own unease.

"I don't know, Ceria," Manvedian said finally as he turned, moving back behind the cover of the rock. "But we'll soon be finding out."

He pulled a waterskin from his bag and offered it to her. Ceria shook her head, despite her dehydration. She was distracted by a different unease now, reminded of that impending journey. It had taken an hour of argument before it was decided that they would go to the Endless in the mountain. Yeoba and Manvedian had argued for; Telde vigorously against, supported by John and Ceria. The deadlock had been resolved, if unhappily, when Yeoba had grudgingly agreed to continue as their guide beyond the mountain, and to lead them to the Regent's lands. Another bitter choice; Telde knew they needed the tribesman if they stood a chance at reaching their destination.

"Telde was right in what she said. It could be a trap," Ceria said.

"Yeah, it could be. But it doesn't feel that way," Manvedian replied. "Why would the half-man send one alone? And why an Endless? They're too valuable to send after some runaways, even a Primitive and a couple resistance members. If he knew where we were he'd send humans, or influence the tribes here. Maybe he has already. But that still leaves this Endless. If it's a defector, we'd ought to fenning know about it. And gods, ain't you curious?"

Manvedian shot a grin at her, but it was unconvincing, as if it had wilted in the sun. Perhaps she simply didn't see the entertaining side – she wasn't curious about the Endless, she was scared.

"It's a risk," Ceria said, aware that she was beginning to sound like Telde.

"Anything worth doing involves some risk. Look where we are. Look at this godscursed desert. And what are we crossing it for? To get to the fenning Regency. For *help*. Us, Ferolians. One little Endless ain't jaller shit in comparison," Manvedian said. Then, in a more even voice, whilst correcting a loose button on his shirt, "It won't change our plans. We won't let it. At worst it'll be a wasted trip, at best it'll give us an advantage in the game."

Always playing a game, Ceria thought. *Always gambling.* If this was his way of reassuring her, then it wasn't working. She remembered something Telde had said in the argument about the Endless: *You know how important Ceria is.* She had whispered it tersely to Manvedian, but Ceria had heard. It was something she had heard before, and never understood. *How am I any more important than anyone else? Why do they always think I need to be protected? Am I both important* and *incapable?* She sighed inwardly, feeling as though she were a piece in this game that was invisible to her.

"Come on," Manvedian said, his hand on her shoulder. "Let's get back before Telde realises you're gone, and ends up tightening your leash even more."

Mercifully Telde wasn't awake when they arrived back at the camp. She stirred as Ceria took a place near her under their tent, but at her enquiring – if sleepy – gaze, Ceria shrugged and said she had been talking to Manvedian. It was the truth, after all. She could tell her about the city later; a few hours wouldn't hurt.

A period of fitful sleep followed. A delirium of imagination and dream brought on by the combination of Spirit and the searing heat. *A finger tracing the rune on her back, pulling the lines out of her, leaving her withered and empty. Then she was the taker, standing over her lifeless body. Radiant with power. Thirsty.* She woke covered in sweat. Dark was beginning to descend outside, yet she felt more exhausted now than when she had first laid down.

Yeoba had returned from Por'syere, where he had been collecting more supplies, and far too soon was ordering them to pack up the tents. Shortly after they were trudging away, travelling again over the bleak rocky ground as the last of the light was squeezed from the horizon. Away from Por'syere; Ceria felt a twinge of loss at that. She glanced back to see a faint blue smog hanging in the distance, glowing gauzily by the light of unseen torches below. In front of her was only featureless black. Perhaps Manvedian was right, she told herself, trying to counter her growing anxiety, perhaps this Endless was truly not under the half-man's control. There could be some good in the species. It was difficult to conceive in such monstrous things, but surely no living creature could be entirely evil.

The jaller had been left at Por'syere. She was grateful for that – it was safer there – even if it left her with one less distraction from the onerous travel. Yeoba told her the animal couldn't follow where they were going. *The lake*, Ceria thought. *Hoa Lake.* But she fought down the murmur of expectation rising in her. It wasn't a lake as they knew them, Yeoba had warned, it's not meant for mortals. She wouldn't allow herself to hope.

Hours passed, characterised by the repetitive, false waves, every jagged peak trailing the same wake of barren seabed. Jago was still the same, all of his previous enthusiasm inexplicably absent. Ceria wished she could help him, but he rejected any of her attempts at communication. She would have thought him a different person if he hadn't retained the same appearance. It was increasingly difficult to ensure he kept up with the group – Manvedian and Telde were both losing patience with his listless pace. She hoped that whatever it was that had been dulled in him would soon brighten again.

Perhaps when they escaped this place.

Telde had remained in a bad temper ever since Ceria had told her about the underground city, not long after they had set off from the camp. *Let her sulk*, Ceria thought. *I was right to go.* She sought out conversation with John to combat a growing drowsiness, but no sooner had she moved alongside him than he began asking about Telde's mother and father. *Does everything revolve around that woman?* John must have seen her grimace and apologised – which made her feel ashamed, and consequently even more irritated – and went on to explain that he knew of their deaths. Ceria was surprised. *Telde told him about her parents?* At another time she might have been pleased at Telde finally lowering her shield, realising that not all were out to harm her or those around her, that trusting someone was worth the risk – but she was still annoyed with the obstinate woman.

Relieved of the possibility of talk, and of caring for the jaller, the desert travel became even more wearisome than usual. Ceria had lost all track of the minutes and hours that had passed by the time she noticed a change to the monotone black ahead of her: a shimmering, fleeting breath of colour on the horizon that she at first assumed to be the product of her tired mind. The spectacle repeated, however, and the others in the group began to comment on it. As they walked on it became more pronounced, bright gusts of scarlet and gold and indigo and green contrasting the dark of the sky. It reminded Ceria of the displays of dancing colour that could sometimes be seen in Ferol skies – *the light of new gods being born*, the Leafshades described it; *portents of angered immortals and coming wars*, the Hearts always claimed. But it was different here, Ceria saw as they drew closer, it was larger, more substantial, even in its transience. Yeoba called it Godsong.

They arrived at a tiny Por camp, two tents and as many inhabitants, and shadows that might have been boats behind them, but Ceria hardly saw it – she was gazing at the nearby lake's edge. The colours of the restless mist above were repeated in the liquid below, but made solid: a shock of thick, writhing vivacity, luminous as if by its own source. The multifarious hues streaked over one another, or blended together in slow whirls, disappearing or appearing anew in the ever changing surface. It was an overwhelming barrage of colour after the desolate land so far, as though the rest of the desert had been drained of its brilliance so that it could be collected here.

She took a step forward to look closer, but there was a hand on her shoulder – Yeoba, handing her a section of cloth and pointing to his mouth. He told the group that they should breathe lightly once they were on the lake. Telde moved beside her and helped secure the material over her jaw whilst she stared out at the liquid.

"It's incredible, isn't it?" Ceria said, her voice muffled from the cloth.

Telde smiled and gave her arm a light squeeze. "Just don't touch it."

A boat was being dragged over to the lake's edge, Ceria saw with a brief glance, then looked back almost immediately – the boat was far from common itself. It was twenty feet in length, with high, elegantly-curved sides, and crafted from an extraordinary transparent material – no, not transparent, or not entirely; Ceria could make out inscrutable traces of colour embedded within the structure. A difficult task to discern the traces then became an impossible one as the boat was pushed into the lake. The liquid seemed to interact with it, producing an effusion of new, complicated colour, and Ceria was unable to attribute any shade solely to the boat or the lake.

One by one the group climbed aboard with the help of the tribesmen, who were remaining on the land. Ceria proceeded as hesitantly as the rest; with the hull almost indistinguishable from the lake it was as if she were stepping into the liquid itself, and she was relieved when instead her feet met with solid matter. Inside, she ran her fingers along the curious material, which was hard but somehow flexible. Yeoba stood in the rear of the boat, holding a long oar crafted of the same substance, whilst the rest of them found places along the bottom and sides. There were no seats to speak of, which resulted in an uncomfortable crouch, but Ceria didn't care. The hull sat low in the lake, allowing her to see both above the surface – where the colours were a child's paints, crude and joyful, yet where subtle flows also existed, semi-transparent streams that seemed to shimmer and shed hues as she watched – and below the surface, where through the interacting lens of the boat a maelstrom of colour whirled, hundreds, thousands of pigments that materialised and merged and were swallowed before she could name them.

Yeoba pushed them off the shore, and the boat glided into the lake almost without resistance. The movement caused the boundary between the hull and the liquid to be even less distinct, and gave the unsettling impression that the lake itself was carrying them. Unsettling but wonderful; Ceria saw her own smile reflected in John and even Telde. Manvedian looked mildly surprised, which probably meant that he was astonished. Only Jago remained apparently unmoved.

The shifting mists above the lake descended to enclose them on all sides, reducing visibility to only a few feet and magnifying the cocooned feeling. Now and then Ceria could make out lasting shadows in the cloud that she took to be rocks breaking the surface. Yeoba steered away from them as the boat made swift progress through the viscous liquid; only an occasional push from the oar was required to send them gliding a considerable distance, as if they bore almost no weight. He reminded them not to touch the lake, but there was little danger of that within the boat's high walls – and the liquid seemed to barely splash or spray, instead acting as an inseparable whole.

"The lake stretches far to the north. Almost to the north-eastern border of the Sea," Yeoba said, in reply to an enquiry from Manvedian. *A shame it doesn't lie the other way*, Ceria thought. Travelling to the south-eastern Regent's lands in this manner would have been a blessing.

She stared through the hull at the chaos of colours below the surface. After a time she thought that she detected a disturbance in the liquid. A dark constant. At first she had the anxious conviction that Yeoba had not spotted one of the rocks, but as the shadow enlarged and drew nearer, it became apparent that it was moving with them, alongside them, and its surface was not craggy but smooth. *Alive,* Ceria realised with shock. She laughed; she could feel it somehow, a benevolent and inquisitive presence. It came closer: a sleek horizontal shape, but massive, the length of the boat and then half again. The colours of the lake seemed to cling to its body, as if reluctant to let go; when they finally did so, they trailed like flamboyant ribbons in its wake.

Ceria pressed herself against the hull, wishing that she could touch it. As though feeling the same, the creature gently nudged its flank against the boat, the collision enough to send the boat swaying and most of them inside tumbling. Telde caught hold of Ceria as she fell backwards, then glanced at Yeoba with concern.

"It won't harm us," Ceria said, looking up at Telde. She hurried out of her friend's arms and returned to her former position. "It's a greeting."

"The Unnhoa," Yeoba declared.

The creature breached the lake surface. On what she took to be its head, Ceria saw a number of glistening orbs that might have been eyes. Its translucent skin contained no shortage of colour itself, and through its flank a prodigious ribcage was partially visible. She recognised the skin; it was surely the same material as the boat. She looked questioningly at Yeoba.

"We do not kill them," he said. "It would be a great dishonour. The Unnhoa grant us their skin when they come to die on the lake edge." There was pride in Yeoba's voice as he went on to describe the creatures, and told of how his tribe knew them to be magical creatures journeyed up from the ocean of the other world.

Ceria watched the Unnhoa below the surface, its long, vibrant body harmonising with the liquid. *There's life even here,* she thought. *Even here.*

All too soon the creature departed; a swift change of direction and its giant form vanished into the thick of the lake. A backwash of turbulent colour lightly rocked the boat. Ceria was left gazing at the lake, hoping that it would return, or that another might appear. *How many are out there?*

She was about to ask Yeoba when her attention was distracted by a large shadow taking shape in the mist ahead of them. It didn't disperse or pass but remained rigidly in front, expanding in its proportions until it was overwhelming: an immense rock surrounded by the lake. Murmurs from the boat made it clear that the others had also seen it.

Ceria's mood sank. She had imagined the mountain to be on the other side of the lake – far away yet. But here it was already, after barely an hour of travel, solemn and demanding. It was happening too fast, after so long spent walking the uneventful desert. Yet at the same time she felt a new strength, a determination to confront the mountain. And the monster within it.

They arrived at land a short time later. Yeoba used the oar to rotate the vessel, until they were sidelong to a rocky platform. Ceria alighted onto it along with the others, keeping the colourful liquid at a safe distance below – although to her, in comparison with the bleak, homogenous rock, the lake seemed a much friendlier prospect.

The ground was disorientating in its stale physicality after the vibrant and incorporeal journey on the lake. The mist, which had thinned as they had approached the mountain, dissipated entirely now, seemingly reluctant to venture more than a few feet onto the island. Ceria was surprised by the sudden darkness left in its place – it had been easy to forget that it was night time whilst within the enclosing luminosity of the lake. The mountain remained visible enough, its barren slopes and snubbed nose of a peak weakly illuminated by the surrounding cloud, giving the stone a sickly aspect. Yet this place exuded a power, she was sure.

Yeoba led the way as they circled the mountain's breadth. They remained near the fringes of the island, near the shifting, enshrouding wall of colour that hid the mountain like an ugly thorn in its flank. Eventually the guide pointed out a narrow opening at the base of the mountain, fifty feet or so ahead of them. The group scrambled over a shallow incline of ragged black rock to reach the cave, which was little more than a crack in the sheer stone. Inside, the passage allowed only for progress in single file. Ceria followed Telde, slowly realising that instead of leading them upwards, as she had expected, the cramped tunnel was undoubtedly sloping down. And it wasn't as dark as it should be; there was a glow from deeper within lighting their way.

Further down the passage took them – *we must be below the level of the lake now*, Ceria thought, imagining the untold weight of the mountain above their heads – until it abruptly widened, and the rough rock gave way to steps cut from a remarkably smooth stone. *The ancestors.* Ceria saw the same conclusion in Telde's frown. The walls were sculpted from a similar blue-veined stone, and began to curve, creating a slow spiral as the steps initiated a steeper descent. *What is this place?*

Deeper they ventured, and markings began to appear on the walls – runes, Ceria recognised. The elegant designs shimmered blue, and seemed to resonate with the group's passing. They whispered: soundless messages that resounded inside her, deep rooted and indecipherable. She could feel the Spirit pulse within this place, the beat of the mountain – she beat in tandem with it. The power was unbalancing. The others in the group appeared similarly uneasy; Telde drew her sword, and even Manvedian struck out a hand for stability. Yeoba pressed on as the spiral tightened. Ceria found it increasingly difficult to breathe; she lowered the cloth from her mouth, but the arid air did little to remedy her panting. They continued to descend, towards the hot heart of the mountain.

She could sense it before they saw it. A scornful presence. Hungry. She knew it was close before its light could be seen reflecting on the tunnel walls ahead. A final coil of the passage, an opening to a wide, low chamber, flawlessly circular, blanketed with glowing runes, and there it was, floating in the centre: a swirling white-brightness, a living light. She felt a disabling nausea. These creatures had killed so many in Ferol and Edemon. With fervour. With pleasure.

The Endless made no move as the group stood at the threshold of the room, and seemed unsurprised by their arrival. Yeoba walked slowly towards it, then knelt before it, uttering some words that Ceria couldn't discern. The Endless hung in front of him, and within its body light began to coalesce. A moment later a tendril of liquid radiance shot out, and Ceria watched in horror as it effortlessly penetrated Yeoba's forehead.

John rushed forward from behind her, clearly intent on intervening.

"Stop we are not damaging you."

The voice came from Yeoba, but it was strange, almost unrecognisable – his voice, but devoid of inflection or accent.

John had his hands on Yeoba's shoulder and was trying to wrench him away from the tendril, straining as though the man was held fast.

"Stop we are not damaging you," Yeoba repeated, in the same lifeless speech.

It isn't him, Ceria realised.

"John, stop. Wait," she said, then again, louder. John paused, looking at her questioningly, his hands still on the tribesman. Ceria summoned the courage to move her gaze to the molten light beside him. "Is this... are we speaking to the Endless?"

There was a brief silence, before Yeoba spoke. "Yes."

John stumbled backwards from the guide as if his hands had been scalded.

"Tell me why we shouldn't kill you," Telde said through gritted teeth, stepping forward, her long sword held in front of her.

"Impossible."

Ceria felt something emanate from the Endless as it spoke through Yeoba. Amusement, superiority. *It's right,* she thought, *Telde's sword is useless against it. But it can kill us with ease.*

"Why did you want to see us?" Ceria asked, trying to keep her voice steady.

"We require you to end Senthis of you in the other land," Yeoba – the Endless – replied.

An uncertain glance passed between Ceria and Telde.

"You want us to kill the half-man?" Manvedian asked, from beside Ceria.

"Yes one here of you is capable of ending Senthis of you in the other land." The constant flow of words from Yeoba, evenly spaced and weighted, made the meaning difficult to discern. *One of us here?* Ceria looked to Telde, who was anxiously fingering the hilt of her sword.

"You go against your own kind?" Manvedian questioned.

"Impossible." An emanation of bemused mirth, as if the notion were absurd.

Do all of the Endless want Senthis to be killed? Ceria struggled to believe that. Perhaps it was doing what it considered best for its kind. Or were the Endless connected to one another in a way humans couldn't comprehend?

It doesn't matter, she decided, taking a step forward. "How do we kill Senthis?"

"One here of you is capable of ending Senthis of you in the place like here in the other land."

"Do you mean in Ferol?" Telde asked.

"No," Ceria interrupted. "I think he – it – means Som'syere. Is there a room like this one in Som'syere?"

A pause, before the Endless answered. "Yes."

"You're not actually listening to this thing, are you?" John asked incredulously, looking between Ceria and Telde. But Telde's eyes were fixed on the Endless.

"How do we use the room to kill the half-man?" Telde asked.

"One here of you is capable of ending Senthis of you in the place like here in the other land," the Endless repeated. It emitted an emotion akin to patient disdain, as if it were speaking to a dumb animal. Telde made an exasperated noise.

"This all sounds like jaller shit to me," Manvedian said.

"You said yourself it could be a defector," Ceria replied. Yet she wasn't convinced of that herself, she realised. It was impossible for this Endless to turn against its kind, especially for the sake of humans – the emanations assured her of that truth. But they didn't need to understand its motives. She turned to Telde. "If it knows of a way to kill the half-man, we should listen."

"I've seen these things, what they are inside," John said. "There's no good there."

Telde took a breath, then faced the whirling intensity. "Why should we believe what you say?"

"We helped you before," the Endless responded.

Telde gave a disgusted grunt. "How?"

There was a second's delay, then Yeoba's sterile voice sounded again. "Senthis of you purposed to take all of you from the other planet we prevented."

"The other planet... are you talking about Earth?" John asked.

"Yes," the Endless answered.

"What do you mean *take*?" John asked slowly.

"Move to planet here."

"Why?" John pressed. "To do what with them?"

There was another pause, and Ceria had the unsettling impression of the Endless searching Yeoba's mind. *What else does it have access to? Is it hurting him?*

"Change."

"Change how?" John demanded.

The Endless remained silent. John ran a hand through his hair and frowned at his feet, as if trying to puzzle the sense from what was said.

"Wait, hold on," he said eventually. "The Russian town. Jago, do you remember?" Jago was standing in the doorway behind them, forgotten until now, staring dully at the Endless. He responded with a shrug. John made an irritated noise and turned to the rest of them. "There was a town in Russia – on Earth – that disappeared a day before the event. Its inhabitants, I mean. And Jago told me that he had found more like it – isolated settlements that were suddenly deserted."

John faced the Endless again. "Did Senthis transport the people of these towns from Earth to Crescent?"

A silence. Then, "Yes."

"Where are they?"

"In the other land."

John looked desperately to Telde and Ceria. "Did you see them in Ferol? Or Som'syere? There would be hundreds of humans, possibly thousands."

"No, I'm sorry, John," Telde said with a shake of her head. "But we were unable to gain access to Som'syere after the half-man's invasion."

Ceria felt a growing apprehension. Two years ago the attack had happened on Ferol, surely only a matter of months after the terrible event on John's planet. Jago had said that the days were shorter on Earth, so it was difficult to be certain – but the two events were surely too close to be a coincidence. John was right when he claimed they were connected somehow. *But how? Where did those people go?* And something else troubled her, a much darker suspicion.

"You said Senthis wanted to take all from the other

planet?" Ceria asked, staring into the light.

"Senthis of you purposed to take all of you from the other planet we prevented," the Endless replied.

John glanced at Ceria, anxiously, evidently picking up on her suspicion. "How did you prevent it?" he asked.

"By ending all of you on the other planet."

Ceria's stomach lurched. Her skin was suddenly cold, despite the heat.

John staggered back a few paces, and leant on the wall for support.

"You killed them," he said quietly. "It was you... you killed them all."

"Senthis of you purposed to take all of you from the other planet we prevented."

"How did you end them?" It was Manvedian that asked, in a detached tone.

"Senthis of you purposed to take all of you from the other planet using energies of the other land we changed energies to end you."

As the words were uttered from Yeoba, Ceria felt something terrible emitted from the Endless: gratification, pride. It was boasting about the act. *There is no good in them*; she knew that now. No empathy, no compassion. *Impossible.* They saw humans as possessions, theirs to toy with, to manipulate and kill. *They think themselves gods.*

"Another of we changed energies to retain selected of you like three of you here," the Endless said.

Ceria was slow to hear the words, sorrow and revulsion storming inside her. She was equally slow to notice John charging from his position at the wall.

"You killed them all!" he screamed as he ran. Telde cried out for him to stop, but despairingly, too late, as John had already reached the Endless. He thrust his hand immediately into the centre of its churning light. At first there was an emanation of amused disdain, but after a few seconds the tendril extending from the creature shuddered, then disappeared altogether. Yeoba fell to the ground, and there was a shift in the intensity of the light; it began to pulse around John's hand, swarm and brighten, until his arm was lost in the tumultuous blaze. Surprise and indignation came from the Endless now, and it was trying to pull away, Ceria saw, its ends arching into a crescent of light, but those extremities were fading as brightness continued to cascade towards John's arm. There was a howl, then a blinding beam of light burst from John's free hand, shooting wildly into the walls and the ceiling, and Ceria had to look away and cover her eyes.

The brilliant glare faded abruptly, and Ceria turned back to see Yeoba on his feet and John on the ground before him. The tribesman had his knife drawn, a lifeless expression on his face. *Is it him?* He stood protectively in front of the Endless, his back to the wavering light. The creature's form was erratic now, skewed; white eddies escaped, haemorrhaging into the air.

Telde raced in, pulling John to his feet and away from Yeoba and the Endless. "*Godscurseyou,* run!" she shouted at the rest of them.

Ceria had a final glimpse of the room – the runes throbbing blue, stone falling from the seared and gouged ceiling, Yeoba standing motionless in front of the Endless – before she retreated hurriedly into the passage. Then they were running, sprinting up the spiral stairs, the glowing runes and suffocating heat and the words of the Endless and the beam of light imprinted on her vision causing Ceria to stagger into the walls; but Telde was behind to steady her. There was an emanation from the depths of the mountain: outrage, pain – and fear. Ceria felt a grim satisfaction. The mountain shook around them, its pulse of Spirit irregular now, as uncontrolled as her own. Finally the smooth steps gave way to rough rock, and shortly after the group emerged into the black of the night.

The five of them stumbled over the craggy surface of the

island, which shuddered and convulsed as great splinters of rock broke from the mountain and exploded upon the ground. Ceria gripped Jago's hand and pulled him after her, whilst Telde and Manvedian helped to support an exhausted John. Yeoba was nowhere to be seen. Telde's terse shouts urged them forward, towards the boat.

Finally Ceria spotted the translucent vessel in the distance. She called to the others and hurried towards it. Upon reaching the boat, the group wasted no time in scrambling inside.

"What about Yeoba?" Ceria asked, as Telde climbed in last.

"Are you serious?" Manvedian snapped.

Telde gave a short shake of her head in answer. She picked up the long oar, then with awkward effort managed to push the vessel away from the rock. They proceeded unsteadily as she rowed, fighting to keep her footing in the swaying boat. Nonetheless they were plunged almost immediately into colour as the mist encompassed them and the vivid lake replaced the harsh material of the island. The imposing silhouette of the mountain remained, however, and Telde strived to turn the boat so that it lay on their left – so they would circle the mountain and head east, Ceria surmised. The lake surface trembled around them.

"I'll find the nearest shore. We need shelter before dawn breaks," Telde announced in an assured voice. "Put your masks on."

Ceria was comforted by the stoic calm of her friend, even if she knew it to be a deception for precisely that purpose. How would they keep their bearings after the mountain was gone? How would they navigate the rocks in the lake? How, without Yeoba, would they find safe passage to the Regent's lands? Telde couldn't have the answers, no matter her confidence.

No-one spoke for a time, and the only sounds were the viscid lapping of the lake and the distant booms of shattering rock. Manvedian was sitting opposite Ceria, but faced away, unreadable. Jago remained predictably sullen, yet his mood was at least in keeping with the others' now. John appeared worn out, distraught, his body slumped against the hull. Ceria couldn't help but feel a pang of guilt; *Senthis brought this terrible event upon his world. Someone from my home, from Crescent.* She felt a responsibility, as if they had failed to control their own evil.

"Are you okay, John?" Ceria asked, knowing that of course he wasn't – *how can he be?* – but she had to say something.

"They killed everyone," John said in a barely audible voice, his eyes down. "Billions of people in a moment. So easily. What's the point in life if it's that easy?"

"You made it fear, John," Ceria found herself saying. "They think they're gods, but you can make them fear."

John didn't reply, and returned to his withdrawn state. *What does it matter now?* Ceria imagined him thinking. *The damage has already been done.* She couldn't help her thoughts moving to her own people: if the Endless did that to John's people, to a whole planet, then the same could happen to Crescent. It felt hopeless to battle against such power, but they had to try. *They aren't gods*, Ceria told herself. *And Senthis is half human still. They can be stopped. They have to be.*

Telde continued to row, and soon they had left behind the mountain of the so-called god. Ceria was relieved to see the vast shadow disappear. She realised her own exhaustion then, her body exhaling as if releasing the last of its energy. She moved to lie on her side, and stared at the slow whirl of colour through the hull. The liquid was somehow distasteful now, reckless in its beauty. It quivered vulnerably as another tremor passed through it.

Ceria closed her eyes, not wanting to see.

20

The sky broiled and pulsed. Heaving black threaded with fine blue fire. The sight was somehow familiar to John, beyond its similarity to the Edemon storm.

The active core of the Spirit storm was a few miles away, but the black swept out from it in every direction, inking out the stars and providing a shadowy canvas on which the ecstatic blue could rove. It wasn't the same as the storm in Edemon. There was no preceding rain – that would have been a blessing – and if anything the air had been stripped further of its scant moisture. To John's relief, he was yet to see any beams of light lancing down. But it still affected the desert: the rocky ground frequently shuddered beneath the black, as if agitated by its proximity, whilst beneath the blue it threw violent spasms. The group had been forced to sail south along the lake edge to avoid that devastating centre of the storm, until there was little choice but to go ashore to escape the toxic air.

Ternerid would be somewhere in the sky above, John knew, but even the moon's light couldn't penetrate the choking black. It felt as though the writhing darkness was intent on extinguishing all who dwelled beneath it, too.

"Are you trying to kill me, Jago?"

It was Manvedian who asked; John returned his gaze to the small campfire at which he sat with the two men. Manvedian was grinning, a gnarled reddish strip held distastefully between his fingers.

"Blame Yeoba, not me," Jago replied. "He obtained the

food from Por'syere. I'm only cooking it."

"Tastes like Ranarin jotu tongue," Manvedian said. "You know there's a reason why no-one likes a Ranarin cook."

The man was more sociable now, John noticed. Whether it was because they had finally escaped the boat, or simply that they were still alive, or, most improbably, that he was warming to their company, John didn't know. He had somehow managed to shave in the hour since they had come onto land, and looked unreasonably well-groomed – especially when compared to the unkempt, bearded forms of his immediate companions. Despite Manvedian's easy smile, John remained convinced that there was something not quite right about him. Something uncomfortably close.

"Stop complaining," Ceria said, appearing from behind Manvedian and giving him a gentle push. "Be grateful we have a warm meal for the first time in days."

"It'll be burning when it comes out of us," Manvedian replied. He gave the length of meat a suspicious shake, before glancing back at Ceria. "Where's Telde?"

Ceria moved to sit cross-legged beside Manvedian. "She's still out there, scouting our route and searching for higher ground. She wants to see if she can make out any stars before dawn comes."

"She needs to rest, or her cough won't get any better," John said, aware of a trace of irritation in his words, which he couldn't seem to shake recently. But he was right about Telde; she was pushing herself too hard.

"You know Telde," Ceria said with a helpless shrug.

"He'd like to," Manvedian added, with a wink in John's direction, and received a subsequent slap on his shoulder from Ceria. John decided that he cared even less for the new, companionable Manvedian.

Ceria leaned over to her right to accept a spit of roasted food from Jago. She took a bite and couldn't entirely hide a sour expression. Manvedian laughed.

"I didn't choose the food," Jago said defensively. He then

held up a raw sample of the meat in front of him to study. "I think it's most likely the flattened appendage of a giant arachnid, or similar. This sticky gloss on the tissue is probably for conserving moisture, and these bristles could be sensory. Yes – see how it bends here – the segmentation suggests a limb of some kind. Or perhaps the equivalent of a pedipalp, given these nail-like extensions. I would love to see a live specimen."

"Fascinating," Manvedian replied without enthusiasm. Ceria prodded his leg with her own charred arachnid limb.

There was a shudder in the ground, forceful enough to dissolve the smiles around the campfire and expose some of the anxiety beneath. John felt a degree of satisfaction in response. *They* should *be upset,* he thought. *How can they laugh and joke after what the Endless told us?* Add to that the proximity of the Spirit storm, and how they were practically directionless in the vast desert without Yeoba, and there was little to be cheerful about.

They're just putting a brave face on things, he told himself. *Do you want them to be sobbing wrecks?* But John still couldn't help a keen resentment as he glanced at Jago. The Brazilian had returned to his old self in the past two days, his depression departing as swiftly and unaccountably as it had arrived.

"What do you think their relationship is with the half-man?" Ceria asked, after a period of quiet. "I used to think the Endless were ruled by him, but I can't believe that any longer. Why don't they just kill Senthis if they want to? Aren't they able? Or is it only some of them who wish it?"

"Gods, I don't know," Manvedian replied.

"I can't remember any of the time in the mountain," Jago said.

John didn't know the answers either. *But she's right about the Endless,* he thought. *They wouldn't consider it possible to be ruled by a human.*

Silence surrounded the soft crackling of the fire. Jago offered John a skewer of meat, which he curtly waved away.

"And what did it mean when it said that it had retained three of us?" Ceria asked.

Manvedian sighed. "Leave it be, Ceria."

"Why? Are you scared to talk about it? It could be important," Ceria said.

"I'm not scared," Manvedian growled. "But you can't trust anything that came out of that godscursed creature. It's a waste of time going over it again and again. It wanted to confuse and scare us, like what it said about that other planet. Lies and jaller shit."

"It was telling the truth," John said tersely. He knew that it was. The Endless had truly done that to Earth, to its people. He had felt the pride of the creature, and somehow a residual memory of the act: the seething pleasure in twisting so many billions of awarenesses into non-being.

The others around the campfire were quieted by his remark, and seemed wary of speaking. John couldn't escape the impression of being regarded as someone who had suffered a recent tragedy. A querulous mourner. *Close enough*, he supposed. But they didn't treat Jago in the same fashion, even though they should, even though he should be suffering just as much. Jago claimed that he couldn't recall any of the period spent in his dejected state, however, and so John was left alone with his grief.

He stifled a cough and put a hand to his raw throat. He looked to the mist that marked the edge of the lake a few hundred yards away. The colours of the cloud were fleeting yet lavishly applied, like an aurora with more constancy; better than the Earthly phenomenon, if somehow, despite willing it, he couldn't find it as beautiful. The group had spent much longer within the mist than they had expected, the better part of three days sailing east – to Telde's best approximation – on the lake, away from the mountain. The multicoloured liquid had stretched determinedly on, as if reluctant to let the boat out of its embrace, and had deployed rocks of increasing frequency and size to slow their passage.

John could make out the shadows of those monolithic stones within the lake. They didn't stop there, but climbed out of the liquid to dominate the land, some upright, many fallen, like an army exhausted by the swim.

The heat whilst on the lake had been just about tolerable – the temperature increased by day, but the mist, stirred into increased animation, seemed to negate the majority of the rise – however the air soon began to take its toll. Inflamed throats progressed to coughing fits and a perpetual, smothering dizziness, which the harlequin surroundings only exacerbated. Telde had the worst of it, rowing from her standing position. She refused to rest, and snapped at John whenever he suggested it – although she had been conversely happy to order him to do the same, following the episode with the Endless. At first he hadn't had much choice; the fatigue was enough that he had frequently slipped into unconsciousness, and the wound where his left thumb had once been had started bleeding again. But it was far less severe than the previous occasion, and his recovery was also much swifter.

Three times now, John thought, closing his eyes. Three encounters with the Endless where they had touched him, and he them. That must be why he felt so close to them; why he felt their taint under his skin and within his head and why he couldn't force them out. Worst of all, most terrifying of all, was the realisation that he *understood* them. He saw the logic in the reasoning of the Endless in the mountain: to prevent Senthis from taking all the humans, kill all the humans. It made straightforward sense, as long as you regarded humans as ants.

He recalled the first encounter in the hotel on Earth, a lifetime away. The headaches, the nestled presence in his mind. No, the two presences – because while the Endless in the hotel was out to kill him, another of its kind had prevented his brain from dying like everyone else's, and somehow allowed him to transport to this planet. He felt like a toy being squabbled over by cruel siblings. *What else did they change in my mind?* They must have given him this language of Crescent, pushed the alien words in so deep they became instinctive, as if he had always known them. And his power – god knew where that came from. Or to what degree, as he increasingly suspected, it had been twisted into something unnatural. *What damage did the tendril do? What rearranging?*

Are you the one? John remembered that first Endless had demanded, hunting for the answer inside his mind. *What one? The one that can kill Senthis? Is that why I was saved?* John felt a fury and guilt at having been spared; chosen as a favourite by this family of mass murderers. He would not be grateful. Nor controlled. Ceria had said in the boat that the Endless were not on their side, not even those who wanted to kill Senthis, and she was right. John had experienced the extraordinary bond that linked the creatures, outside of which nothing was of a significance beyond amusement. The Endless might disagree with one another, but it was like an argument within blood ties, or within yourself; swearing allegiance to the termites because of it was absurd.

The others around the campfire were talking quietly, John became aware as he opened his eyes. As if not to disturb his reverie. He licked his cracked lips and fought down a rising annoyance.

"It's a shame about him. I would have liked to hear more of his tribe's stories," Jago was saying. "You can learn a great deal through such tales, and the tribes here are rich in culture. But not as rich as my country of Brazil – that's a place where the wealth of diversity and culture would astound you. Iberic, Amerindian, Catholic, African – these heritages make my country what it is, a land whose stories have no bounds. The indigenous tales are the best. My grandmother used to tell one that I eventually traced to the Tupis of the Amazon, about the creation of night.

"There was a time when only day and its endless sunshine existed," Jago began with hardly a pause. "The secret of the night was kept at the bottom of a river by a giant cobra – this is a limbless animal with scaled skin –" Jago made an illustrative sound and movement with his hand "– who was also a powerful witch, and had a beautiful daughter with fire for hair. This daughter sought the secret of the night for her husband, as his people and all the animals of the daytime suffered greatly in the perpetual sunlight.

"Three servants were sent to the giant cobra to collect the secret. The cobra couldn't refuse the request of her daughter, who was as powerful as she was beautiful, and so gave the servants a coconut – a large nut with a hollow centre – and warned them not to open it. But on the return journey they heard strange sounds from within the coconut, chirps and squeaks and howls, which was the noise of all the animals of the night-time. The servants couldn't control their curiosity and split it open. They were immediately enveloped by darkness and the night animals that spilled out into it. The husband and his people and the animals of the daytime despaired, for they couldn't live in the perpetual dark. And so the daughter, who was as wise as she was powerful and beautiful, plucked a strand of fiery hair from her head. She placed it between day and night, forever separating the two by dawn and dusk, and allowing both times to exist in harmony."

Ceria smiled at Jago as he concluded his story. "I'm glad you're back to normal."

Manvedian coughed, either in dispute or involuntarily, then searched out a flask from a bag at his feet. He took a swallow, before offering it to Ceria next to him. She grimaced following a thirsty mouthful. "This isn't water."

Manvedian grinned. "It'll help with the throat. And get rid of the fenning awful taste of Jago's food."

Ceria couldn't prevent a slight smile from spoiling her otherwise disapproving glance. She took another sip of the flask then offered it around, but John and Jago both waved it away.

"What happened to you anyway, Jago?" Manvedian asked. "You were as quiet as a L'pen oathtaker. Not that I wasn't appreciative."

"It's a condition I've always had," Jago said, ignoring or not noticing the insult. "Most days I wake and I'm myself – I can't wait to explore the limitless knowledge of the world around me. God is in that weight, and he shows me the path through – the way to be nearer to him. When I'm discovering what he has put before me, I recognise my place in the world. I know what I'm made for. But sometimes I wake and find that same weight has become a terrible thing – all the unknown and indefinite presses down on me, and I can't find my direction, and then I'm not me anymore. I was given medication for it once, but it only made me lose myself in another way. I've grown to accept it. I always come back to myself afterwards."

"Sounds convenient," John said, not disguising the bitterness in his voice.

"Now I've returned to myself," Jago continued, "and I'm happy to feel God again."

"How can you be happy when we just found out what we did?" John asked angrily. "How can you simply continue?"

"Knowing the cause doesn't alter the result, John," Jago replied.

"Yes it damn well does! We know we were murdered now. Billions of people, in a second. Murdered by the Endless as if they were nothing. And you're acting like them, like it doesn't matter. Do you feel anything? Do you fucking care?"

"John…" Ceria tried to intervene.

"All that life being destroyed means the life remaining is more precious," Jago said.

"Go to hell, Jago," John spat back. "You're a coward. Hiding in this supposed condition. *Not yourself* – so you don't have to face the truth. Just like back on Earth. Everyone was killed, Jago. Everyone. Was that in your head, like all of this? Or does none of it matter if you weren't yourself?"

"Stop it John!" Ceria shouted, then immediately pressed a hand to her temple, as if her balance had wavered.

"Are you okay?" Manvedian asked with concern, moving a hand to her arm.

"Yes, I... I just feel tired all of a sudden," Ceria replied with a frown.

"It's been a long day. You should get some sleep," Manvedian said. "Want me to walk you to your tent?"

"No, I'm fine. But yes – yes I think I'll get some rest," Ceria said, getting falteringly to her feet. "Remember that we're all on the same side," she added, with a pointed look at John, before walking away from the campfire.

Silence descended over the three of them once she was gone. John still bristled with anger. But he had lost the words to channel it into, and perhaps the target too. He clenched his jaw and didn't look at Jago.

Manvedian began whistling quietly to himself, apparently lost in thought. He idly plunged his spit of meat into the fire. John watched it blacken and curl and was reminded of an apartment on another planet, filled with the acrid smoke of burning violins. He remembered pressing against the point of pain, of loss, and couldn't believe it had taken such effort when now he felt it piercing his being from every angle.

Eventually Manvedian stood and told them he was going to find Telde. John was glad to see him stride away, but less happy to be left alone with Jago. The latter was presently reading a book by the weak light of the fire. *Indifferent again*; but there was less venom in the thought now. Another shudder passed through the ground, causing Jago to drop the volume before he hurriedly retrieved it from the brink of the flames.

John breathed a sigh and ran his hands slowly over his face. He needed some sleep himself, he knew. But he was too restless, too frustrated. *What is it I'm grasping for?* he asked himself. *What am I angry at?* It seemed the answer should be obvious: that it had happened, that everyone had died – but he had known that for a long time now. The Endless for doing it, then. And the others for not caring enough, for not being as outraged as him. Yet there was something else, contained within that outrage. A dissatisfaction. The end of humans on Earth had been without fanfare and without reason, he had originally thought. But then he had come to this planet and realised there must be a connection, a cause behind the event. Now he had that answer, or a large part of it, and it wasn't grand enough, not sufficiently meaningful. The movement into death was too effortless.

He was angry at the universe for making things this way. For making the distance separating life and death so small, so easily pinched together. What was the point if the design was so unbalanced? If life was so exceptional yet so unexceptionally snuffed out? John needed to kick and scream the unfairness of it, but the universe was unmovable, disinterested.

"Not everyone died, John."

It took a moment for John to realise that Jago had spoken.

"What?"

"You were wrong in what you said," Jago remarked, looking up from his book. "Not everyone died on Earth. There's you and me, and there's the inhabitants of the towns transported here."

John was surprised, and a little abashed. He gave a faint nod in reply. "Do you think they're still alive?"

"I don't know," Jago responded simply, and returned his attention to the book.

He was right, John thought. The people from the Russian town and the other settlements – they hadn't died on Earth. They could be somewhere on Crescent, still alive. *Changed*, the Endless had said. *What did it mean?* He felt as if he was scratching at the edge of a dark truth, but it wouldn't yet reveal itself.

Give your head a rest, he told himself. *Accept what Jago has given you – a small measure of hope to work with.*

He gazed out at the desert, a landscape made of shadows and silhouettes, over which the Spirit storm hung like an open secret. He found himself softly humming a tune. It was a melody from the past – from his childhood, something from Earth. An old pop song, or the theme to some long-forgotten television show. He wondered what had suddenly put it into his head. *You really are tired, John.* Instead of staring into the dark he should be talking to Jago. *At least ask him about the book.* He leant forward with that purpose, but the question suddenly lodged in his throat as a shock of comprehension shot through him.

"Oh Christ, Jago. I know why Manvedian's so familiar to me," John said. "He's from Earth."

Jago looked up from his book in surprise. "Manvedian is from Ferol. He's part of their resistance."

"No he isn't – I mean yes, he's part of the resistance. But Telde said herself that she'd known him for less than two years," John said. "That tune he was whistling, I remember it. I've heard it before – on Earth, years and years ago. How else could he know it? And there's more besides that. I told you before he was familiar, even though I've never met him – but I have, in a way. You have, too. You must have noticed how people on this planet move differently – only subtly, but it's in their expressions, their body language, unconscious things I can't describe. But not in Manvedian, despite his words and accent. The way he moves is familiar, do you understand? Because we've seen it before. He's been lying, Jago. He's not from Crescent."

"Why would he pretend?" Jago asked.

"I don't know. But it can't be good," John replied. He struggled to think of more he could say to persuade Jago of his conviction, but the man's face abruptly changed, as if in realisation. "What is it?"

"We changed energies to retain selected of you like three of you here," Jago recited. "That's what the Endless said in the mountain. Me, you – and Manvedian."

So he does remember, John thought. But that didn't matter now. "I have to warn Telde."

"There could be many explanations for the deception," Jago said as John stood.

"Go wake Ceria and tell her," John said. "I'll find Telde and Manvedian. He can explain the reasons himself."

John waited until Jago assented, then turned and ran. He aimed for the general direction in which Telde had previously gone, yet soon realised his approximation was a vague one, and, moreover, that he had no idea how far she had travelled. But at least the eerie light of the distant storm granted him some degree of visibility in the rocky terrain. He hurdled the smaller protrusions of stone, circumvented the larger aggregations, searching in vain whilst the towering monoliths watched on like unhelpful sentinels.

Soon he was breathing hard and sweating profusely in the heat. *Damn it. This is taking too long.* He hesitated, then began calling out Telde's name, with increasing volume, as he continued his search. Finally a shape emerged out of the dark in front of him; dull crimson glimmered as it swiftly approached.

"Blood and gods man, stop shouting," Telde whispered sharply upon reaching him, the effect marred by a rasping cough that obscured her last word. She recovered, then saw his expression. "What's happened?"

John glanced past her, but could make out no other figures. "Where's Manvedian?"

"What? I haven't seen him since the camp," Telde said with a frown. "What is it, John?"

John took a deep breath. "He's from Earth, Telde. Manvedian is from my planet, not Crescent."

Telde studied him, then shook her head wearily, annoyed. "You go too far this time. Manvedian is part of the resistance. He had a wife in Ferol."

"Did you ever see her?" John asked. "Did anyone know him before he joined?"

Telde considered that for a moment before answering. "There are many in the resistance with unclear pasts. It's not a coincidence. They're drawn to us, as they have no other ties left. Climbe trusts Manvedian. I know you have something against him, but –"

"Telde, listen to me," John interrupted, grasping her arm. "I'm certain in this. Trust me." He let the weight of his words linger, and saw a resultant change in Telde's eyes – if not quite belief, then at least uncertainty. "If he lied about this," he added, "then what else?"

"Where is he now?" Telde asked, at length.

"He said he was coming to find you."

Telde looked away in thought, then snapped her gaze back to him. "Ceria."

The name had barely left her lips before she was sprinting away, back towards the camp. John struggled to keep up with her pace; his throat felt as if it were on fire. On several occasions he lost track of Telde's shape in the gloom, only to be rescued by the pale flash of the sword on her back. For the first time John began to question whether he might be wrong. What if he was creating all of this fuss for nothing? Or simply due to his dislike of the man? But he quickly dismissed the thoughts. He was sure. He should be wishing that he wasn't.

When John reached the camp, where their makeshift tents huddled under an overhanging claw of rock, Telde was already searching beneath the stretch of cloth that she and Ceria shared. It was clear by her expression that no-one was here. John noticed that there were only two tents; Manvedian's was gone, along with his belongings. Telde's eyes met John's. He saw an increasing panic in that dazzling green, which at that instant he realised he would do anything to appease. But he didn't have time to dwell on the awareness, as Telde again raced away. John followed, too breathless and occupied with the task of keeping up to ask where they were going. The answer was soon evident, however, as he saw the expanding colours of the mist ahead of him. *The boat.*

They swiftly covered the few hundred yards to the lake. Telde then turned and dashed along its edge. John spotted in the distance the immense slab of rock – a fallen monolith protruding over the lake – at which they had moored the boat. He thought he saw figures on top of the stone. He sprinted towards it, arriving just behind Telde, who had stopped a small way in front of the raised platform. She was staring at the figures above her, which now resolved themselves: Manvedian and Ceria were standing together at one end, the boat below them – no, he was holding her up, John saw with dreadful comprehension, she was unconscious in his arms, and he held a dagger to her throat. Jago stood at the opposite end of the vast stone, his hands up, repeating *don't, don't*.

Oh shit, John thought, *oh god*.

"That's close enough, stop there," Manvedian called down as he saw Telde. His voice was calm and cold. It matched his expression.

"What are you doing, Manvedian?" Telde asked stiffly, unsheathing the sword from her back.

"I'd have thought that was obvious," Manvedian replied. "Throw your sword in the lake. Do it, or I'll open her throat and drop her in instead."

Telde stared back at Manvedian, her eyes hard and furious. "You work for the half-man."

The shifting wall of colour behind Manvedian illuminated half of his face, and reflected off the silver-white of the dagger as he pressed it against Ceria's neck. "I'm either taking her or killing her, Telde. Toss the sword."

Telde hesitated, then, to John's dismay, threw the long, double-edged sword into the lake without further protest. There was a faint fizzing as the etched blade sank slowly into the liquid, before it was enveloped entirely by the thick colours. Somewhere in the distance the land rumbled.

"How can you do this to Ceria?" Telde asked, turning angrily back to Manvedian.

Manvedian let out a bitter laugh. "Do you even realise

what a hypocrite you are? So fenning self-righteous – and yet you're no better than me. We both seek to use her for our own gain."

"It's for Ferol, not for myself," Telde replied.

Out of the corner of his vision John saw Jago make a small movement towards Manvedian, who instantly brought the blade under Ceria's chin in response.

"Jago, don't," John called out, hoping for once his friend would listen to him. *This can't be happening.*

"Why don't you tell your little followers the truth, Telde?" Manvedian asked, pointing the dagger momentarily at Jago and John. "Tell them about you and Climbe's plan. To sacrifice Ceria."

"You know nothing of it," Telde snapped back. "Ceria would be the first to understand."

"Would she? Then you've told her, I suppose – told her how you would use her against Senthis," Manvedian said contemptuously. "You know she wouldn't have a chance of survival. Even if by some miracle she managed to get close enough to use her abilities against him, you know what it would do to her. All that power, all that corruption going into her. You're not only prepared to kill her, but to turn her into a monster. Would she understand that?"

John glanced at Telde: was that the truth? *She wouldn't do that*, he thought. *Not to Ceria.*

Telde glared up at Manvedian, her face twisted with rage, but when she spoke her voice was level. "You're right, she doesn't deserve that fate. So take me instead. If it's me you resent, then take me."

"*Godsblood,* Telde. You don't get it – this isn't personal," Manvedian replied. "You've lost already. Why don't any of you see that? Shit, I wish you were the winning side. I do. But you've got to face the truth. This is about survival."

"You wouldn't say that if you were from Ferol," Telde said.

Manvedian was taken aback. He glanced at John, his head

cocked, before returning his gaze to Telde and shrugging. "No, I'm not from Ferol. So there'll be no convincing me," he said, stepping back towards the boat.

"You won't survive the lake air," Telde said quickly. *Desperately,* John thought. He had been expecting her to say or do something to stop this, he realised, but she was as helpless as him. Manvedian was going to take Ceria. They couldn't stop him. *Oh god.*

Manvedian started to reply but his words were swallowed by a sudden shudder in the ground around them. The quake rapidly increased in force until John was thrown off balance, along with Telde. When he looked up Jago was running towards Manvedian, too fast for John to call out, and the dagger moved unnaturally, pointing away from Ceria as the two men came together – but John lost sight of them as a powerful tremor knocked him from his feet. He thought he heard someone cry out, and when the shaking had subsided enough for him to look again he could no longer see Jago, and Manvedian was lowering Ceria into the boat. Telde charged past John, sprinting toward the end of the fallen monolith, where a jagged ascent led to the platform above. John pushed himself up and quickly followed as she scrambled up the stone.

When he pulled himself over the lip of the rock seconds after Telde, he could see that the boat was already a distance away, fading into the mist. Jago was lying at the far end of the stone and – *Oh no.* John rushed to him, and saw the blood soaked through his light grey robe, the dagger buried in his chest. Jago gasped wetly for air, his eyes wide with shock. *Oh shit oh god what do I do?* John looked to Telde for help – but she was preparing to leap after the boat.

"No!" he exclaimed, hurriedly moving in front of her. "It's too far!"

Telde pushed him angrily aside. "Get out of my way!"

"You can't reach them," John implored. "You can't help her if you're dead."

Telde didn't respond, but stood staring after the boat. John returned to Jago. He knelt by the man's side as he rasped and coughed up blood. He moved his hands to the hilt of the dagger, seized by panic and uncertainty. *What do I do?* He looked up at Telde, who had remained stationary at the edge of the rock. "Help me," John cried out. "For god's sake help me!"

Telde finally reacted, and moved to kneel on the opposite side of Jago. She pushed John's hands away from the dagger hilt, then ripped open the robe around the blade, her face emotionless as she studied the wound. John could see nothing but blood, dark and thick. Telde took John's arm and tore the sleeve from his shirt. She bundled the cloth against the wound, pressing it down with both hands. Jago grunted weakly beneath her. John thought there was something else in her expression, but he refused to acknowledge it.

He looked down at Jago, taking the man's hand. "You're okay, Jago. You're alright."

Jago tried to speak but only blood bubbled out of his mouth. John found it difficult to meet his eyes. His hand was trembling.

"It's in his heart, John," Telde said. John hated her for the finality in her tone. He refused it.

"You're okay, Jago. You'll be okay."

Jago began convulsing and retching more blood. Telde kept the pressure on his wound but made no other move. *She's a soldier,* John told himself, *she knows what she's doing.* He waited for an instruction from her, some canny field surgery that would fix this.

At length she stood, and at first John was relieved that she was taking action and would tell him what to do. But the feeling was replaced by a rush of outrage as he realised her stance was one of acceptance.

"What are you doing?" he asked incredulously. He moved his hands to the cloth, pushed it back down on the wound, felt warm blood on his fingers. "Help him!"

"I'm sorry, John."

John kept his hands on Jago's chest and whispered to him that he would be okay, and repeated it, over and over, because he needed to know that Telde was wrong, that she had given up too soon. Jago had stopped heaving and gasping and John took it as a sign of improvement. But his chest wasn't moving and he had the sudden apprehension that the pressure might be preventing him from breathing. He quickly removed his hands and glanced at Jago's face which was surprised, questioning, and almost caused him to move them back in apology, but the expression was fixed, and John felt tears in his eyes and wiped them away angrily. There was blood on Jago's chin and he tried to clean it off, but his fingers were covered in blood and when he searched for a clean part of his shirt he saw blood everywhere there too and he stumbled backwards and crawled away from Jago in abhorrence.

Telde was staring into the mist. John couldn't breathe. He could feel blood filling his throat, thick and dark and choking him, but when he turned on his side to vomit only a scarce pale matter was ejected. Near his head Jago's bare legs stuck out from the tattered edges of his robe. John could see rashes on his skin from the heat, scratches and bruises from the travel – fresh proof that at any moment he would jump to his feet. *It can't be this quick,* John's thoughts protested and raged, *it can't be this easy.*

But another, cruel voice kept pronouncing the truth and wouldn't be supressed. *Jago is dead, and Ceria and Manvedian are gone.*

PART IV:
SACRIFICE

I am Maurice Joshua Vedian, he tells himself. It is important that he remembers this but he does not know why. He sits on the edge of his bed and looks out of the open window at a telegraph pole surrounded by blue. He is hot and knows that in this heat fat black flies will come in and buzz close to his ears and land on his skin but he is not afraid of them as he used to be. Because his mom told him the truth. The flies came to him because they were lost and knew he could show them how to get outside again. So now he was not afraid and liked to find them and take them to gaping windows and doors.

But there are no flies currently because the air is thick and charged with something he dreads and he goes out into the hallway and is relieved to find his mother in the bathroom. She is putting on make-up even though it is the middle of the day. He wonders why but he knows why (is this the past?) and then she is gone and he hears her downstairs with him. *The shouting starts and he retreats to his bedroom and closes the door and turns on the television. His favourite program is on. He turns up the volume and the theme tune drowns out everything. He hums and whistles along.*

But he knows what is happening and now he is downstairs hidden in the closet as they argue and there is another thud and a cry and he knows what he has to do. There is a long silver-white dagger in his hands. He whistles to himself and knows what he has to do. But as he looks down at the dagger he realises that this is the past, this is old hurt and he knows what happens after and that his mother will betray him. Tears sting his eyes. How can she take his *side over her son's? How can she send her son away and lock him up in a terrible place for saving her?*

Not this time, he tells himself. This time he knows the truth of the world and he knows he is alone. He drops the dagger and runs. They are behind him, chasing, blaming, and the front door that should be there isn't but he sees the entrance to the basement and rushes through. He runs down the stairs and enters a cavern of concrete filled with cars. There are two men in the car park and he rushes to them, screaming for help.

But as he reaches their hard expressions he remembers they cannot help him and he can only rely on himself. He recognises the men. And he is embarrassed and confused that he asked for help when all he needs is himself. These men are beneath him. He worries that he is still young but feels his face and hair and knows he is older now and he looks into the faces of the men with confidence. He remembers that fear and respect are vital in this game and as he sees it in their eyes he is pleased and soothed to feel this control. He looks down for his gun and finds blood on his hands and sleeves.

When he looks back up the men are lying on the ground like everyone else on Earth. But I didn't kill them, he tells himself, I'm not to blame.

The concrete walls are moving around him, enclosing, and they are no longer concrete but soil and roots and rock. They darken and close until he is in a living tunnel that he knows so well. Moist earth presses against his body, it urges him forward (towards?). He feels the pulse of the land surrounding him, but it is much weaker now (than when?).

He emerges into the heart. Faint blue illuminates the circular chamber. Ancient runes pulse with the land and whisper desolation and pain and ending, but their voices are fading and almost gone. Across the room he can see it, the wild dark, the shadow from which it comes. It has escaped already – the elemental presence is here, he can sense its boundless power. He cannot look at it, he cannot turn towards it. Preserver and destroyer, blackness and light, bloom and ruin. Take it, the land wills him, the wet earth thrills him towards it.

But he cannot, he tells himself, he tells the land. He refuses (if he takes it, what will he become?) and the land is too weak to hold him and he breaks free of its embrace. It is too much to risk.

He escapes, upwards, towards the air, and below him Som'syere wails.

21

Manvedian woke up clawing at air, before realising that he was free and it was only a weak breeze that held him. *Goddamn dream.* He had hoped it would plague him less often, or at least be of less intensity, now that he was clear of the Spirit-soaked desert. But the dream and its inhabitant continued to dominate his sleep.

He stretched out his arms and winced at an ache in his neck. The seat at the front of the carriage, which in truth was little more than a protruding wooden ledge, creaked and listed under his weight. He cursed himself for falling asleep in the first place. The two harnessed jallers in front of him had taken the opportunity to stop and graze the scant vegetation at the side of the road, and had dragged the carriage into a ditch as a result. He turned to search out a flask from his bag to soothe both his throat and his irritation, and couldn't help a glance into the covered trailer behind him. At its far end was a shape enclosed by blankets. He uncorked the flask and took a long drink.

Focus, he told himself. *This is the easy part, don't fuck it up now.* He removed the wide-brimmed leather hat that had been sheltering his eyes from the afternoon sun, and let the brightness dazzle him awake. The travel on the lake, and after it, had left him in a weakened state, Manvedian knew. But it was simple from now on – all he had to do was continue north. Get to Ferol and reap the benefits of all the months of work.

He scratched at his neck, only realising the unconscious action when he felt the sting of the wound beneath his shirt collar. A souvenir from the lake; from when the Spirit storm had passed near the boat, convulsing the viscous liquid enough to send a shower of colour over the tall walls of the vessel, searing his skin where it landed. A tensun later and the lesion didn't seem to be healing, and its prickling pain increasingly nagged at him. He was annoyed to discover a trace of righteousness involved with the suffering. *Leave that shit for Telde.* Guilt was a fool's distraction.

He left the flask on the seat and jumped down from the carriage. The soil was almost as hard as stone, but it was still soil. Along with the vegetation and trees, though sparse and equally desiccated, its presence meant that the landscape was a vast improvement over the black nothingness of the desert. Manvedian walked to the front left wheel of the vehicle, and saw to his relief that the rut in which it lay was not too severe. The jallers would be able to pull the trailer back onto the relative flat of the road, if he could coax them that way.

Half a miracle the wheel didn't snap, he thought, scowling at its slim wood and absent spokes. Behind it the trailer's shallow sides were a faded burnt orange, the old cracks in the wood filled with tar, whilst the more recent fissures had been left to prosper. Above, the once-white canvas was stretched over an arched frame and brandished a number of garish tassels alongside its stains and tears, further evidence of a more glamorous past. Manvedian wondered where the trader had found it. Or, as was more likely, from whom she had stolen it.

He moved to the front of the jallers, locating the rope harness that hung between their shaggy heads. Large bovine eyes stared dumbly at him. At least they appeared a sturdy Tvennik stock – more reliable than the vehicle they hauled. From the front, with its canvas drawn over the foremost arch and cord tied across the opening, the carriage reminded Manvedian of something out of the Wild West, if more oriental and dainty. He was about to chastise himself for thinking in such Earthly terms, as he had trained himself so rigorously to do, before he realised that it was no longer necessary. He didn't have to hide anymore. He didn't have to think like them.

Once he had guided the animals back to the road – employing the bribe of a water pail filled from the supply held within the carriage – he pulled himself back onto the front seat. He glanced behind him at the bundled shape within the trailer, then replaced his hat and took up the reins. The jallers began moving after some initial stubbornness, and soon the vehicle was jolting along the dirt road at a reasonable pace. Manvedian felt vaguely ridiculous presiding over the rickety carriage. And a restlessness, a lack of certainty within himself. But the transport wasn't responsible for the latter, he knew. *Wait it out.*

At least he didn't expect to encounter anyone else travelling the road. A long disused trade route, Mercy's End Pass was named after the far-flung outpost it had once linked so prosperously to the south of Ireldelor, before the nearby Black Sea tribes had ceased trading with the town, stripping it of its exotic exports and of its population in consequence. Now Mercy's End was a conversational byword for riches swiftly lost – which was how Manvedian had heard of it in the first place.

After Edemon but before they had reached the Savage Lands, he had managed to send away several messages, each containing a separate contingency dependent on where he eventually exited the Black Sea's border. Mercy's End had been one of the preferable options, if unlikely – he had not expected to be able to leave the desert at such a north-eastern point. But the lake had been a godsend, allowing for such swift travel almost to the border of the Sea, and for him to avoid the south-eastern Regent's lands, towards which Telde would surely be forced to continue. On foot, over the scorching black wasteland. She stood no chance of catching him now, Manvedian thought with some satisfaction.

As thorough as the plans held within his messages had been, and as substantial the rewards promised, it was still with some surprise that he had found the trader waiting for him at the Mercy's End outpost. Relief, too, after the punishing walk from the edge of the Black Sea, where he had had to rely on scrawled maps that were comparable only in their sparse detail. The dour face of the trader, sunk into a thick trunk of a neck, consumed by a sexless lump of a body, welcomed him with immediate complaints about how she had waited in the abandoned town for days before his arrival. She had sputtered an obviously fake name from a mouth left to hang perpetually open, as if it wasn't worth the unpaid work to close it. He knew exactly what kind of trader she was, but that was what he had wanted; she was more likely to be discreet.

She had brought all of the supplies he had requested: clean clothes, food and water, the shackles, the jallers – if two instead of three, and if attached to an impractical trailer. She had demanded more money for her time, but Manvedian would have been concerned if she hadn't. Her questions about the girl he was carrying ended when he told her she had died during the travel.

The carriage rattled on. Its wheels squealed in protest at the hard road, and were joined by the concurring grunts of the jallers. As the hours passed, the flat landscape began to lift itself into hillocks and gentle wolds. Even if fairly devoid of life, the dreary greys and infrequent dashes of green remained a soothing replacement for jagged black or dizzying, kaleidoscopic colour. The further he travelled into Ireldelor, Manvedian knew, the more the vegetation would venture upon and eventually conquer the bare land. And with it would come rain – he anticipated that like some precious pleasure after the weeks of parched heat. His mind roamed briefly to the forests of Ferol: he saw the early morning haze that regularly bathed the ancient woodlands, and wondered why he thought of it now – he had never paid much regard to such scenes.

He pushed the image from his mind, scratched his neck, then glanced at his sleeve and was momentarily surprised to find it clean and white. The clothes from the trader, of course. The shirt was not exactly to his tastes – too much lace, and the cuffs were overly voluminous – but it was preferable to its sodden and stained predecessor.

Eventually the skies began to dim, the sun diving for shelter behind a distant arch of hills. Manvedian removed his hat and gladly felt the relative cool of the evening. After a time there was rustling from behind, followed by a series of coughs.

"I asked you not to give me that poison again," a hoarse voice said.

Manvedian didn't reply, and kept his eyes on the road.

"Did you hear me?" Ceria continued, her voice regaining some of its character. There was a rattling from within the trailer. Manvedian knew she would be discovering the metal clasp and fetters attaching her ankle to a beam of the vehicle's frame.

"Where are we?" she demanded. On receiving no answer, there was further rattling, then a loud succession of clatters and bangs. The carriage began to sway unsteadily.

"Stop that!" Manvedian finally retaliated. He turned and peered into the dim light of the trailer behind him: a pair of black eyes glowered back.

"I'm not an animal you can chain up," Ceria said. "I'm not merchandise for delivery."

Manvedian returned his gaze to the road. "That's exactly what you are."

"You don't believe that," Ceria replied quietly, after a time.

Soon she would be pestering him again about it being *not too late*, Manvedian thought. Telling him that he *didn't truly want to do this*, that he was *a good man in his heart*. Despite his disinterest, which he went to great lengths to communicate, she had repeated similar appeals every time she had been conscious in the last week.

"So you're truly going to deliver me to the half-man?" Ceria asked disbelievingly. "He will imprison me. Torture me or kill me. Or worse. And you will simply give me to him, as if I'm an animal to be slaughtered."

"Like Telde would have," Manvedian replied.

"It's not the same. You know that."

He had told her about the plans of Climbe and Telde, how they had intended to use her as a weapon against Senthis. At first she had refused to believe him. That had eventually changed into a stoic acceptance, a submission to her sacrificial role. *Telde would be proud,* Manvedian reflected scornfully. He had also revealed that he was from Earth, not from *her* Ferol, in the hope that she would stop attempting to appeal to his sense of allegiance.

But he hadn't told her everything. Not about Jago.

"There's clean clothes in the chest," Manvedian said in a neutral voice, "as well as water and food."

"Is it laced with poison again?" Ceria snapped.

"It's not poison," Manvedian said, irritated. "It's a sleeping draught, nothing more. It was for your own protection."

"Because my health is your principal concern."

"Merchandise is more valuable undamaged," Manvedian replied, and immediately reproached himself for rising to the bait. He regretted more than ever the fact that his supply of the sleeping draught was nearly at an end. *Godscursing girl.* Awake she wouldn't allow him a moment's peace. But it didn't matter. He could deal with her. All she had to fight with were her words, and they were of little power against him.

The carriage began to shake again. Manvedian did his best to ignore it. He whistled under his breath and twitched the reins to reassure the jallers. After some minutes the swaying ceased, and a short silence followed. Then movement; he heard the opening of the chest, Ceria drinking. The rattle of chain and a loud sigh.

"You need to take this shackle off my ankle if I'm to change my clothes."

"Make do with a shirt for now."

A few murmured curses. More rattling. Manvedian looked back into the trailer. Ceria stood facing away from him as she pulled her jerkin over her head. A shaft of light passed through the perforated canvas and rested upon the smooth skin of her back, the side of a breast. He saw the markings of the rune whose lines and curves seemed to flow with her contours, as if a language summoned by her body. Ceria noticed his gaze, and he quickly turned away.

A small derisive laugh. "So you will kidnap me, but you're too courteous to leer at me naked."

"Don't make me tie that mouth of yours," Manvedian muttered.

He glared at the road, which stretched apathetically on, and spurred the jallers to a faster trot. The hills were increasing in magnitude on both sides; if the maps were correct, they would eventually form an enclosing valley that was days in length.

A memory forced its way into his mind: black monolithic stone, a wall of shifting colour, blue pulsing the sky. A bloody sleeve. The shock on Jago's face. Why did it haunt him? It wasn't as if he hadn't killed men before. *But the others were men like me.* Men that deserved it, or at least knew the game they were playing. *Goddamn idiot, why did you have to do it? Why try to be a fucking hero?* Jago had used his power. Manvedian had warned him but still he made the attempt. He had made his choice.

"This is a man's shirt," Ceria said from the back of the carriage. Then, after a few moments, "Remove this shackle, so I can put on the leggings."

Manvedian ignored her and picked up the flask next to him. *It's done,* he told himself as he took a large mouthful. *Let it go.* It was regrettable, but that was all. Any guilt he felt was pointless, counterproductive. *Don't be weak. Not now.*

"You'll have to at some point," Ceria continued, "unless you expect me to relieve myself in here."

Besides, any feelings he might have, any guilts or doubts, were to be expected. Expected, and not real. They didn't belong to him. Two years he had spent in the resistance, after being sent to the half-man by Niscem; two years of playing the part, of posing as a Ferolian, a Crescentian. Sharing the loves and hates of his colleagues, their jokes and sadnesses, their victories and losses – forging his own history and identity alongside them. He knew from experience the best way to infiltrate a group was not only to behave like those around him, but to think and feel like them. Not posing as a Ferolian, *being* a Ferolian. It had required that he bury the core of him that didn't fit, forget the self behind the act.

"Where did you find this carriage? Did you hurt anyone to get it?"

Of course it would have its effects. This restlessness he felt, this emptiness, it was simply a by-product of those two years. The space left from abandoning the role. The questions that came in his half-sleep, always at cowardly times – Does the other you really exist? Who is he? Are you sure you want to become him again? – were the incidental results of spending so long in character. *Wait it out.* The doubts would eventually lose their voices, and then he could return to himself. *Remember why you did all this. Remember that Manvedian doesn't exist.*

"How is your neck? That wound will only get worse, you know."

The bloody sleeve invaded his thoughts, followed by Climbe's gaunt and ravaged face, then the god in the mountain. But his mind had slipped up with the last: that was comfortable territory, he was confident with his decisions in regards to it. Yes, he had delayed his taking of Ceria, but rightly, and not for any other reason beyond convenience and opportunity. To see what advantage the lake could give him, and to discover the truth about the Endless in the mountain. The latter was valuable knowledge, especially if it turned out to be a defector. The more cards he held, the better.

But *okay*, he conceded, *alright*, he hadn't expected the rest. What the Endless had told them. The merciless scale of it.

"You will never forgive yourself if you do this. Manvedian. I know you can hear me."

He was indebted to the Endless for saving him from Earth. *No, not indebted,* Manvedian thought, *such obligations don't exist.* Appreciative, then, that they had yanked him from the dead world, even if the reason remained a mystery. But at the mountain he learnt that the Endless had been responsible for the human extinction to begin with. The Endless and Senthis. He had suspected that truth before, he realised – after all, he knew what the half-man had done to the towns he transported – albeit he didn't know how or why. Yet he hadn't faced it, even after what the Endless did to Ferol, and to Edemon, after he had witnessed what they were capable of. Was that the offence his mind was charging him with? Was that what it wanted him to see? But *so what* – even if that was the case, Manvedian thought, even if he had refused to recognise the truth, then *so what?* It was the smart choice. He couldn't change what had happened. He had no control over that, only over his own fate. And this way it was easier to do as was necessary, to take the side of Senthis. It wasn't his fault the winners had already been decided.

"You're not like Senthis. You can still go back. It's not too late."

"Godscurseyou shut up!" Manvedian turned sharply to shout. "I killed Jago, Ceria. And I will kill you if you don't shut up."

Ceria stood in a black shirt that stretched halfway to her knees, staring back at him with a startled expression. "You're lying."

"I stabbed him in the heart and left him to die."

"No, you didn't. You wouldn't do that."

"You don't know me," Manvedian replied. "He got in my way and I killed him."

"Stop saying that!" Ceria cried out. Tears filled her eyes. "Please, Manvedian. You're lying. Tell me that you're lying."

"No, I'm not," Manvedian said, keeping his eyes fixed on hers. Then he turned, feeling a cold satisfaction as he faced the road once more. No more weakness. He had severed the lingering bond that needed to be cut. For some time there was a soft weeping from behind him, then silence.

"Why?" Ceria finally asked. "Jago would never hurt anyone. Why?"

"He tried to stop me from taking you," Manvedian replied, not looking back. "He gave me no choice."

"You had a choice. You always have a choice," Ceria said. "You decided to kill him."

Manvedian clenched his jaw and forced a shrug.

"I was wrong. You're exactly the same as the half-man and the Endless. Evil. A murderer."

"Gods, will you stop being so fenning naive?" Manvedian said, turning to her. "There's no such thing as good and evil, Ceria. Morality is wishful thinking. There'll be no punishment for what I did. Do you think the world cares? Do you think Senthis will be made to suffer for his sins by wrathful gods?

"There are two types of people," he pressed, unable to stop himself, "those who survive, and those who get used up. Those strong enough to face the reality of the world – and recognise it's a game of power and nothing else – and those who die suddenly and uselessly, wondering with their last thoughts why they couldn't do a fucking thing to stop it. A game of power, that's it. No other rules. You can deny it all you want, smother it with gods to hide the truth, to make you feel better – but the sooner you accept it, the better chance you have at surviving. Because that's all there is – scraping together as much power as you can to protect yourself."

"You're wrong," Ceria said, her dark eyes defiant. "Life is more. You are wrong. I'd rather die than live such an empty existence."

"Then you'll die, and your sacrifice will be forgotten and meaningless. Just another used up body. I plan on living. On making the most of a rigged game." He waved an exasperated hand. "That's what you and Telde and Climbe and all the others in the resistance always failed to understand. *You can't win* – you can't change the design of things just because it's unfair. Just because it isn't right. Those with the power win – Senthis wins. Anyone too blind to see that deserves what they get."

"Do I deserve it? Do you think Jago deserved it? His death – his life – is not meaningless, even if you treated it that way. He is why we fight against people like you, why we will always fight against the world you would allow," Ceria said, not taking her eyes from him. "I will never forgive you, Manvedian."

Manvedian was about to reply that her forgiveness didn't matter – how could it in the world he had described? – but he was stopped by a noise from the road ahead. He turned to stare into the gloom in front of the jallers, the road barely visible beyond a dozen yards in the scraps of evening light. A clatter of hooves. And *there* – movement. Something was travelling rapidly towards them.

"Lie down and cover yourself," Manvedian said brusquely. Ceria began to protest, but he interrupted her. "Do it now!"

It wasn't clear whether she followed his instruction or not, as he couldn't risk looking back into the carriage. Three riders had materialised out of the darkness, and slowed their gallop as they approached. Three men, Manvedian quickly discerned, along with the glint of metal: weapons, armour. The mounts he recognised as jahtis, half-breeds that were swift in both their step and lifespan – and were accordingly expensive. If a coincidental meeting on the obsolete trade route was unlikely before, the dress and mounts of the men extinguished any such innocent possibility. Manvedian's hand moved instinctively to his boot, but the dagger he sought was no longer there; he quickly retrieved a smaller blade from within his sleeve and rested it on his thigh, beneath his palm.

He had no option but to slow the trailer to a stop as the men reined in their mounts in front, blocking the path. The ungainly jahtis gulped down air, long strings of saliva hanging from their jaws. Two of the riders remained stationary before the carriage, whilst the third trotted his mongrel casually around the side, inspecting the canvas. Manvedian glanced at him, then shifted his gaze to the left rider of the two in front, who possessed an obvious air of authority: a heavyset man, his skin, cropped hair, and week's growth of beard an indeterminable colour beneath a homogeneous coating of dirt. He wore layers of heavy leather with smatterings of chain, and two axes protruded above his shoulders. *A mercenary, and confident enough not to hide it.* The man licked dust from his dry lips and stared at him, sizing him up just as Manvedian was doing the same, and he waited, letting it be known that he was at ease, that he was in control.

"Manvedian, is it?" he asked finally, in a speech so thick it was almost slurred. "We're here to escort you to Ferol."

"I'm touched," Manvedian replied, "but I'm sure I'll manage on my own."

Godsdamnit. The messages. He had known they were a risk when he sent them. Somewhere along the line – the messengers, the recipients, the trader at Mercy's End, it didn't really matter – the information of his whereabouts had been sold. Manvedian had hoped that the news of Ceria's death – if the trader was as open-mouthed as her appearance suggested – would put off any others working for Senthis, or those sniffing around for opportunity. But it was always a far-fetched hope.

The man spat on the floor, then inclined his head toward the carriage. "She in there?"

"Who?"

The mercenary grinned. "We ain't interested in your

girlfriend. We've been tasked to get you to the city in one piece, that's all."

Manvedian knew that further argument was useless. Both of them were aware of the subtext: the mercenaries would not be leaving, Manvedian would not be able to escape on this road, and when they had the chance to take Ceria and receive the credit themselves – it was tacitly understood in those few words and scrutinising stares, one mercenary to another, nothing personal – they would not hesitate. *Godsfuckit.*

The three riders settled their mounts into step a distance ahead of the cart as Manvedian drove the jallers forward, if at a reduced pace now. *Their pace.* The men talked languidly amongst themselves, muttered remarks preceding low laughter; they were confident that Manvedian was trapped. *And they're right.* Why hadn't he seen this coming? Night began to enclose the travellers and so too did the valley, the hills lurching up into the encouraging dark of the sky. One of the men lit a torch and carried it as he rode. The jahtis continued their loud wheezing even at the slower pace, as if never able to consume a sufficient amount of air.

After a time, Ceria spoke in a hushed voice from behind him, asking about the men. He told her they were mercenaries, sent by Senthis or acting on their own power, and that they would try to take her for themselves.

"You don't want that to happen, believe it," he added under his breath. "They're much worse than me."

"Will you kill these men, too?" Ceria asked.

"It's very likely."

"Your master sends thugs to take your prize, that's how little he cares about you," she whispered. "He doesn't hold any loyalty for you."

"Of course he doesn't. Did you listen to anything I said?"

"What's the point of surviving if your life contains only killing and betrayal?"

Manvedian left the question unanswered and stared grimly forward. The carriage creaked and shuddered on, the jallers grunting, the jahtis wheezing. The man with the twin axes glanced back at him, a small smile on his lips. It would take at least three tensuns yet to reach Ferol, Manvedian knew. He wondered when they would make their move. Not that it mattered; he would be ready when it came. Or he would deal with them before that.

Ceria is mine. He would be the one delivering her to the half-man. *Focus. Get it done.* He whistled quietly to himself, and pushed down the rage that he felt, forced it into the same place as frustration and uncertainty and guilt; he had no use for those weaknesses.

They wouldn't take away his control. *She is mine.*

22

"Are they gone?"

"I don't know. Stay quiet."

"They must've passed us by now."

"Stay quiet."

John sighed, quietly, and rolled onto his side, facing away from Telde. It was almost pitch black beneath the immense slice of rock, which was wedged at an angle into the land like a shard expelled by a colossal explosion. The two of them lay concealed in the trench it had gouged. John could see a slither of sky in the interval between the edge of the rock and the land; a sky equally dark apart from its spray of starlight. He wiped sweat from his brow. It felt as though they were being swallowed by a desiccated mouth of the desert.

He heard the soft clink of Telde's armour as she shifted next to him. Her slow breathing.

"They'll be far away by now," John whispered.

"Shut up." John felt a sharp jab in his back, and fought the temptation to make a noise to spite her.

Silence followed. He brushed a lock of sodden hair from his eyes, then ran his hand over the heavy stubble covering his jaw. *Close to a full beard by now,* John thought. He hadn't seen his reflection in weeks. As he licked his cracked, painful lips, he reflected that that was probably fortunate.

A sound from above: a faint flutter – a slow beating?

"What was that?" John asked after a few moments.

"I don't know."

Another noise; a rush of air, a distant shriek. *Not a human sound*, John thought. *But if it's not the tribes, then what?* He inched closer to the gap to peer through, but found only darkness in his limited view of the surface. In the newly revealed section of sky, however, he could see a moon: one of the smaller satellites that orbited the planet along with Ternerid, just large enough to exhibit a rusty fingerprint of colour. Its light seemed to flicker momentarily as he watched, as if something had passed in front.

John waited, but saw and heard nothing further. Inventions of his exhausted mind, no doubt. The conclusion gave him a momentary déjà vu. He sighed inwardly and forced his tense body to relax. It wasn't only his mind that was tired, it was all of him, a weariness that had sunk through to his core. The sweat-soaked clothes, the scorched skin, the blistered feet, muscles that cramped and struggled to heave a leaden body – it was almost as though this was his default condition, he couldn't recall any other state of being. *Or is it that you don't want to, John?*

Two tensuns of the relentless and numbing heat, of the hot black that blanketed everything and made progress invisible. Two tensuns of avoiding the tribes that traversed the desert like it was prairie beneath their feet, and not the jagged rock that cut and clawed at John and Telde. Of the constant anxiety due to those close calls, or their dwindling water supply, or the cancerous gnawing that insisted they would never escape this place, there would never be anything else. *Is that what you want?*

During those weeks Telde had become increasingly withdrawn. Not that John felt much of an inclination to talk himself, but he nonetheless felt the dull pang of loneliness the silence exposed. Both of them were in mourning, he knew. And both were punishing themselves. *You don't deserve another life, is that it?*

Two tensuns since Jago and Ceria.

"Get up, we have to keep moving," Telde said abruptly.

"Now? I need to rest. We both do," John added, knowing it would annoy her.

"We need to keep going."

It was a well-worn argument between them by now, as repetitious as the travel: Telde pushing them forward, John pulling back, and the bond between them stretching thinner by the day. She seemed to rely more and more on that resolute aspect of her personality, to the exclusion of all else. There was a hardness to her that made her a stranger again to John.

"How long until we reach the border?" he asked.

"You know that I don't know. It could be a day, it could be another tensun. Get up."

Their water supply wouldn't last another tensun, John knew. He managed to stop himself from making the comment, however. A small victory over the self-pitying part of him that he despised but could not banish recently. He was fed up with Telde's suffering, too. He wanted to shout at her to snap out of it, to tell her what had happened wasn't her fault. But he couldn't find the energy or will to do it. Or to convince himself of the same.

"Get up or I go without you."

John complied, finally, mutely, and soon they had scrambled out of the trench. They left the rock behind, and almost immediately it was lost amongst innumerable duplicates in a landscape populated by the giant shards. John imagined the two of them as gnats crawling between the armoured plates of a vast dinosaur's back. He wondered what Jago would have made of it.

He quickly dismissed the thought and concentrated on following Telde, stepping clumsily over the ridges and pits between the immense rocks. Without the light of Ternerid in the night sky he could hardly make out his own feet, let alone the terrain in their proximity. They couldn't use a torch, of course, it would serve as a beacon for the tribesmen who already smelt foreign blood on their land. He was almost sorry for the absence of a nearby Spirit storm; he would have welcomed its violent blue light, if not the accompanying convulsions of the land. But the storms had seemed to cling to the lake, following where John and Telde could not, a final spiteful gesture, and subsequently they had seen no sign of one for days. He hoped it meant they were getting closer to the desert's border.

John cursed as his right boot, which had gained several tears to complement its original gaping hole, was pierced by an unseen thorn of rock. Ignoring the stinging in the sole of his foot he quickly pried the spike loose, knowing that Telde wouldn't slow for such a trivial injury. He wiped sweat from his palms onto his shirt. The night had taken the shirt's colour, but he knew the stains were still there. The blood. He couldn't help but think back to the lake: how he had futilely scraped at the desert rock, unable to penetrate the hard surface. The lack of tools had made it impossible to dig. In the end, with an impatient Telde watching on, he had gathered a collection of loose stones and broken rock, barely enough to cover the body. The ragged stretch of cloth they had used to wrap Jago was visible through the gaps between the stones. John had been ashamed of the pitiful grave, and couldn't even think of any words to say. He had said goodbye to his friend silently, insufficiently.

He gritted his teeth through the pain in his foot, and hurried to catch up with Telde. She glanced back, and he was uncertain whether he imagined her admonishing expression through the darkness. She then returned to her habitual alert posture: scanning the landscape, listening and watching for any disturbance in the surrounding murk. It was the same vigilance, almost paranoia, that John had seen so often from her in the past. But he knew it was for good reason.

Their first encounter with the bands of tribesmen had been one of the closest. Telde had pushed hard that night, and they had kept moving beyond the time when they should have been finding shelter from the following day. Dawn was breaking – an inferno climbing over the lip of the world – when they had seen the group. A cluster of three or four figures in dark clothing, far in the distance. It was clear the tribesmen had already spotted them and were approaching rapidly. John and Telde had raced away in the fierce and still rising heat, fuelled by an unknown reserve of adrenaline. Eventually they had taken refuge beneath the low overhang of a sizeable shard of rock, wedging themselves into the shallow elbow where the stone penetrated the surface, in what was to become a performance repeated almost nightly. The calls and piercing whistles had pursued them, as they had numerous times since, nearing their hiding place, becoming louder, before, to John's substantial relief, they finally began to fade.

On one night's travel they had come upon a body, or what remained of it. A tribesman judging by the shreds of leather, his body torn up and mutilated as if by a large animal. But surely no such predator could exist here, John reasoned, which left explanations too grisly to contemplate. Telde had been more careful since then, ensuring they found cover before the first hot breaths of dawn. Yet the encounters continued. During the latest, a few hours earlier, they had heard footsteps pass their prone position.

Do they know what happened at the mountain? John wondered. *Are Yeoba and his people hunting us? Or is it some other tribe? Or several? Did we step into the middle of a battlefield?* The truth wasn't of great consequence. He knew that their capture in any circumstance was likely to be fatal.

Telde was coughing. John saw her body shudder with the effort of stifling the fit. As ever she was too stubborn to stop walking, which was no doubt a contributing factor in the persistence of the illness. *Not just stubbornness*, John told himself. *Strength, too.* Sometimes he forgot that, he took it almost for granted. Her strength to keep going with the cough weakening her body, the weight of her plate armour, and the weight of losing Ceria. And in the face of such bleak prospects. Her spirit that kept him alive. He felt small and ungrateful when contemplating it.

John reached into his bag and retrieved a waterskin. "Here, you need to drink something," he said, keeping his tone neutral as he offered it to her. "Please, Telde."

She gave him a scrutinising look, at least as far as he could make it out, then stopped to take a few sips. "You too, John," she said, passing it back.

The water was a fresh blessing to John's parched lips and throat, even lukewarm as it was. He glanced at Telde as she adjusted the loose shirt worn over her crimson armour to prevent any glimmers of light, unlikely as that was on a night such as this. He couldn't detect the auburn shade of her hair, and even the brilliant green of her eyes was lost in the dark. *We're outlines of people,* John thought, *our details blackened out.* Telde's expression was obscured too, but he could usually discern her mood from her voice. He realised that a tacit rule of communication had developed between them over the past weeks: they would only use each other's names when what they were saying was sincere or vital. Never in the midst of argument, to attach aim to barbed remarks, or even during small talk.

Now you're really imagining things, John chastised himself. Even if it was true, it was simply a practical tool, used in a situation where clear communication was crucial to their survival. *What do you want it to mean? A closeness?* He felt an indistinct guilt as he wrestled with his thoughts.

Once they had started walking again, John asked about their plans after they managed to escape the desert. Telde dutifully explained in a low voice how they would travel to the Regent's lands in hopes that the two armies were still there; they would learn more about the march on Ferol and find a way to influence their plans, to use the resistance to help them defeat the half-man's forces with as little damage to her city as possible. And they would find a way to get Ceria back. John knew all of it already, but it was comforting to hear. For both of them, he hoped.

"Do you think we can catch up to Manvedian?" he asked.

Telde paused before answering. "I don't know."

"I can't believe he passed himself off as a resistance member for so long. And that he was from Crescent."

"Just say it," Telde said with sudden sharpness. "You've been wanting to for tensuns now."

"What do you mean?" John asked, taken aback.

"You want to know how it's possible I didn't suspect the truth about Manvedian earlier. You think I should have stopped him before it happened."

"What? No, that's not how I meant it."

"Why else would you keep mentioning it?"

"It sounds to me like it's you who thinks you're guilty," John replied. He wanted to tell her that he was relieved – he had been convinced that she thought *he* should've done more, after all he hadn't realised the truth in time either – and to reassure her that it wasn't her fault, neither of them was at fault, but he couldn't force the words out.

"You blame me for your friend being killed," Telde said.

"Jago. His name was Jago," John said, feeling a prickling of anger. "I don't blame you. But you don't seem to give a damn about him dying. You've said barely a word about it."

"He is dead, nothing can be done for him," Telde said. "What's important is finding Ceria."

"So you can use her against the half-man?" John asked before he could stop himself.

Telde stopped and turned fiercely to him. "Don't speak of things you know nothing of."

"I know enough," John replied. "I've seen what happens to her when she uses her power like that. She's lost to all the energy she takes – like with the Queen's Claw. Even if she *could* do the same to the half-man, who knows what it'd do to her? She said she'd never even used her power on a human before. And if Senthis is half fenning *Endless* too... Manvedian was right about one thing – if she's not killed outright, she could become a monster. She could become everything she hates."

"You can't know any of that," Telde said.

"You can't either!" John retorted, then made an effort to lower his voice. "She thought you were protecting her. But all this time you were planning to sacrifice her."

"What do you know of sacrifice?" Telde took a step closer to him, hissing the words through her teeth. "If you'd seen the things Senthis has done, what he's done to my city – he brought the Endless upon us, and all those other ungodly creatures. He doesn't wish power alone, he wants pain and cruelty and death. Ferol and Edemon won't be enough, he'll infect the entire world with his misery. He has to be stopped. He has to be. But every godscursing thing we've tried has failed. I've seen arrows pierce his chest and he continues walking. Poisoned blades, flames – Fen take us we've tried. He lets us, he revels in our failure.

"You're wrong about Ceria," Telde continued. "She lied to you. She's used her powers on a human before. In her youth, on one of the Elders in the forest. That's how we know she's our best chance to defeat Senthis. Our only chance, before it's too late. If she only weakens him it might be enough. Understand that I'd do the same whoever it was that held her power – any price is better than allowing the half-man to rule Crescent. Godsfuck you and your judgements. Don't you think I've wished it not to be Ceria? Don't you think I'd give anything that it wasn't, that it was me in her place?"

"You know what? I'm not even sure," John spat back. "I mean this is perfect for you – what could be more of a sacrifice? Not giving your own life, that's too easy, that's not nearly enough. No, the life of your best friend, the woman who's a sister to you – now that's sacrifice. The betrayal and guilt of it. Knowing you'll despise yourself the rest of your life. You'll be the ultimate martyr."

Telde pushed him in the chest, hard enough to make him stagger backwards. She began to reply but her words were cut short by an unexpected noise from her armour, as if something had ricocheted off its side. As she looked down, there was a skittering sound from a nearby rock, and John was puzzled to see in the gloom what appeared to be a thin line marking the ground.

"Arrows – run!" Telde shouted, seizing John's arm and pulling him after her.

As they sprinted he could hear the brusque gasps of arrows cutting the air around them, rattling against the rocky terrain, unseen but fearfully close. He couldn't even tell the direction from which the arrows came, let alone from who. But Telde seemed to know as she led them on a zigzagging route, using the great shards of stone as temporary cover. Before long a spate of whistles and shouts from behind confirmed her intuition. The sounds of pursuit continued, and John was convinced they were becoming louder, the arrows ever closer. *They're catching us.* Then there was a noise that caused them both to skid to a halt. Out of the dark ahead of them: a low, resonant whistle; an answer to those trailing them. It sounded again, and a moment later was joined by calls from somewhere to their left. *Oh god. They're surrounding us.* He followed Telde as she turned and ran in the only direction remaining open to them, dreading that a telling note would soon be heard from that bearing too.

The rain of arrows had subsided, however John couldn't find relief in that; he was certain it was only because the tribesmen were confident of their prey's capture. But as yet there were no sounds ahead of them, and now a dark smudge appeared at the far reaches of his view. John at first took it to be an enormous rock, but it was surely too long, too uniformly low. *A wall?* His heart sank with the thought, until subsequently he discerned variations in the black surface: shadows, stripes; a swarm of thin pillars. *Trees*, he realised. It was a forest, similar to that which they had seen so long ago when starting their journey on the other side of the desert.

Telde headed with renewed vigour towards it. John breathlessly followed. As if realising their plan, the shower of arrows began anew, landing in a hungry chatter around them. They were almost at the forest border when John felt a searing pain in his right calf, causing him to stumble and fall. Telde was there instantly, hauling him up and supporting his weight as they crossed the final few yards and plunged through the foremost row of trees.

Inside, the world immediately slowed. The surrounding gloom was thick with presence: trunks and boughs and silhouettes. The sky was replaced by a canopy of harsh limbs. John reached down to feel the back of his leg but there was no arrow, only a dampness corresponding to the burning pain.

"I'm okay, I can keep going," he quickly whispered in reply to Telde's enquiring glance.

She nodded and they continued, John limping but able to keep up. Their passage was unavoidably slow as they navigated the trees. The ground crunched and cracked beneath their feet, anxiously loud despite their careful tread. But the whistles, which had changed in pitch, seemed to remain a fixed distance away, as if reluctant to follow them into the forest.

It holds nothing but death; John remembered Yeoba's words, as the guide had taken them on a wide berth around that first forest. *Did he mean it was dangerous? That the plants are poisonous maybe? Or did he simply mean the trees were dead?*

Those trees were difficult to make out in the dense dark, but snatches of recurring features eventually formed an overall image: a tangle of roots that lifted themselves above the ground, like the legs of a spider, out of the centre of which a thin and sinewy trunk reached high above John's head; some ended in a web of branches forking over one another, whilst others possessed a black mass at their crown, like a gigantic bud. He was certain, even in the achromatic night, that the plant's bark was black too. It felt charred and withered as he ran his hand over a central stem, tough and brittle as he snapped off a branch. *They seem dead enough,* he thought.

He kept close to Telde as they crept through the forest, the gangling roots doing their utmost to trip them. Their progress was reduced to little more than walking pace in the congestion, which allowed John to become aware of an odour to the place, a fetid breath. And there were noises around them: creaking, fluttering, as if the plants were contradicting their lifeless appearance and shaking themselves awake. A dull beating. A gust of air over them. Telde and John exchanged concerned looks, both containing the same appeal for haste. But movement was increasingly arduous, and they could only scramble clumsily over the glut of roots.

They came to a stop, their attention caught by a tree before them that appeared to be trembling. It was the giant bud at the top, John saw; its vibration was shaking the rest of the tree. Then, as he watched, it began to bloom. Two prodigious petals unfurled, ridged at their edges, a gossamer sheen to the swathes of black that stretched and fanned out until they began to take a familiar shape. *Wings,* John comprehended. *Christ, they're wings.* Telde cursed in astonishment next to him.

Then they were running again, clambering over the roots, not daring to look behind. John felt a renewed blaze of pain as several of the rigid tendrils scraped against his calf. The forest was coming to life around them. A rising clamour of rustles and flaps and unearthly shrieks. He witnessed countless more of the winged blossoms occurring throughout the forest.

"They're on the fenning trees!" John exclaimed over the noise.

"Keep running!" Telde yelled in front of him. "There must be –"

Suddenly a dark form swept in from their left, crashing into Telde and knocking her to the ground. A vast wing whipped back and buffeted John, sending him hurtling into a heavy tangle of roots. Stunned by the impact, he struggled to regain his bearings, unable to discern up from down in the confusing and murky world. There was a deafening shriek, and he fought through the stiff arms that held him to see a bird-like creature towering over Telde. The tremendous outstretched wings shimmered a diaphanous blue, and jutting out far below their crest was a skull dominated not by a beak but a snout. The creature stalked and snapped at Telde, who crawled backwards. She attempted to push herself up only for the bird to swing its head and knock her down again, as if toying with its food.

John shook off his stupor and scrambled up. *Not Telde,* he thought desperately. *No more life will be taken from me.* He took hold of a broad, tapering branch that had been broken off by his impact, and he charged, losing his balance over the uneven ground so that when he reached the bird he was half falling. But the inadvertent momentum proved an advantage as the creature turned, spreading its appendages in hostile reaction, and the keen point of the branch lanced its filmy wing. The impetus drove it backwards until the bough collided with a tree, impaling the trunk and pinning the creature to it. The vast bird emitted a terrible screech, its head jerking side to side, its muzzle hanging open to reveal rows of serrated teeth. The free wing flapped furiously at both the protruding branch and John, but he had already rolled away and out of reach.

He got to his feet and hurried to Telde, finding her dazed but otherwise intact.

"We need to get out of here," he said breathlessly, helping her up. She nodded quickly.

The screeching continued from behind as the two of them made their escape, and as they weaved in and out of the trees, remaining as close as possible to the tenuous protection of the slim trunks, the sound was echoed from all over forest. *A giant fucking nest of them,* John thought. He realised as they ran that his shoulder bag was missing; he must have dropped it in the snarl of roots. *Shit, the water. But* – sudden hands on his shoulders yanked him backwards, as at almost the same instant a vast shadow passed within an inch of his face; a gust of foul air brushing his skin. Telde pushed him forward with equal force and barked at him to move.

John had no time to thank her as they rushed onwards, picking their way over the masses of roots, climbing up to gnarled trunks then scurrying down towards the next such waypoint, expecting at any moment a deadly shadow to detach itself from the black surroundings and envelop them. The sky was filled with beating and flurries of air. He didn't look up.

Finally the trees were becoming more spread out. The roots correspondingly subsided, allowing for faster progress, if the reduced cover made it more anxious still. They kept low, skirting around the nearby shrieks and changing direction frequently. Then, without warning, they broke free of the trees and spilled out upon hard, rugged rock. The abrupt change caused the two of them to halt in surprise. But a moment later John looked at Telde and saw the same desperate realisation: they were out in the open. Exposed.

They bolted away from the forest. Out into the gaping black, its nothingness even more unwelcome now. John ran awkwardly, his body heavy and languid beneath him. A blaze of pain shot through his leg every time his right foot connected with the ground. He glanced behind to see a swarm of shadows blocking out the stars. *They're coming.*

Telde shouted something. John saw her dart away in a different direction, and turned sluggishly to follow. She reached a shard of rock embedded at a low, almost horizontal angle in the land, and slid immediately feet-first into the narrow space beneath it. John replicated her manoeuvre but with considerably less success, the craggy ground ripping at his back and stopping his body only two thirds of the way in. There was a gust behind him, a shriek that resounded like a klaxon inside his skull, and in the next moment Telde had dragged him the rest of the way beneath the stone. He wriggled further in on his back until he was pressed against her side, both of them panting so hard he couldn't tell his breath from hers.

But it was clear they were far from safe. Countless birds surrounded them, their presence evidenced by an excited chorus of shrieks, and the beating and pounding and scraping against the rock above. That shard of rock was smaller than John and Telde's previous shelters, covering them with only a few feet to spare. *Not enough to protect us.*

A leathery snout suddenly appeared next to his arm, pushed through the crevice; he felt the hot stench of its breath, saw its tumescent tongue roll between barbed teeth as it snapped at him. Telde reached across as he drew back in reflex, slashing at the snout with a silvery dagger. There was a shrill squeal as the creature withdrew its bloodied muzzle, but almost instantly another had replaced it, then more yet alongside and on the other sides of the rock. Spiteful heads and now the tips of flattened wings forced themselves inside, as if they were ferreting for insects inside a cranny. Telde continued to hack at them with the blade, but their numbers only grew.

John and Telde retreated into each other, back against back, but it wasn't enough: he felt something grasp the hair on his head; he kicked out at a wing scraping his leg. The stone above them was lurching under the frenzied weight of the birds. *Shit shit shit.* There was no escape. The creatures would reach them and tear them out, or the rock would crush them, or by some negligible chance it would be upturned, revealing the ripe bugs beneath.

I don't want to die, John thought. *Not here. Not now.* He was shocked by the strength of that conviction, after he had spent years on Earth so apathetic to the thought of his death. Where it had been a comfort, a promise of rest. But now he had allowed himself to hope for more, to want life. *I'm not ready.*

An abrupt silence fell; the shrieks and clawing stopped, and a moment later the snouts and wings retracted from beneath the stone. A dissonant drumming arose, the sound of innumerable giant wings taking flight. The rock ceased swaying.

The creatures' departure was so startling that John wondered briefly if it was caused by the power of his thoughts. But shortly after he heard the birds' ravenous, high-pitched clamour resume in the distance, intertwined with the unmistakable screams of humans. *The tribesmen*, John comprehended. They must have circled the forest to see if their quarry would emerge.

Telde was tugging at his arm. "Come on!"

He followed as she slid out from under the rock. Pulling himself to his feet, he looked fearfully back at the stone, but could detect no avian shadows in the dark. He turned and ran with Telde, away from the forest and the abhorrent sounds. She was coughing heavily by now, and John wasn't in much better condition as he gasped for air, attempting to sustain a body that was increasingly unresponsive. The agonised screams continued from behind. John felt a surge of nausea and thought for a moment he might vomit, but he doubted his body contained either the matter or energy required.

After several minutes the screams became more intermittent, then ceased altogether. John, previously desperate for them to end, presently felt a keen anxiety at the absence: would the birds return to their previous prey? Telde must have shared a similar thought, as she stopped and hurriedly surveyed their surroundings. John had hardly taken notice of that landscape until now: clusters of rock behemoths protruded from the land, at least half of them broken so their fragments – the largest in themselves the size of a car – lay scattered about their progenitors, wedged into shattered ground or leant against one another or broken into further piles of shards.

Telde rushed towards a nearby heap, climbing over the rocks to inspect the recesses between. John watched as with an agility belying her surely exhausted state, she gripped the top of a rock and swung her body inside an opening. She reappeared a moment later, motioning for him to follow. He duly clambered up after her, his shoulder colliding heavily against stone as he stumbled through the gap. But the pain barely registered; he drowsily perceived the jumble of rocks that enclosed the hollow, then crawled past Telde to a comparatively flat area and collapsed onto his back.

"Do you think they'll come back?" he asked with what breath he still possessed.

"I don't know," she answered. "We can hope they've eaten enough for now."

John felt his stomach react to her words, but it was muted by the thick tide of fatigue rapidly consuming him. The sounds of shrieking and screaming still rang in his ears, and his mind conjured images as an accompaniment: vast winged forms battering bodies, teeth ripping away flesh.

He closed his eyes and tried to escape them.

It might have been minutes or hours later, John didn't know, but when he opened his eyes again dim light was seeping into the cramped space.

He coughed and pushed himself up onto his elbows. It felt as though every part of his body wished to communicate its own acute ache or pain. He was hardly any less tired, either, but was annoyed at himself for having abandoned Telde for sleep so readily. She was awake and alert, of course, peering through a chink of light between the enclosing rocks. She turned to him and answered the question in his eyes with a short shake of her head: *the birds had not returned.*

John was determined that he stay awake, to share the burden as he should. And so that he might stop feeling quite so useless. The hollow they were in was larger than he had first thought, if its slanting ceiling made it too low for them to stand upright. He saw the jagged corrugations of the black rocks surrounding them, as well as the dubious way in which they supported one another. He wondered how much stone was above their heads in the miniature mountain.

Telde had blocked the entrance with another chunk of

rock; muddy light oozed around its outline. *It must be nearly dawn*, John thought. But not yet. The cavity would become an oven when the sun breached the horizon in earnest. His head was already pounding a protest, and it was joined by a scorched throat, a shoulder that refused to rotate, and the lacerated complaints of his feet and back. But the miserable collection was forgotten in an instant as he moved his right leg, and he couldn't help but gasp as fire seemed to engulf its lower half. He looked down to see a bloody tear through the leather leggings, across the outside of his calf.

Telde crawled wordlessly over to him. She placed her hands on his leg and peered at the wound. John tried his utmost to not let any further noises escape him.

"What are you doing?" he asked.

"You'll slow us down if it's not treated," she replied as she pulled out a long, silver-white dagger, and began cutting at the leggings just below his knee.

"You kept it," John said, nodding to the weapon. *The dagger that killed Jago.*

"My sword is gone. We need any weapon we can get," Telde said, then glanced up at him, her green eyes ablaze. "I plan on returning it to Manvedian."

She hacked through the remainder of the legging's diameter, then cut down lengthways to its end so that she could peel the section of leather away. John was embarrassed at the stale smell of sweat that resulted, but Telde didn't appear to notice as she studied the wound again, flicking away dried blood with the edge of the blade.

"It's not too deep," she said, before retrieving a piece of cloth from her bag. She dampened it with a trickle of water from a flask, and John tried not to think about how thirsty he was. Once she started dabbing at his wound, however, he desperately tried to return his thoughts to that thirst, rather than the far less preferable pain seizing his leg.

"I lost my pack."

"I know."

"At least things can't get much worse," John said after a moment, for the sake of any conversation to distract his mind.

"If we escape this desert," Telde replied, "and we make it to Regent's lands, it's likely they'll execute us on sight." She said it with a grave glance, but even for her the combination was excessively solemn, and as John stared into her face that was encased by dirt, bruises, innumerable scratches, and she, returning his look, surely saw the same dishevelment in him, both of them paused, and then broke into laughter. Quiet and hoarse laughter, interspersed with coughs, but laughter all the same.

"You really have a gift for lifting morale," John said.

Telde raised an eyebrow, then dabbed at his wound a little more firmly than was strictly necessary.

John gave a slightly pained chuckle. He felt a fresh layer of sweat form on his forehead, partly due to Telde's cleaning of his wound, but also because of the increasing heat. The light framing the rock at the entrance was more intense now, and further brightness was trickling in between the irregular stones forming the walls. Colour was returning with alien clarity to John's vision: Telde's chestnut hair, albeit streaked and dulled by dust; the dark red stains on his shirt.

"I didn't mean what I said earlier," he remarked at length. "About you and Ceria."

Telde remained quiet while she tore a section of the cloth, evidently to use as a bandage.

"Because of Senthis and his Endless billions of people on my planet were killed," John continued. "My whole civilisation wiped out. I'm on your side, Telde. I want him dead as much as anyone. I want to help." *But not with sacrificing Ceria,* he added silently. He wouldn't let Telde go through with that. And he realised that he didn't believe she would.

Telde gave a faint nod in response. She began wrapping the bandage carefully but tightly around his leg. "I do care about Jago. His death matters to me," she said slowly and awkwardly, not meeting his eyes. "But I have to focus on the future, on those who can be saved. Else the noise of all the lost would ruin me."

"I think I understand," John said. "I don't think I ever really faced the loss of those on Earth. How do you even comprehend such a loss? Jessica alone was enough for me. It's been years since she died and I still can't let her go."

"Are you sure it's her you grieve for?" Telde asked.

John was surprised and puzzled by the question. It seemed tactless, but she hadn't said it unkindly.

"Don't answer," Telde added, with a shake of her head. "Describe her to me."

"Jessica?" John replied, uncomfortable at the request. But he began to tell her – about Jessica's appearance, her occupation, her upbringing – the words coming out stiffly, in disconnected clumps. It felt surreal in the circumstances, conjuring her up like this, yet he was uncertain why he was finding the task quite so difficult. Not painful, but simply difficult, as if his mind encountered an obstruction, or had to dig especially deep to retrieve the details with which to describe her. Which was absurd, John knew, as barely a day passed that he didn't think of Jessica. *So why is it so hard?*

A realisation started to form, and wouldn't be dismissed despite John's repeated efforts. He began to understand what Telde had meant. The woman he was trying to describe wasn't the Jessica who had been rooted in his head for so long. That Jessica was something else: a cold and heavy semblance, vague yet unyielding, wrought out of a flawless material. An unquestionable good to hold up against all the evil of loss. *Not Jessica.*

John was shocked by the discovery, and anxiously tried to recall the characteristics of the real Jessica, her likes and dislikes and quirks and imperfections. Her passion for the creative world even though hers was a careful, scientific mind. Her cynicism of anything unproven. Her focus when it came to what she wanted from life and how she would get it.

The point on the back of her neck that was more ticklish than anywhere else on her body. The hidden tattoo on the inside of her thigh. Her short blonde hair that John had always secretly preferred to be longer. She would always buy an abundance of fruit, but eat only those that had rinds to peel. She loved how the ink from newspapers stained her fingers, and had confided in John that she had pursued a career in journalism because her younger self yearned to have her own words leave similar marks. She loved beaches but only at night; it was the reassuring atmosphere of it, she told him, how the tides continued even in the dark. She was an expert on films but fell asleep in the cinema because it reminded her of her childhood. She argued furiously with her father but loved him dearly, and somehow didn't see her likeness to him that was so apparent to John and her mother...

He told Telde all of this. The details poured out of him. Jessica the flawless object began to dissolve, and in its place was Jessica the woman, the flawed human of infinitely more worth. John felt a painful and precious loss as he continued to describe her, as much to himself as to Telde. It was as if he only now allowed himself access to his memories of her, memories that he could hardly believe he had kept buried. He had regained her, even as he accepted, finally, that she was gone.

After he finished talking, Telde left him to his thoughts for a time, the bandaging of his leg completed long ago. He scarcely felt the wound any longer. He sat shaken, gripped by sadness. Yet he was freer somehow, as though a weight had fallen away.

"John. Quick, come and see," Telde said suddenly. She had moved to the rock at the entrance to peer through the gap.

John's pulse quickened as his preoccupied mind stirred and leapt to thoughts of tribesmen and monstrous birds. But although Telde's words had held an urgency, it didn't seem a worried sort.

He crawled over to kneel alongside her. She pulled him

closer, her cheek brushing his as she pointed through the crack. He followed her gaze, and saw how the dawn had spilt its blazing deluge over the desert, revealing the ragged black that stretched on for miles and miles until – until, he realised with an intake of breath, the expanse was ended abruptly at the horizon by an immense wall. A cliff-face that extended laterally without end, its rim dotted by the diminishing glow of torches. *The border. The end of the Black Sea.*

Telde turned to smile at him, her light rivalling the sunrise. "Tomorrow is a better day."

23

Ceria lay on the wooden floor of the carriage, a shiver passing through her. The night had brought a keen chill to the air, but to feel it was almost a pleasure, as if her body were shaking off the last vestiges of the clotted desert heat.

Through a tear in the canvas roof above she could see a scattering of stars surrounding the small moon Nothir, named after the god of newborns who was said to have a similar complexion to the moon's russet face. It was also known as Irek'andalon in the older parts of Ireldelor, after the king who had perished in battle; on the night of his death, the moon had absorbed his noble spirit so that he could forever watch over his people. Ceria remembered the story from her youth. At that age she had held a fascination with the inhabitants of the night sky, and the Elders in the forest camp had been only too pleased to furnish her enthusiasm. The moon was called Nothi'malir in some of Ranarin, she had been told, where the god's true purpose was disputed; Warden Of The Sea in the L'pen Isles, the people of which had their own gods; an augury of good fortune in the West; the vengeful eye of Fen according to the Hearts. *There are many contrary ways to view the same thing*, Elder Nefehed had said, a prospect that had exasperated the young Ceria – especially when the Elder had refused to tell her which was the correct belief.

The Fivemoons had at least ten separate titles and biographies for each moon orbiting Crescent, Jago had explained to her, dependant on such things as their location in the sky, the position of the other moons, the date and weather, the age and sex of the observer. The memory was unbearably recent in Ceria's mind.

She shifted to sit up, leaning her back against the large square chest positioned at the rear of the carriage. There was a faint jangling as she moved, produced by the metal chain that attached her ankle to a beam of the vehicle's frame. She looked to Manvedian, who lay sleeping near the opposite corner, but he hadn't roused at the sound. She watched his slow, slightly irregular breath. *Not yet.*

She hugged her knees, her hands disappearing inside the sleeves of the voluminous black shirt. The cloth leggings she had picked out of the chest – in the absence of any alternatives – were little better, and only remained about her waist due to a thin cord she had fastened around them. An array of colourful designs were sewn onto the leggings, which reminded Ceria of the time spent travelling with the merchant caravan. It felt an age ago now. She saw Telde practising her flowing forms in the night, and felt a piercing, complicated pain.

From outside the carriage came the sound of wheezing, followed by a loud, wet snort; the perennial noises of the jahtis, animals that even Ceria found unsightly. Beneath their rasping, and the infrequent gusts of wind that whistled through and around the carriage, she could make out the guttural murmur of the mercenaries. *Drinking again, most like.* Initially after their arrival Manvedian had remained awake most of the time, and was especially alert at night, poised at any irregular sound – or lack of sound – from the men. But now he was weaker. Ceria saw it, despite how well he hid it from the mercenaries. *It has to be the wound on his neck,* she thought. He wouldn't let her see it, and she was sure he had been increasingly favouring his left arm over the past few days. She studied his supine form, which was showing increased signs of a feverish sleep. *Not yet,* she told herself.

She rested against the chest and felt the cold air that filtered through the numerous holes in the canvas and the

315

carriage's shallow wooden sides. The climate was becoming noticeably more mild the further north they travelled. *We must be far into Ireldelor by now,* Ceria thought. She wondered why Manvedian had not made a move against the mercenaries. It had been nearly a tensun since the men had appeared, and of the ensuing travel along the solitary valley pass. The bordering hills – which she had watched swell into behemoths of earth and stone, their contours smoothed by pale grass so it felt as though the carriage were trickling between the vast dormant muscles of Crescent – had dwindled into little more than foothills now. Ceria had the impression that the mercenaries were content to be patient, to let Manvedian handle the chore of looking after her whilst they waited for him to make a mistake. It was a long way to Ferol yet.

But she couldn't explain Manvedian's inaction. Yes he was outnumbered, however she doubted he was concerned by that. She had seen him fight before. She remembered when he had saved Benuitis from the gang of Hearts conscripts; the speed with which he had killed two of them, the fierce and clinical routine of it that had sent the remaining attackers fleeing. Surely he could hold no qualms about killing these mercenaries. It was possible that he was waiting for an escape route, but if he was growing weaker as the days passed then wasn't it better to act sooner rather than later?

She hadn't questioned him about it. A knot formed in her stomach when she thought of the violence; she didn't wish to provoke that kind of bloodshed. And she didn't want Manvedian to think she was on his side. *He's as bad as them,* she reminded herself. *Worse.* Yet she couldn't help but fear being left in the mercenaries' hands. She had no delusions about how the men would treat her. *But I'm not defenceless.*

The wind was picking up outside; an infiltrating breeze tousled her short hair. She ran her hands over her face. She felt changed, older. More than simply the months that had elapsed since she had left Ferol. During all of that time spent travelling with Telde she had longed to return to her city, to how things used to be – to how she used to be. But now she was returning as some prize possession for the half-man, for him to do gods only knew what with, and she knew life had changed irrevocably. *Merchandise,* Manvedian had described her. Out of anger, perhaps, but it was the truth. She was the goods that would earn him a profit. And Telde and Climbe had regarded her in the same way.

She had asked Manvedian earlier that day, resentfully, for what possible reason they could all want her so badly. He had been quick to denounce her ignorance. *You know why. You know what you can do.* The words had startled her, and while she had attempted to deny it, claiming she didn't use her ability on humans, and never in *that* way, it was a weak appeal; he knew what had happened in her youth, in the forest camp that was once her home. *You didn't move to Ferol city because of the razed forests, Ceria. You could've gone with the camp to another place. But you didn't. Because you knew that you didn't belong anymore, after what you did.*

She repeated his words to herself; a fresh layer to the old torture. *Nefehed was sick,* Ceria had protested, like she always protested to herself. She had thought herself capable of healing the Elder, just as she helped the forest animals, despite the woman's vehement refusals. She had tried anyway, stubbornly, arrogantly, against Nefehed's wishes. But she couldn't control it. The saturating torrent, the glorious power. She couldn't stop. *Those in the camp, previously your friends, your family, they were scared of you, Ceria. You were scared, too. Of what you could do and what you could become. And so you should be.*

She felt tears stinging her eyes. A stream of bitter anger. Anger at herself, and at the truth. At the gods for giving her this curse. At those who had been betraying her all along: Manvedian, the resistance, Climbe. Telde. She felt the pain of that reality, the loss it entailed. *Why didn't she tell me? Why didn't she ever say?* Ceria despised the idea of using her power the way they wanted – but she would have done it willingly. For Telde, and for Ferol. *She must have known that. Why did she choose to use me instead?* They had protected her only because of what she could do. *Does she care for me at all? Or am I just a weapon to her?*

And they were all wrong, anyway. She couldn't kill the half-man, she was certain of it. It wasn't a truth simply because they wished it. *One here of you is capable of ending Senthis*, the Endless in the mountain had said, but Ceria refused to believe the implication. It was just as likely that it had been referring to John, or Jago, or Telde herself – if the hateful thing was even telling the truth. But now Senthis wanted her, surely because of that possibility. Because she had been made into a weapon by those she trusted the most. She had sworn never to use her ability in that way again, yet now she would be forced to.

She wiped at her eyes and glared across at Manvedian. His body was twitching, his jaw working soundlessly. He was having the dream. *Now.*

Ceria got quietly to her feet and moved to the beam of the carriage's frame, around which the circular clasp at the end of her chain was secured. She placed her hands on the metal and tried to force it upwards; it grated against the enclosed wood and refused to move. *Come on.* She leant her shoulder to the clasp and pushed with increased vigour. At last it gave way, jerking several inches up the beam with a loud jangling of chain. Ceria glanced back at Manvedian, but he displayed the same signs of agitated sleep. She was confident he wouldn't wake. He never did during the dream, which she had concluded was some recurring nightmare.

She looked up at the beam and followed its arch, which curved with the canvas over her head and down to the other side of the cart. Doubts began to form in her mind, but she shook them off. *You can do this.* She took hold of the beam and pulled herself up, so that she stood on the thin verge of the carriage's low wooden side, then pushed the clasp higher until she felt the chain attached to her ankle tauten. With considerable effort she hauled herself up after it, her legs straddling the beam. The chain rattled but she couldn't turn to look at Manvedian now. She would have to hope that the dream persisted for a while yet.

She repeated the same manoeuvre: slowly but steadily inching the clasp along the wood, then shimmying her body after it; all of the time spent climbing trees in her youth was finally proving beneficial. Halfway along the arch, as she hung upside-down, an audible crack emanated from the wood. She could feel the frame bowing as she clung to it. Even dreaming as he was, Manvedian couldn't fail to wake if it broke and she crashed to the floor next to him – and that was besides the likelihood of her neck snapping in the process.

With her muscles ablaze from the strain she pulled herself forwards, the beam creaking pessimistically. She moved a hand to the clasp, which had stubbornly wedged itself against the wood, but the sweat on her fingers caused them to slip from the metal, and she gasped as her arm fell and her body pitched with it. For a moment the carriage floor whirled in her vision – before she realised her legs still straddled the beam, and with determination she was able to pull her upper body back up again.

She took a deep breath. *Come on.* With the palm of her hand she forced the clasp on, then continued along the beam as it began curving downwards, the strain on her arms and legs only intensifying as she descended head first. Eventually, hand over hand, she came to the end of the canvas, where the fabric was fixed to the side of the carriage. She endeavoured to reach the floor through an awkward combination of climbing and falling, but as she did so the clasp again caught on the beam, tensing the chain behind her and wrenching her ankle in mid-air – Ceria barely managed to suppress a cry at the resultant shooting pain. She twisted her body uncomfortably to place her free foot on the ground, then, hopping, moved her hands up to the manacle. At length she was able to work it down to the base of the arch, and gratefully place both of her feet on the floor.

She panted heavily and winced at the throbbing in her ankle, which she found too tender to put any weight on. But she had made it. She looked to Manvedian who, previously in the opposite corner of the carriage to her, was now on the same side due to her exertions. And much closer. He was still dreaming, she saw with relief, murmuring in his troubled sleep. *Som'syere?*

She stepped towards him. As the chain became rigid behind her, she shifted to her knees, then lay flat on her stomach, edging forward and stretching her hand out in front of her. Manvedian's left arm lay by his side, still a foot away from her fingers. She strained every inch of herself forward, her ankle grating agonisingly against the fetters, the wooden frame groaning behind her. It felt as if her foot might be torn away by the metal, but now her fingertips brushed the edge of Manvedian's hand, and with torturous effort she was able to grasp a finger to pull it closer. She immediately gripped his hand fully in hers. Manvedian stirred but didn't wake.

Hurry. Concentrate. She closed her eyes and tried to find it: the boundary between them. But it was difficult to escape the noise of her body. The pounding of her heart, the aching of her ankle. And she felt a deep-rooted reluctance, a revulsion at using her ability in this way. *Think of Jago. This man is a murderer.* She banished her doubts and the outside world, and searched for that thing beyond touch, beyond skin and blood, beyond designation. She could sense its radiance. She urged it towards her, opened herself, diminishing the barrier separating them. The torrent was suddenly there, a fierce bright surging into her. *Don't slow. Take it.* It felt so good giving in to the thirst, allowing the energy to gush unrestricted. The exalting inundation, the sweet stress to contain it. *Don't stop.* A convulsion in him; a shiver in her. *Take it all.* A void, a leaching tear; his wound was much worse than expected, a distant thought told her. And something else. She felt it even beyond the roar of intensity flooding into her. Something behind it. An opening, a presence slowly revealing. Immense, impossible. *Stop,* a voice cried out. But it was coming, she could feel it, she could almost glimpse –

Oh gods – sheer and elemental – wild and absolute – Oh gods oh gods – brilliance and black – No – protector and destroyer – Stop – boundless – No!

Ceria fell away from Manvedian, expelled either by her own force or his. Her body shook. Her senses wouldn't work. The saturating torrent still coursed through her, making her ache for more; she was distraught at the sudden deprivation. But as potent as the thirst was, it was engulfed by the shock of that staggering glimpse. *So much power. So much.*

"What did you do!" a voice demanded. It was Manvedian, but she couldn't see him yet. She touched her face, numb fingers against numb skin, and closed her eyes, willing the radiance to fade so that she could think. *What was it?* Desperately, dreamily, she fought to recognise herself through the tempest in her mind.

A hand gripped her arm. A dull pain. She opened her eyes to find a dark blur in front of her.

"What did you do, Ceria?" Manvedian whispered fiercely. "You stupid fenning girl, what did you do!"

Slowly the carriage was materialising around her: wooden beams rose up against her legs; a dull grey canvas descended above her, its surface breached by stars. She could hear her own quickened breath.

Manvedian had moved back, and was leaning against the side of the cart. As Ceria's vision cleared she saw that he was drenched in sweat, his hand on an arch for support.

"What... what is it?" she managed to utter. "Inside you. What is it?"

Manvedian glared back. "I don't know what you're talking about," he snapped, his voice unsteady. "You used your fenning powers on me."

"You must know," she pressed. "What is it?"

"I should kill you for what you did."

So much. Boundless. Even her thirst had shied away from that unconditional energy. *How can it be within him?* But it was, she knew what she had seen. *With such power he could do anything. Why doesn't he use it?*

"Tell me. Tell me, Manvedian. It's in you."

"There's nothing fucking in me!" he exclaimed, visibly shaking.

How much did I take from him? She remembered that his neck wound was a great deal worse than she had thought. There was a sound to her left, and a face appeared at a tear in the side of the canvas. One of the mercenaries.

"What's the racket? You lovers not getting along?" He glanced at Manvedian, who despite obvious effort couldn't conceal a shiver.

Manvedian stared icily back nonetheless. "Why don't you come in here and find out?"

The man peered at Manvedian. *For a moment too long,* Ceria thought, although he eventually shrugged with a grin. "You can sort your own problems. Just try not to bruise that pretty face of hers."

The man disappeared from the tear, and Manvedian immediately moved to a bag, cursing as he searched through it. He retrieved three small, handleless blades – throwing knives, Ceria guessed – which he tucked away into his sleeve. He felt his boot, where she presumed another weapon was hidden, then flicked his wrist within the other sleeve to reveal a larger dagger.

"You've done this," he said quietly.

"They're going to attack?" Ceria asked, but she already knew the answer. The mercenary had seen Manvedian's weakened state.

"I won't let them have you," Manvedian breathed. He moved towards Ceria with the blade in his hand.

Ceria backed away as he approached, knowing at the same

time that it was a futile effort. But as Manvedian reached her his hand disappeared into a pocket, and he produced a small metal key. He knelt at her ankle and took hold of the fetters. She frowned a question at him.

"If I win, which I'm going to, I will find you," he said, attempting to steady his fingers as he unlocked the clasp. He looked up at her. "You won't escape me, Ceria. You are mine. Know that."

The clasp snapped open and Manvedian stood, the blade again in his grasp. He moved to the canvas next to them, the opposite side to that on which the mercenary had appeared, and hacked through a number of the rope bindings that held the stained fabric in place.

"When I go out there," he said, "wait a few seconds, then slip out on this side. Cut two of the jahtis loose, take the third and go."

Ceria struggled to keep up with the pace of events; too many emotions battled inside her head. Combined with the mournful ache of the fading radiance, and the shock that still held tightly on to her being, consequently the world felt surreal and insubstantial. Manvedian had moved to stare through the tear on the other side of the carriage. He glanced back at her, his expression unreadable in the gloom, then wordlessly walked to the front of the carriage and, too abruptly for her sluggish awareness, climbed out onto the seat behind the jallers and disappeared from her view. There was a short silence before she heard his voice from outside. She couldn't make out the words, but he sounded calm; there was a muttered response, a short laugh.

Maybe he's wrong. Maybe they're not going to attack. But it didn't matter; she had her chance to escape. She pulled the fetters away from her ankle and moved to the side of the carriage. As she climbed over it the unsecured canvas gave way to her body, and she slid down the other side, dropping the last few feet to the ground outside. She grit her teeth at the subsequent pain in her ankle, yet at least it shook away some of the stupefaction clinging to her.

Muddy night surrounded her now: the listing black of the hills, the sky smeared by stars. A cold wind gusted against her. The mercenaries were out of sight on the other side of the carriage. A brief shout from that direction; the sounds of struggle intermingled with the breeze. Ceria rushed away, limping towards where she knew the animals were kept – a distance from the camp due to their unpleasant habits. Once she had moved ahead of the carriage she looked back to see dark forms moving in front of the revealed campfire. Grunts; a cry; the ring of metal. She couldn't discern the details.

She hurried on, fearful that her escape would be detected at any moment. But the mercenaries would be focused on Manvedian, she told herself. They wouldn't have expected him to set her free. *Why did he? To spite them? Does he hate losing that much?*

She could smell the jahtis long before their awkward shapes emerged in front of her. Upon reaching them she hastily untied the ropes securing two of the animals, receiving enquiring wheezes and whines as she did so, then slapped their haunches to cause them to bolt away. She untied the remaining animal and mounted it, with some difficulty owing to its gangly build and disgruntled fidgeting, as well as her still languid agility. But the jahti was at least willing to gallop away – after the persuasion of a heel in its flank – and rasped eagerly as it set forth along the road with startling speed. Ceria leant forward to keep her balance, gripping the wide collar around its neck, and tried to steady her own breath. *They won't catch me.* The jallers were too slow, and by the time they retrieved the two jahtis she would have a considerable lead. She realised that she took for granted the fact that Manvedian would not win the fight. He couldn't, no matter what he had said. She knew how much she had weakened him. Surely he must have known, too.

But it didn't matter. She couldn't have hoped for a better outcome than this. They could busy themselves killing one another, and she would escape in the meanwhile. *He's a murderer,* she reminded herself. *A mercenary just like them.*

The overgrown dirt road made for a jolting ride, which was only amplified by the jahti's bony spine. The animals were designed for speed, not comfort. *But not a natural design,* Ceria thought. They were half-breeds, disproportionate creations; their legs too long and thin for their bodies, their mouths too large for their skulls. The creature wheezed on, the facing wind billowing through Ceria's oversized shirt. Frigid fingers seizing her bare skin. She couldn't help but think of what she had felt in Manvedian, that terrible absolute. *Why didn't he use it?*

Keep going, she told herself. Continue north along this road, then north through Ireldelor, and she could make it to Ferol on her own. She could contact the resistance and Climbe, and eventually find Telde and John. Yet there was a bitter attachment to that thought, the welcome tainted now she knew how they had planned to use her. Defeating Senthis remained the most important concern, Ceria was convinced of that, but she was determined not to be controlled any longer. She would fight on her own terms, by her own will.

She swore loudly and turned the jahti around. She knew what she had seen.

When she reached the carriage again, after a fretful gallop on the jahti, Ceria leapt from the animal, ignoring the spasm of pain in her ankle, then immediately raced towards the campfire. She slowed as she discerned only one upright figure. As she snuck closer she saw that the man was standing with his back to her and kicking someone on the ground. He held an axe in his hand, and another was strapped to his back. Two other bodies lay on the ground nearby, unmoving.

The mercenary leader was cursing and laughing as he kicked the man, who didn't seem to be moving either, save by the force of the kicks. *Manvedian.* Ceria recognised his still shape as the mercenary took a short run up to execute a savage blow to his chest. *I'm too late.*

Ceria considered using her powers on the man, but swiftly decided against it. She instead picked up a spiked mace lying next to one of the fallen mercenaries and crept up behind the man, who was too preoccupied with his brutal assault to hear her approach. She raised the weapon above her, its substantial weight requiring both of her hands, and swung at the mercenary's head – however her unwieldiness and a shift in the man's posture resulted in the mace coming down upon his shoulder, heavily enough for several of its metal spikes to penetrate his leather spaulders.

The man fell down with a surprised cry, but only upon one knee; he quickly rose again and turned, pulling the mace from his shoulder with a loud curse – the jarring impact had caused Ceria to let go of the weapon – and throwing it to the ground. He glared angrily at her for a moment, but then, as he looked her up and down, revealed a grin full of bloodied teeth.

"Gods, girl, I'm going to fuck you raw," he growled.

He stepped towards her, but an instant later halted, his eyes widening as he emitted a choking noise. Blood lapped out of his mouth as he clawed at the back of his neck. He fell to his knees in front of her. Ceria moved instinctively away, then slowly circled to see a blade projecting from the base of his skull. Manvedian was suddenly behind the man, another blade in his hand, and Ceria looked away as he took it to his throat.

As the man collapsed forward, Manvedian fell back onto the ground, clutching his side. He was covered in blood, Ceria saw, a deal of which was his own judging from the tears in his shirt. There was surprise in his eyes as he stared up at her. It was his turn to ask the unspoken question.

Ceria took her time, composing herself, remembering her resolution. She moved to stand over him.

"You're a coward, Manvedian," she said. "You claim the world is only a game of power. That you have to take what you can to survive. But you have this power in you, this unspeakable power. You could do anything. Take all you want. Rule Crescent like Senthis. But instead you live like this, like one of the half-man's pets, fighting over what scraps of power are tossed to you. You are a coward."

Manvedian rolled onto his side to spit out blood. "What in gods are you talking about?" he asked in a ragged voice.

"You're the one who can kill the half-man," Ceria said, keeping her eyes fixed on him. "You're the one the Endless in the mountain meant."

Manvedian coughed a laugh. "Is that what brought you back? You're a bigger fool than I thought if you believe I can kill Senthis."

"And yet you'd so readily believe that I could?"

"No, I don't believe that," Manvedian replied. "But Senthis does. At least enough to want you for his collection."

"I don't belong to anyone," Ceria said, her jaw clenched.

"But here you are, walking right back into my grasp. Mine again."

"No, I'm not." Ceria knelt down, placing her hand next to his. He flinched, pulling his fingers away from her. "You couldn't chain me now if you tried. But you don't need to, anyway. We're going to Ferol together."

It could have been because of his injured state, his vulnerability, the threat of Ceria using her ability against him, but it remained the first time she had seen Manvedian appear discomposed. Anxious. There was a certain pleasure in taking away his control and making it her own.

She stood up and, before he could speak, aimed a hard kick at his head, taking a deal more satisfaction in the connection. *He deserves much worse,* she thought, staring down at his resultantly insensible form.

"You're going to make up for your wrongs, Manvedian."

24

John knelt before the small mirror, trying in vain to locate a clear reflection in its blemished surface. He raised the scissors to his cheek and began clipping his beard. The metal blades were delicately engraved with what John assumed to be a Regency crest – two faces above a lavish ship – but they weren't especially sharp, and it was consequently hard work to cut through the tangle of hair.

A scattering of black locks lay on the floor around the wooden basin beside him, or floating on the water within, from his previous efforts at cutting the hair on his head. The resultant haircut was far from perfect – although it was difficult to judge just how imperfect in the fogged mirror – and there was sure to be numerous stray tufts he had overlooked, but it was at least better than its wild thicket of a predecessor.

Sunlight beamed through the tent entrance to his left, filling the square interior, warmly irradiating the pale canvas around him. It felt like a different sun here, John thought. A much milder character than the unforgiving steward of the Black Sea. He wet his fingers to work out a thick curl in his beard, the water still lukewarm against his skin. It had been boiling when it was brought in for him; an alien luxury. He had also been given three bowls containing suspicious-smelling ointments for the task, as well as a small cloth, a selection of combs, and a razor crafted from a dark, glass-like substance. John had quickly discovered the keen sharpness of the latter, and hadn't yet summoned the courage to bring either it or the ointments near his face.

It was clear the Regency populace held personal grooming in high regard, which might have explained the distasteful glances he and Telde had received when arriving at the camp in their bedraggled state. The adjutant assigned to them – a *Principal Conditioner* as he referred to himself, resulting in a poorly disguised laugh from Telde – had acted as though it were an insult to have such coarse creatures in the camp's neatly arranged midst, and had immediately rushed both of them to separate tents. *To improve yourselves.*

John had felt uneasy to be separated from Telde – who might have felt the same, or was at least distrustful of the situation, if her glance back at him was to be judged – however he welcomed the rare opportunity to be able to clean himself up in comparative leisure. As he had washed the dirt and weariness of weeks from his body, cut his hair and now his beard, so more of his skin was revealed. A face not seen for what felt like an age: blue eyes, thin aquiline nose, prominent cheekbones that were perhaps sharper now. He was surprised to recognise the features, as if he had expected to have changed as significantly on the outside as he felt he had inside. This old face should no longer be his. But there was the scar under his eye from when he had fallen off a bicycle as a child; there the dot of a mole at the top of his cheek. And above it, on his temple, the small patch of mottled skin from the car crash before the hotel. There were more marks in addition: abrasions and cuts and bruises on his face and his bare chest and arms, as well as a thumb missing from his left hand. *I'm both men*, he thought. All of this history was him.

He looked down at his body and saw the outline of his hip bones and lower ribs. The new leggings he had been brought by the adjutant – John had insisted on cloth ones this time – were slim around the waist, but remained fairly loose nonetheless. He had also been given sandals, and a clean shirt lay on the collection of vividly-coloured pillows on the floor behind him. His previous clothes, with their tears, their stains of dirt and blood, their wounds of the desert, had been taken away by the adjutant with a display of repugnance, probably to be destroyed. *Good.* He was glad to be rid of them. And of the Black Sea.

He glanced around the rest of the tent. The space seemed larger than its modest dimensions, due to the fresh afternoon light, or perhaps its sparse contents: a clay jug of water, a plate of fruit, a few tall candles, a claret and gold drape behind the pillows. It felt strange being alone, John reflected. He had rarely been left to himself since he had arrived on Crescent. A familiar apprehension settled in his stomach: if he let life escape his gaze, if he didn't watch it carefully, it would vanish once again. He realised the largest proportion of that fear was centred around Telde.

But that was only natural, he told himself. Ever since the events at Hoa Lake they had barely left one another's sides. That closeness hadn't changed when they had escaped the Black Sea.

John's mind roamed, placing him back in that half-starved and desperate state where, without an alternative, the two of them risked climbing one of the winding paths carved out of the cliffs that bordered the desert. They didn't avoid detection, as they knew they surely wouldn't, and it was only luck that a group dressed in black robes apprehended them.

They were taken to another Nightsteppers' town, eerily similar to the first. Its Spirit Seer, with his pale nakedness, bald head, and blue-stained teeth, was almost indistinguishable from the previous province king. He somehow knew all about their journey to the mountain, which placed them in some regard: it was deemed the god had judged them favourably, given that they still lived. The Seer nonetheless interrogated them on the events – John and Telde answered carefully, omitting many details – before granting them an escort to the Regency border, along with jallers and much needed supplies of food and water.

The two of them took turns to sleep on the journey, wary of the tribesmen. They relaxed once their robed escorts left them at the Regency border, if continuing to watch over one another with the implicit trust that had developed between them. One would sleep awkwardly on a jaller, leant forward, head against the animal's neck, while the other guided their mounts south-east, navigating by the sun or the stars. John always secretly hoped that when it came to her turn to sleep, Telde would do so with her face turned towards him. On one occasion, travelling in the blissful novelty of a cool night, he allowed himself to reach across and stroke a loose tuft of jaller fur from her hair. He realised then. When he felt the fear that she might open her eyes to discover his hand; when he felt the contradictory part of him that wanted her to.

The landscape bloomed around them as they rode. The Regent's lands were hot, but it was a fresh heat, a coastal air, increasingly suffused with the colour and fragrance of plants and animals and life. So too the conversation between them burgeoned. Telde spoke of Ferol, her resistance colleagues, her life as a soldier – she recounted her first battle, without fuss whilst John listened astonished, in which she had helped to defend outlying Ferol settlements against a Gol warband – and what she knew of the Regency and how different its people were. But she had never previously travelled far beyond Ferol's borders. *I feel lost out here,* she told him, *and more the coward with every step I take away from my home.*

He reciprocated with descriptions that he found mundane in comparison, but Telde seemed fascinated by: his old life, England, his family and friends, his work as an illustrator – an artist, he explained, not knowing how to describe the difference. He told her that people were his preferred subject – *individuals stripped of their surroundings, so the viewer has to consider that person alone* – and then admitted he hadn't been able to draw for a long time. *My mother was fond of drawing,* Telde said, *and encouraged the same in me when I was a child. But I stopped after she died, when I saw the pain it caused my father.*

John described various technologies of Earth, always a favourite topic for Telde, who was both captivated and highly distrustful of devices that could carry disembodied voices or images instantly across the world, or music without an accompanying performer, or vehicles that could convey people into and beyond the sky. The two of them went on to share their planets' histories, as well as their own, and found with surprise the number of common threads, the recurring patterns of human life.

Despite all that had happened and the dangers ahead, or perhaps in part because of them, John found himself to be entirely content during the days of travel. He felt better, too, no longer in that state of physical and nervous exhaustion the Black Sea engendered. Telde's cough finally began to recede. The roads became busier as they travelled south-east on the jallers, and they passed an increasing number of villages and towns. They encountered other travellers: traders, farmers, villagers going about their daily tasks, the ordinariness of whom seemed to mark them as little different from those in Ireldelor or Ferol, Telde had to concede. *They can't be so dissimilar if they speak the same language,* John thought.

It was with some disappointment on his part, alongside a new apprehension, when it became clear by the growing magnitude of the traffic and surrounding settlements that they were nearing their destination: the Regency capital that lay in the corner of the continent. They arrived at a large guard post positioned in the bottleneck of a road, the passing multitudes inspected by soldiers dressed in neat black leathers with high collars and thin yellow sashes across their chests. Telde informed them, in a decision made previously with some consternation, that they were both part of the Ferol resistance. The news was accepted with little fuss, however – it appeared their arrival was not wholly unexpected – and they were designated two soldiers to escort them the remainder of the journey.

The subsequent route along high bluffs and steep rocky

paths afforded a generous view of the encompassing country. John suspected the soldiers were trying to show off their land, with some justification. On one side of them a tremendous ocean rolled out to the edge of the world. At first it was glimpsed between trees and hills, the breeze carrying its scent as if preparing them for the later unobstructed view. *The Shatter Sea*, a soldier declared; *A real sea this time*, John thought. Its deep olive was broken only by the ashen grey of rocky islands, and then the necessarily immense barriers of the cliffs. The view inland only continued the theme of majestic scale, manifested in its inexhaustible hills and mountains and valleys and woodlands. As they neared the capital John saw palaces and statues and walls, constructions imagined on a huge magnitude, as though trying to compete with the surrounding land. Telde scoffed at their ostentation, but he remained quietly impressed.

The path became a long and winding descent, ending at a tumultuous marketplace lying half in the shadow of an enormous wall. The latter's light grey length curved between two mountains, numerous bowmen visible over its parapets. The soldiers led them through a gate in the wall, and John was surprised when, instead of the buildings he had expected, he was confronted by row upon row of tents. Beyond the town-sized camp lay another great wall, the embellished spires and domed roofs of palaces rising above it, and then, on higher ground, yet another wall and palaces that were grander still; so continued the pattern, repeating at least five times as far as John could discern. *The Regent's Crown*, one of the soldiers called it as he explained that the city was tiered, each subsequent level more fortified than the last. *And exclusive*, the other soldier muttered, evidently less impressed. *No opposing army has breached even the outer wall*, the first continued, ignoring his colleague's remark.

The camp was populated by army and Regency officials involved in the war effort, as well as other affluent figures, the soldier went on to partially explain; the rest John could see for himself. Adjutants buzzed in every direction, and might have been mistaken for servants were it not for their haughty carriage and the reproachful glances aimed at John and Telde and their escorts; it appeared that adjutants were higher up in the hierarchy than common soldiers. The prominence of that social hierarchy was evident all around them: the high-ranking and wealthy were never without several adjutants in tow, or as a vanguard noisily announcing the passage of their patron. *Most are here only to be seen here,* the second soldier remarked as they were passed by an individual submerged within a capacious amber dress, their gender unclear. John recognised the truth in the soldier's words; the site held the atmosphere of a fashionable society event rather than a military gathering.

Although the clothing of the camp's inhabitants was severely neat for the most part, as was clearly the convention for Regency attire, it was apparent that the higher the strata of society, the more freedom and ornamentation was afforded to appearance – if the meticulous aspect was maintained even in the most elaborate of costumes. The uppermost echelons, those with the greatest number of adjutants attending to them – *like bloodflies around a carcass,* the unimpressed soldier said – wore wigs of matted hair, ascending into the air in implausible coils and twists, or descending to form intricately woven masks. The inflated curves of their robes, maintained by some unseen internal structure, were coloured in rich reds and oranges and golds, with sashes as further adornments.

The soldiers guided them through the throng, eventually reporting to the lavish tent of a senior officer. The man visible through the tent opening was dressed in impeccable leather armour, his yellow sash of a prodigious width, his collar high enough to lift his jowls. A kneeling adjutant painted his fingernails as he cast a brief and disinterested eye over the new arrivals. They were subsequently treated courteously enough – to Telde's surprise and annoyance – and were informed by the soldiers that they would be furnished with tents and an adjutant. Of much more interest to Telde was the news that a meeting would be arranged in the evening, involving the Ferolian resistance members and Regency officials. It was only with some insistence that the soldiers deterred her from immediately attempting to seek them out.

She should make the most of the luxury, John thought presently, shaking off his reverie. *And I should, too. Who knows when we'll get the chance again?*

He hesitated, then picked up the razor next to him. Its dark, glass-like surface reflected the light and the pink and black smudge of his face. He glanced at the bowls of ointments, but decided against using them.

After several minutes of ineffectual and somewhat hazardous efforts with the razor, there was a change in the light behind him.

"You're holding that wrong."

John turned to see Telde standing in the entrance, and couldn't help the smile that immediately found its way onto his lips. However his expression froze in surprise as he took in her appearance: she had obviously washed and groomed herself as well – more successfully than him – and her light auburn hair was let loose, free to spill over the shoulders of a simple yet elegant pale yellow dress, its lace sleeves the sole concession to extravagance. She held her armour and bag as a bundle in her hands, looking noticeably uncomfortable and perhaps a little irritated because of it, but also unquestionably beautiful.

She apologised and glanced away, and it took the still-gaping John a moment to realise her meaning; he rose and moved to pick up the shirt lying on top of the pillows, quickly putting his arms through it. He was dismayed to discover its fluted cuffs and high collar.

"You look…" John started, but was interrupted by Telde.

"It wasn't my choice. The dress. You should have seen the other obscenities that man tried to force me into. The Regency has the taste of a blind beggar."

She looked much younger, especially when she gave the small awkward smile – if somehow alongside a glowering gaze – that she did now. Younger and transformed. John was almost afraid to look at her.

He desperately searched for something to say. To his instant regret, he ended up indicating his shirt. "What do you think?"

"I preferred the old one," Telde said, placing her belongings on the floor. She moved to the jug of water and filled a cup. "Don't let me interfere," she added.

John comprehended slowly as she nodded to the mirror that she meant his shaving. He had the impression that she wanted to make him uncomfortable, in return for him doing the same to her. Kneeling before the mirror he picked up the razor again, wilfully relaxed, determined not to let her have the minor victory. But he doubted his success; in addition to his inexpert use of the tool, he knew that he couldn't escape her presence.

"Well, they didn't execute us on sight at least. How's your tent?" John asked as he wet the blade and brought it to his neck, his skin protesting at the raw contact. He could feel her eyes on him.

"It's fine."

John shifted on his knees so that he could see her indistinct reflection in the mirror. She was sitting on the pillows, but continued to adjust her position every few seconds.

"But?"

"You can't understand. The Regency has been an enemy of Ferol for hundreds of years. The recent peace is only a thin veil, it doesn't change what's behind. They are everything we stand against. To be in their midst like this, being pampered like a guest, it feels... unnatural. A betrayal of Ferol." She shifted in her perch again, then put down the cup and simply stood. "It's like lying in a nest of jestai. I feel naked."

John sucked in a breath as he nicked his skin with the razor. He cursed and put a finger to the bright spot of blood that appeared.

"Let me help," Telde said, walking to his side. She knelt next to him and picked up one of the small bowls of ointment. "You have to use this – don't you shave on your planet?"

She didn't wait for an answer, or his permission, before dipping her fingers into the bowl and spreading the substance liberally over his jaw. There was a faint odour, somewhere between ammonia and coconut, and a slight fizzing on his skin. She took the razor from his hand and, evidently seeing the concern on his face, gave him a disappointed frown. But there was a degree of enjoyment in her expression too, John was sure.

"I used to shave my father," she said.

Telde brought the razor to his cheek, then shaved downwards in a surprisingly smooth and painless motion. She studied his face as she continued. John didn't know where to look.

"You might not like this dress, but – don't try to speak – but my submitting to wear it meant I was finally able to get some information out of that adjutant. Hold still. There's at least six resistance members here – hold still, I said – and by the description one has to be Edodani. Only the gods know how he made it here, as he was supposed to be at the Candar'laon meeting – if you insist on fidgeting, you'll lose an ear."

"That's good news, isn't it? About Edodani, not the ear."

"No talking," she scolded. "It might be. We don't know the situation yet – or if the resistance's voice carries any influence here. But at the least we can gather information about the armies set to head north."

Telde's face was close to his own as she carefully shaved his upper lip. He could feel her breath as she spoke, and thought he could sense her smell beyond that of the ointment. It was impossible to look directly at her green eyes.

"I like the dress."

"No talking."

Despite her instruction, Telde proceeded to ask him numerous questions as she worked. *Have you always had a beard? What clothes did you wear on your planet? What was the weather like in your country?* John tried to answer in the intervals when she was cleaning the razor in the water. She was intrigued by the idea of such dramatically varying seasons.

"It must be like you're witnessing nature's life cycle," she said, and smiled as if the reflection wasn't entirely her own. "Ceria would like your country."

When she had finished Telde placed her hands under his chin to observe her work, then finally gave a satisfied nod. "I've never seen you barefaced," she said.

She dampened a cloth and dabbed away the remnants of ointment from his face and neck. Then, picking up another of the small bowls, she began applying the substance within, this time in a more modest amount. The ointment possessed a sweet, fruit-like fragrance, as well as a cooling property; she gently massaged it into his skin with her fingertips.

John wasn't certain if he imagined her touch lingering on his cheeks, and fought the temptation to close his eyes. But surely now her fingers were tracing his jawline. Then the palm of her hand rested on his cheek, and those brilliant eyes were staring at him. He met them and couldn't look away. He was caught in the fervent green that communicated so much: challenging and confiding, fierce and vulnerable. A gaze he could never hide from. He leant forward to kiss her, and found her lips hesitantly responding, unbearably soft.

He didn't know how long the kiss lasted, time was suddenly unreliable, but then she pulled away from his arms and stood. She walked to the tent entrance, away from him. John concluded, with considerable regret, that she intended to leave.

She paused at the entrance, however, and remained there for several moments. He saw her take a long, deep breath. She then moved her hands to lower the tent flap, and slowly turned back to him. Keeping her green eyes trained on his, ablaze even in the diminished light, she lifted her dress over her head and dropped it to the floor. She stood naked before him, smooth skinned and lithe, her breasts small and pert, her nipples the shade of her hair.

Then he had moved to her, and her to him, his shirt stroked from his shoulders, their hands and lips exploring one another, feverishly, impatiently, the intimacy they already shared now expressed and affirmed and unrestrained as they allowed their bodies to speak.

*

The light had turned to that of early evening when a figure appeared at the tent entrance. Telde was picking through the plate of fruit whilst John sat on the pillows examining her crimson armour; they had opened the entrance again to await the arrival of the adjutant.

But the figure was certainly no adjutant: a stocky man perhaps in his late forties, his face was dominated by a hooked nose and heavy scarring that covered almost half of it. The disfigurement extended over his bald head and down the side of his neck, and John couldn't quite tell if he was also missing an eye. He was dressed in plain leathers, and held a wooden cane. He took in Telde with a solemn nod, with perhaps a hint of surprise at her dress, and gave John a scrutinising glance.

"Edodani," Telde said with a smile, rising to meet him. She gave the man a somewhat perfunctory hug, which he appeared uncomfortable at enduring nonetheless. "It's good to see you."

"And you, Telde," he replied, retaining his sober expression, which Telde didn't seem to interpret as any ill omen. John quickly surmised it to be his usual manner.

"This is John," Telde said, turning to introduce him. "He's... on our side."

John put down the armour and stood, uncertain how to greet the man – handshakes were foreign here, and *Hello* seemed foolish. In the end he simply nodded, hoping the gesture wasn't as clumsy as it felt.

Telde turned back to the man. "How did you get here? Who else is here?"

Edodani lifted a hand, soliciting patience. "After certain events in Ferol, I chose to travel directly here instead of attending the meeting at Candar'laon. A worthwhile decision, considering the arrests." He used his cane to further lift the tent flap beside him: an invitation for Telde to go through. "I'll tell you more on the way. I want to show you something."

Telde nodded, before glancing back at her armour.

"You won't need that," Edodani said.

She walked back anyway, retrieving a crumpled dark cloak from her bag and wrapping it around herself. John followed as she left, wishing he had a cloak to conceal his high-collared shirt.

Edodani walked with a limp and leant heavily on the cane, yet seemed hardly slowed as he strode rapidly through the camp. The handicap and his appearance were somehow strengths rather than weaknesses: the man had unquestionable stature, no small part of which was intimidatory. Even the adjutants moved quickly out of his path. Telde had previously told John that he was one of the founding members of the resistance, and Climbe's closest advisor. When her father was alive, she had said, the three of them had been like brothers.

Telde hurried to move alongside Edodani. John attempted to do the same, but was frequently slowed or forced behind due to the narrow, crowded paths between the tents.

"There's something I need to tell you," Telde said, glancing at Edodani with some unease. "It's about Ceria."

"I know," Edodani said simply, not looking at her. "Manvedian has taken her. Was she hurt?"

Telde was taken aback. "How did you know?"

"I knew you were approaching the city. I have Leandra keeping track of everyone coming in and out. She's formed a useful relationship with the guards – you'd be impressed how far the girl's come since you last saw her. I also knew you were travelling without Ceria, and with a man that wasn't Manvedian." The three of them barely avoided a collision with a bulbous vermillion dress and an orbiting pack of adjutants, and John was left on one side of the group whilst Edodani and Telde continued on the other. With tents flanking him, he had no choice but to wait until the procession passed – suffering the daggered looks of the adjutants as it did so – before finally rushing to catch up.

"...aware for some time about him," Edodani was continuing. "We attempted to get birds to you, but they must've been intercepted. Was she still alive when he took her?"

"Yes," Telde answered distractedly. "Yes, she was. I couldn't follow, they –"

"I know," Edodani interrupted. "You wouldn't be here if you could have pursued them."

John managed to draw alongside the two of them as they passed a long yellow- and white-striped tent, pristine guards stationed along its perimeter.

"He won't hurt her, she's more valuable alive," Edodani said, then evidently saw a question in Telde's expression. "There were suspicions about Manvedian's allegiance before we knew the full truth of it. Incidents in Ferol accumulated until it was obvious we were compromised – abductions of those secretly working with the resistance, attacks on meetings only our members could have known about. Senthis and the Hearts were always a move ahead of us. And shortly after Manvedian left the city, Peledis encountered him in strange circumstances. What happened isn't clear – Peledis is of little help on the matter – but it was wood to the fire. Manvedian told us he was going to the meeting in Anat's

Dark, but he was chasing you and Ceria. He knew how important she was to us, and therefore so did Senthis. Tiyaden was attacked in Edemon, before he could meet with you. He would've told you the truth. And Manvedian undoubtedly prevented you from finding out what I must tell you now." Edodani paused with a frown, plainly not used to mixing delicacy with his words. "Climbe has been missing for months. We suspect that Manvedian killed him."

Telde paled, frozen in place. She searched Edodani's face, then looked down. "When we didn't hear from him for so long I just thought... and then Manvedian told us Climbe was fine, and I – I was so relieved. He can't be gone. Are you certain? If he's gone..."

John saw the pain in her expression, frustrated that he didn't know how to alleviate it.

"Enough, girl," Edodani said crossly. "Many have died, and many more will yet." He grasped her arm to pull her after him as he resumed walking; John felt a flare of anger in response. *Let her have a damn moment.* He was about to repeat the thought out loud, but Edodani continued.

"Climbe would spit fire if he thought we'd crumble without him. You know that, Telde. You know we must continue. Else we'd be pissing on all he's done. We must prepare Ferol for the armies coming north, we must ensure this war is won. We'll get Ceria back, and we'll cleanse Ferol of Senthis, the Endless, the flesh beasts, the Hearts, and any other godscursed shit fouling up our home. Ferol is ours. It'll be ours until the gods fall out of the sky."

Telde seemed to gain strength as Edodani spoke, nodding as they walked on, her face adopting the stoic bearing that John knew so well. He had to admit that Edodani's words were rousing, even if part of him was sorry to see Telde's hardened manner. It was clear why the man was a leader in the resistance. John couldn't imagine many others who could refer to Telde as *girl* without losing the capability of speech shortly after.

They reached the great wall enclosing the camp, and Edodani headed towards the gate through which they had entered earlier that day. The soldiers standing guard nodded at the resistance man, letting the three of them pass without challenge. On the other side the marketplace was as busy as the camp, if considerably more disordered; people bustled and argued and laughed between wooden stalls and flimsy gazebos, the sellers announcing their wares and denouncing those of their competitors. John watched the lively scene with pleasure, wondering absently if he would ever possess money to spend on this planet – and whether one day such pragmatic concerns would become important again. Edodani took them on a path skirting the majority of the market, its clamour making conversation difficult. But Telde seemed reluctant to speak in any case.

"Are we going to the meeting?" John asked as the stalls began to thin out, stepping hastily aside to avoid a woman bearing a pile of linens that rose a foot above her head.

Edodani looked at him as if it was a foolish question. "The meetings are a waste of time. If we're not snubbed entirely by the Regency, then they'll send some dim-witted officers with no more authority over the armies than the ticks on a jaller have over its course. Denyn and Lefes will show their faces, to play the resistance's part in the pretence, but our true influence will come via other avenues. I'm gradually gaining the ears of two Queen's commanders who have some sense about them, and possibly one of the Regency's also. Leandra is spreading word and rumour throughout the ranks of both armies – she'll have them all believing the Ferol resistance are the progeny of the gods before she's done.

"For now we have to remain patient," he continued, glancing across at Telde, "and allow both sides to indulge in their spectacles of war. When the real affairs are closer, when the commanders start to hunger for individual glory, then we'll show them the cards we hold. Our knowledge of Ferol, the use of our men inside the city walls – we're the difference between conspicuous victory and humiliating difficulty. They'll be crawling over each other to get into bed with us. That's when we'll make our deals, and ensure our city comes out of this intact."

John sensed that Edodani was speaking for Telde's benefit rather than his. Before long she was requesting exact details and plans, names and places that were presumably resistance members and sites in or around Ferol. The two of them began discussing the intricacies of tactics and contingencies and, as much as John attempted to keep up with the conversation, he felt increasingly like a third wheel.

They had left behind the last stalls of the market now, and the land started an upwards slope. They followed a road that snaked over the gently undulating hills ahead of them. Sporadic clumps of impenetrable bronze-leaved bushes lined the route, and John could see the same vegetation growing en masse on the bordering hills and distant mountains, ignited as if a last rebellious act of the falling sun. Between the molten scrubs were streaks of bare grey rock, or the neat geometries of farmed lands, or man-made furrows that transformed grassy banks into a giant's staircase. The numerous forests that lined the hilltops cut a stark contrast out of the blushing sky, and, to his right, the ocean was sometimes visible in between the heights, as though pooling in the valleys. An unrecognisable bloom of glimmering purple and silver in a far off field reminded John that this was the scenery of a different planet, but he struggled to feel that sense of alienness anymore.

By now John had given up trying to follow the talk, and watched Telde instead. There was a new hardness about her as she walked alongside Edodani, as if she had iced over any weaknesses in her armour. John wondered if that included him. She seemed a different person to the one he had been holding in his arms only an hour ago. He could still feel her skin, sense her taste and smell. When they had lain together on the pillows, sweat-covered and out of breath, bare in every way, her green eyes had belonged entirely to him. John ached to have that time again.

A small ornate carriage passed them on the dirt and ashen stone of the road, its wooden frame pulled by a single jaller. Its two wheels were painted white, along with the roof that curved acutely upwards at the front, revealing both the driver and, behind him, an elaborately-dressed and again seemingly genderless occupant, winking jewels aloft in his or her woven hair.

John recalled Telde describing the sibling rulers of the Regency – Regent Amuur as the two were jointly referred to, a combination of their abandoned names. Once they had ascended to leadership their separate identities had ceased to exist; they were now one entity. The system worked, as Telde told it, with the principal rule that any family of those in the Circle of Regents – made up of the most powerful Regency houses – who conceived a brother and sister were entitled to claim the future throne for their offspring. Twins, like the current pair, were especially favoured. This had led to centuries of rampant reproduction in the families, as well as tales of kidnapping, murder, faked pregnancies, swapped or stolen babies, and wives who, with or without their husbands' encouragement, would seek out men who had given women mixed twins, or, the lengthier but surer gamble, those who had given only females, followed by those who had given only males. John wasn't certain how much Telde had exaggerated.

On how the sibling rule had come to be, she was less illuminating. But it seemed the Regency populace considered such a leadership pairing an ideal, judicious whole. *Like how two sides make a coin,* Telde had shrugged. It would explain the androgyny seen in the upper classes, he thought.

"John?"

He turned to find Telde staring at him expectantly.

"We were talking about Edemon," she said.

"It seems Ferol is indebted to you for saving Telde and

Ceria," Edodani said, peering at John with his good eye. "This power that you used against the Endless – can you use it again?"

Telde was looking at John with an expression containing a trace of pride, combined with something else he couldn't identify. John felt awkward under both of their gazes. He should be the grateful one – after all, Telde and Ceria had surely saved his life many times over before and after that day.

"Can you use it against Senthis?" Edodani asked.

John shook his head. "If Senthis is like Telde describes, if he's principally a man, I doubt that I can. It's hard to explain. It's not... physical, I suppose. It works against the Endless, but I'm not sure I can control it, or if I even still have it in me." He paused, unhappy at how unwilling he sounded. "I can try to use it against them. I *will* try."

"The Endless killed John's people," Telde added.

Edodani studied him, before giving a sharp nod and walking on. John and Telde followed. He was glad that Telde had kept her comment vague; he didn't want to explain about coming from another planet. *Will she tell him about Manvedian coming from Earth?* John wondered. *Does it matter?* He was beginning to realise that he increasingly felt as if he belonged here. Or that the feeling of being a part of something was being restored after his years of isolation. Telde and Ceria had not only saved his life, they had given him something to live and fight for. But also something to lose again.

They ascended a rise, then Edodani unexpectedly led them away from the road and through a dense thicket. Before John could ask why, they had pushed their way through the undergrowth and emerged into a clearing at the top of the hill, and he found himself speechless at the sight before him. The land fell away precipitously, revealing a flat expanse below that stretched on for miles, every inch of which was filled with tents and carts and animals – and thousands upon thousands of humans.

"Blood and blackness," Telde muttered under her breath.

Fires were being lit in the fading evening light, and John could make out the recurring white and chain mail-silver of Queen's soldiers, in addition to a gigantic standard bearing the design of a barbed stem twisting into three full scarlet flowers. There was a different standard on the opposite side of the valley, amongst the more tidily arranged tents that looked like rows of blunt teeth: two faces above a prodigious ship, gold against deep claret. The innumerable animals were spread throughout the camp, in pens or pulling carts or carrying people. Besides various unrecognisable shapes, John identified jallers, a row of immense grey and russet forms that had to be jooruns, and the graceful, sidling silhouettes of Queen's Claws. The latter still made him uneasy. Almost below where they stood, a hundred feet or so down, was a large area set aside from the camp that contained soldiers sparring or moving in vigorous unison; noises from the drills drifted up to them, along with a trace of the robust aroma of the encampment.

Edodani pointed with his cane. "Look over there, beyond the trebuchets. Do you see the fenced area? That's where the Primitives are – all of the hundreds taken from Ireldelor in the arrests. Not just so Senthis couldn't get his hands on them, but to use them in battle – even though most couldn't amuse a child with their supposed powers. They'll end up as little more than fodder."

"But some could be Primitives like Ceria, couldn't they?" John asked.

"She doesn't like being called that," Telde said, staring at the encampment.

"Perhaps," Edodani answered, after a sideways glance Telde. "But I suspect Senthis sought out the most gifted before the arrests – and the reports suggest many Primitives disappeared even after being captured by Queen's soldiers. Killed most like, if they couldn't be taken. It's obvious that Senthis' influence runs rife throughout the Queen's army. The arrests at the resistance meetings proved that – the majority of our people vanished en route."

John returned his gaze to the vast armies below, unsure whether he was meant to be cheered or terrified by the sight. "If Senthis controls some of the Queen's army, how can we trust them?"

"We can't," Edodani said, as if it were obvious. "And we can trust the Regency even less. But Fen take me if you have some better allies in mind."

"All of these forces, it will take tensuns for them to reach Ferol," Telde said in a detached voice, still focused on the multitudes below. "By then it might be too late."

Edodani tapped her arm with his cane. "Follow me."

He led them on a path along the brink of the hill, and after a few minutes the ocean could be seen emerging from behind a distant mountainous rise. As they walked on, a prodigious harbour was revealed, its timber skeleton extending far into the water. The ocean beyond was a motley brown and black, and it took John a moment to realise, with some shock, that the colouration was due to hundreds of ships floating on the surface. Even from this distance he could make out individual masts; the ships had to be considerable in size, and the flotilla itself seemed to be without end.

"The boats will carry a vanguard of more than half of the armies' numbers," Edodani said from behind them. "I'll make sure we're on board."

John glanced at Telde, who was eagerly studying the fleet. The events surrounding him suddenly seemed so huge, so real – surely he had no hope to influence the future when the consequential machinery was of this scale. The fate of life was out of his hands, just as it had been on Earth.

No, he told himself, *it's not the same.* This time he could fight. He could try. For Telde – for his own life. He wouldn't be left on the outside again, a helpless witness. He would fight.

"When do we leave?" Telde asked, her green eyes fixed on the ships.

He crouches behind the tree in the darkness, gripping a vine attached to the trunk. He calms his mind. He remembers who he is and clings on to that truth. Manvedian. I am Manvedian.

He concentrates on the consistent patterns in this world that is not his. The vine comes into focus and swells and slithers over the wide trunk. Leathery leaves are around him and now he is in a forest. He ignores the rest: the errant images, the fragments of places and faces and textures that do not belong here. Follow the coherency he tells himself. See what she sees.

He knows the dangerous part has passed. The deluge of sensations and emotions and thoughts had swamped his mind on entering but he held fast to his purpose and to himself. Rain starts to drum – has always drummed – on the leaves surrounding him. He is aware. This is her dream.

He occupies the same space as her, he is where she is. He is confident of his control and opens himself to her. Their senses combine. He does not let her discern his presence, he does not interfere. She and he crouch, they hold on to the vine. They feel panic. Dread and helplessness. Something is chasing her, she tells him, she tells herself.

They look back and see lights within the dark of the forest. Torches. Shouts are carried on the wind. Faraway, nearby. Run, she tells herself. Hurry.

They are running and branches and leaves buffet them. Why doesn't the forest help? She cannot understand and he feels her frustration. Their feet are bloodied and burning from the hot jagged rock beneath them. The rain thickens and the wind howls colour. The shifting mist chokes their throat. Low whistles penetrate the air.

They look back into the forest and it is not the tribes but the Hearts following them. She hears their hunger. A white temple appears, a body hanging in front of a blood red window; he quickly dismisses the image and reminds her to run. Their body is heavy and the forest tangles their limbs. But the Hearts are unimpeded, she knows, scores of them race through the trees. He feels her rage and indignation. This place does not belong to the Hearts but she cannot stop them, the forest will not stop them. Why won't it act?

The Hearts are trying to catch her but he and she realise that she is not afraid of them – she never was – and she is chasing something, she is trying to find something. He feels desperation. She has to reach it before they do. The hunters are no longer chasing her – they never were – they are pursuing the jalren.

Run she tells herself. Come on. But he feels the crippling pain in her feet and the wind and rain blind their eyes. He helps: he suggests that the ground is soft and grassy. He whispers that the wind is weak and the air is clean of rain and mist. He feels exhilaration as they sprint unhindered: he recalls how he loves this world, its different rules and its consequence before cause and his control over it. She stumbles confused; disorientated and carefree. He reins in his thoughts. Focus, he warns himself, don't let your emotions into hers. He reminds her that she has to find the jalren. Hurry, she agrees.

Their limbs are light and they pass freely through the undergrowth. She looks back and sees brightness between the trees, not torches but a white fire that is living and whirling and Endless. Crackling fills the forest. They smell burning flesh and see a tumorous monster ripping apart a woman. Trees are falling like slow pillars. The forest is being torn down and she is losing her home. He feels fear and sadness and guilt (hers or his?). The land shudders beneath them.

She remembers that she finds it in a clearing and it appears before them: a wounded jalren. They kneel and place their hands on its arm and suddenly it is Manvedian lying on the ground: he is surprised to look down upon himself and wonders if he caused this change, but is sure that he did not. She tends to the Manvedian. Concern and affection. She moves their hands to the Manvedian's neck but it rears its head and its daggered horns impale her chest. No! he shouts and separates from her. He moves to her side and she recognises him: the air fills with relief. He puts a hand to her wound and tells her she is lucky it barely scratched her skin. He helps her up. Her back is bare and her markings glow. She smiles over her shoulder at him.

He senses a tension. She is starting to remember, she is summoning a new feeling and he knows it is his betrayal. He stops the pathway and eases her away from the knowledge.

She is soaked and shivering and water drips from her short hair. She points to the buildings at the top of a hill. He recognises Ferol. We have to get to Telde she tells him. This is a dream Ceria he tells her. She is puzzled and shackles appear on her ankle. She is dry and wearing a shirt too large for her. He struggles to control his emotions.

There is a light behind them. Ternerid is rising she tells him. But it is the wrong colour: it is bright black and wild white and inverting and both and neither. Its brilliance turns the forest dark. He knows what it is and he tries to contain his fear. No, stay aware. He tells himself where he is who he is but now the trees are all black and he reaches out and touches wet soil.

He is enclosed by moist earth and roots and stone, by these living passages that he knows so well. Som'syere she says alongside him. She is still here. He is surprised but wonders where they have been and who she is. He moves through the tunnels that pulse the land and she follows him. He knows the path: he is urged on by the land and by her. Faint blue whispers urgency, but so much weaker now (than when?). Her back is a rune that glows like them.

He feels as if something is falling away from his mind but the land thrills around him, it embraces him and he continues (towards?). There is pain in the land she tells him and you can make it better and he agrees. It feels right, this alignment.

He emerges into the heart chamber and it is there: the presence that is light and dark and death and life. Take it the land says she says (if he takes it what will he become?). He reaches out. It roars abundance and utterness (preserver or destroyer?).

No, he remembers, he resists. He cannot. He cannot take it. Why don't they understand? It is too much to risk.

He tears himself away, he is torn in two, he is losing himself, he is swimming up through dirt as the land and her cry out from below.

25

"There was a TV show when I was a kid – TV, television, imagine, I don't know, a play in a box. It doesn't matter. It was my favourite, a cops and robbers show – city guards and thieves – and the cops, the police, they were the heroes. They were powerful, respected. They always caught the bad guy in the end, it was black and white like that. Justice was always served. They were how my father should've been – he was a cop too. A real one. I pretended he was that way. But the truth is he was weak, he was too straight, too down the line. That doesn't work in the real world. It doesn't pay. He took his failure out on my mother. I guess it gave him the power and fear he didn't get as a cop. Didn't know how to get."

The rain was driving down upon the carriage's canvas roof, its angle of assault shifting with the fitful, howling wind. Water cascaded from a tear in the centre of the roof, landing in-between the two of them: Ceria sat in the corner near to the chest, Manvedian opposite to her, leaning against the cart's front panel. The wooden boards were damp against his back, but he hardly noticed. The leaden clouds had turned early evening into premature night, yet he could see her looking at him, felt her large black eyes studying him, evaluating. Outside, the jallers moaned and brayed, their complaints merging with the whining and creaking of the storm-beaten carriage.

Manvedian winced from the burning in his neck as he moved his head. He was sweating even in this cold, and he knew the fever could be heard in his words. His accent was slipping, too, but it wasn't important – there was no need to hide such things from her now.

"I stopped him, eventually," he continued. "I thought I was doing the right thing. But afterwards my mother stood by him, not me. She chose him. I was sent to juvie – a jail for kids. I paid for my mistake. But I learned from it. I grew strong – in the ways he never could. I learned how to gain the power he always wanted but was too weak to take. I grew and I recognised them both as the small, helpless people they were. Shit, I should thank them for forcing me to see it. The truth of the world. For my clarity of vision."

His right hand was shaking. He moved it to his knee and placed his other hand on top of it.

"What did you do on your planet?" Ceria asked quietly, from her corner. "You weren't a – cop – like your father?"

"No, no I wasn't. I was one of the criminals – one of the bad guys," he said with a dry chuckle. "You know what I loved about that show? It was the simplicity of it. The good versus evil – it sucked you in. There was no choice to be made. Good always won. The world isn't built like that – my planet or yours. That isn't how the game is. It's freeing, once you realise it. Once you know the rules. No – it's focusing. You know what you have to do to get what you want."

"Did you kill people?"

"Sometimes. When it was necessary. I was involved in all kinds of things. Drugs were always the easiest. The biggest margins. Imagine Dredora's Vine or Seeing Leaf here, or Spirit even. But I was versatile, that's what got me ahead. Versatile and focused. A fenning chameleon they called me, before I was above them and they wouldn't dare say a word I hadn't put in their mouths. I had power, I'd protected myself – do you understand? I was safe. Then everyone died, of course. Shit, that proved I had it right if nothing did before – the universe killed all the virtuous, the quiet and the well-behaved, the cops and the priests and the children, the great and noble minds, but it spared me. I survived."

"It wasn't the universe that spared you, it was the Endless."

"Right, yeah, yes. It was. And what they did couldn't be stopped – no-one even knew there was anything to stop. Just flip, dead, lights out, so long." Manvedian made a gesture of flipping a light switch, which was expectedly lost on Ceria. He felt suddenly dizzy and tired.

The wind blustered against the carriage, billowing the stained canvas. A leaf blew in through one of the holes in its side. Manvedian could hear the gale ransacking the trees outside, and the drowned-out trills of wildlife caught in the storm. *Ferol country.* Tensuns of travelling north and now they were here, in Ferol, within a few miles of the city.

It wasn't the situation he had envisioned, naturally. During those long months of the chase, the countless tensuns playing the game. Things had changed. From the night of the mercenaries' attack, when Ceria had come back, saved him, declared that they would go to Ferol together. *No,* Manvedian corrected himself, *it started before that.* That night had simply solidified the change. In the days following she had helped him through his fever and treated his wounds, until he had regained enough strength to care for himself. But he was lastingly weakened, he knew; from the fight with the mercenaries, from Ceria using her ability on him, from the Black Sea poison that ate away at him still. And from Jago. Shackling Ceria again was pointless – besides the risk of her using her power again if he attempted it. Things had changed, and she was no longer his prisoner. *Rethink your strategy,* he had told himself.

Their progress north had been slowed when one of the carriage's wheels had cracked – *A wonder the wood lasted as long as it did,* Manvedian thought – and they had stopped in a village near the Ferol border to have it repaired. He hadn't been concerned by the delay. There was no great rush to reach the city now, and his mind was busy rearranging a new order inside of him.

I won't heal you, Ceria had said on that night in the village, jaw clenched, almost instructing herself, *I won't try. I know,* he had replied. She had come to regard Manvedian with what he took to be a cold acceptance, viewing him as a tool that she could make use of. *Good,* he thought. She was growing stronger as he became weaker.

How long were you working for the half-man whilst in the resistance? she had asked afterwards. She meant, he knew: *How could you do that to us? How could you drink and laugh and spill blood with us and do that?*

I was never on your side, he told her, unsympathetic, forcing the reality home. *I made sure the resistance was successful, that we – you – rendered the city defenceless in time for Senthis' attack.* Although, admittedly, he hadn't expected that level of slaughter. Not that many of the Endless or the other monsters. He had underestimated what the Endless and Senthis were capable of, misjudged their motives.

Climbe never knew, Ceria had said, more statement than enquiry. *No,* Manvedian thought, the gaunt and bloodied face invading in his mind. *The old man didn't see it coming.*

That night he had entered Ceria's sleep. He wasn't sure why he did it, what he was searching for. Her intentions, perhaps. To understand her. Or as a childish response to her using her power against him, to prove he had a few tricks of his own yet. He remembered the forest and the running; her relief when she had seen him. But he had spent too long in her dream, he lost control and let his own seep in. It came faster than usual, and he hadn't been able to react – it appeared he was weakened even in that domain. He had been dragged again into that place, Som'syere, to the presence he knew but couldn't comprehend. And Ceria had seen it again.

She seemed unsurprised by his ability to enter her dreams, and had barely mentioned it. Instead she labelled him a coward once more for not using his power – she called the presence that, *his power,* as though he could contain it. *But she doesn't understand,* Manvedian thought. *She would regret it if I did.* It was indifferent to the world's concerns. He would lose himself in that absolute power and it wouldn't care, couldn't care, if he chose Senthis' path over Ceria's. And he would, he was convinced of that. He would take all he could from the world, bleed it dry – why wouldn't he?

"The world *is* simple," Ceria said presently, staring at him across the carriage. Her hair was longer than Manvedian had known it before, the gusts of wind blowing dark strands across her forehead. Most of the jewellery once decorating her ears was now absent. "At this moment, it is. The half-man and his Endless are evil and they need to be stopped."

"You're right, they are. Evil exists. But the point is that it doesn't mean anything. It's not of consequence," Manvedian replied, brushing back his own hair, which was in an uncommonly tangled state. He waved a hand, showing he was tired of the matter. "We were built to look out for ourselves. For survival. Ferol's had its share of blood on its blades over the centuries in that respect, just like any other country. Eventually your so-called allies will prove they live by the same instinct." He added the last comment casually, almost as if by accident, whilst busying himself with searching out a flask from a bag next to him. The bait was left for Ceria to chew on.

He took a large swallow from the flask, the liquor warming his throat as he looked through the opening in the canvas behind him. Beyond the beaded waterfalls issuing from the top of the fabric he could see the backs of the jallers, the impacting rain creating a chaotic mist above their matted fur, and beyond them the reeling limbs of trees, the suggestion of distant forested hills. He knew that he had allowed weakness in, that he was allowing it in still. He wasn't presently strong enough for Senthis' world. The episode with the mercenaries had proved that. He had delayed too long in dealing with them, telling himself he was waiting for the right moment while in truth he wanted to be certain of their guilt – certain it was the only option, when he had known from the start it would be. Jago had got to him. Weakened him. The realisation had caused him no little alarm at first, but he had quickly come to accept it. He had to adapt. There was a way to turn any circumstance to his advantage.

Manvedian forced himself, as he had repeatedly since that realisation, to think of Senthis and the Endless. The Endless who had killed billions of humans on Earth. Because of Senthis – to stop what he was going to do, what he had already achieved in part, a fate worse than death for those he had managed to transport to this planet. *Change,* the Endless in the mountain had said: Senthis had changed all of those people. Manvedian knew the horrendous truth of it, as well as what the half-man was doing to the Primitives. *How could you be a part of that?* he accused himself, but not convincingly; it was not yet his voice. *The same will happen here as it did on Earth,* he instead thought. The half-man and his monsters will tear civilisation away from Crescent, or simply flick the switch on its existence. *Then what will you be left?*

Senthis wasn't playing for survival, to gather enough power for control over his life and over others', but for all power. To destroy everyone and everything and in that destruction prove that he was a god. *You didn't allow yourself to see it before,* Manvedian thought. There would be no winning side, no life, if the half-man succeeded in his plans. He convinced himself of this new reality. *This is the game you have to work with now. And you need a new self to play it.*

"What do you mean by that?" Ceria asked. "Do you know something about the Queen's and Regent's armies?"

Manvedian allowed himself a small inward smile. He waited, outwardly deliberating, drank again from the flask, then gave a resigned shrug.

"The Regency are going to betray the Queen's army, and Ferol," he said. "They made a deal with Senthis months ago. Their forces will ambush the Queen's army before the attack on Ferol city – there'll be no attack."

Manvedian imagined Ceria paling as she leant forward. "Why?" she asked disbelievingly. "You're lying. No. Why would they?"

"The Regency have no love for Ferol, you know that. They don't need much enticement to turn against you – Senthis has provided that and more. Their share of power. Ferol lands disputed since the White Age – Ro'laon and Tursen Fens – as well as future territory in Ireldelor. Shit, maybe he'll gift them Ferol itself – Senthis won't care much for it after he's used up Som'syere. They'll get their cut of the Spirit mined from the island, too."

"Their greed will end us all," Ceria spat out, now standing. "Because they only think of themselves, Crescent will perish. How do they not see that?"

Manvedian shrugged again, then fought off a momentary nausea as he scratched his neck. "Put yourself in their position. Ferol is their oldest enemy, and Senthis and his armies are the likely victor in this war. Siding with him is the logical choice. I told you, it's about survival. Senthis will turn on them eventually, of course, once he's done with the other nations. But perhaps they know that. Maybe they *do* see, and they took the deal anyway. Why die today when you can die tomorrow?"

Ceria made an exasperated noise. "They ruin our sole chance at stopping the half-man. If they do this he'll be too strong – with the Queen's army shattered there'll be no-one to stand in his way. Gods, don't you understand that?"

"Yes, I do. It's too late to change the Regency's decision now – but you can at least even the playing field," he said, fixing his gaze on Ceria. "The resistance can warn the Queen's armies. Maybe they'll even listen."

Ceria paused for a few moments, staring suspiciously back at him. "Why are you telling me this? What's in it for you?"

"Does it matter?" Manvedian replied.

He wondered, somewhat light-headedly, if he possessed the answer to her question or if he'd even allow himself to see it if he did. Did he truly believe that Senthis winning this war would be the end of things? Or did he simply not want Ceria to be taken away from him – to not lose his control? *Are you lashing out to show you can still affect things?* He told himself he cared about what happened to this world, but he didn't know if there was sincerity behind the instruction or if this was just another role to be enacted, one that suited his weakness. Perhaps he was playing for time himself, levelling the sides in order to keep Senthis occupied; he could escape in the ensuing chaos, the weak and the not-worth-the-trouble, the cockroach that survives the nuclear blast. *Have you shed your skin or adopted a new one?*

Manvedian rubbed at his temples and struggled to rid his mind of the dizzying glut of thoughts. *Focus.* He didn't need to know the answers. *It doesn't matter. It's not of consequence.*

"Later tonight," he began, attempting to keep his voice steady, "I will go into the city. Alone. There's something I need to do."

"You're not going without me," Ceria said firmly.

"No, listen, you have to stay here," Manvedian said, then interrupted her protest. "I'll come back. I will. Then we'll go into the city together. Trust me in this."

"Trust you," Ceria scoffed. "I will never trust you, Manvedian. How do I know you'll return? You're just as likely to run away. Or come back with Hearts by your side."

"You should know by now I don't work well with others. But even if I did come back with company – you wanted to go to Senthis, didn't you? And if I don't return, you can simply go and tell the resistance yourself."

"I want *you* to go to Senthis," Ceria replied. "I'm going to be there to make sure you do the right thing."

Manvedian shook his head with a sigh. "I could've got away from you a hundred times on the journey here if that was my aim, even in this state. You must realise that. But I'm telling you that I'll come back. I know where and when the ambush will happen, and a lot more besides. Information that's crucial to the resistance."

"So the resistance can't afford to kill you, you mean," Ceria scowled. "What is it you have to do in the city?"

Manvedian gave her a weary smile. "Allow me a final mystery."

*

The sullen glow of the coming dawn banded the horizon as Manvedian approached the bridge arching over the canal. The storm of the night had dissipated, leaving behind raw, fragile air. He snuck over the bridge, and saw how the woodwork of its sides – intricate waves curling towards a hilly island – was obscured by untidily-attached metal girders, their thick widths thrusting into the water below. So that the construction could bear the weight of the half man's creatures, Manvedian supposed.

He turned right at the end of the bridge, following the water's edge until the squat shape of a granary appeared on a rise ahead of him. He hiked upwards, cutting a path that passed before the stone building, then through the trees dotting the embankment beyond it, and quickly down towards a scattering of small buildings. The outskirts of the amorphous Geadard's District, named after the ancient bladesmith that gave the district its craftsmanship flavour.

He kept to the outlying houses, away from the district centre where the prodigious forges were found, the proprietors forced into ceaseless service by Senthis since his occupation, and slipped through the spacious grassy avenues between the buildings. He was careful to keep to the walls and shadows, avoiding the torches that had doubled in frequency throughout the city, although he knew it was unlikely that any Hearts or city guards – those who had pledged allegiance to the new order instead of being executed – would take the trouble to patrol this far out. Despite his tiredness and the dull burning in his neck he moved swiftly, instinctively: his body remembered its territory. The Hearts' curfew ensured the quiet, yet the emptiness seemed more complete than when he had left those months ago; there were probably fewer people remaining to disturb it.

He had always liked Ferol city, it was safe to admit that. It was unlike other cities, on Earth or on Crescent, hardly a city at all in the conventional sense. It was almost an opposite to Edemon, that other metropolis that had soaked into his veins – gone now, he had to remind himself. Instead of its buildings and inhabitants being packed so efficiently and uncomfortably together, the Ferol capital was spread out over its miles of wild, rolling terrain. The districts that formed the city were like neighbouring villages and towns that happened to collectively fall behind the extensive outer wall. Vegetation and wildlife were not excluded by that stone barrier as in other settlements, there was no dividing line between human and the rest of the living. *The trees and the animals are the city, too,* Manvedian remembered Ceria once telling him, the spark of passion in her eyes that she gained whenever she talked about such things. *Without them Ferol is not whole.*

Forests of trees were as common as the forests of baked brick and mortar, the two often mingling or even, in the more devout districts, forming a symbiotic relationship. The buildings themselves were simple and sparse to the point of dullness. *Extravagance is for soft southern hearts,* so the saying went; for the Regency and their ilk. Canals crisscrossed the land in vitalising furrows, and the streets, rare as they were, were broad and only cobbled on the most frequented routes. It was a city that suited the unencumbered and staunchly self-reliant spirit of Ferolians, or, as other nations claimed, put them in touch with the baser sides of their nature. Manvedian liked both interpretations.

He abandoned the edges of Geadard's District and ventured over a gentle ascent where a small forest used to be: the trees had been half-cleared in the time before Dalinde's rule – Ceria had told him that, too – whilst the remainder

Manvedian had himself seen incinerated during Senthis' attack. He remembered the electrical hum emanating from the bracers around the flesh beasts' wrists, his surprise – quickly masked – at the balls of lightning shot from their hands. The people had mistakenly run for cover amongst the trees. He had reined in his emotions then, during the attack. It was too late, he had chosen his side. Allowing doubt a voice would have helped no-one, especially not himself.

He slipped between the charred remnants of the tree trunks, the ground alternately crunching and softly crumbling beneath his tall leather boots. It had been as easy as expected to navigate the city undetected, once he had made it beyond the outer wall. Knowing the details of the guard changes in the latter, the blind spots in its vast and meandering length, in addition to a good deal of patience, was enough to get a lone man through the boundary. He had other means of getting into the city, of course, but didn't want his return to be known to anyone in either faction. Not yet.

He looked beyond the blackened stumps and saw a pair of watchtowers in the distance, their outlines exposed by the approaching dawn. Like the torches they had doubled in number, and for similar motives. The wooden towers that had always guarded the city wall had been joined by those erected throughout the districts, eyes now trained on the prisoners within rather than invaders without. They represented a city that had turned on itself, a notion inconceivable to Ferolians; Manvedian recalled the sentiments from one of Climbe's better speeches. The old man had understood that ingrained disbelief in the people that their own neighbours could betray Ferol's principles. *But so did Senthis,* Manvedian thought, *that's what made his subjugation so easy to achieve.*

The two towers were to the north-east, he concluded, watching over the Root District – now known as the Hearts District. It was the only district to possess an outer wall of its own, pre-dating even the city wall. Included within was the imposing city hall, the white brick and blood red glass of the

Hearts Temple – which, since its reconstruction, rivalled the city hall for size and surpassed it in embellishment – and the embankment that displayed the debris of the razed governors' mansions from six years ago. *Dalinde's sole worthwhile act,* Telde had always bitterly repeated, speaking of his mandate to have the buildings destroyed on the day of his election. The remains were left – laughably now – to remind of worse times. Telde had been one of those let down the most by the governor's subsequent manipulation by Senthis.

The Hearts District also contained the great confluence of canals known as The Join, and the remains of its commemorative fountain, destroyed in Senthis' attack. Following the slaughter, after allowing his deformed beasts to satiate their bloodlust, and the Endless to indulge their fascination with cruelty and death, Senthis had stood triumphantly upon the fountain's shattered stone. Before the crowds of defeated and dying in the flooded courtyard he had revealed his true self, half man and half Endless, and declared the new way of things, his ownership of a city that thought it could never be owned.

Careful, Manvedian. He reminded himself that he'd hardly known Ferol before the attack; it had only been a pretence, a method of infiltrating the resistance so that they could be used, via their misguided insurrection, to weaken the city's defences. Then afterwards so that he could keep a watchful eye on the group, negate their efforts, remain close to Ceria. And, when the time came, to kill Climbe. *You're no Ferolian. Your feelings aren't real.* He hadn't lived here all his life, hadn't had a wife murdered by the Hearts – even if he had made himself believe it, felt the pain of it, and of the wounded city, and shared the burden with his new family in the resistance. He leant both hands on a tree stump, fighting a moment of disorientation: who was he meant to be now? What was he meant to feel?

Focus, he instructed himself with some annoyance. *Remember what you're here to do.* He looked up and traced the skyline, counting another five towers and then pausing on the sixth, situated to the north-west, which he knew marked the Sellsoul District. He whistled a tune under his breath, ignored the fire in his neck, and set off towards it.

One of the lesser moons hung in the sky ahead of him as he walked, the flaxen orb gradually being wrested of its lustre by the light of the coming sun. Somewhere below it, beyond the channel of water that separated it from the mainland, would be Som'syere, the island that haunted his dreams. There was a black line scoring that channel now, he knew, the bridge a thousand feet in length that reached out to the island; one of the products of all the forges and the masonry and the hundreds of lives expended in slave labour. For centuries previously Som'syere had lain virtually untouched, according to the deeply lodged belief, contained within even the most sceptical of citizens, that the land belonged to the gods. Manvedian had always suspected that part of the reason for the bridge was that the half-man wished to humiliate Ferolians with the perpetually broken taboo, the crude finger penetrating their most pure of lands.

But he knew what Senthis was doing over there was infinitely more damaging: the mining of Spirit, the use of it and the land's energies to twist and deform humans and Primitives, the creation of the flesh beasts and worse; pulling the Endless into this world and somehow controlling them.

Half an hour later he came to the first stocky buildings of the Sellsoul District. He slipped through the alleys between them, plunged almost immediately into the thick of the community: the construction was more clustered here than in other districts, not out of necessity but preference, a sense of huddled solidarity. Its official designation of the Downberry District had never stuck, with critical outsiders and proud residents alike instead adopting Sellsoul. The district had the reputation of attracting the more adventurous, the morally diffuse, the down-on-their-luck, the downright crooks;

Manvedian had headed almost directly here on arriving at the city two years ago.

But the previously boisterous spirit of the district had now burnt out like so many of its buildings. There were more such stone skeletons since he had left, Manvedian noted, and he wondered how many people remained. He saw parchments nailed to the doors still standing, and didn't need to look closer to know their contents: evictions, warnings, doctrines, judgements.

He avoided the main avenues, yet couldn't help the glimpses of familiar sights. The fishmongers' market, the brothel, Raleben's tannery – all closed now, of course. Kelled's inn, where on so many evenings Dem Cleaver's wife would be cajoled to sing; the unfortunate truth that the men wished for an eyeful rather than an earful usually ending the nights in a brawl. Gadhallud's shop, the tailor whose revealing nightwear had led to his expulsion from the Hethea District; an idle pastime for many Sellsoulers was to identify his clandestine clients hailing from the wealthier districts. The house of Metimbe, vermin catcher and doctor. The small courtyard where the Hearts had hung Benuitis' son.

Manvedian stumbled over some debris, and leant a hand against the corner of a building to steady himself. The previous assurance in his body was fading, his legs felt weak and his head light; he was a silhouette moving through these echoing streets. The full light of dawn now fell upon the district, and the flaxen moon had dissolved into the sky. Some of the echoes were real, he realised: the sounds of voices and activity, the remnants of the community stirring into life. *Focus,* he repeated to himself and hurried towards his destination.

He arrived at an unremarkable building in the shade a large tree, relieved to find it intact. The surrounding bustle was rising by the minute, doors opening and figures appearing in windows; the Hearts' monotone chanting could be heard amongst the clamour. He took a nearby lit torch from its bracket and moved to the alley beside the building, pushing away the crates that he knew obscured a cellar door. When the wooden hatch was revealed, he drew a dagger from his sleeve and cut through the knotted rope by which it was secured. He ignored the tremor in his hands and the sweat on his brow that even such a minor exertion produced.

He pulled open the hatch and proceeded down the steep steps within, closing the doors behind him. He reached the cellar below, which was filled with an untidy stockpile of empty casks and broken crates. The building belonged to Heredem, a trader who had previously made his coin due to a diverse array of imports – mostly illegal – and an exceptional lack of scruples. When the borders were closed he had lost his income and become increasingly desperate. He had been perfect for the job.

Manvedian headed to a rear wall, then moved aside several barrels until a large hole was revealed, accompanied by a gust of cold, fetid air. He pushed the torch in ahead of him and crawled into the narrow tunnel, the low ceiling only allowing for progress at a crouch. The scamper and squeak of rodents – or at least Crescent's equivalent, jopiks and jons – sounded along the tunnel's length.

The passage eventually heightened enough so that he could continue upright, and after a time he came to a roughly hewn stairway leading further down. As he descended, the foul stench permeating the tunnel only escalated. At the bottom of the steps was a large door, no window set in its plain wooden face. He searched the wall to his right until he found a loose stone and, behind it, a set of rusting keys.

He took a breath, straightened his jerkin, then turned back to the door to unlock it. The mechanism grated noisily, and the heavy door swung open. He stepped inside.

The darkness in the chamber was profound enough that at first it appeared empty. The stink suggested otherwise, however, and after a moment the light of the torch gave shape to a bundle of rags in a corner. Manvedian was momentarily concerned – and angered – by the possibility that Heredem had allowed the man to die, but then there was a movement in the heap, followed by the rattle of chain.

He moved closer and the bundle became a body; a hand shielded a face enveloped by dirt and sores, a ragged grey beard covering the jaw – a face unrecognisable to Manvedian until the hand withdrew and he saw the eyes that at first widened slightly in surprise, then narrowed in hostility.

"Manvedian," said a voice scoured of its timbre.

"Hello, Climbe."

Manvedian moved to place the torch in a bracket on the wall. The remains of food and rodents and excrement littered the floor of the dungeon. He resisted the strong compulsion to cover his nose and mouth.

"Tell me, traitor, have you finally come to finish the job? Have you the courage to kill me this time?" Climbe rasped from the floor, his gaunt countenance turned up to Manvedian.

"Don't tempt me, old man," Manvedian replied. He felt the pulse of assurance returning to him, the certainty and control in what he was doing.

"What, then? Do you intend to parade me in a Hearts' execution?" Climbe peered at him, then tilted his head. "No... it's not that. You want something else from me. What is it?"

"You know," Manvedian said, reaching into a pocket for his flask, "I was hoping some time alone might make you less talkative."

"I will tear out your throat, traitor."

Manvedian grunted and took a long swallow from the flask. He could enjoy the dominance for a moment – it was the last he would allow himself for some time. He reflected that he had been right to secretly defy Senthis and keep Climbe alive. At the time he had assured himself the decision wasn't due to sentimentality or doubt, and it wasn't: he was simply abiding by the wise precaution of not killing a person who could be of future use. It had taken a considerable quantity of coin to keep the matter quiet, but it was the correct move.

"You don't look well, Manvedian," Climbe said with dry venom. "Are you no longer your master's favourite?"

"You're not exactly a Tvennik dancer yourself. Move." He knelt next to Climbe, trying to ignore the stench, and unlocked the shackles that held both of his ankles.

Climbe struggled to his feet, unable to disguise the exultant tremble that ran through his body at its sudden freedom. One of his legs gave way and Manvedian caught him, for a moment feeling how exceptionally thin he was beneath the rags, before Climbe pushed him fiercely away. He leant a fleshless hand against the wall for support and stared at Manvedian with hatred and rage: the look of a man who had been stripped of everything and was faced with the demon responsible.

But also, despite that surely overwhelming intensity of feeling, alongside it even now, he could see that Climbe was thinking, calculating, analysing. *We're not so different,* Manvedian thought, not for the first time, and remembered just how strongly he disliked the man.

"I will see you gutted and fed to jallers for what you've done to me," Climbe pronounced slowly in his broken voice. "But you're aware of that. You have a reason why I can't. You had better tell me it quickly, boy."

Manvedian resisted the temptation to laugh off the threat. Despite Climbe's age, and the ten years the imprisonment seemed to have added, he knew the man should never be underestimated. And he couldn't escape the weakness that permeated his own body; the exhaustion in his mind, the acid in his neck.

"The armies are on their way north, probably no more than a tensun away by now. But the Regency have secretly allied with Senthis, as you once feared. Together they'll destroy the Queen's forces – unless the latter are warned. I know the details of their plans," Manvedian continued, "and I can get to the half-man. You need my help if you've any chance of saving Ferol."

Climbe considered the information, no emotion showing on his withered face. "And Ceria?"

"I have her."

"Telde?"

"I left her alive."

Clime made an effort to stand unsupported. "So I'm to believe that now you fight on the side of the resistance."

"What do you think?" Manvedian answered with a shrug. He took another drink from the flask, then offered it to Climbe. The man batted it angrily away onto the floor of the dungeon.

"You should thank the gods that my revenge is not as important as saving this city."

Manvedian had to admire the old man's focus; how he was able to place apart his immediate emotions and desires in favour of the greater objective. *A clarity of vision.* It was the rare attribute Manvedian had been relying on.

"You'll not be protected forever, Manvedian. Remember that," Climbe said as he took a step forward, hollow eyes glaring. "Now get out of my way. I have work to do."

26

John left Telde sleeping, closing the door quietly on their small cabin. He climbed up a short wooden ladder and through the hatch at its summit, then stooped across a narrow corridor to a steep set of stairs, his shoulder colliding with the enclosing wood as his balance wavered. A submerged swell of laughter sounded from within the walls. He climbed through another hatch, navigated another cramped passageway, hauled himself up the sturdy rungs of the subsequent ladder, and emerged suddenly into blinding light and a world that creaked and gushed and billowed and boomed.

He stood motionless as his senses attempted to adjust to the bright storm of input. Voices cried out monosyllabically around him. Conflicting smells filled his nostrils: damp wood, sweet smoke, the tang of the ocean, something resembling hot tar, and an underlying rancid odour that he had almost learned to block out. The wind whipped the sun's heat from his cheeks. A weight bundled into his shoulder; a sailor carrying several buckets cursed back at him as he continued on his way.

John quickly scanned the vast deck and located a bald figure standing a distance away at the portside. He hurried towards the man, dodging the barefoot deckhands and trying to maintain his balance despite the swaying of the ship, an expertise that evaded him even after weeks of practice.

Edodani acknowledged his presence with a brief nod, without turning, as John moved to stand beside him. He gripped the wooden handrail at the side of the boat with some relief. The resistance member was looking out to sea with that critical air and his cane leant against the side, his arms folded, his balance seemingly untroubled. John couldn't tell whether his focus was upon the fleet of ships encompassing them or beyond, where a thin smudge of coastline provided an unconvincing frame for the ocean.

"Telde?" Edodani asked.

"She's sleeping," John replied.

"Good."

The short exchange was followed by a much longer silence. John, turning away from the sea spray, but careful to keep a hand on the rail, looked back over the length of the ship. Its series of prodigious rectangular sails were bloated with wind, the foremost of which bearing the design of a thorny stem entwining beneath three ample scarlet blooms. The deck below – a patchwork of sections either darkened by water and shadow or dazzled white by the sun – was even busier than usual. The sailors were engaged with the additional preparations, and groups of soldiers, previously stowed beneath in their crowded berths, gazed and commented upon the evolving coastline. The sight put a knot in John's stomach.

"What is it, John?" Edodani asked, keeping his eyes forward.

"Nothing," John replied, aware that Edodani would know better, but also that he wouldn't press him on it. "Any news?"

"A bird from Lefes. He's on Edem's Ire, another Queen's boat. The command there is uncommonly on edge, too. Ever since the message."

"It could just be the landing," John suggested, hoping that he didn't give his own feelings away.

"Soldiers show nerves of an upcoming battle, not the generals," Edodani replied. "No, something is going on. Something has them riled. Commander Bunadere has refused to see me since the last time. I need to know what that godscursed message said."

John's eyes were drawn instinctively to an area near the stern, where a tall figure stood perched atop the gunwale. The ship's Birdspeaker. Most were Primitives, Telde had told him, and they were often taken aboard larger vessels and warships. When John had once ventured near her, close enough to see the colourful coat adorned with small shards of mirrors and glass – and to earn a terse warning from a sailor not to disturb her – he had recognised the thick smell of Spirit, and perhaps a whistle that lay at the uppermost fringes of hearing. He had witnessed from a distance, on his own ship as well as others in the fleet, the great turquoise birds that seemed to materialise out of nowhere to land on the outstretched arms of the Birdspeakers, their tarsi bearing messages from neighbouring ships or from much further afar.

It was following one such message three days ago that Edodani, Telde, and John had been summoned to the Commander's cabins. There she had shown them the end of a letter – a seemingly senseless phrase followed by a set of symbols – and asked Edodani to confirm its authenticity. *There's no doubt it's from the Ferol resistance,* he had told the woman, going on to assure her of their robust code system. But to his and Telde's considerable irritation, Bunadere had refused to show them the rest of the message. At the time John had been concerned that the vehemence – and profanity – of Telde's remonstrations would result in them being thrown overboard.

"Leandra has found truth in the rumour about the missing Queen's boats," Edodani eventually continued. "Four of them have disappeared. One was laden with Primitives."

"Do you think they sank?" John asked. More than once night storms had ravaged the ocean and the fleet balancing on top of it – and then there was the much discussed threat of pirates as they had sailed through Gol Edge waters. But surely someone would have seen something in either case.

Edodani gave a brief shrug, not replying. They had discussed it before, and the man didn't like to repeat himself.

Especially when there was no clear answer.

"Has there been word from Denyn?" John enquired instead. The Queen's ships were not the only disappearance; the resistance members residing on Regency vessels had gone silent in the past few days.

"No, and nor from the others. But conspiracy is not the only conclusion, despite what Telde believes. It's a plain truth that the Regency dislike us as much as we do them. I can imagine it's been a constant temptation for them to simply toss our people into the sea during the night – they know the Queen's would make little fuss of it. It was a mistake to place them on the boats." Edodani spoke dispassionately, but by now John could recognise the signs of simmering anger: his body more rigid than usual, his words even more brusque.

"We had to. For the information, and to play the commanders against one another. To get the best deal for Ferol." John worried momentarily that he had overstepped a boundary by adopting the shared responsibility, and by reassuring Edodani of matters he understood better than John ever could. However he received only a silent nod in reply.

John reflected on how he took for granted the fact that Edodani would now talk about such matters with him, even without Telde present. In the beginning he was sure the man had seen him as some awkward hanger-on, but that had changed over the near two weeks spent at sea. They weren't exactly on friendly terms – he had difficulty imagining Edodani having that kind of relationship with anyone – but by all accounts he seemed to consider John a part of the resistance. He suspected the improved opinion was due in no small part to his closeness to Telde, with Edodani perhaps having respect for any man that she chose. He couldn't deny feeling a little pride in that too; that she would choose him, that she saw something in him that was worthy.

In the privacy of their cabin, he had asked Telde about Edodani and his past. *He's like Climbe and my father,* she had said. There was a slight tension in her body that John wasn't sure whether to attribute to the missing resistance leader, her father, or both. *But he wasn't always that way. I told you they were like brothers – Edodani was once the jester of the three. I'm telling the truth,* she had insisted, nudging him in the ribs at his disbelieving noise. *I remember him that way when I was young. Then his family were killed in a fire, murdered by the same faction responsible for the night of knives. It made him a different man. But after my mother died he was always there for me – I saw more of him than my own father.*

He cares more than anyone about Ferol, Telde had added, after a pause. *He'll do whatever it takes to free it.*

John felt a keen spike of anxiety as he gazed upon the deep olive of the sea. He knew they were close to their destination now. It was the Ferolian coastline visible on the horizon. However much he might wish that the ocean was endless, that this journey never came to an end, the grey brushstroke of land told of the reality. Tomorrow, or even tonight, the fleet would land, and soon after would come a battle of thousands, larger than imagination, where loss would be real and arbitrary and beyond his control. He feared losing Telde and this life he had gained – regained – and the love he had allowed in despite the risk. He feared the pain. He wanted to ask Edodani about it, to be granted some reassurance about what would happen, but he knew the man was unable to give it. For a brief moment John thought that it might be better if he had never taken the risk.

Telde was anxious too, he knew, despite her public stoicism. Her armour. Over the past few days their lovemaking had become even more intense, fervent to the point of desperation. It was as if fuelling their passion was a knowledge that their time was coming to an end, that the world was set on reclaiming them.

As they became ever closer indoors, however, out in the open they seemed to be growing more distant. Yesterday they had argued about Ceria again. Initially he had wanted to comfort Telde, to tell her they would find Ceria – and

Manvedian, too. But as swift as their travel was at sea, John knew, and Telde went on to reiterate, Manvedian's head start and shorter journey meant he would have surely arrived at Ferol already. *If we get her back, will you still sacrifice her?* John had asked, not able to stop himself. There was something in her anger that he had needed to see, a revealed glimpse that worried him more than anything else. When the hurt and uncertainty in her eyes gave way to a coldness – as though he were a weakness, as though he were in her way. It sometimes made him hope, guiltily, that they wouldn't find Ceria at all.

John studied the ocean and felt the welcome distraction of the wind in his hair, the sea spray wetting his skin and his clothes; he had thankfully managed to find a plainer replacement for the high-collared Regency shirt, as well as a pair of boots made of a soft leather. He looked at the surrounding ships, countless in number, blotching the sea. He regretted, not for the first time, that he had barely any experience of sailing, besides an ill-fated yacht trip once taken with Jessica's father. Jago would have reeled off hours of unsolicited information.

He was at least able to recognise the clear contrasts between the two nations' fleets: the Queen's ships were long boxy arcs, ungainly giants with pale wood and square masts, whereas the Regency vessels were smaller and faster, sleekly cut out of a dark wood, almost midnight blue to John's eyes, with triangular sails and rigging more complex yet as tidily maintained as the rest of the ship. However both fleets shared the ballistae or trebuchets on their decks, the projectiles from which could rip through their neighbours. Both held the thousands of soldiers within their ships' hollow stomachs, as well as the animals and Primitives and the piles of blades and bows; all sailed with this war machinery of flesh and bone and wood and metal north, to Ferol, to the half-man and his armies.

John could make out soldiers lining the deck of a nearby Queen's ship, their tunics bleached white in the sun, a few of them already dressed in full armour, judging by the glint of metal. He imagined a tension in them, like the soldiers on his own ship, becoming more palpable as they neared their destination; their laughter too loud, the fights more frequent. Then there was the rumour that the Queen's command had not received any word from the substantial reinforcements left to travel north on foot. Edodani had told John that no communication had been received from the resistance member left with the armies either. *Surely Senthis couldn't have got to them already?*

"Are you listening, boy?"

John realised with a start that Edodani had been speaking.

"You should have a drink," the man said testily. But he had also turned to him for the first time, the scars prominent over his face and bald scalp. "Something strong. It will help."

John became aware that his knuckles were white from gripping the handrail. "Maybe later," he said, relaxing his fingers with some effort. "I'm fine."

Edodani nodded, then gestured back across the deck. John turned to see Telde striding towards them, only slowing to scowl at a sailor who was bold enough to cross her path.

"Why didn't you wake me?" she demanded upon reaching John, her green eyes smouldering. The combination of those eyes and her dark, sharply angled eyebrows was somehow even more alluring when she was angry, he thought. But she soon looked away.

"How long?" she asked Edodani.

"A day at most," he replied. "Perhaps half that, depending where we land. We passed Hannidan's Fjord an hour ago."

Telde nodded impassively. The hilt of a sword was visible over her shoulder – Edodani had obtained the new weapon for her, though it was markedly plain compared to her previous one – and she had loosely wrapped a cloak around herself, covering the crimson armour that she habitually wore when on deck. She liked to practice her forms when the ship was quieter, and the sailors had quickly learned not to interfere. John had watched her one evening, mesmerised by the flowing, elegant movements, until she had noticed his presence and chased him away.

"What news?" she asked, moving between the two men to peer over the side of the ship.

Edodani grunted and turned away. John answered in his stead, repeating what little there was to tell, and avoiding the temptation to add that she had missed nothing by remaining in the cabin. Telde listened inscrutably, a soldier again. She rarely met his eyes.

"Fen take that idiotic woman," she eventually complained, meaning Commander Bunadere, John knew. "She has no right to keep resistance information from us. We should go and demand it from her."

"She almost had us thrown off the boat last time," John replied, then gave a small shrug as if to dislodge Telde's subsequent glare.

"Look," Edodani interrupted gruffly, pointing his cane ahead of the ship. On the horizon was a growing speck; a small vessel, rapidly approaching. "Scouts. A few of them went out in the night," he explained. "Surveying the landing sites, no doubt."

The vessel eventually pulled alongside, and one of its occupants scrambled up the rope ladder that was thrown down. Once aboard, he sprinted in the direction of Commander Bunadere's cabins.

"It seems they have something to report," Telde said.

It didn't take long for the news to filter back to them, passing through animated sailors and soldiers alike. The scouts had discovered the Ferolian docks to be empty and unguarded. Invitingly so, suspiciously so – but even with the possibility of a trap, Edodani remarked, it was an opportunity the commanders wouldn't be able to resist.

"They may be right," the man went on to admit. "A few boats sent to scout each way along the coast, that would give ample warning of any advancing forces on land or water. The closest forests or hills that could hide an army are too far from the harbour for an ambush. And as large as the North Gate is, it would greatly limit any host coming through it." He frowned, shaking his head. "It makes no sense."

"It's his arrogance," Telde said. "The half-man is telling us that we're no threat."

Over the next hour the three of them watched uneasily as the sky filled with turquoise birds, ships' sterns glinting with Birdspeakers, and several of the largest vessels moved alongside one another. The Regency leaders argued strongly for taking advantage of the empty docks, they soon learned, and, as the skies cleared and the scores of ships took formation, it was clear the Queen's command had acceded. The fleet was going to land.

John glanced at Telde and found her gazing intently at the coast. He couldn't help but feel that the world was about to take back its property.

*

The jaller grunted beneath John. The mounted group around him shifted nervously, impatiently. Telde and Edodani stared ahead from their animals. Behind him was a deafening tumult.

They had landed during the night. Or at least began to – the task of berthing a fleet of enormous ships and unloading their thousands of occupants and supplies was a lengthy and logistically challenging one, even at the commodious docks into which they had sailed. By the time the majority of the ships' contents had spilled out onto the land, converting the mild terrain of grass and stone into a broiling cacophony of colour, the light of dawn had arrived an hour previously.

John twisted his body on the jaller to gaze back upon that sea of human activity. It was difficult to gauge the scale of the armies from his low vantage point, but the ceaseless noise attested to its immensity. He knew there were upwards of twenty thousand men gathered here. The two nations were divided: the white and red of the Queen's forces were on the right as John looked back, whilst the black and claret and gold of the Regency were on the left. If it wasn't for the predominant number of faces turned towards him, or at least towards what lay ahead of the mounted group, it might have been tempting to imagine them as opposing forces about to do battle.

A deep rumbling: one of the trebuchets was being slowly rolled through the midst of the crowds by a score of soldiers. Nearby, another group were involved in some kind of construction – huge timber beams were being levered upright and fixed into place – and, not far from that, John saw a stack of exceptionally tall ladders. Innumerable banners already fluttered over the multitudes, and around them was the perpetual buzz of organisation: the officers barked orders and incitement, the soldiers sharpened swords and restrung bows and checked armour. John was unsurprised to see that the Regency regiments were quieter and held neater formations.

The brays and cries and roars of hundreds of animals added to the din. John picked out jallers and similar-sized creatures, the huge grey and russet shapes of jooruns, and, on the Regency side, animals taller yet, if narrower, balanced by a thick reptilian tail and with canopied seats or handfuls of archers upon their backs. The thronged crowds continued all the way up to the distant docks where the fleet of ships lay discordantly static, the life squeezed out of them.

It should have given him a great deal of confidence, John reflected, witnessing the tremendous strength of the two nations' armies. But the sight on the opposite side of him, which he turned to face now, quietly cauterised any such optimism. A vast wall, its motley grey and light brown length stretching away without end. Two towers formed its suitably imposing gatehouse, rising up to twice the wall's height, and a handful of dark figures could be seen in the uppermost echelons or along the parapets above the prodigious wooden gate. It was the silence that troubled John. The lack of reaction. The city of Ferol seemed almost indifferent to the armies gathered at its door.

It was the same kind of indifference that had allowed the fleet to sail so freely into the Ferolian docks. There had been no trap when they had landed. No sign of an army cleverly hidden and lying in wait. There was only a solitary message from Senthis, attached to an arrow shot from atop the wall, offering a parley inside the city. If giving them the docks was a show of contempt, John thought, then it had been an effective one; it only reinforced the part of him that insisted Senthis held the upper hand. After all, he knew what monsters lay under the half-man's power.

"Blood and blackness," Telde muttered from the jaller next to him. "How long are we to wait here?"

"It's deliberate. He's making us play by his terms," John responded.

"And we obey him, trotting like docile jotu into his pen," Telde said darkly.

"Would you prefer it if we remained outside?" John asked, knowing well the answer, which was confirmed in Telde's glare.

"Perhaps he intends to surrender," said a Queen's soldier on the other side of John. "Your half-man glimpsed our forces and now he's kneeling in his piss repenting to the gods."

"He won't find any mercy in my blade," another soldier remarked.

"Get in fenning line. I had family in Edemon," muttered someone in front.

"He's not *our* half-man," Telde said through gritted teeth.

"Quiet," Edodani demanded, a jaller down from Telde. No-one was foolish enough to defy the scarred man.

John studied the group around him. He saw the white armour of the Queen's soldiers, the wooden shields on their backs bearing thorny stems and scarlet flowers. Most of the men and women shared the same tense expression. A few rows ahead the dark leathers and yellow sashes of the Regency soldiers could be seen. Both armies had accepted the terms of the parley, and Edodani had been quick to arrange the inclusion of the three of them in the Queen's contingent. *It's your own risk,* Commander Bunadere had declared as they joined the assembled band, *I will hold no responsibility for you. And I will use you as necessary,* John had continued her sentiments, if internally.

Near the front of the group were riders in markedly more elaborate armour: fluted and ridged suits of gleaming white plate alongside immaculate dark leather with prominent sashes and high collars; helms shaped like beasts next to labyrinthine weaves of hair. Bunadere herself was contained within one of the Queen's ornamental suits; Telde had grudgingly given the woman credit for coming in person. But the Commander and the other esteemed leaders had been made to wait like the rest of them, for an hour already, whilst the frigid coastal air rifled through them and the hot smell of jaller urine rose from around their feet. They waited for the North Gate to open, a quietly ordered knot in front of the turbulence of thousands.

The jaller shifted beneath John, straining against the reins as it reared its head. He absently soothed the animal by stroking through the thick tawny fur at its neck. Beside him Telde was keeping a watchful eye on a Queen's Claw and its armoured rider as they prowled along the perimeter of the group. John reflected on the strange fact that they were now a part of the Queen's contingent, when once they had ran so desperately from the same forces. *When Telde had fought and killed them,* he reminded himself. This was the army that had carried out the arrests across all of Ireldelor, abducting Primitives and anyone else suspicious or who happened to get in the way. For the larger purpose of using them against Senthis, perhaps, or at least to prevent him from taking them, but it was nevertheless a ruthless action against its own people.

John wondered what had happened to Wimda, if she managed to escape after the distraction that had surely saved the rest of them. Or if she had been taken, if she and the others from the village were locked away somewhere. Or if she had simply disappeared along the way. He felt guilty for not wondering before now, for not keeping track of all the wrongs occurring around him, and he resented the design of life that made it impossible to grasp all of its strands at once.

More than ever he admired the Ferol resistance for working with these dubious allies; the blunt force of the Queen's, the ancient enemy of the Regency. *Whatever it takes to free Ferol*; John recognised the strength of that determination. *My father sacrificed his wife, my mother,* Telde had once told him. *He sided with those who murdered her, so the resistance would have an advantage. No matter how it fouled his heart. Do you understand? Long before he was killed, he gave his life for Ferol.* She had been telling him about herself too, John knew.

He fingered the pommel of the short sword attached at his belt. Telde had given it to him in the hours before they had landed, during their last time together in the cabin. She had also insisted on the somewhat dilapidated chain armour that he wore under a thick cloak, despite his complaints of the weight. Once she had finished helping him dress, they had kissed, softly, sadly. He told her that it would be okay, and she nodded. But he had seen the ending in her eyes. He sensed the acceptance in her.

They had returned to the deck afterwards and saw how the land had resolved into tangible matter: honey-coloured cliffs and jagged rocks striking out of the sea, and then the outer wall of the city, endlessly rising and falling with the coastline. Telde explained that behind the stone barrier the city lay scattered over the expansive land, and described the different districts, the forests, the canals, the markets, the festivals, the people. As John listened he had allowed himself to imagine that he was a welcome guest here, a tourist, and that Telde was showing him her home for happier reasons.

When they had come to the harbour, positioned within a wide sickle of a bay, skinny wooden fingers resting upon the water, he had seen a large island in the distance. The dark line of a bridge appeared to tether it to the mainland, and above the island's undulating outline hung a prickly mass of inky black that caused the hairs on the back of his neck stand up. If the island was the mile or so away that he estimated, then the Spirit storm was of an enormous size. *Som'syere,* Telde had whispered.

"Something is happening," said a soldier ahead of John. "Look – above the gate."

He was right, John saw, his attention snapping towards the wall. Figures were moving hurriedly through the gatehouse and behind the parapets. The group around him seemed to stiffen and sit upright on their mounts. John glanced at Telde, whose eyes were fixed upon the gate. There was a loud grinding of metal and a thin thread of light appeared, slicing the great wooden tablet in two.

John could hear the pounding of his heart. He stared at the strip of brightness as it thickened, the doors swinging slowly outwards, and feared the appearance of malformed giants and liquid light. But when the gap was wide enough, it revealed only human figures: a group mounted on jallers. Half were dressed in red hooded robes – *Hearts,* John was certain – while the other half, flanking them, were soldiers in studded leather cuirasses and skirts with tall pikes on their backs. At the front were several men and women enveloped by more extravagant robes, the layers of crimson lavishly brocaded with silver and gold. The terms of the parley involved half of the Ferol delegation remaining outside of the city in exchange, Edodani had explained, including two of the Hearts' high priests. *They don't understand Senthis,* Telde had said, *these people mean nothing to him.*

The Regency and Queen's leaders moved forward from the group to converse with their opposites. John was struck by the incongruity of the situation – this act of courteous ceremony when soon the same site would surely hold a battle where thousands would die, where humans would revert to the most savage of instincts, to animal violence.

Now the Ferolian contingent was dividing itself; half were continuing toward the armies behind, while the remainder moved to the front and flanks of John's group. A few moments later the group began trotting forward as one. The immense portal of the gateway loomed. Figures peered down from the parapets as they passed through and into the city of Ferol, leaving the armies behind them. Telde and Edodani were impassive next to John, hard-faced like the rest of the group. It reminded him again that he wasn't a soldier. But he also knew with certainty that he didn't want to be anywhere else than beside Telde. There was a peal of hollow thunder as the gates closed behind them.

The group proceeded quietly, eerily. John was surrounded by the clink and jangle of metal, the creak of leather. He saw the Queen's soldiers exchange appraising glances with the Ferolian soldiers. *The City Guard,* Telde and Edodani called them. The collection of functional stone buildings leading from the gatehouse soon gave way to open land; shallow foothills, dense lines of trees, and not a hint of an opposing army. If he hadn't known otherwise, it would have been easy to believe they had left the city's territory rather than entered it.

Telde was staring at a flanking Ferolian soldier. At first John took it to be a sign of her intense dislike of the City Guard – she had told him how those who had remained as guards after the occupation were enemies of Ferol, carrying out the bidding of the Hearts and Senthis – but then he saw her nudge Edodani, bringing his attention to the man. The guard looked directly at them, and gave a barely perceptible nod. John might have thought he had imagined the movement, if it weren't for the frown on Telde's face.

She leaned across to whisper in John's ear. "He's in the resistance."

John was left wondering how to interpret the information, as Telde had already turned back to Edodani. *Has he betrayed them? Or has he infiltrated the City Guard? Why is he here?* The man's position in the group at least suggested that he wanted them to be aware of his presence.

"Where are we going?" a Queen's soldier asked loudly, earning a stern rebuke from a commander. But the sentiment was too prevalent amongst the other soldiers to stifle.

"We are going to the Hearts District," a monotone voice eventually answered. One of the Hearts – a pale, youthful face protruded from a crimson hood.

"Root District," Telde muttered in amendment.

"You are to be highly honoured on this day," the Heart continued. "You will witness the Master God himself."

John saw Telde and Edodani exchange a look of concern. He leant across to Telde. "Senthis?"

Telde nodded. "But he very rarely leaves Som'syere."

John leant back on his jaller. Soon then he would meet this man, this half-man who was responsible for so much suffering. Who had destroyed Edemon and brought about the death of billions on Earth. The man for whom Manvedian worked. He felt a fury burning in him, and was surprised to find its intensity eclipsing even his fear. He wanted to meet Senthis. He wanted to kill him.

The procession continued in silence. John adjusted his position on the jaller and felt the chain mail shift uncomfortably beneath his cloak. He saw that an adjutant near the front of the group was balancing atop his mount to attend to the soaring woven hair of a Regency officer. The latter's expression was remarkably calm, as though he were simply out for a morning stroll. With the hills and forests gently rolling past them, the distant districts and farmlands as handsome patches sewn onto the land, the ornate bridges – if strangely appended with metal – with which they forded the numerous canals, it should have been that pleasant journey, John thought, but for the purpose hanging sombrely above their heads.

As if emphasising this latter truth, the land began to exhibit an increasing number of scars: a bridge with its back broken, small collections of burnt out buildings, copses that were similarly blackened. Next to him, Telde's expression grew harder.

After half an hour the group came to another wall. It was nowhere near as large as the city's outer wall, but was nevertheless striking in its ancient-looking stone and the gateways along its length which allowed the ingress of numerous canals. Above the wall John could make out the tops of buildings and, thrusting far above those, two wooden watchtowers. *The Hearts District*.

The mounted group were led through a gate and almost immediately found themselves on streets swarming with people; a startling contrast to the wilderness of the preceding journey. In front of the plain buildings and lining the sides of the road were city guards, the red robes of Hearts, and, in the majority, men and women who by their appearance were normal citizens. The latter were mostly moving in the same direction as the group, their stares half-starved and desperate, or, worse, vacant of emotion. John noticed that Telde didn't look at them.

They rode on through the unnatural atmosphere. John couldn't escape the impression that the people had been forced out in order to see the group. He wondered, with growing unease, what it was that would make the parley such a spectacle.

The escort of Hearts and city guards eventually led them to a large and crowded courtyard situated at the core of the district. To the general surprise of the group, they were brought to a stop in the cramped midst of the onlookers. On the left side of the courtyard John could see the complex coming together of numerous canals, in front of which were

387

the broken remains of what might have once been a gigantic fountain. Enclosing the courtyard ahead and to the right of him were impressively grand buildings, a departure from the modest Ferolian architecture seen so far. The most imposing was directly in front: a towering white construction with intricate stone reliefs, arching buttresses, and a vast blood red window. A platform had been erected near its foot, which was currently empty apart from a small number of the City Guard. John and the rest of the mounted group were thirty or forty yards away, hemmed in by the jostling crowds who peered both at them and the platform. The jallers whined restlessly in the stifling heat and noise.

John heard Bunadere's voice rise above the din, strong but concerned. "This is not what was agreed."

"Do not be alarmed," a Heart intoned for all of them to hear. "You are to bear privileged witness to the justice of the Master God."

"It's an execution," Edodani said grimly.

The people weren't brought out for us, John realised. *We're part of the audience, too.*

There was an increase in the clamour of the courtyard, a bustling and shouting near the front, and then at each end of the platform appeared two tumorous giants. The creatures' size meant that the raw, twisted flesh of their upper bodies was easily visible above the height of the crowds. Large spaces had opened up around them; people were straining to move further away, but were prevented by the choked masses or the forceful pushes of the city guards. John's attention was then drawn away by an unmistakable luminosity. Floating onto the platform, almost too bright to look at, were several shapes of impossible fluidic light.

All around him were gasps and curses. He felt a malevolence tainting the air. In-between the swirling luminosities appeared a figure, that of a man. Beside such supernatural creatures he looked small and unremarkable, dressed entirely in white. John strained to see more, but could only make out a pale face and equally colourless hair. *It can't be Senthis,* he thought. But the intense hatred in Telde's eyes said differently.

Several guards were leading individuals in chains onto the platform. With pikes at their backs, the captives were forced to kneel before Senthis and the Endless.

"We have to do something," Telde said.

"No," Edodani replied, a hand on her arm.

Someone called for silence. Fear was palpable throughout the thronged courtyard, apart from in the hungry expressions of the Hearts. An electrical hum; the sound sent a shudder through John's body. One of the flesh beasts' wrists were pressed together, and growing around them, causing its mass of pallid muscle to gleam, was a ball of crackling, fitful lightning. Muffled cries from the crowds. A signal from Senthis. The flesh beast lifted his arms and before John could think the ball of light had disappeared from the creature's blackened hands and white fire was enveloping two of the prisoners on the platform. High-pitched screams. The silhouette of a body curling into a foetal position. Many of the soldiers around John turned away but he continued to stare, a lack of sensation washing over him. The air was filled with the smell of burning flesh. A third prisoner had been caught by the blaze, John saw, but was still alive. He was writhing on the floor of the platform, shrieking, reaching out. One of the guards moved to him, lifting his pike to finish the man, but before he could do so the flesh beast bounded with shocking speed across the stage; it swung a prodigious arm at the guard, who was propelled through the air and into the front rows of the crowd.

The flesh beast retreated as one of the Endless slowly glided forward. John watched as it moved in front of one of the remaining prisoners. A shimmering tendril coalesced and snapped from its body of light, entering the forehead of the kneeling woman. She convulsed briefly and then fell to the ground.

Telde is right, John told himself, *we have to do something.* But the thought was strangely distant, paralysed. The Endless was floating towards the next prisoner. The man's pleading cries could be heard above the quiet of the courtyard, above the low feverish chants of the Hearts.

There was a sudden stirring at the front of crowd; someone broke free of the line of guards and scrambled onto the platform. He seemed to throw something at Senthis – a blade, by the metallic flash – but in an instant Senthis changed: the corporeal dark of his body burst into vivid light, violent eddies at its boundaries, radiances that drifted and surged. The projectile passed through the ephemeral form without effect. There was a curious high-pitched oscillation. *Laughter,* John thought.

The intruder was swarmed by guards, but at a signal from Senthis – whose body had become a contortion of gauzy matter and whirling brightness – they stepped away from the man. The thing that was Senthis moved forward with outstretched arms that became projections of gushing light. He stopped and the appendages lengthened and shot into the two closest Endless; subsequently a thick beam of light threaded between them and the other Endless on the stage. There was a series of otherworldly howls and their shapes began to waver and stretch. The tethering beam intensified, then Senthis made a movement and blinding light fired out in multiple directions and engulfed the entire platform; John was forced to cover his eyes and turn away.

When he looked back he found that the beams of light and the Endless and all of the figures on the stage apart from Senthis had disappeared. In their place were only wisps of fading, turbulent light, and a scattered collection of bodies. One of the flesh beasts at the edge of the platform was flailing about wildly, half of its torso absent. It crashed to the ground with an impact that shook the entire courtyard.

There was a period of shocked silence, before the chanting from the Hearts began anew. The monotone recitations were taken up by those in red robes around John, and even a few of the City Guard. The guards near the platform – those who were still alive – were climbing up and clearing the space, pushing bodies and severed limbs and hunks of bloody meat over the edge. One of them was gagging into the crook of his arm. Senthis had stepped back a pace, in his original human form once again, his hands clasped calmly over his stomach.

John stared numbly. *We can't fight this.*

A gasp from Telde next to him caught his attention. He followed her gaze to one side of the platform, where an old, white-haired man in chains was struggling up the adjoining steps, surrounded incongruously by three guards.

"He's alive..." Telde breathed.

Before John could ask who the man was, he saw more figures coming onto the platform. Two others that – *oh Christ.* Feeling suddenly came flooding back into his body; an agonising dread seized his veins. It was Ceria. She stood with her head lowered and her hands tied behind her back. And beside her, his hand gripping her shoulder, was Manvedian.

"Gods, Ceria," Telde said. "Gods... we have to stop this, Edodani. Don't you see them up there? We have to stop this!"

John glanced across to see that even Edodani appeared startled by the events before him. Telde was drawing her sword, and moved as if to jump down from her mount.

"Wait," said a voice next to them. It was the city guard Telde had recognised as a resistance member – he had manoeuvred his jaller so that he was nearer. "Wait," he repeated, looking insistently between them.

John looked back to the stage. The old man – *Climbe,* he realised – was at the centre, forced onto his knees by one of the guards. Ceria was standing at the rear of the platform, Manvedian restraining her; it seemed as though Senthis intended her to watch. *Like all of us,* John thought. All of these people brought out of their homes. The Regency and Queen's group. Telde and Edodani. He wanted everyone to witness the execution.

Senthis was walking towards Climbe.

"Edodani!"

"Wait!"

Something was happening around John, a low stirring of activity amongst the Queen's soldiers. But he couldn't take his eyes away from the platform.

Senthis was standing before Climbe. He held the appearance of a man, but his features were too pale; there was a suggestion of light barely contained by his skin. He began to say something, but there was a movement from Climbe and the metal bindings seemed to fall away from his wrists. The white-haired man rolled away and at the same instant the scene erupted into conflict: the city guards near him were punctured by arrows; those guarding the front of platform were attacked by members of the crowd and seemingly some of their own; individuals were climbing onto all sides of the stage. Ceria was loose, John saw, and surely that was Manvedian acting swiftly to prevent a guard from assailing Climbe.

Much closer in front of John, Commander Bunadere unsheathed her sword, turned to scream something at the mounted soldiers behind her, and in the next moment had driven the blade through the chest of the adjacent Regency officer. John glimpsed a stunned face beneath elevated waves of hair before his view was blocked by the response of the Queen's soldiers, who were following their commander's lead and attacking the Regency soldiers around them, most of whom fell before they could react. Some of the City Guard were defending the Regency, and themselves, but others were aiding the Queen's soldiers, as well as turning on the nearby Hearts. Fighting was suddenly everywhere about John, in the group and in the courtyard and on the platform.

"Come on!" the resistance soldier shouted at them, wresting a bloody sword out from the back of a guard in front of him, then jumping down from his jaller. Telde and Edodani followed, and to reach them John clambered across the backs of the panicking animals, grasping clumps of fur before he tumbled to the ground.

Then he was in the maelstrom: incredible noise and violence enclosed him, bodies wrestling and stabbing and slashing and crying out, the Regency and Queen's and Hearts and the City Guard and those in no uniform all involved in the fighting, some seemingly on both sides. John stayed close to Telde and the small group – made up of Edodani, the resistance man, another city guard, and a woman in plain clothes – as they battled their way towards the stage. He caught glimpses of that platform as he looked up: the remaining flesh beast was staggering unsteadily, a flock of arrows piercing its swelled tissue, an erratic spluttering of light around its wrists. And Ceria was next to Senthis.

John's view was interrupted as a man charged into their group and collided heavily with his shoulder; Telde turned swiftly, long sword in her hand, poised to strike, but the man only gave them a frantic look as he scrambled up and continued into the tumult. The crowds became even thicker as the six of them forced their way through. Bodies tussled and buffeted them on all sides. John constantly feared the barb of an unseen blade in the congestion, but there were as many people simply jostling to escape, he realised, as those engaged in battle. He looked to the platform and saw that Ceria had both of her hands on Senthis' arm, and the man appeared to sway momentarily in reaction. But a few yards away the flesh beast was finally falling, and as it hit the ground there was a flash, followed by an explosion that ripped through the stage. The platform was briefly obscured by a cloud of wood and splinters, and when it cleared John saw that both Ceria and Senthis had been knocked from their feet. Senthis was the first to rise. A blaze of pulsing light enveloped him, and when it faded he had vanished.

John lost sight of the platform again as they entered a pocket of more intense fighting. Someone swung wildly with an axe, either at them or some other target, then was knocked down by a blow from behind. One of the guards who had been helping them fell to a Heart; Edodani buried a sword in the assailant's stomach a moment later. Only now did John remember to draw his own short sword. A sharp scream sounded from close by. The ringing of metal. Arrows sliced above their heads. Telde gave a frustrated shout. John followed her stare to see that the broken stage was now empty. They were a distance away yet, and the fighting that blocked their path was only fiercer.

The resistance soldier turned to shout at them, pointing in a direction away from the platform. "That way! They'll head to Sellsoul – go!"

Telde hesitated in front of John, then cursed loudly as she followed the man's instruction. She pushed past him and began leading the way towards the left side of the courtyard. A man stumbled and fell at John's feet, his hair matted with blood. A jaller careered across their path and crashed into someone's back. John thought he heard the sound of distant horns and an accompanying roar. *Another battle?*

Telde continued at pace, pushing or throwing those in the way, or, more rarely, using her sword to combat them. Their passage began to ease as most of the crowds seemed to move in the same direction. And because many by now had fallen, John thought as he stepped over another body. A noise drew his gaze to the right: a figure in the ornate robes of a Hearts high priest lost the last of his guards and was engulfed by opponents. A push in his back and a gruff command from Edodani kept John moving. Ahead of him Telde hacked across the midriff of a city guard, before kicking his bent form to the floor.

Then they were climbing, alongside countless others, over huge blocks of stone. *The wreckage of the fountain*, John realised. He heard more horns, closer but this time from the opposite direction, followed by a thunder that vibrated the rocks beneath them. He clambered on, following Telde's agile progress, and pulled himself up and over a stone verge.

Rising to his feet, he found himself on the circumference of a once circular structure, its smooth basin cracked and lopsided. An archer was perched on a nearby ledge, shooting at unknown targets below. John turned to help Edodani, who appeared to have received a deep gash to his arm. The resistance man in City Guard armour came behind – but a brief shake of his head told John that the woman previously with them wouldn't be following.

They descended the other side of the fountain's debris, then crawled over the collapsed wall of an adjoining canal, bodies clogging its shallow water. John scaled a further wall, and saw that beyond another narrow canal was a row of intact buildings, the streets and alleys between filled with scores of fleeing people.

He looked behind him to find the courtyard still turbulent with battle, the white building with its vast window like a bloodthirsty eye revelling in the slaughter, before he followed the others, climbing down, out of sight.

27

The Spirit storm hung above the land, a crawling dark engulfing the gentle wilds, the far-flung districts, the walled city in all its commodious breadth, and still it grew, thickened, its turbulent black draining the light from everything beneath. The day had disappeared into shadow, a gloom only interrupted by the synapsing blue within the cloud. John stared transfixed as he knelt behind the wooden barricade.

"He was alive all this time? In some dungeon?"

"Yes. For months."

"Blood and blackness. Manvedian did this?"

"He must have had help from Heredem, it was beneath one of his buildings. But when Manvedian brought Ceria back to us –"

"Brought back? He fenning kidnapped her, Peledis. He killed to take her from us."

John clenched his jaw and gazed out over the makeshift bulwark. The barrier had been erected between two buildings at the eastern edge of the Sellsoul District, so that the view in front of him was of the lightly forested hills that stretched back towards the Hearts District. That district was only a distant smudge on the horizon, but the Spirit storm above it was starkly clear. The writhing black seemed at its thickest there, and the brilliant veins of blue were similarly concentrated, as if pulsing towards an epicentre. John thought he could hear the faint sound of horns and the roar of battle, but it may have been his recent experiences still ringing in his ears.

"Yes, right, anyway, when he... returned, he set Climbe free. Climbe organised all of this. He's given us a chance."

"I can't believe Climbe trusted him. That godscursed jestai will slither under the sheets of whichever side most benefits him."

John turned towards the two speakers: Telde was crouched next to him and a gaunt, nervous-looking man faced her. About ten or so others were around them, members of the Ferol resistance dressed in patchworks of leather armour. A man peered over the barricade with a spyglass held to his eye, whilst two women beside him clutched crossbows in their hands.

The resistance man who had helped them in the courtyard – Raleben, his name was – had led them here after they had finally escaped the Hearts District, exiting via a breach that had been torn through its outer wall. In contrast to the desperate townsfolk streaming out through that hole alongside them, regiments of Queen's soldiers had been rushing in to the district. On the subsequent passage to Sellsoul – a twenty-minute sprint from which John's lungs were still burning – Raleben had pointed out more of the Queen's cavalry flooding in from the south, as well as the distant streaks of similar groups from the north.

"Climbe is doing what's necessary," Edodani said. "Manvedian is an advantage, and he's making use of that." The scarred man sat close by, leant against the wall of a building whilst another man bandaged his wounded arm.

"He is still a murderer," John said. "We can't let him get away with what he did."

Telde shook her head slowly. "Edodani is right. We must do what's best for Ferol. If Climbe can postpone his thoughts of revenge, then we can do the same."

John looked at Telde: thin strands of auburn hung loose from her ponytailed hair, blood and dirt streaked her face, and the raised shine of a developing bruise could be seen on her cheek. She had dispensed of her cloak, fully revealing the crimson armour beneath, its interlocking scales enclosing her shape like a second skin. He felt a resentment of this hardened warrior who had taken his lover's place.

"You did say that you wanted to return his dagger," John said quietly. "Perhaps you can make it a gift."

Telde turned her green eyes on him, fierce and examining. In them was a warning; an appeal.

"He saved Climbe on the platform," the gaunt man said.

"Gods, Peledis," Telde said angrily, directing her glare upon him instead.

"The events on the platform, they were part of Climbe's plan?" Edodani asked, more an assertion than a question.

"Yes," Peledis said. "Manvedian handed Climbe and Ceria over as prisoners in order to draw out the half-man for the execution. So that Ceria could use her abilities on him."

"But it didn't work," John said.

"It might have," Peledis replied defensively, "but she was interrupted. Climbe intends to try it again – that's why we need to get Ceria to Som'syere."

John had been anticipating those words with some apprehension, and couldn't help but glance at Telde again. He began to feel a frustration that he hadn't in some time. A constriction. A voice told him that he should be taking action.

"The message received by the Queen's ships," Edodani said, "that was from Climbe."

Peledis nodded. "He warned them of the Regency's betrayal. They had planned to turn on the Queen's army before they ever entered the city."

"Fen worshipping bastards," another resistance member hissed. "We'll send them back south with their innards in their hands."

"Bunadere was aware all this time…" Telde said.

There was a distant crash from within the district, followed by an inhuman shriek.

"The Queen's reinforcements travelling on foot would

have already been ambushed," Peledis quickly continued, as if to drown out his anxiety with words. "There was nothing we could do about that. But their silence at least served to convince the Queen's commanders. They knew they'd have to turn on the Regency first. We helped by infiltrating and recruiting the City Guard – many were eager to fight on our side after their treatment by the Hearts, and the things they've been made to do."

Telde muttered something inaudible under her breath.

"If all has gone to plan," Peledis said, "then the Queen's forces outside the North Gate will have set upon the unsuspecting Regency, and we will have opened the gate for them. The half-man expected the Regency betrayal to end the invasion before it began, so he hadn't concerned himself with the defences at the walls. By now the South Gate will be open too, admitting several ships' worth of Queen's soldiers."

"The ships that disappeared from the fleet?" John asked.

"Yes," Edodani said, as though puzzling out an answer. "Yes. This initial surprise is essential, Climbe knows that. The defeat of the Regency and City Guard, and the entrenching of Queen's forces within the city, needs to occur swiftly, before Senthis' army arrives." He smiled grimly, and pointed his cane at the sky behind them. "You're correct Peledis, Climbe has given us a fighting chance. But now the true battle starts."

John turned to look along with the others, and saw that there were filaments of brilliant blue above the Hearts District, connecting it to the Spirit storm. It could almost be imagined that the district had lashed itself to the cloud, but he knew in reality the beams were striking downwards; he knew the churning devastation that lay at their bases. He glanced up uneasily at the black mass suspended over Sellsoul, part of the same prodigious storm that had drifted, or expanded, from Som'syere at such a startling rate. It was becoming more opaque even as John looked: waves of viscous dark overlapped, blackness spilt again and again over itself, suffocating the air. Intermittent flashes of blue. A low thrumming, a vibration on the edge of perception.

In the pensive quiet that had descended over the group, John thought back to the courtyard and the brutal disarray of the fighting. It wasn't the way he had envisioned battle. The confusion of it, the uncertainty of who was on whose side, of what was happening. It didn't seem right that people could die in such unclear circumstances.

At least the surely imminent arrival of the Endless and the flesh beasts, an unambiguous enemy, would resolve things into a plainer picture. *But it's still not clear,* John thought. *Not comprehensible.* Why were such creatures here in the first place? What drove their desire for slaughter? Telde said that Senthis wanted power and destruction. He had previously been a member of the ruling council of the city, before the reformations, and afterwards he had remained quietly unnoticed, manipulating the eventual governor Dalinde from the shadows. No-one knew a great deal beyond that, or what his motivations might be. But this apparent thirst for power and cruelty wasn't enough, John thought. It couldn't adequately explain all the death he had caused.

It would always be that way, he knew. Even if they discovered further motives behind Senthis' actions, if they learned of some crucial event that had twisted him into a being of pain and rage, or of what was broken or absent from his brain, it would never be satisfactory – there would always be that disparity between cause and effect. Yet neither could he accept the idea that one man had acted and an entire world's population had died. It wasn't true. There were a thousand events outside of the half-man's control that had allowed it to happen. Just like those other omnipotent forces seemingly operating the gears of the world, The Queen and her Central Seat, The Regency, Ferol, the West, L'pen, Tvennar, Besgenin, the unseen entities that would always turn out to be mortal minds, tiny and confined, Senthis wasn't accountable for the direction of things. There was no story to be divined from the arbitrary generator of a billion motives in collision. It made loss unbearable and meaningless.

You have to do something, John.

"Where are they? And where is Raleben?" Telde asked impatiently. She was standing now, sword in hand, alternately staring out over the barricade and into the streets of the district behind them. "They might have already arrived. They might be waiting for us within Sellsoul."

"Neither Climbe nor Ceriande have come this way, we would have seen them," said a woman holding a crossbow near her.

"Raleben will soon return with news," Edodani said.

Raleben had ventured further into the district shortly after their arrival, in order to locate the other resistance groups positioned around Sellsoul. He had urged the rest of them to remain here in the meantime – the eastern site was the most likely point of arrival for Climbe and Ceria.

"He should have returned by now," Telde said, not appeased. "They might be here. Or trapped within the Root District."

She paced, frustrated, eager for action. Eager to fight. John watched her and felt the opposite. He wanted to stay here, and to delay finding Ceria for as long as possible – he knew what would happen after that.

"Soldiers. Coming this way," the man with the spyglass announced. "Queen's. Mounted."

"Is anyone else with them?" Telde asked.

"Only – yes, a city guard by the looks of it."

John peered over the barricade: soon the approaching group was close enough for the white of Queen's armour to be visible. Peledis stood next to John, waving a section of pale fabric above his head. The group visibly adjusted their course and headed towards them.

They slowed their jallers as they neared, and a man in City Guard dress, leather-plated cuirass and skirt, tall pike on his back, came forward from the group. He was heavily bearded, and wore a white cloth tied around his neck.

"Resistance?" he asked gruffly, stopping before the barrier.

"Yes. Come through," one of the men answered. The barricade was heaved aside, and the bearded guard gave a nod to the Queen's soldiers, who then proceeded through the opening. The thirty or so men and women passed John with a heavy jangle of chain.

"Where have you come from?" Peledis asked the guard as he climbed down from his jaller. The barrier was pushed back into place behind him.

"Geadard's. The Hearts and City Guard are long defeated there," the man replied in a thick accent. "Heard it's alike in Hethea's and the other southern districts. Was told to bring the Queen's here. Lots more on the way."

"You finally fight for your city, then," Telde said, with some hostility.

The guard turned sharply to her. "Ain't seen the resistance out on the streets these last months. Ain't seen you putting a stop to any executions."

"Shut up," Edodani snapped, cutting off Telde's reply as he walked up to them. "Guard. Take the Queen's soldiers into the district. Get them in a defensible position – Kelled's inn is well-suited. Leave the jallers here."

The guard tore his stare away from Telde, then nodded at Edodani and moved to the waiting group.

"I will go with them," Telde said, continuing before Edodani could speak, "I have to see if Climbe and Ceria are here. If they aren't, I can return."

Edodani studied her for a moment before giving a faint nod. "My wounds keep me here," he said, with an edge of frustration. "Be careful, Telde."

Terse though the latter instruction was, contained within it was more concern than John had seen the scarred man show before. But an instant later he had turned to issue further orders to the guard.

"Perhaps you should remain here, too," Telde said as she looked to John.

John knew why she suggested it. "I'm coming," he replied resolutely.

Telde didn't argue it further, and the two of them joined the Queen's group, who had dismounted from their jallers. Peledis wished them gods' fortune from behind, whilst Edodani told them to hurry, causing John to look reflexively up at the storm. Lightning blue shot through the cloud as they set off from the small encampment.

John followed Telde as she moved to the front of the group, beside the bearded guard. They led the Queen's contingent through the infrequently cobbled streets of the district, narrower here than in the Hearts District. The buildings were placed together in companionable bunches, and had a more rudimentary look than even the unadorned standard John had witnessed so far in Ferol. Many had been destroyed, reduced to charred frames or untidy piles of rubble. There were signs of more recent fighting, too: they passed a number of unmoving bodies in City Guard uniform.

John caught fleeting glimpses of faces peering out of windows, but for the most part the district appeared empty, quiet apart from the ringing crunch of chain mail as they moved. Many of the Queen's soldiers had pulled the sturdy wooden shields from their backs to hold alongside their swords. But any sense of reassurance issuing from the armour-clad contingent was spoilt by the presence of the Spirit storm, hanging so closely over them. The dense cloud pulsed blue continuously now, and the thrumming had grown into a deep bass resonation that trembled the dust from the district.

They passed a building with a wide window and a collapsed wooden awning in front. Brown vines and decaying plants lined the stone face, and John was reminded of a restaurant window from a different lifetime. *From another planet,* he reflected almost as an afterthought. *When did that become such an ordinary fact?*

Ten or so more minutes had elapsed, the sky amplifying its

slow, throbbing drone, as if a colossal heart beat above their heads, the group marching further into the thick of the district, when a figure appeared at the end of the street ahead of them. He stood at the corner of a building, and seemed to scrutinise them briefly before making a signal to someone out of sight. A white cloth was subsequently produced and waved. The Queen's group, who had instinctively paused, swords and shields poised, now lowered their weapons and moved forward at the word of the bearded guard.

John worried momentarily about the possibility of a trap, but other individuals presently joined the man or peered curiously around the edge of the building; a child ran out and was swiftly retrieved by an adult. As the group approached, a man in City Guard dress appeared: Raleben. Telde rushed toward him. When John caught up a few moments later she had evidently already pressed the resistance man with questions.

"No, but Climbe passed by a resistance group on the northern outskirts," Raleben was answering loudly, in order to compete with the din of the sky. "He was separated from Ceria in the Hearts District – don't worry, he's sent more men back to help, but he expects they're already on their way. Manvedian's with her."

"Is that meant to be a fenning comfort?" Telde replied.

John saw that in the alley behind Raleben was a large group of people: civilians armed with swords, knives, or makeshift clubs, several city guards with either white cloths around their necks or white markings on their cuirasses, and an unarmed majority that included the injured and the elderly, children clinging to mothers, families huddled together, their faces illuminated by the cloying blue of the storm.

"They'll most likely take the canal path to the north of the Hearts District," Raleben was continuing. "It's the safest route here currently, according to Climbe. He's gone ahead to arrange the forces near the bridge. Find Ceria and get her to him."

Telde nodded. "You're not coming?"

Raleben gestured to the crowd behind him. "The half-man's armies will soon be here. I need to help these people, and to defend Sellsoul. It's my home district," he added, then nodded at the Queen's soldiers. "Where are they headed? I could use them."

"I'm taking them to Kelled's inn to dig in there," the bearded guard answered.

"Then we'll join you," Raleben replied. "But we'd do better aiming for the inn at Red Tree yard – it has a larger cellar for those who can't fight."

John glanced at Telde. "Maybe we can go with –" he began, but was interrupted by an explosion that shook the ground and knocked several people from their feet.

He regained his own balance and looked behind to see a blinding beam of blue firing down from the sky, its churning base throwing up a tempest of stone and wood as it tore through a nearby building.

"Come on!" Raleben was shouting above the roar, both to the soldiers and those in the alley.

Many in the latter group appeared to be on the verge of fleeing in panic, but the Queen's soldiers reacted quickly to keep order. Half of the armoured group formed a line a short distance up the street, whilst the other half took a position at the rear; Raleben shepherded the majority of people out of the alley and into the space between them, although John saw a few run in the opposite direction, and a small number evidently refused to leave the alley. With an exasperated gesture, Raleben left them.

John and Telde joined the right of the group as it began to move, its initial progress anxiously slow. The beam of light could be heard thundering through the buildings behind them. Soon the group organised itself into a faster jog, however, with many hands and shoulders aiding the slower or injured. John stared at the backs of the helmed soldiers arranged in a rigid line ahead of him, grateful for their discipline. He began to hope that Telde would choose to join them in the defence of the district. Then, as they turned a corner, there was a split-second of a high-pitched wail, and the ground erupted beneath the front of the group.

John shielded himself from the rock and dirt that showered the rest of them. When he looked again, expecting to see a blinding light where the explosion had been, there was only a great plume of dust rising up from the broken ground and the silhouettes of bodies scattered around it. Arrows were slicing through the cloud, and most of the group retreated behind a building on the corner; however Telde was pushing her way forward and onto the street.

John followed in alarm, not understanding until he saw her dragging back one of the soldiers. He gritted his teeth and rushed out to do the same, crouching in the swiftly dissipating cloud whilst the brusque exhalations of arrows passed over his head. He saw a broad fissure in the ground – and then the bodies, buried amongst the rubble or lying motionless around it. There were groans and pleas, but in the haze it was difficult to tell their source. A leg close to John jerked upwards, and he moved quickly to grip the attached boot. He pulled but without effect; the upper half of the soldier was wedged under debris. There was a sickening crunch as an arrow sank into a nearby body.

Someone moved beside him, taking the other exposed leg and helping to dislodge the soldier. As they dragged the body backwards, John glimpsed a number of Hearts and City Guard archers positioned at the opposite end of the street. There was something hideous in the centre of them, like a flesh beast but thinner, angular, a deformity possessing too many limbs. *No, there's two of them,* he realised, *linked together.* His view was blocked as numerous others hurried past to retrieve the fallen, the Queen's soldiers providing cover with their shields. John heard the thuds of arrows impacting the wood, and a whisper of disrupted air close to his face, then he was behind the shelter of the building again.

With the other man's help John pulled the soldier a few yards further back. He saw that it was an unconscious woman, her helm split on one side, a dark trickle of blood running down from her temple. There was a deep curse from the man next to John, and he recognised the bearded guard as he knelt down to tend to her. John looked up to see Telde returning – she must have gone out again – and, following her, the Queen's soldiers with shields held above their heads, as the last of the survivors were dragged back to safety.

He moved to Telde, who was wiping dust from her eyes as someone else saw to the soldier at her feet. "What in Christ was that?" he yelled.

Telde shook her head, but if she answered then it was lost in another deafening blast from behind; John turned to find a second beam firing down into the district, closer to them than the first.

Raleben was shouting to the bearded guard, then in the commotion reverted to hand gestures. *We have to charge;* John understood the clear message. There was little choice with the infernos shredding their way through the district at their backs, and no other route available to bypass the attackers in front.

The guard turned to yell in the ears of the soldiers. The message was passed down and those who were able took formation again, despite many wild and fearful expressions. The armed amongst the civilians joined them, whilst the others in the group, treating the wounded or hunched together, were signalled to wait behind the building. John drew his sword, gripping its hilt tightly in his right hand. Those around him were already moving to the edge of the building.

Moments later he was advancing with the group around the corner, past the bodies and the tear in the ground, then running through the remnants of the dust cloud, the Queen's soldiers forming the vanguard with their shields held aloft.

John was deafened by the thrumming and the roaring and the battle cries. He caught sight of the group at the opposite end of the street, before Telde pulled him forcefully toward her as a flurry of arrows clattered against the shields. The barrier couldn't block all of the projectiles however, and men and women were falling and clutching at arrows in their chests and arms. The group thrust on towards the opposing Hearts and City Guard, who were fewer in number. John glimpsed one of them take a hesitant step backwards.

But now there was a high-pitched wailing, a shrieking that pierced the heavy layers of sound. He saw the two abominations, their scrawny limbs linked. The air between them seemed to shimmer and blur. They motioned with their arms and instantly the ground erupted in a straight line, tearing through the group. Several to John's left fell in the explosion of uprooted stone, but he managed to remain on his feet as the momentum of the rest of the group carried him forward.

They covered the last few yards and careered into the enemy. Telde was one of the first to reach them and flew into the City Guard archers, cutting down two with a powerful sweep of her sword. A second later John had made it to her side and slashed wildly at an advancing red robe; he was surprised when he felt the sword connect with something solid and by the cry of pain that followed. A Queen's soldier slammed his shield into the side of the Heart's head, silencing his scream and knocking him to the ground, before he drove his sword into the man's stomach. A few feet beyond, a city guard's face contorted in terror before another Queen's soldier slashed across his neck in a spray of blood.

An agonizing screech filled John's ears, and he turned to see the abominations wheeling as several attackers hacked and beat at them with swords and clubs. They were still clutching one another, their defective limbs attached to thick leathery trunks, their heads crooked and barely recognisable. Someone wielding an axe chopped through an attenuated arm and with an intensified wail the link between the creatures was severed. The attackers rapidly overwhelmed one of them, and John saw Telde leap at the other, hacking frenziedly at its gnarled flesh, viscous black blood spurting out as the creature staggered and screamed. Finally, with a two-handed thrust of her sword, it collapsed beneath her. Telde fell with the creature and rolled away, her sword breaking and the greater part of the blade remaining in the weakly thrashing body.

John realised the rest of the fighting had also ended, and was shocked at both the brevity and the fact that they had seemingly won. Many of their own lay amongst the fallen guards and Hearts, however, and behind them a trail of dead and wounded littered the street. The unarmed portion of the group had emerged from behind the corner building and were hesitantly navigating the sundered earth, helping up or tending to the fresh quantity of injured.

John stood dazed, nauseous and exhilarated, his heart pounding. The two beams were visible in the distance, as well as several more now, so that it was impossible to look in any direction without being dazzled by twisting blue. Above, towards the centre of the storm above the district, the opaque clouds seemed to be parting. No, John corrected, they were unfolding, disgorging a contradictory black that human eyes struggled to decipher. He remembered the sight from Edemon.

He tore his gaze away and quickly located Telde. She was kneeling over a fallen man only a few feet away, blood splattered across her face and hair and armour. It was the bearded guard, John realised as she gave a terse shake of her head.

A distant wail sounded beneath the booming drone of the sky. A hand gripped John's shoulder, and he turned to find Raleben facing him.

"You have to go," the man shouted.

"The Endless are coming," John said.

"I know," Raleben replied. "Get to the group in the north.

Find Ceria and get her to the bridge."

Telde had moved to them and answered before John could. "We will," she said, her hand clasping the man's forearm. "Gods protect you."

"Today we take back our city," Raleben said.

The words had barely left his mouth before Telde turned and dashed towards a side street ahead of them. John shouted for her to wait as he rushed after her, but she either couldn't hear or chose not to. He ran the length of a long alley choked with thick-stemmed grass, and caught up with Telde as she stopped at its end to peer out. She had drawn a silvery-white dagger that John knew too well. He glanced up: light was pouring out of the black folds in the sky, floating down in fluidic shapes to the district below.

Telde signalled for quiet, before sprinting across to the opposing buildings. John followed as she slipped through the backstreets and pathways that crisscrossed the district, trying to keep up with her mazy run, avoiding the trees and bushes and rubble from collapsed walls. He wondered how she could move so swiftly in her plate armour, when the weight of the chain mail shirt beneath his cloak felt as if he carried another person. He pulled off the thick cloak and threw it aside as he ran, but it did little to combat the weary disorientation caused by the exertion, the overwhelming noise, the blinding beams, the slowly descending light.

Halfway along a narrow alley a small group was huddled in a recess. A family; a middle-aged man stood protectively in front of them, clutching a rusted sword with both hands. Telde raced past them with only a cursory glance. John followed, then skidded to a halt. He turned and frantically searched his mind for the name.

"Go to the Red Tree inn!" he yelled finally.

He had no time to see if the family acted on his instruction as he raced after Telde, who was already turning a corner at end of the alley. There was a trace of something in the air. A malevolence, John realised. He sprinted to Telde, who was crouched behind a tall tree bordering a wide road, and grasped hold of her arm before she could cross the open ground. She struggled out of his grip, but his urgent look gave her pause. Her expression changed as she evidently sensed the same taint.

They hurried to the burnt out remains of a nearby building, stepping through its collapsed entrance and over the blackened debris within to duck behind a partially intact wall. Telde was restless beside John, peering through a gap in the stone, until a pounding noise accompanied by an electrical hum made them both hunch low behind the cover. The malevolence became stronger, tangible, a cruel taste lining every breath. He felt them, so close now. *The Endless.* A section of wood groaned beneath his weight. A charged crackling, raising the hairs on his neck. The malicious emanations grew, and it was as if he could once again sense that astonishing connection the Endless shared. He remembered their inscrutable energy occupying his mind, he felt the bond between them that reduced everything outside of it to trivial amusement.

To John's relief, the impression finally began to fade. The creatures must have passed the building and were moving away. The taint lingered behind them, a contaminating film that clung to his skin.

Telde moved to the corner of the building and peered over the diminished wall. A frustrated shake of her head told John that the way was not yet clear.

"Godscurseit, we need to move," she complained under her breath. "Ceria may already be here."

Some of the blood on her face was her own, John saw; there was a deep laceration across her right cheek.

"We should go back to the others," he whispered, experiencing a new, rising apprehension. "We can help at the inn."

She would think him a coward, but that didn't matter. *No –* he saw it now in her glance at him, in how she looked away immediately afterwards. She knew that wasn't why he had said it.

The world seemed to slow around him. The noise of the storm disappeared. He could feel the grain of the wood beneath him, pressing against his palm, and the charred, velvety black that crumbled softly between his fingers; he could smell the seared debris and the rich ash that coated the floor. He was aware that these moments were crucial, that they were more dangerous than any of the battles that had come before.

He knew by now that he would sacrifice anything, anyone, for Telde. But that wasn't the point. If he allowed her to sacrifice Ceria, then he would lose her forever. She would be destroyed by doing it. She would never forgive herself. And she had accepted that fate – it was her sacrifice.

He felt a constriction seizing his body. His hands were trembling. He had to act. *Don't let the universe do it again. Don't let it take her away.*

"You can't do it," he said.

Telde stared out over the wall, silently, as if she had been expecting his words.

"I won't let you. Do you hear me, Telde?"

"I hear you, John."

There was a long pause, and then she looked back with green eyes that told him everything. Passion and pain and determination. A plea both desperate and cold-blooded: *Don't get in my way.*

"The street is clear," she said, "we need to move."

John stood up, obstructing her path. He met her gaze. He showed her his own conviction.

"This has to be done. For Ferol," she said.

"I don't care about Ferol, I care about you."

"Get out of my way," she said, pushing his shoulder, but he planted his feet. She glared at him, irate, resentful. "This is more important than us. Than Ceria or anyone else. Why don't you understand that?"

She tried to pass him, but he blocked her shoulder with his. She pushed him harder, causing him to step back a pace, but he quickly recovered to resume his position.

"I won't let you," he said. "Listen to me. I won't let you do it. If I need to I'll block every inch of your path. I will never let you reach her."

All of the emotion seemed to drain from Telde's eyes, even her anger. She held the silvery dagger out before her.

"I need to get to her," she said slowly.

She attempted to move past him again, but John barred her way and forcefully pushed her into the wall. Almost immediately she sprang back at him, too swiftly for him to react, and when he did lift his hands he suddenly possessed no strength, as if he were winded from her impact. He stumbled backwards, confused as his legs gave way beneath him and he landed heavily on the debris. It was difficult to breathe. He looked down to see that the dagger was in his chest, a tear of metal chain around the hilt. He didn't understand; she couldn't have done this.

He looked up to Telde, who was staring at him with wide eyes. She would explain it, John was certain, she would fix it.

"I have to find Ceria," she said instead.

She moved past him, to the collapsed entrance. He watched, puzzled, disbelieving, as she appeared to leave the building.

His gaze remained on the entrance but she didn't return. He fell onto his side, coughing. Now there was pain, branching out from his chest, an agonising tremor passing through his body.

Above the wreckage of stone and timber he could see the Spirit storm. He could feel the dense black pressing down on him, seeping into him, his head was heavy with it, his body thick with its resonation, its beating, beating, beating harder than his heart. He surrendered to the dark.

Ceria could taste blood. She leant against the wall, panting heavily. She spat on the floor and wiped her mouth. She saw the blood smeared across the back of her hand, felt the stinging in her lower lip. The pain was a good sign. A relief. It told her that she was regaining sensation, she was returning to herself.

"You alright?" Manvedian asked, next to her.

Ceria swallowed, then nodded quickly. He looked in a worse state, after all – his face bloodied, his hair slick with sweat, his dark leather jerkin slashed and torn so that the wound on his neck was visible, inflamed and pale yellow. She didn't know how he was able to ignore his exhaustion.

"There's a few guards," he said, turning to peer around the corner of the building. "But we can make it."

The Spirit storm throbbed above them. Its inky dark enveloped the Hearts District, shaking the buildings and only adding to her disorientation. She struggled to find a way through to her own thoughts, to fight the dazed state in which her mind had been since the platform. Since Senthis. She pressed her teeth against her split lip, gasping at the pain, concentrating on it.

It was her sluggishness that had allowed the city guard so close. The man had knocked her down with a blow from the wooden shaft of his pike, and it would have been much worse had Manvedian not been there in the next instant. The guard had collapsed next to her, choking, and she had watched the blood lap over his hands as he pressed them to his neck. She had felt nothing. The world around her was unreal, its sights and sounds occurring as if at a great distance. It was empty and mundane compared to the ferocious energy that had flooded her body, overwhelming her, glorifying her; the power that echoed through her still. She ached from the deprivation.

"Come on!" Manvedian shouted, gripping her arm and

pulling her after him.

They rushed down the adjacent street. She saw a Heart and several city guards in the centre, singling out men and women from the crowds streaming past, beating and spearing those who were caught. Manvedian skirted the buildings bordering the road, then slipped behind a small group as they passed the guards. He tugged Ceria urgently after him as she gazed back.

They ran on. She heard the ringing clash of metal from somewhere nearby but out of sight. They took a left turn only to be confronted by a blinding beam of light sundering through the buildings, its thunder surrounded by shouts and screams. Manvedian turned sharply in the opposite direction, dragging Ceria behind him, and she slowly realised that the sky was striped by brilliant blue, that the district was filled with the roar of the columns, it was being torn apart, and she told herself the horror of it. At the centre of the storm waves of black were unfolding onto themselves, and she stared in fascination at the light that spilled out like blood from a wound.

Manvedian cursed loudly in front of her. She looked past him to see a large band of guards blocking the road. He stepped backwards in retreat but they had already been spotted; one of the men pointed a long pike in their direction. With a growl Manvedian pushed Ceria behind him. He held up his arms in surrender as two of the guards approached. But as they came within a few paces a dagger appeared in his hand and without hesitation he leapt forward and slashed across one of the men's faces; his target had barely let out a cry before Manvedian stepped to the side, avoiding the lunge of the other guard's pike, and, in the same movement, thrust the blade forcefully into the second man's neck. A third guard was rushing at him, but he quickly withdrew the bloody dagger – the man dropped to his knees beside him – and threw it into her chest before she could bring her pike within striking range.

He produced another blade almost instantly, clutching it in his left hand and snarling a challenge as the remaining guards moved towards him. Ceria knew that even though his right side was weakened, and he essentially fought one-handed, he was more than a match for the individual guards. But now as they came in greater numbers, angered yet wary, it was clear that they intended on using their advantage to overwhelm him from multiple angles. She could see his shoulders rise and fall with his heavy breaths. He wouldn't be able to stop them all.

Suddenly there was a mighty crash – the ground rocked beneath her and a body flew shrieking through the air – and the enormous shape of a flesh beast burst from the buildings to the right of them. It was close enough for Ceria to see the twisted exaggerations of its limbs, its irregular patches of dank hair. The creature tore its way through man and woman alike, both the city guards and the citizens running past, batting bodies aside or crushing them beneath its immense weight. In front of her Manvedian was knocked down by a guard tossed like a cloth doll into him. Then the monster pounded towards her, until it was within touching distance, a seething mass of flesh towering over her. She was filled with its stink, febrile and fetid, raw meat rotting in the sun. She looked up and saw liquid black eyes staring back at her, sunk deep within its huge, misshapen skull; she saw its pallid skin, veins bulging, and its shrivelled charred hands as, with time slowed to a crawl, it lifted a prodigious arm high above her head.

Then the creature let out a pained howl and spun around, and Ceria glimpsed numerous arrows embedded in its vast back. A distance along the street was a line of City Guard archers, a new band with white markings on their cuirasses. Queen's soldiers were streaming around them, charging at the flesh beast with swords and shields in their hands. There was a crackling hum, a flickering of light, an explosion that knocked her from her feet.

Manvedian was beside her in the next moment, pulling her up and after him. They ran together, past the scores of soldiers attacking the flesh beast, the screams of battle, the burning bodies. Manvedian pushed her into a wall as a gleaming black animal bounded by, only narrowly missing them – a Queen's Claw, she realised. There was another explosion from behind.

Still more soldiers rushed past them, a river of jangling white and silver; Ceria and Manvedian fought through the current along with the escaping district citizens. *They must be coming from the north,* she thought in a voice finally recognisable as her own. *That's where we are going,* she continued, slowly, determined to keep a hold on herself and the reality around her. The western passage out of the district had been blocked by fighting and the beams of light, and they had been separated from Climbe in the confusion. Yes, she remembered now. Most of the resistance members with them had remained behind, fighting the City Guard and Hearts, giving them the chance to escape. *I should have stayed to help.* But she knew that at the time she had been barely aware of the surrounding world after the events on the platform – and besides, they wouldn't have allowed her to anyway. She hated the sacrifice, how it felt like she was abandoning them and the district. Yet it gave her the resolve to do her part. *We have to get to Sellsoul. To Climbe.*

She shook off Manvedian's hand as they continued, with a look that told him she was able to think for herself now. They reached a point of comparative safety, away from the fighting, the roads packed with Queen's soldiers as they made their way further into the district, as well as a deluge of those like Ceria and Manvedian moving in the opposite direction. Ceria saw the northern gate up ahead, or at least what remained of it; the gate and the surrounding sections of the district wall had been blown apart. They were nonetheless slowed into a bottleneck pace on approaching the breach, as people pushed and grappled and shouted, the unrelenting drone of the sky ensuring no calm could reach the minds beneath it.

The crowds finally eased once they had passed through the remnants of the gate, those escaping the district scattering in all directions. There were hundreds more Queen's soldiers outside the wall, Ceria saw, and more yet were arriving in the distance, funnelling over a bridge that spanned the nearby canal. *Climbe's plan must have worked,* she thought. The great North Gate of the city was open, and the Regency had surely been defeated before they could carry out their treachery.

She looked back, shielding her eyes from the columns of blue fire that engulfed the district. Amongst them was a pillar of conventional flame – a watchtower ablaze, she realised – and smoke rising from a hundred other fires, a smog that weakly imitated the tumultuous black above. But dominating the sight was the twisting vortex of light issuing from the centre of the storm cloud, liquid and dreamlike. *So many of them.* The more Ceria's thoughts and senses came back to reality, the more nauseous she felt. All of those remaining in the district would be torn apart by Senthis' army. The flesh beasts were monstrous and terrifying, but at least they were physical things – they could bleed and die. No amount of soldiers could hope to defeat the Endless.

Ceria turned away, and with Manvedian cut through the regiments of soldiers and headed towards the canal. The resistance member was there, as she was supposed to be: a young woman standing pensively by the low wall enclosing the water. Ceria was grateful for the innumerable contingencies that Climbe always worked into his plans. The girl ran forward as soon as she spotted them; Ceria thought she recognised her as the younger sister of Leandra, but couldn't recall her name.

"Ceriande, thank the gods you made it out," she said breathlessly upon reaching them, if sparing a glance at Manvedian that communicated the sentiment wasn't especially extended to him. "You should get to Sellsoul as quickly as possible."

"Is the way clear?" Manvedian asked, unperturbed by the look.

"As clear as we could hope for. We'll follow the canal, it'll take us most of the way to the district. Stay here," she said, already moving away and shouting over her shoulder, "I'll be back with the jallers."

The girl disappeared into the throng of soldiers, and Ceria moved to the canal, glad for a moment's respite. She leant on the shallow wall and looked at the waters below, which appeared incongruously peaceful. Manvedian rested next to her, retrieving a flask from his pocket and taking a thirsty swallow. She glanced at him and saw the festering colour on his neck, which had almost reached his jaw.

"I'm fine," he said crossly, catching her look. He pulled up the collar on his jerkin.

Ceria reflected on how she had suddenly come to rely on Manvedian, on his wits and his protection. For some reason she held an implicit trust for this man, this murderer. *Or you simply have no choice,* she told herself. But he had been true to his word when it came to Climbe's plan, and his reactions had saved both of them on the platform. If only she had not failed in her own task.

Her mind returned unbidden to the executions. To the sickening rituals of Senthis and his monsters, the display of power and sadism. The stage was slick with blood when she had been led onto it, rivulets pooling and soaking into the wood and dripping in-between the boards. She had stood facing the frightened and enthralled multitudes filling the courtyard. Her people, Ferolians, cast into unrecognisable shades of themselves. She had been shocked to see Telde and Edodani in the crowds, conspicuous amongst a mounted group of Queen's and Regency soldiers. John was there, too – he had looked different, healthier, his hair shorter, and somehow as if he belonged alongside them. The wave of relief she had felt at knowing they were alive was tinged by the bitterness that now always followed her thoughts of Telde.

419

But none of that mattered, only defeating Senthis did. Friends and enemies merged in the shadow of that goal. She might have failed on the stage, yet for a moment her power had affected the half-man. For the first time he had shown vulnerability; in her grasp she had felt him waver. But also, so rapidly after forming the connection, she had felt herself slipping away. The half-man's power was incredible, like nothing she had experienced before. There had been a reluctance in her core, a warning that she was nearing a point from which there would be no return, that she would forever lose her self in that ferocious inundation of energy. But she wouldn't have stopped. Only the explosion from the flesh beast had prevented her from taking more, and her body howled at the disconnection as though a limb had been severed.

Now Climbe's plan was to get her to Som'syere, then somehow fight their way to the half-man so she could try again. Alongside her anxiety of that confrontation was a knowledge that part of her longed for it, to once more feel that radiance surging into her. To surrender herself to it.

"You don't have to do it, you know," Manvedian said, as if reading her thoughts. "You gave it a try. They can't ask for more than that."

Ceria found his dark eyes intent on her, and she wondered just how clearly he saw her. "Yes they can," she answered, the sound of her own voice restoring some of her resolve. "They can, and I choose to do it."

Manvedian eventually looked away, to her relief. He shrugged and took another pull from his flask. "Fearless of fortune, and resigned to fate," he said after a pause. "I heard that somewhere once. It stuck in my head, but I never believed it. There's no fate, just other people." He chuckled to himself, and Ceria worried that the wound might be making him delirious.

She had never understood him. In the past the mystery surrounding the man had both fascinated and scared her – but she had felt safe around him nonetheless. A lie, of course; she had been fooled like all of the others. More so, perhaps. The mystery was nothing more than the layers of disguise he had conjured around himself. She was angry that he had forced her to hate him. It could have been different. He was capable of so much more – why else had he been given such singular gifts? Above all the extraordinary power that resided within him, that wild and boundless entity she knew was there no matter how he denied it. There had to be a reason for its presence. Her conviction that he could use it against Senthis had diminished somewhat, but she was determined that he at least try.

The young resistance member returned, with three jallers in tow. She ushered them onto the animals, and once mounted they immediately set off in a westward direction along the canal. They passed the mouth of the bridge from which Queen's soldiers were still issuing, then spurred their jallers to a faster gallop in the comparatively open land beyond. Ceria could discern the position of Sellsoul in the distance ahead; the district itself was not visible, but the blaze of striped blue above it was impossible to miss. Scanning the land around her, she saw similar streaks of light attached to the black canvas of the storm cloud, each surely indicating its own besieged district.

Ceria tightened her fists around the reins. The wind billowed through her thin shirt, freezing the layer of sweat that had previously formed on her skin. She hardly felt the cold, her mind consumed with outrage at the destruction that surrounded her, and by the sharp pangs of loss. But the latter had been present even before the battles had started. Two days ago, when she had entered the city with Manvedian, for the first time after so many months away, she had known immediately that both she and her home had changed. Something had ended, regardless of what happened in the days to come.

The three of them covered the land swiftly, the journey a

muted contrast to the commotion in their wake, apart from the sight of a collection of farm buildings that had been set ablaze, and a group of City Guard archers taking cover behind the canal wall and shooting at an unknown target on the opposite side; they took their jallers on a wide berth around them. Eventually they left the canal altogether, turning on a south-west bearing toward Sellsoul. The outlines of buildings could soon be seen, and, to Ceria's dismay, an immense vortex of light was now funnelling down upon the district centre. The roar of the blue beams and the thrumming of the sky rose as if in anticipation of their approach.

The resistance girl led them towards the northern border of the district, where she said a camp would be situated. Upon their arrival, however, they found only the shattered wood of what might have been a barricade, and a building next to it that appeared to have recently collapsed.

"They should be here," the girl yelled as she stared frantically around the remains of the camp.

"We'd do best continuing to the bridge," Manvedian said, his eyes fixed on the descending spiral of light in the distance.

But he had barely finished his sentence before a cry reached them, followed by more shouts and a deep rumbling. Ceria swung her jaller around and raced into the district. The others followed as she navigated the twists and turns of the short avenues, aiming for the source of the sounds which was surely close by, though with the oppressive din of the Spirit storm it was impossible to distinguish clearly.

Finally they turned upon a cul-de-sac, and Ceria pulled her jaller so abruptly to a halt that it reared up in response. Twenty yards away was a malformed creature that at first she took for a flesh beast, until she realised it was a degree smaller and thinner. Bodies surrounded it, and the street was lined with collapsed buildings. It stood with its back to them, in front of one of the few structures that remained intact and pressing an outstretched limb against the stone wall.

There were people visible through the building's window,

and more on its roof, attempting to rain arrows or stones down upon the creature, but struggling to keep their balance as they did so; because the building was shaking, Ceria realised, as if by the creature's will. The movement became more violent, and there was a loud crash as a section of the roof collapsed and two figures disappeared with it.

Ceria jumped down from her jaller, ignoring Manvedian's protestations, and sprinted towards the building. The creature began to turn as she approached, but before it could react she had leapt onto its back, throwing her arms around its awkward body and gripping tightly as it wheeled and bucked in an attempt to throw her off. Her senses were congested with the unnatural animal: its overripe flesh, its wheezing, its feverish heat, the sodden hair that stuck to her cheek. She dug her fingers into its skin and hurriedly sought for the connection. She was able to bridge the gap between them with much less difficulty than usual – there seemed to be little or no resistance in the creature, as if its energy was already on the verge of leaking out. But as she began to guide the flow, opening herself to its elemental intensity, she felt something familiar, if twisted and changed, something that... *Oh gods.* The shock of the realisation caused her to break her grip on the creature and she fell, landing with an impact that knocked the breath from her.

The creature spun about as though disorientated, before a shape collided heavily with it and both were sent crashing to the ground. It was Manvedian, Ceria saw, and now the resistance girl had clambered onto the flailing creature alongside him. He shouted some instruction, and together they pinned down its arms as he drew a dagger and began to hack at one of its wrists. The creature managed to wrestle its other limb free, however, and the girl let out an agonised scream as it gripped her arm. Ceria pushed herself up, but others were already there before her, men and women jumping onto the creature, ensuring that it couldn't rise and following Manvedian's example of suppressing its arms.

There was an awful squealing as they slashed and tore at it – someone lifted a severed limb victoriously above his head – before finally the beast ceased its thrashing. Several individuals continued hacking at the body nonetheless, but Manvedian got to his feet and moved to Ceria.

"*Godsblood,* are you trying to kill yourself, girl?" he shouted fiercely.

Ceria was still staring at the deformed body. "It felt human," she said slowly, not quite believing the truth of it yet. "How is that possible?"

She glanced at Manvedian; he frowned, but didn't appear surprised.

"You knew?" Ceria asked. "Were all of them once…?"

"Yes," he said simply, looking back at the creature with some distaste.

"Gods, Manvedian… they were *human.*"

"It makes no difference now."

The resistance girl was in discussion with a man nearby, but presently left him to hurry over to them. Her right arm hung limply by her side, and there were tears in her eyes from the pain, but she clenched her teeth through it. "Climbe was here. He's gone on. Go. Get to the bridge."

"Are you okay?" Ceria asked.

"Does it fenning look like it? Just go!"

"Come on," Manvedian said, pulling Ceria after him.

She followed in a daze, this time not as a result of using her ability – she had barely touched upon the creature's energy – but from the revelation that had struck her like a heavy and deceitful blow. *Is this what Senthis is doing on Som'syere?* she asked herself, even though she already knew the answer. All of the Primitives, all of those taken from John and Manvedian's planet. *Changed.* The Endless in the mountain had killed the rest of the people on that world so the half-man couldn't turn them into these abominations.

The jallers were gone. Manvedian cursed, but soon gave up the search; the animals had no doubt taken fright, and there was little hope of finding them now. Instead they continued on foot back towards the northern fringe of the district, past the ruptured buildings and bodies, through avenues lit by the fitful blue of the beams that ripped through mortar and bone without discrimination. She felt the malevolence of the Endless, a befouling gauze that descended with them, coating the broken district. The sky thundered its pulsating rhythm.

The abandoned resistance camp was within sight when Ceria heard shouting from behind. She turned and was shocked to recognise Telde sprinting towards them, unmistakable in her crimson armour. Ceria rushed forward to meet her and saw how the armour was covered in blood, and that she held no weapon. Telde's face was bloodied too, and there was a prominent gash across her cheek, but what made her so unrecognisable was her expression – a look of desperation that Ceria had never seen before.

She almost collapsed upon reaching them. Ceria supported her with an arm. "Telde!"

"You have to come with me," she managed to utter between breaths, her eyes fixed on Ceria's.

"It's okay," Ceria said. "We're going to Climbe now – to the bridge."

"No," Telde quickly replied, shaking her head. "I need you to go to John. I… he's hurt."

"But what about Senthis? I think I can –"

"Please, Ceriande."

She hesitated, knowing what Telde asked. Could she even use her abilities on John in that way? After what had happened with Elder Nefehed she had vowed never to attempt to heal a human again – she didn't have the strength to resist the temptation. Especially now, after the day's events. After Senthis. *No, I can't,* she told herself. And she felt a reluctance that stemmed from a different source. The thirst within her that ached for the half-man's energy.

But as she looked at Telde and saw her fraught expression,

the open distress, she realised that her friend's defences had been broken. Her armour was completely absent, even in front of Manvedian. She realised that Telde was in love with John, and that she was choosing him over Senthis, over Ferol, over all else.

She looked at Manvedian. He understood without her having to speak.

"I'll go on," he said. "I'll find Climbe and see what can be done."

She couldn't have said why, but in that moment Ceria believed him. He would at least try to stop Senthis. A part of her suspected that this would be the last time she saw him, yet as she glanced up at his face, at those eyes that would never hold an answer for her, she felt a regret that might not have belonged solely to her, and couldn't bring herself to say goodbye.

She turned back to Telde. "Take me to him."

I *must be out of my fucking mind*, Manvedian thought.

He trudged along in the unnatural dusk, through the long grass of the shallow Ferolian hills, avoiding the shadows of trees and bushes. He had stopped jogging a few minutes earlier, a heavy weariness sinking into his body now he was alone. *They can wait a while longer.*

It was quiet, peaceful in a way. The black of the Spirit storm still hung above, as it did over all of the land, but the thrumming of the cloud was subdued here, like a distant, angry hive. Only the occasional shout or gallop of hooves reintroduced the concept of urgency into the gloom. Accumulations of lurid light marked out the far-flung districts, the majority by now possessing the intense glow of a central vortex. The closest luminosities were behind him – although he didn't look back at Sellsoul – and directly ahead of him where even in the absence of a vortex the ecstatic blue coursing through the dense cloud ensured its prominence. It felt as if he walked the dim abyss between hells.

Not far now. He had already passed over two canal bridges – both held by Queen's forces – and he knew there would be no more before he reached the city's outer wall. The brightness in front of him steadily grew. The storm above Som'syere, pulsing, thrilling. He could almost feel its pull. The pain in his neck had long since faded to a numb heat, and he could no longer lift his right arm. As he loosened his collar and the top few buckles of his leather jerkin, he felt the sweat that coated his feverish body.

He wondered how he had ended up here. He had made some bad decisions, some stupid moves, there was no doubting that – though he couldn't say precisely which. It was a waste of time analysing it. *I should turn and go the other way. Get out of the city.* Even if the chance of making it out alive was slim, and likewise of besting this weakness that had taken over him, it had to be worth a shot. But he continued towards Som'syere.

Encountering Telde had been a surprise. Even more so when she hadn't taken a blade to his throat, as he had assumed would be the case if he ever saw her again. But she had hardly been aware of his presence. He couldn't understand it. If anyone was cut of a brittle enough material for the game, it was Telde. Perhaps he had overestimated her. After all of her self-righteous talk of sacrifice, she had turned out to be as desperate as everyone else. As selfish. He wasn't sure whether to take satisfaction in that fact or to scorn his faulty judgement. At any rate, she had granted him an unexpected favour in diverting Ceria away from her foolish mission.

He wondered if she would be able to heal John. Not that it mattered, as long as it kept her from Senthis. The relief he felt at that was natural enough, he told himself. It didn't mean anything. She had caught Senthis off guard once, perhaps, but it wouldn't happen again, and she couldn't hope to overpower him on his own territory. It would be a waste, that was all.

He remembered how she had come back for him in the valley pass. She had saved his life, and saw something in him that wasn't there. It pissed him off. Her naivety. Her ridiculous hope in people.

He stumbled over a bramble, disorientated from the thoughts clouding his mind, the different voices that fought for recognition. He cleared all of them away without discretion and forced his fatigued body on. The land slowly rose and fell, and the city's outer wall began to emerge, an unending black barrier that made the blue of the storm beyond appear more brilliant still. Eventually he discerned the broken shapes of buildings, as well as human sounds; the commotion of a large crowd.

Hundreds of figures materialised out of the gloom. Queen's soldiers and city guards and resistance members, a small army gathered amongst the shattered structures. The site had once held a regular festival market, Manvedian knew. He had seen it in the light of day. Spread amongst the stalls had been a number of religious constructions – stone statues, a shrine to Hethea – notable for their rarity; Ferolians didn't often indulge in displays of worship, preferring to keep their beliefs securely within their breasts. *Closer to the heart,* so the saying went. But Som'syere was always of particularly sacred concern.

He buckled his jerkin to the top and pulled up his collar, straightening the dark leather as far as was possible in its torn and stained condition. By the time a resistance soldier confronted him, he had turned his step into a purposeful stride. He interrupted the man before he could finish his challenge and insisted, in a calm, loud voice, to be taken to Climbe.

The man led him through the swarms of soldiers. The atmosphere held the anxious, impatient quality that always preceded battle. Climbe had evidently already received word of his arrival, and Manvedian spotted the old man stalking towards him, stern and skeletal.

"Where is Ceria?" he immediately demanded.

"With Telde," Manvedian replied. "They're staying in Sellsoul."

"What do you fenning mean? What did you do?" Climbe's gaunt eyes were accusing. "If you betrayed us again, gods curse me I'll make your death last a lifetime."

"I had nothing to do with it," Manvedian snarled back. "Ask Telde. It was a fool's notion to use Ceria in this fight, anyway."

Climbe turned to issue hurried orders to those around him, instructing several men to go to Sellsoul and find the two women, before returning his attention to Manvedian. "Why did you come here? And what reason do we have to keep you alive?"

Climbe stared at him with open suspicion. He was hunting for a motive, Manvedian knew. For the self-serving advantage that had to be there. The man was right to look of course, although he couldn't say what there was to discover this time.

"I'm going across the bridge. To Som'syere," Manvedian said.

"We're not moving until Ceria is here."

"I meant alone. I can get to Senthis."

"Why in gods' shit would I allow that?"

"There's nothing I can tell him that he doesn't already know, old man," Manvedian replied. "And you know as well as me that he won't let me leave the island, even if I were to change sides."

Climbe seemed to bite back a remark, then paused to study him; his gaze flicked momentarily to Manvedian's neck, and he knew that the man recognised his weakness. He saw the change in his eyes. The resistance leader was reclassifying him as unimportant. "What do you hope to achieve? They'll tear you apart."

"Perhaps," Manvedian shrugged. "So what have you got to lose?"

"I'll not send any men with you."

"I told you I'm going alone."

Climbe sucked through his teeth and took his time to scrutinize the surroundings; the former prisoner was making it clear who wielded the power over fate now. "Ceria seems to believe you can somehow prove useful to us," he finally remarked. "It's only by her word that I'll permit you to try."

"Then stop your fenning prattle and get out of my way," Manvedian said.

"Allow the traitor by," Climbe shouted over his shoulder, "we'll let his masters deal with him." He clasped Manvedian's arm as he moved past, continuing in a lower voice. "We will fight our way to Som'syere as soon as Ceria arrives. You'd best hope you're already dead by then."

"I'll be waiting for you in hell, old man," Manvedian replied, shrugging off his grip.

He made his way through the groups of soldiers, who offered an abundance of hostile stares and curses but stepped out of his way nonetheless. Soon he was free of the crowds and the buildings, and he trod the flat, featureless ground towards the city wall. The gateway was easy to discern even at this distance; whereas once it had been only a tiny break in the stone, a door the width of a person, reflecting the fact that barely any Ferolians were allowed upon the island beyond, it was now a razed section a hundred yards across. Collections of liquid light hovered in front of it.

As Manvedian advanced, he picked out flesh beasts and other, unnamed deformities, their shapes made more grotesque yet by the uncanny glow of the Endless. He quickly lost count of their number as the wall expanded to fill his vision. A few of the giant shapes began to move towards him. A faint crackling stirred the air. But the creatures stopped abruptly – an Endless glided in front of them, churning its liquid brilliance, an impossible entity no matter how many times he witnessed them.

Manvedian clenched his jaw and didn't slow. He kept his eyes forward and passed within a metre of the Endless. He felt the crawling sensation over his skin. Its emissions. Malice, inquisitiveness, hunger. All around him were the guttural grunts of the other monsters; the viscid stink, the heaving flesh.

But no tendril of light snapped out to stop him, no immense limb smashed him to the ground. The creatures only watched him pass. He couldn't help but make the comparison to the walk through the human soldiers, and reflected wryly upon which army might dislike him the most. He didn't belong to either side, that much was certain. A man apart. Did that mean he yet possessed some control? Or did his enemies sense that he was lost? *Senthis knows I'm here,* Manvedian thought, forcing his mind towards more useful conclusions. He was still alive, so the half-man must have granted him entry.

He passed through the hordes of monsters, through the vast gulf in the city wall to the last expanse of land before the continent crumbled into the sea. Untidy heaps of timber and stone remained strewn over the barren ground, tasteless monuments to the hundreds of Ferolian lives lost here, their final, miserable days spent as slaves building the bridge that was anathema to their civilisation, in the vain hope they would be spared, and in that way demonstrating their allegiance to self-love above the love of invisible gods. The right decision, Manvedian reflected, if still a futile one. The bodies of those who weren't torn apart or eaten or tossed into the sea remained here, rotting on soilless land that wouldn't accept them. Ahead of him, the bridge was a leaden line scoring the channel between the mainland and the looming shadow of Som'syere.

A minute's walk brought him to its mouth, where it plunged into the land amid furrows of displaced rock. He instinctively held his breath as he stepped onto the bridge, a symbolic action no matter how he tried to deny such notions. There had been no going back for a long time now, he told himself.

The ugly union of stone and wood and metal stretched away in front of him, arrowing into the murk at the horizon. Manvedian was unable to separate the outline of Som'syere from the dark waters around it; the Spirit storm above seemed to cling possessively to its luminosity. It had been a gamble that he would be allowed entry, he admitted as he walked. He had relied on Senthis' curiosity, that he would humour him even after – or because of – his betrayal. The half-man wouldn't have taken that disloyalty personally; he didn't view Manvedian as significant enough to elicit that kind of sentiment. He would simply want to have his fun, perhaps make a show of his superiority, before he killed him. Because Manvedian was no longer useful. Because he was weak.

The bridge was deserted. The monsters must have poured out en masse into the city already. Or travelled via the storm. He could hear the rushing of the waves below as they lapped the enormous abutments. Between the irregular parapets the black sea swelled and listed, tipping his weary body along the bridge. He tried to focus; he thought about Senthis' abilities. Some he knew well – his ability to transform into that otherworldly light of the Endless, earning him the half-man appellation used both as insult and adulation, rendering him invulnerable to conventional attack. His ability to teleport himself, a more recent talent, indicative of his still growing power. He could somehow see, or experience, through the Endless – it was the only explanation for his ubiquitous awareness – and could direct them, at least to a degree. Manvedian wondered just how far that connection extended. It could prove crucial.

The bridge stretched on, strangely bereft of wind. Sections of it glimmered blue; Spirit must have been used in its construction, he thought sluggishly. The lodes left dancing apparitions on his vision. He tried to whistle but couldn't find the breath, couldn't recall the melody. The vivid blue pulsing the storm cloud blurred into a single, uniform brightness.

He knew that this was ridiculous. It was suicide. But despite himself he couldn't shake the feeling that the act of it, the gesture, held a significance. How was that possible, if his actions ended up having no impact? It didn't make any sense. But somehow it mattered.

The end of the bridge appeared abruptly, the island hauling its leviathan mass out of the sea and drenching the sky. There were more Endless, he slowly realised. Lingering at the periphery of the bridge. But their liquid light remained hovering at a distance, and he felt only their malign emissions reach out to him as he stepped onto the island, the ground turning to thick, cloying mud beneath his feet. He ascended a rise and the landscape unfurled before him. The digging was far more extensive than when he had been here last, the smooth contours of the island's hills sliced apart by a maze of crisscrossing tunnels and gouged by deep, black craters. Illuminated by the Spirit storm, the scene looked like a surreal battlefield. Something within him spoke outrage. He ignored it.

He followed the undulating land for a time, before he came to a trench and half climbed, half dropped into it. The cloud reverberated above him. No, it was the land; he felt its throbbing as he continued along the narrow tunnel. The walls rose on either side of him until he was enclosed by dark, moist earth.

His body was heavy with exhaustion. The power radiating from the walls and the sky was disorientating, dislocating. He walked endlessly through the tunnels that branched and tangled and suffused the land like a network of veins. But he knew instinctively where to go. He was urged on by the land, by these passages he knew so well. There were runes along the walls, stone patterns that glowed faintly, a fading blue. They whispered to him. He felt increasingly dizzy. He couldn't hear his own thoughts, the doubts that might question his path. It was too late now, anyway. The land drew him further in.

Finally he emerged into a large excavated pit. The passages had led him here, to their heart that had been torn open to the sky. It was the chamber from his dreams, part of him said, though he was having trouble recalling the difference between imagination and reality. Runes covered the walls of the circular space, pulsing a slow rhythm, and he felt the waves of Spirit that saturated the air, making it difficult to breathe.

On the opposite side of the pit was Senthis.

The half-man was unmistakable, dressed all in white, his small body turned partially away from Manvedian. The irradiating blue of the runes and the storm caused him to appear even more pale and insubstantial. He stood near a wall, his hand held out in front of him whilst a stream of mercurial light issued from a rune, snaking and enveloping his arm which transformed into a translucent brightness in response.

"Manvedian," he said simply, his voice its usual strange combination of delicacy and dispassion.

He continued to bleed light from the rune, not reacting further to Manvedian's presence for a lengthy interval, as if operating on a timescale apart from the rest of the world. Or as if in demonstration to pronounce much the same. Manvedian remained silent; he struggled to form cohesive thoughts, to find a voice with which he could speak. He leant against a wall, his hand digging into sodden earth so that he could maintain his balance. The land pounded around him.

"It is difficult to believe that once, when I was mortal, I came to this island simply to mine its Spirit," Senthis eventually continued in his high, measured pitch. "I was yet to recognise this place for what it is, and the true reason that I was drawn to it. It had been waiting for millennia. Buried and wasted. Waiting for me. It is a conduit for powers you could not comprehend. My conduit. It is nothing without me."

With considerable effort Manvedian pushed himself away from the wall and took a few steps towards Senthis, who turned to him as he approached. The flow of light from the rune thinned and then ceased, and the half-man looked down at his arm, which fluctuated between transparency and physical shape. Manvedian attempted to focus on the being in front of him. He saw a blanched face, fleshy red lips, fine, colourless hair. As more features resolved – the too-large mouth, the gaps between his teeth, eyes that bulged from deep hollows – Manvedian remembered that he had always thought him to look like a sickly, petulant child. He took strength from the recollection, and noted that Senthis' body was covered even more than in the past, the white cloth swaddling him like bandages and splattered with blood from the earlier executions. He could discern an area of dry, cracked skin on his neck, the powder residue of make-up.

"The people of Crescent believe this is a war," Senthis said. "They think in terms of swords and shields, armies and allegiances. They haven't the imagination to see beyond such mundanity. I cannot be *fought*. They are animals that oppose the sky by throwing stones above their heads. This is not a war. I watch and I play and when I grow tired I will change them all. I had intended as much with your planet's population, but the Endless were correct. It was more interesting this way."

"Why?" Manvedian asked, his voice a hoarse whisper. "Why destroy it all?" It wasn't what he had expected to say.

"There doesn't have to be a why," Senthis replied. "It is immaterial. I thought you understood that."

The half-man moved within a few paces of Manvedian. He stretched his arms out to the sides and light began funnelling to him from multiple runes, wreathing his limbs, becoming them. Manvedian felt the viscous stirs of Spirit surrounding and permeating him. He felt the land shiver as it was drained. Senthis let out a soft groan, his lips peeling back. His skin shimmered; a surface tension for the volatile energy beneath.

"Do you know what it is to become God, Manvedian? It is an awareness that can never be taken back." Senthis' body flickered back to solidity. "I am the only relevance in the universe, outside of me there is no meaning. It is liberation from consequence. It is isolation. In the same instant that the world became entirely mine, it became entirely unimportant."

Part of Manvedian wanted to respond but it was stifled by the noise around him, by the delirium fogging his mind. His weight swayed and he felt his control ebbing away. He glanced up at the sky, its rapturous blue swirling in his eyes. He felt the strained beating of the land. Something close howled for him.

"Ceriande might be capable of understanding. I allowed her a taste of godhood. She will return for more. I will change her into a more interesting animal."

The obfuscation surrounding Manvedian seemed to momentarily clear, and he found his voice. "No. You won't."

Senthis let out an abrupt peal of high-pitched laughter. A mocking comprehension. A boredom. It would be soon now, Manvedian knew.

"I can reach into other worlds, I can tear creatures into Crescent. Even the Endless belong to me. What will I make of you?"

An echo rose up inside of Manvedian, an old self. *Get on with it.* He flicked a dagger out from his sleeve and in the same motion threw it at Senthis. The half-man shifted instantly, becoming a turbulent luminosity; there was a warped squeal of a laugh as the blade passed harmlessly through him. Light from countless runes around the chamber began streaming to him, and his radiant form rapidly increased in intensity, eddying and surging and cascading in front of Manvedian. He raised an arm and there was a burst of blinding light; Manvedian was knocked back several yards onto the ground. Blazing pain engulfed the right side of his body.

He clenched his teeth and pushed himself up. His vision

was failing; Senthis was a nebulous sun in front of him. Without warning there was another blast of agonising light, forcing him back to the ground, searing his left flank. The half-man was toying with his kill. Manvedian could smell his flesh burning.

He clawed at wet soil to pull himself up. But no sooner had he managed to stand than he was struck again, this time with a sustained inferno that pinned his body against the wall and enveloped him entirely. Cauterising fire. A scream that could have come from him. When at last the light abated, Manvedian collapsed limply to the ground. Every nerve raged excruciation. A distant shrill laughter. Mud pressed against a face that was no longer his.

But the pain was receding now. A prickling numbness. A relief. His senses were dimming and the world faded with them. His self was slipping away and he welcomed the descent, the chasm.

Not yet.

The voice (his voice?) pierced the void and brought pain back with it. It wouldn't allow him to rest. There was something he needed to do but he couldn't call to his mind what it was.

He glimpsed a brightness, a shape that was familiar. He crawled towards it. A pattern of light: curved lines and elegant loops. A rune consisting of three symbols. *Hers.* The same as the markings on her back.

Life is more, she said.

He couldn't stay awake. The chasm tugged at him. Was he already asleep? But he remembered. He knew why he had come to this place. It was here. He needed to take it. To give himself to it.

The wall changed in front of him. *He sees wild, deep dark; a slither of light. He knows what it is. Boundless elemental. Preserver and destroyer.*

It emerges, it reaches out to him. Bloom and black. Bright ruin. Take it, the land urges.

But a part of him resisted. He was uncertain. He couldn't be trusted with such power. How would he use it? *He shudders rejection.* A voice told him not to relinquish control, to cling on to his identity. *It is too much to risk he tells himself.*

His body was convulsing, he was remotely aware. Shedding its life. The substance of the outside world was vanishing. He heard laughter. *No. Remember.* With determination he pushed past the resistance, the doubt, the fear. He faced the presence.

He reaches out. He opened himself. *He allows it in.* He embraced it.

A roar of utterness. Ferocious abundance. The exultant land resonates: other lands answer. It expands; its presence breathes through Som'syere, it bridges to the other lands, it increases and encompasses more and more, it spans continents and worlds, distance becomes nothing and all pulse as one, and still it breathes out and sweeps through more, it expands and it is too much too far and he tries to stop it.

It slows, lurches suspended.

It breathes in; it contracts through worlds, gushes through the lands, through this disfigured place, through Som'syere and it is here, beating unstill. He strains to hold it; it is too much to control. He remembers. He senses the being that is close, the one that is striking at a body uselessly. Senthis. He releases some of his hold and it surges out and seizes the being's energy. It twists and bends it, pulls it in and breaks it open and there is agony and the being is trying to open a pathway to leave this land but it is prevented with ease.

It beats unbound unrest and will soon breathe out and he cannot stop it. Let it, he tells himself. There is no urgency concern doubt, no limitation. But he has a purpose he shouts, he strives to remember. He cannot stop it.

It breathes out. It expands pulses but he gives it direction, he guides it into Senthis into the Spirit storm into the Endless. Yes, he feels them; it rushes through the beings, through their connection, it grows until it fills them all and there is no more space to breathe into. It grasps them. It contracts, dragging ripping the connected beings with it (there is surprise and powerless opposition) it breathes them in; energy inundates satiates and it is overwhelming him, he is losing control and himself, wait, he tries to stop it slow it but more and more is drawn in and the torrent increases escalates (he is scared; what will he become?) a deluge obliterating he clings on but losing consuming can't –

Ceria stood turned away. The markings on her back were glowing, and her skin was impossibly smooth. She smiled over her shoulder at him.

He lets go. The deluge roars over him through him and the last part of himself dissolves into it.

It breathes out and the world is light.

28

John woke with a gasp of pain. His hand immediately moved to his chest. But when he looked down he found only a clean white shirt and, as he hastily pulled it up, his skin intact apart from a large purple bruise near his heart.

He was lying on a bed in a small room, the space illuminated by the gauzy light issuing through its sole window. A door to his right opened, and Ceria walked in.

John sat up with some effort, a tight pain in his ribs protesting the movement. "What happened? Where's Telde?"

Ceria smiled, as if his concerned words held a significance. "Telde is fine," she said, moving to the bed. "She's outside, like she has been for all of the days you've been unconscious. She's scared to come in."

Ceria gently pushed aside his hand so that she could examine his chest. John remembered the burnt out remains of a building, the charred wood, a tear of chain.

"She stabbed me."

"Telde brought me here to heal you," Ceria replied. She turned her eyes upon him, speaking with some deliberation. "John, she found me and brought me to you. Instead of Senthis. Do you understand?"

John managed a nod, though in truth he was having trouble untangling all of the thoughts and emotions that assailed him. Ceria crossed the room to fill a cup from a pitcher of water.

"I thought you couldn't use your healing on humans," John said.

Ceria brought the water to him. She looked tired around her eyes, but there was a relief there, too, John was sure. She sat on the edge of the bed whilst he drank thirstily.

"It took a lot, you were badly wounded. And I almost..." She hesitated, then gave a faint shake of her head. "No matter. It's good that you're awake."

"I don't know what to say. Thank you." It sounded wholly inadequate to his ears.

Ceria smiled, a little embarrassed, but with that relief again. She was silent for a few moments, before evidently detecting the question in his gaze. "It's over, John. Senthis and the Endless are gone."

"How?" he asked in surprise.

"No-one knows for certain. In the midst of the battle there was this sudden, awful howling, and you could sense... I don't know, agony, I suppose. And indignation. It was the Endless. They withdrew into the Spirit storm – were dragged into it, most describe it as. They must have gone to Som'syere, because afterwards... well, you will see for yourself." She paused for a moment, looking down. "I think Manvedian did it. He is gone, too."

John was puzzled. How could Manvedian have possibly stopped the half-man and the Endless? He was about to ask as much, but he saw a pain in Ceria's expression that caused him to suppress his words. Instead he drank more of the water and attempted to settle some of his own questions. He remembered the argument. The dagger in his chest. He remembered lying amongst the ash, unable to breathe. The black skies suffocating him. *She really did it. She left me there to die.* He couldn't help but glance towards the door.

Ceria offered him a hand as she stood. "Come on."

She helped him out of the bed. His legs were weak, but he managed to pull on his boots without much aid. He followed Ceria outside, shielding his eyes against the sudden brightness. He slowly came to recognise Sellsoul around him; the streets looked vastly different when filled by daylight and people. Many of the latter were repairing or searching through the devastated buildings, whilst a man beside a cart was handing out buckets of water and sticks of bread. The sky was a fresh aquamarine, the air correspondingly chill. There was no sign of the Spirit storm.

He quickly scanned the surroundings, and found her a short distance away to his right. Her crimson armour gleamed in the sun. Ceria said something from behind him that John didn't hear, then walked away.

He moved towards Telde. Bitter anger filled him; he felt the wound of her betrayal. *How could she do that to me? How could she leave me?* But the words stuck in his throat as Telde turned at his approach. She appeared drawn, hesitant, almost meek; a smile touched her lips as she saw him, but was quickly replaced by a frown as she looked away.

"John, I... I'm glad to see you awake," she said in a quiet voice that he barely recognised. "Are you healed? Do you feel well?"

"I'll survive, thanks to Ceria," he replied.

He saw her jaw tense. She kept her eyes from him. Confusion paralysed him; he felt the intense pain at what she had done, at the cold heart she had turned upon him – but also a conflicting warmth. She had asked Ceria to come to him instead of Senthis. He understood the significance of that decision. What she had abandoned for him. He realised that he would forgive her, in time. Their relationship was hardly the stuff of fairy tales; it was blemished, fragile, a risk. *But it's real.*

He moved to stand beside her. There was a brilliant light at the horizon that he had previously assumed to be Crescent's sun, and only now realised his mistake. It wasn't spherical but lens-shaped, upright with sharply tapering ends, and not beyond the planet's atmosphere but within it, perhaps only a few miles away. The central body was almost impossible to look at directly, both because of its luminosity and the restless, irreconcilable nature of the light. It gave the impression of having been torn directly out of the air.

"What is that?" he asked.

Telde shook her head, but appeared grateful for the new subject. "The Endless were pulled into the Spirit storm, and the storm in turn to Som'syere. There was... it's hard to describe. The light of the sky changed, as though it drained towards the island. Then there was an explosion – the entire world seemed to shake in its berth. The sky turned completely white, and when the light finally receded and the skies returned to normal, that thing you see remained on Som'syere. Nobody knows what it is. We can't get near it – the bridge to the island was shattered, and the surrounding waters are too fierce for sailing."

"Ceria thinks that Manvedian killed Senthis," John said.

"Perhaps. I can't say. But the half-man is gone, that I'm certain of. The flesh beasts and all of his other godscursed creatures seemed to lose their purpose after the explosion. They were still dangerous even in their disorientation, but without the Endless they could be overwhelmed and cut down. The Hearts and city guards aiding them met their fates much more swiftly." Telde let out a small sigh, but quickly continued. "The battle is truly over. I can't say we won, not with the losses we've suffered – but what remains of Ferol is saved, and that's the most we could have hoped for. A number of the Queen's commanders and the resistance have formed a temporary leadership. Climbe and Edodani have never been busier, or more ill-tempered."

John detected an awkwardness to her as she spoke, as if she continued only out of anxiety. "Telde..."

"The Root and Hethea districts suffered the most damage," she persisted breathlessly, "besides this one, I mean. The remaining Regency forces have been tasked with helping in the reconstruction – it might earn them their lives. The city gates are open to outsiders for the first time in years. Some ships from Dereselon have already arrived. Raleben survived. He –"

John reached out and took her hand. She paused, closing her eyes. He felt her body tense. A tear ran down her cheek, a glistening trail over bruised and abraded skin.

She finally met his gaze, her green eyes open, explicit, telling him all that he needed to know.

After a time John turned, allowing his attention to drift over the remains of Sellsoul: the broken buildings, the desperate and determined people, the brilliant rift at the horizon, the bare skies. Telde looked out with him.

"What happens now?" he asked.

"Life continues," she said.

ABOUT THE AUTHOR

Matt Bone lives and writes in Bath, UK, where he is steadily working through the city's supply of caffeine. He has degrees in both Astrophysics and English Literature, supporting his ambition to be entirely unemployable.

His website can be found at www.writingmattbone.com.

The *Crescent* series continues with book two, *Rifts*.